THE

Ebony

THE Ebony

CHARM OF SAINT HELENA

HEATHER FISHER

SWEETWATER BOOKS
An imprint of Cedar Fort, Inc.
Springville, Utah

ISBN 13: 978-1-4621-4056-5

Published by Sweetwater Books, an imprint of Cedar Fort, Inc.
2373 W. 700 S., Springville, UT 84663
Distributed by Cedar Fort, Inc., www.cedarfort.com

Library of Congress Control Number: 2021936730

Cover design by Shawnda T. Craig
Cover design © 2021 Cedar Fort, Inc.
Edited and typeset by Valene Wood

Printed in the United States of America

10 9 8 7 6 5 4 3 2 1

Printed on acid-free paper

I would like to dedicate this book to my sister, Jenn. Jenn you were my rock throughout this whole journey. I will always cherish our late night chats as we laughed and discussed my entries. Brainstorming ideas with you have brought my story to life. Thank you for believing in me.

Prologue

1795

Jane swallowed the terror and cried out above the wailing wind, "Hold on, Millie!" She quivered, staring blindly into the dark cabin in search of her handmaiden. The merchant ship tilted sharply forward, plunging into the stormy sea. Squeezing her eyes shut, she clung to the bedpost. Her body rolled across the blanket, flinging her legs off the mattress.

"This is just a dream," Millie, cried somewhere in the cabin. "We're home in Bombay."

Jane's fingers cramped, clinging to the wood post with what little strength they had left. Light flashed through the water-streaked port window, brightening the cabin room. Peeking over her shoulder, she saw Millie, laying on the wood plank floor with her feet pressed against the wall and arms spread flat away from her body. A wave collided against the ship, dipping it to its side. Terrified she watched the floor tilt, forcing Millie to collapse against the wall.

"Millie!" Jane called. She released her grip and allowed herself to slide down the floor, plowing into the wall. She drew in a sharp breath when her knees smacked against the wood panel from impact. Ignoring the shooting pain, she looked to her handmaiden. "Are you hurt?" Under Jane's touch, Millie shook uncontrollably. Through the flash of light, she watched as the young maid stared at Jane with large, petrified eyes.

"Why didn't your uncle decline the job at Oxford?" she began to mutter. A low rumble of thunder echoed through their quarters. Jane's body gave an involuntary shudder. She smiled softly at the girl. She knew Millie didn't mean what she said. A storm like this would make anyone doubt any decision that got them there.

"Come," Jane yelled over the ruckus. Unable to balance on her feet, she brought herself to her hands and knees. "Let's get you to your bed, before we're thrown all over this room." She felt Millie move beside her, but then collapse to the floor. Her groan was drowned out by a clap of thunder.

"Here," Jane's hand trembled as she felt for Millie's arm. "We'll do this together." Blindly, they began to crawl across the unstable floor with Jane holding Millie's arm for support. "That's it," Jane encouraged. "A little faster." She released a slow, shaky breath as she tried to ease the churning in her stomach.

Fierce waves splattered the window. "Miss Jane," Millie yelled over the roaring wind, "I think this may be the worst storm we've encountered."

After having to endure many storms along their journey, she couldn't agree more. It was the most fearsome storm yet. And hopefully the last. They reached Millie's bed and, in an instant, brightness flooded the room. Jane's eyes snapped wide with fear. Taking advantage of the light, she quickly felt along the bedding until she found what she was looking for. Her hand clung to the rope that was attached to the bed frame. She and Millie had thought it was there to dry their clothes, but it wasn't until Jane had overheard a sailor mentioning how he had been tied into his hammock, that she realized its true purpose.

"Take this and hang on to it until you can find the other half, then tie yourself in."

"Other half?"

"Yes, on the other side!" Jane yelled over the clap of thunder. Suddenly the ship tilted hard to the side. The two collided into each other as they clung to the rope. Jane wrapped her arm around a section to secure her grip. Their feet slipped from the floor and began to dangle as the ship began to climb.

"Please let us make it," Millie whimpered. "Please let us make it. I promise I won't complain ever again! I'll even write my mama every week. Just please don't let me die!"

Jane winced as the coarse rope dug and pulled against her arm. Her other arm wrapped around Millie, not daring to let her fall into the wall below them. "Amen!" she breathed, dangling for what felt to be an endless second. The ship began to even out and panic soured in her stomach. What goes up, must go down. Scurrying to her feet she helped Millie climb onto the bed. "Millie, quick! Get the other rope!" The ship began to groan and shift downwards.

"I got it!" Millie exclaimed.

"Lay down!" Jane ordered.

"But Miss Jane, no. You should be—"

"I'll be fine!" With trembling hands, Jane pushed Millie against her bed and ignored her protests while she fumbled with the rope over her petite frame. "Come on," she mumbled, feeling her body leaning against the wall. Her stomach lurched as the ship began its dive. With years of practice, her hands swiftly moved around each other without hesitation. She tied what she felt would be the easiest knot for her maid to escape from. Left over right, right over left. With the coarseness of the rope, the square knot should hold. Pressing her body between Millie and the wall, she braced herself. The panels around them creaked and groaned, like they were going to snap in two from the hard impact. With a jerk of the ship, Jane flew from the bed to the floor. Her cry hitched in her throat as the impact knocked the air from her chest. An intense ache shot from her hip to her stomach. Gasping for air, she rolled to her back.

"Miss Jane," Millie cried from above. "Are ya hurt?"

Drawing in a sharp breath, Jane blew her mangled, mahogany curls out of her face. "I'll be fine," she rasped. "Just stay where you are."

Salt water began to pour in from under the door. She shrieked from the chill of it, prickling her body like tiny daggers. Helplessly she kicked her legs free from the shackles of her twisted dress. With chattering teeth, she unlocked her arms from her shivering body and spread them out to keep from rolling. The ship tilted abruptly towards the port window. A cry escaped from her lips as her body, along with the sea water, bounded across the slippery floorboards, crashing her into the bed's wood frame. Groaning, she wiped her heavy curls out of her face. After heaving herself onto her bed, she closed her eyes and tried to think of anything other than the storm.

It was only ten weeks ago that the chancellor of Oxford University visited her uncle. He had traveled from England to discuss with her uncle a position at the University. The position entailed teaching students advanced surgeries that her uncle had perfected. Jane knew, without a doubt, that as Her Majesty's finest surgeon, the chancellor couldn't have picked a finer doctor to be an instructor. His experience in India during two of the Mysore wars had refined him into an elite, skillful surgeon. His highly practiced hands had saved many lives and offered alternative procedures that preserved men's limbs from amputation. Not many surgeons dedicated their time to perform such tasks. They were too focused to end the surgery as swift as possible, without caring to preserve the soldiers' limbs. That's what made her uncle successful with his patients. He cared for them, and cared that their future was in his hands.

Jane's body rocked on the narrow bed, magnifying the unsettling sloshing in her stomach. A lump formed in her throat, and she fought to swallow it down. A clap of thunder boomed through the cabin. Her heart pounded fiercely against her chest, racing with the hollowing wind. From the other side of the room, she heard Millie's sob.

"It's just an elephant trumpeting to its master," Jane assured, attempting to calm her handmaiden. The ship banked sharply. Unable to find her rope, she gripped her blanket to keep from tumbling to the floor.

"Or tigers roaring at those provocative monkeys!" Millie cried in reply.

The storm instantly quieted from the perturbed thought. Jane looked in Millie's direction and laughed, welcoming the wonderful distraction. "I believe you mean provoking!"

"Yes, miss! That too!"

A flash of light lit their cabin, but all Jane could see was the water sloshing against the window. A rumble echoed through her stomach followed by a prickly sensation crawling up her back. Unwelcoming heat spread to her cheeks. She swallowed hard in hope to alleviate the parchedness in her mouth.

"Oh no," she panicked as it intensified. "Bucket, bucket, bucket," she murmured, fumbling along the bed, and clasping the hook that held the pail. She squeezed her watery eyes shut and quickly brought the bucket to her clammy face. Having endured enough, her stomach waved its white flag and gave up the brutal battle. She groaned into the bucket and began to wonder if their journey was a prelude of what was to come.

Chapter One

"Not too tight, Millie," Jane gasped as her handmaiden pulled the strings on her corset.

"I'm so sorry, Miss Jane." Millie's fingers gripped and tugged on the constricted strings, loosening the suffocating garment. Jane let out a sigh of relief as the discomfort in her weak stomach immediately began to ease. She leaned into the ship's quarter wall, inhaling deeper.

"That's much better, thank you," she whispered and released a breath. Staring down at her stocking-covered feet, she rested her head against the vessel's wall, welcoming the coolness of its planks against her flushed skin.

Six weeks at sea, and they were over halfway to their destination, Oxford, England. From there Jane and her uncle planned to settle in a rented townhouse for two years before returning to her treasured home in Bombay, India.

England, pish, Jane grumbled to herself. She traced a knot in the wood with her index finger. There was a brief moment when she had been thrilled with the thought of accompanying her uncle to England. It occurred during the blissful minutes she pictured herself along his side, aiding him in the classroom duties, and learning more in-depth knowledge of anatomy and surgical procedures. She closed her eyes. Sadly, her wishful thoughts were put to an abrupt halt due to proper etiquette.

Her dreams and hopes of becoming the first female surgeon were dashed by society as a whole. No lady had ever entered Oxford's door as a student, let alone as a professor's aid. She understood the reality of the matter, but it tortured her how close in proximity she'd be to learning more of her passion. It was as though one dangled the college in front of her like a delicious chocolate pastry but forbade her to eat it. Heaven only knew how difficult it is to avoid such a sweet.

Jane frowned at the knot in the wood. If she removed one letter *s* from "Miss," and added a *ter* at the end, Mister Jane Sawyer could be walking around campus without any disapproving glares.

The warmth of Millie's hand on her arm caused her to start from her reverie. "Are you feeling any better today, miss?"

She shifted her attention from her thoughts to the young maid. Millie's shiny blonde hair was tied back in a loose braid that draped down her thin, long neck. Above her freckled nose and sharp cheekbones, her young shimmery blue eyes stared with concern.

With a halfhearted smile, Jane offered her assurance. "Yes, thank you, I'm just a bit tired."

"I would be too, miss, if I had gone through what you did. The journey from Bombay to this town here in Saint Hell-ina, was filled with nothing but turmoil for you."

Jane bit her lip to keep from laughing. Millie always had a way of distracting her from her unpleasant moods. "It's pronounced Saint Helena," she explained, taking care to correct her in a tender manner. "Yes, it's been quite the ordeal for the both of us." *Hell-ina,* Jane chuckled to herself. It did sound fitting. Their journey had been nothing but Hell-ina.

"Oh, Saint Helena, yes," Millie remarked, her round face turned towards the ceiling as though contemplating the word.

Jane grimaced when her fingers brushed the bruise on her hip that was branded there by the storm. "To think we left a few weeks earlier than planned, with hopes to get ahead of the winter's monsoon season. Unfortunately, Mother Nature had the same idea."

By the time the winds had calmed, Jane was shaking with exhaustion. She had awoken the next afternoon too weak to crawl on her bed to see Jamestown's harbor.

When Uncle Duncan entered her cabin to inform her of their arrival, he nearly cancelled his day of exploring the southern Atlantic island. Not wanting to have him spend another day on the dreadful ship, she refused his offer to tend to her. After explaining that she was going to spend her time sleeping, she convinced him to go. And sleep she did. All through the day and into the night.

Ever since she'd awakened this morning, the unsettling dreams of crashing waves, howling winds, and torn up sails had left her in a groggy state of mind. She squeezed her eyes shut, letting out a quiet groan.

"Come, Miss Jane." Millie's gentle hand rested on her slender shoulder. "We must arrange your hair for the evening."

Breaking away from the wall, Jane took a seat on an uneven stool. Her coiled muscles graciously unraveled, melting into Millie's calm touch as she twisted and pinned Jane's curls on top of her head. Tenderly, her fingers easily slid through the now silky curls—courtesy of the bucket of fresh water they received for a wash. Poor Millie had helped Jane scrub and comb the treacherous strands for an hour.

With curiosity, Jane began to wonder if the rest of her appearance would be as tolerable as her curls. Millie turned from Jane's hair to grab more pins. Finding her moment of opportunity, she reached for a small silver hand mirror that laid on her trunk. She raised the oval mirror, bracing herself for what she may see.

Dull, hazel eyes framed with dark, thick lashes, stared back at her. She didn't recognize the woman and her ghastly, pale complexion. Even her heart-shaped face was gaunt from the intolerable diet their ship's chef had kept serving over the course of their journey—that indistinguishable brown mush he called stew. She traced her fingers over her pale lips.

"Are you certain you're well enough for tonight's dinner party?" Millie's doe eyes looked to her with lack of confidence.

Understanding Millie's hesitation, Jane quickly turned the mirror over on her lap. "Quite," she replied. Straightening her back, she pinched her cheeks until they were on the verge of being bruised. "I can't miss an evening with Governor Keaton and his family." She pressed her pale lips together, bringing back their rosy tint for a mere moment. "He's invited some of his close friends and associates."

As weak as she felt, she preferred she didn't stay another night in the confined cabin.

"Which gown would you like to wear, miss?" Jane turned to see Millie holding up two evening gowns that hid the maid's petite body. Millie's round eyes peeked over the exquisite fabrics of a dark blue muslin dress and an emerald satin dress, their skirts tarrying in the trunk.

"The green gown, please." The shimmering emerald gown was one of her favorites and tonight, after spending weeks on the blustery sea, her time on land called for a celebration. She loved how it brought out the green in her green-blue eyes—and, at that particular moment, she was desperate to brighten her appearance in any flattering manner.

Stepping into the full-skirted gown, Millie helped bring the bodice over Jane's curves to her shoulders. Sliding her arms through the satin sleeves, she used the wall for support while Millie tied the laces on the back of the heavy gown with swift motions.

"Do you know the Keaton family well, Miss Jane?" Millie inquired, while securing the strings. As a handmaiden, Millie never steered to the rules of formality. Quite the contrary, she— like her mother, their cook in Bombay—voiced her opinion and spoke so often that Jane felt it was refreshing. That was why she had asked her uncle if Millie could be her handmaiden when she came of age. Graciously, he agreed, and Millie had been with her for two years.

"I do," she released a breath as Millie pulled the strings tighter across her shoulder blades. "They've visited us in Bombay on a few occasions over the past eleven years. They even came this past year. Don't you remember? I believe you assisted the lady a time or two." Jane pressed her lips together holding in a gasp as soon as Millie tightened her waist.

"Ah yes, I recall Miss Keaton. She's a spirited one! I've never heard a woman talk as much as she."

Jane smiled. Spirited—an excellent word to describe her friend. A year younger than Jane, Governor Keaton's only child, Elaine, loved talking about the latest trends or her most recent infatuation. She had a new one every time she visited Bombay.

The last time Jane had seen Elaine, she was gushing about her most recent beau when suddenly, she had gone quiet.

Jane glanced at her friend. Elaine stared at her with an impatient expression. Her mind must have wandered off—again. "I beg your pardon, Elaine, what was it you asked?"

"I simply asked if there were any gentlemen that you have your eye on? Surely, you must have someone you fancy."

She refrained from chuckling at the absurdity and offered Elaine a small shrug. "Not yet."

Elaine's shoulders dropped with disappointment.

Jane always seemed to lack the details Elaine craved when it came to gentlemen callers. Growing up in the middle of a war over territory, she had gotten to know many of the gentlemen quite intimately at the hospital—certainly not in the ways of lovers but more as a younger sister. She was twelve when her afternoons consisted of mingling with the injured soldiers. They kept her entertained after her lessons, while she waited for her uncle. As the years passed and she started to blossom, many of those same officers and soldiers instinctively took her into their care like a herd of elephants with its young, keeping a watchful eye over her. Whether there were ever any potential suitors, she knew not, for all gentlemen were always pre-warned to stay away from her. England was certainly going to be different without having the officers hovering over her conversations or sending deathly stares at any new possible suitors. She smiled to herself, thrilled with the idea.

"All done, miss." Millie took a step away to grab Jane's slippers.

"Thank you, Millie." Without a tall mirror to see herself fully, she took a step back, shaking out the wrinkles in her skirts. "Do I look alright?" She pinched her cheeks again.

"You look as beautiful as ever, miss."

She gave Millie a warm smile and slid on her shoes. Straightening her bodice, she gave a quick embrace to her beloved handmaiden. "Shall we?"

"Yes!" Millie exclaimed, smiling brightly up at her. Knowing Millie felt just as eager to get off the ship, they quickly departed the room.

"Oh!" Jane exclaimed, nearly bumping into the officer guarding the door. The sailor's blue naval frock with saltwater stains appeared a size too large. *Perhaps he has had enough of the stew too,* she smiled to herself. "Private Whitby, I dare say I was so eager to leave our quarters, I had forgotten your presence."

The gentleman broadened his grin, exposing his yellow-stained teeth, and offered her a bow.

"Miss Sawyer, nice to see you on your feet again." He bowed to Millie, standing behind her. "Miss Millie."

As one of their assigned guards during the journey, Jane appreciated how he treated the young maid with the same respect he gave her.

Millie bobbed down into a curtsy. "Private Harry."

His weathered cheeks flushed in embarrassment, but his smile remained. *Poor gent, I'll have to remind Millie to use his surname.*

"Well, my ladies, shall I assist you to the carriage?"

"Yes, thank you," Jane calmly spoke, hiding how anxious she was for fresh air.

The swollen planked stairs creaked as they made their way towards the welcoming light outside. Jane stopped, baffled by the mayhem that spread before her on the deck. The orange sunset cast an eerie glow across the torn-up sails. Ropes scattered across the vessel in organized piles of chaos. A large mast that had snapped into two, dangled over the edge of the ship. It appeared the crew had been trying to maneuver it off the boat but had given up, as no one was in sight.

"I can see why we're now delayed for over a month on this island," she whispered in astonishment.

"Aye, miss. We're lucky to be alive," Private Whitby murmured.

Their original three-day stay for supplies turned into at least a month of repairs due to the storm's damage. *One month!* Jane shook her head. When her uncle told her the news, to say she was relieved was an understatement.

Governor Keaton shared her excitement for their delay. Not only did he insist on having them stay at his plantation, he also insisted on throwing a few dinner parties to celebrate their arrival. Jane didn't mind the celebration. Anything to distract her from the journey they had just endured.

In the distance, she heard men hollering at each other on a separate pier. They were loading a few vessels with supplies. Other piers appeared busy with dozens of ships docked to them. She gazed at where they berthed. Being the longest pier in the port, it was the quietest with only two large ships anchored to it. It was odd how desolate the deck and pier were compared to the others. "Where are the crew?" she asked Private Whitby.

"You'll find all the crew at the pubs and taverns. A few of us stayed behind to man our posts, but they're below deck. It being the dinner hour and all."

Jane nodded with understanding. Taking a couple unsteady steps, she looked around, astonished to see the large harbor. The town snuggled along a steep-sided valley with a cobblestone street running through the center towards the pier.

The luscious green volcanic island stood magnificently high above the ocean with its valleys and ravines. Considered a fortress, with three sides of rocky cliffs that stretched high above the water of the large bay, the c-shaped harbor was the only port of entry. She smiled at her friend's detailed description of the island. It appeared exactly as Elaine had described it to her—breathtaking.

Drawing closer to the rail, she anxiously took a deep breath of the heavy air. A stabbing pain shot through her stomach as it took a turn for the worse. What she had hoped to be fresh air filling her lungs was a far cry from what she expected. Fish from the fishing boats tainted the air, prickling her tongue with a mixture of the salty humidity. *Not again!* Her hand flew back to her mouth. Normally the smell of fish never bothered her, but tonight with her stomach being still in such a tender state, she felt as if she were entrapped in a stuffy glass container that oozed the scent of stale fish carcasses.

Confound it. If she were to get sick in the presence of Private Whitby, he'd order her to be returned to her quarters immediately, ruining any hopes of being on land. Due to her weakened condition, she and her uncle had already stayed an extra night on the ship after their arrival in the harbor. Being more alert and less sick than before, she couldn't fathom the thought of another incarcerated night. Not while a soft, feathered, *stable* bed stood in a fresh, airy room merely miles away. A cold tingle sensation ran up her back.

"Private Whitby?" a low voice called out. They turned to face a young sailor standing in the doorway. "We're needing your help below deck. A few of the men are in a huff with the cook." The sailor's voice dropped. "Something to do with demanding the captain's rum supply."

"Why aren't you informing Lieutenant Howard? He's the officer on deck."

"He's left the ship with a few of the other officers."

"He's left his post?" Private Whitby's mouth fell.

"Aye," the sailor rolled his eyes and scoffed.

"Who's supposed to take charge in his stead?" Private Whitby's eyes darkened, his friendly countenance growing cold.

"He nominated you, sir."

"And none of the other officers corrected the ridiculous notion?" His face flushed with irritation.

"Nay, sir."

Private Whitby shook his head with disgust. "Of course. That blasted, indolent man. I may as well be promoted to an officer, seeing how I carry on his duties," he grumbled under his breath.

Jane bit her tongue to refrain from agreeing with the private. Not wanting to discuss the lieutenant's disgraceful nature and seeing a chance to escape, she addressed the disgruntled man.

"We'll manage from here, private." The pang sharpened again as she inhaled a short vile breath.

"But—"

"You mentioned the carriage is waiting for us at the end of the pier, correct?" She took a few wavering steps.

"Yes, but—"

Knowing he'd insist on escorting them to the carriage, she held her hand up. "Splendid," she spoke cheerfully, keeping the urgency from her tone. "Now Private Whitby, I don't want to delay you any further." His mouth opened in protest but paused when he turned towards the anxious sailor in the doorway. "You've been gracious enough with your time, sir. Millie and I can manage from here to the end of the dock." She curtsied him a farewell and stumbled from her weakened state. Swiftly, she hid the motion by stepping over a rope. "Thank you, private." She smiled again when he tipped his hat to her.

Hastily walking over another rope, she moved along to the gangplank, attempting to avoid reliving the last couple days of torture. She overheard Millie mention something regarding their trunks to the private before she hurried to catch up.

"Millie, will our trunks be arriving immediately after we've arrived at Governor Keaton's home?" She kept her voice even and calm. Every step she took, her stomach whirled in discomfort. She was hoping she had all her belongings immediately—just in case.

"Yes, miss. I informed Private Harry to have everything taken over to the Governor's home as soon as we've left."

Jane bit back a smile. "Millie, you need to address the gentleman by his surname, Private Whitby. Besides, I believe the private prefers it."

"Oh, but I've heard the other sailors call him Private Harry all the time. I just assumed that's what he liked with all the laughter."

If Millie had seen his face when they called him by his first name, she would have realized that he didn't. The crew was always taunting the poor private. She could only imagine how he was counting down the days until his next promotion.

Millie hurried behind Jane, attempting to keep her pace. "Miss Jane," she called out with a labored breath. "Your uncle told me he'd inform the hostesses you'll arrive later this evening, there's no rush."

Oh, but there was. Jane's stomach churned when another waft of the rancid aroma tickled her nose. Her hand flew to her mouth, while she stepped onto the unsteady pier. Goodness, the dock felt as if it weren't anchored to any of the posts in this choppy harbor. *Perhaps, that's why it was vacant,* she thought while taking smaller, cautious steps. Surely, they wouldn't allow ships to dock here if it wasn't secure. Would they? She glanced over her shoulder to see if Millie managed the gangway alright but felt herself stumbling to her left in the process. *Good heavens, the dock is now tilting to its side!* Jane abruptly focused in front of her to see if any of the barrels were rolling into the harbor. Nothing. They were sitting perfectly still on the dock. *Wait*—she attempted to stop, but her wobbly legs took over, taking extra involuntary steps in an attempt to regain her balance. *Oh no!*

"Miss Jane!" Millie's soft steps quickened down the ramp, but she was too late.

With no rope or rail for Jane to catch herself, she quickly stumbled to the edge of the secure dock. She sucked in a scream. Her eyes widened with horror. Weightless, she plummeted fast towards the *calm*, murky water.

❧ Chapter Two ❦

Deep in thought, Captain James McCannon stood on his ship's deck watching the orange sun slowly fade into the horizon. The war against the French had been intensifying over the last few months and their island had become a point of interest. As one of the most important ports of call for the East India Company, many ships restocked at Saint Helena with provisions.

After many failed attempts of trying to overrun the island, the French had since moved on to attacking the trading company's supply ships. There had been another attack on one of their merchant ships last week. Fortunately, the crew was spared, but all the supplies and armory were confiscated, making that the third attack this month.

James sent a request to the Royal Navy asking that they send more frigates to Jamestown. They needed more convoys to protect and accompany the suppliers. Frustratingly, they had been told it was a matter of months before they would receive reinforcements. Until then, his ship, along with two others, were assigned to patrol the surrounding waters while many of the vulnerable merchants sailed on their own, defenseless.

"Are you delaying your departure for Governor Keaton's dinner party?" Thomas Fletch, First Lieutenant on the Ebony, strolled across the quarterdeck like an arrogant peacock. James shook his head as he watched his best friend. "If you delay any longer, Miss Keaton may become anxious and send out a search party." Giving a mischievous smile, his cheeks barely broadened over his thick neck.

He always enjoyed teasing him about the infamous, clingy Miss Elaine Keaton. She's had her eyes set on him for months.

"If she hasn't already," James muttered.

Thomas brought his calloused hand to his squared chin and rubbed it like something weighed on his mind. "I've put very little thought into this," he mused. Above his laughing caramel eyes, he raised a thick chestnut brow. "And I decided you two would make an adorable couple." With a devious expression on his face, he clapped James's back with reassurance.

The man was being insufferable. Just a couple inches shorter than James, Thomas was no stranger to hard work. Laboring most of his life in his parent's orchards and then years aboard a ship earned him a lot of strength—but as his best friend, James voluntarily worked alongside him in the same orchard, performed the same drudgery tasks that are mandatory on a ship, and grew tempted to knock the wicked grin off his face.

James drew in a breath and offered Thomas a sly smile instead. "I hate to disappoint you, my friend, but I'm afraid no couple could possibly be as endearing as you two were." Thomas gave a shudder.

They were twelve when Thomas and James were walking to school in Jamestown. The young Miss Keaton practically ran to catch up to them. It was then that Thomas had made the gentlemanly mistake of offering to carry Miss Keaton's books. And it was then that his school term took a turn for the worst. The innocent act twisted into a year filled with rumors of affection he had for her. Gossip that was started by Miss Keaton herself. Thomas had a miserable time as his classmates constantly tormented him. It wasn't until the following year that he caught a lucky break. A new boy had joined the class and, unfortunately for him, Miss Keaton had found her next prey.

"Ah yes, we shared some unforgettable times together," Thomas countered at his friend's jab.

James's stomach released a low growl, interrupting their banter.

"I believe your stomach is giving you an order to conquer tonight's dinner, and save your damsel from distress," Thomas stated with a playful smile. "Shall we go?"

James scowled at his friend. He was obviously enjoying himself a little too much. Before they retreated from the banister to depart for James's unpleasant evening, the sound of soft feminine voices floated across the water towards them. Both gentlemen stopped to peer over the rail. Two women were crossing the deck of what appeared to be a dreadful looking ship that had encountered a battle or faced a storm.

"What do we have here?" Thomas inquired. His curiosity matched James's. Women rarely wonder this far out on the pier unless it was bickering fishwives or sultry pub girls. And these were not that. Quite on the contrary, one sounded sophisticated. James leaned against the banister to get a better view. The tall woman with brown hair seemed to be in a hurry, swaying across the cluttered deck, ahead of the shorter woman with a blonde braid.

Thomas chuckled. "It appears the lady found the barrel of rum."

James wanted to agree with his friend, but he didn't hear any slurring of words or loud laughter. He focused on the staggering woman clasping the wood rail of the gangway. Not wanting to look like a brute staring at her through the spyglass, James squinted to study her face. All he could see was a ghostly, white blur with feminine features. She must use white powder for her face because she was a lot paler than any of the ladies on the island. She stumbled and caught herself. *Unless she is unwell.* Dread shot through him when she reached the dock. She began to totter sideways towards the edge of the pier. Unwell she is! Quickly he removed his boots, then threw his blue officer frock and the last of his clean waistcoats onto the deck. Leaping up to the rail he heard a slap against the water. A splash and ripples spread across the surface, with the woman nowhere in sight.

Over his shoulder he yelled to Thomas, "Get to the pier!" before he dove into the smooth dark water.

His body submerged into the chilly harbor, sending a jolt of shock from the crown of his head to the tips of his toes. Fervently he swam through the murky, cold harbor, thrusting his arms and kicking his legs towards the direction he saw the splash. With unsettling thoughts of her not being able to swim or her gown anchoring her to the ocean floor, he pumped his arms faster. His chest ached with his breath locked into his lungs. Through the roiled water the storm had caused two nights prior, green fabric floated into view. Kicking harder, he saw the woman was motionless. The fabric of her gown flowed effortlessly around her like the seaweed below. *This isn't good, not good at all,* he thought to himself.

Reaching the unconscious woman, his lungs began to burn. Fervently, he wrapped his arms around her tiny waist and kicked using all his might against the water that pulled them to the bottom. Through multiple thrusts they made a gradual ascent. James glanced towards the glass surface, his stomach sank. He still had a few feet to go until they reached the top. His lungs blazed with fire, ready to burst. Desperately he kicked again, this time holding one arm around her waist while the other frantically pumped, clawing his way upward. It helped slightly, but not enough. The muscles in his body began to contract. He desperately needed air but there wouldn't be enough time to surface and retrieve her. The longer she stayed under, the less chance of survival she'd have. Having enough air for a final attempt, he tightened his grip and pushed her towards the surface. But it was useless. He was now fighting her dress like it was a sail tangling him in the water. *The blasted dress is going to drown them both!* His lungs convulsed as the last of his breath seeped from his lips. *Please forgive me,* he prayed, hoping she'd understand for the abrupt decision he had to make in order for them to survive.

He pulled out the dagger that was tucked in the holster on his pants. One swift motion he cut the laces off the back of her gown, promptly freeing it from her slender body. Immediately the treacherous anchor drifted off her, gracefully folding into itself. James wrapped his arm around the curve of her waist and kicked rigorously to the surface. *Finally!* Instant relief rushed through him as they burst above to the surface. He gasped, gulping in the salty air, filling his lungs with invigorating breaths.

Above, Thomas kneeled over the dock with a determined expression on his face. Panting from his run, he threw a rope to James, the cord slapping a piece of lumber that floated by. The young lady that had accompanied the unconscious woman, stood by Thomas's side whimpering; her hands covered her mouth as she trembled with wide watery eyes.

"Grab on and I'll pull you up!" Thomas bellowed.

James swam them to the rope, keeping the limp woman's head above water. Grabbing the line, he draped her over his shoulder like a wet sack of flour. Careful not to be thrown off balance, he climbed the remaining ten feet, wrapping the rope around his free arm, pressing his feet to the dock's post for support. Her body swayed side to side across his back like a ragdoll with each step he took. Towards the top, Thomas promptly pried the young woman from James's solid grasp and laid her on her back.

"She's not breathing!" he panicked, leaning his ear to her mouth.

James heaved himself onto the dock. Not pausing to catch his breath, he hastily crawled to the lifeless woman. He remembered a method he'd seen a sailor use years before that had saved a man who'd drowned. He wiped his mouth and prayed he would be as successful. Pinching her delicate nose, he took a deep breath and pressed his mouth around her parted, blue lips and pushed air into her lungs. In front of him, the blonde woman let out a horrified gasp of alarm. He knew how indecent it appeared. But, he wasn't going to let her die because of formality. It's absurd! She won't lose her life. Not on his watch. Ignoring her and the rules of propriety, James carried on.

From the corner of his eye, he watched the unconscious woman's cheeks expand with each breath. After a few attempts, and pauses in between breaths, a choked cough sounded from her, with water surfacing in her mouth. Swiftly, James leaned back on his heels and rolled her to her side. With hopes to help release the fluid she had inhaled, he awkwardly patted her back above her corset. She gasped and coughed, rasping in shallow breaths of air.

"That's it," James encouraged, relief washing over him. He continued to gently pat her back. "Nice, easy breaths." He sank back and sat looking to his friend with astonishment. Thomas towered over them, meeting James's stare with disbelief. James nodded at him in agreement. It was remarkable that what he did even worked.

The young companion collapsed to her knees and threw her arms around the feeble woman's shoulders. "Miss Jane!" she sobbed on her, searching for solace. "Miss Jane! Thank heavens. Are you alright? I was so worried." Never pushing the young lady away, Miss Jane sat up on one arm, and with quiet raspy words, seemed to reassure her distraught companion.

Funny how the one who almost drowned did the comforting, James thought, while collapsing onto his back.

Feeling completely winded, James gazed at the vibrant pink and orange sky, focusing on steadying his breaths. His chest expanded while he revived his lungs with the salty, fresh air. All his tensed muscles relaxed, melting into a state of exhaustion. Having already committed to the night's engagement, he decided he'd have to make an early departure for a good night's sleep. A cold, weakened hand clasped his shoulder, startling him from his thoughts. He turned towards the woman and suddenly forgot how to breathe. She looked at him dazed with soft, glistening eyes. He couldn't help but stare, gaping at how her eyes reminded him of tropical water on a clear sunny day. He felt himself sinking into their depths, consumed by tranquility.

"Thank you," she whispered, in a hoarse whisper.

He blinked, resurfacing from their captivating lure. Even when she wasn't smiling, her pale full lips curved up at the corners. Her petite nose, pink at the end, matched the slight flush on her high cheekbones. Her wet hair curled around her pale face, draping past her slender shoulders. Realizing he gawked at her like a buffoon, he clamped his mouth close and swallowed, making some grunt of an inhuman noise, acknowledging whatever it was he'd forgotten she'd said. Shaking his head to rid his incompetent thoughts, he stood and held out his hand to assist her while Thomas aided the other young woman. She placed her cold hand in his, holding it tight while she staggered to her feet. Without a thought, James grabbed her waist to balance her but hastily lifted his hands as though his skin scorched from the indecency of his action. Awkwardly, keeping his eyes locked above her hair, he felt uncertain how to help her in her indecent state of dress—no thanks to him. Quickly, he grabbed her elbow and hand when she staggered towards him. Behind her, Thomas shrugged out of his jacket and discreetly placed his large coat over her shoulders. Grateful, James relaxed his gaze and let out a breath he forgot he held.

"What happened?" Jane's legs teetered, trying to gain strength. Last she remembered was how one minute she was falling towards the not so choppy harbor, and then the next she laid on the dock coughing up water.

"Miss Jane, you seemed to have lost your balance or possibly fainted and fell off the pier. This gentleman dove in and rescued you," Millie exclaimed.

Jane didn't hear Millie's frantic response. The pounding at the back of her head distracted her from the words. She flinched as she reached up and barely grazed the large bump that formed. She had definitely been knocked unconscious. *But how? Drat, Uncle Duncan!* After he hears about this mishap, he'd certainly insist she stay in bed the rest of the evening. She groaned inwardly at the thought of another night, shut away from engaging with others. Perhaps she'd best tell him in the morning after the night's entertainment. Then they both could have an enjoyable evening. He, not worried sick, and she, out of a confined room.

Satisfied by her self-given counsel, she calmed herself and allowed her eyes to drift down to assess the damage the salt water had done to her favorite satin evening gown. Suddenly, every muscle in her body tensed. Her breath shortened with constraint from the sight of a large, weathered hand, securely clasping her arm. How did she not notice him still standing there? *Wait!* Her eyes grew large, as she continued to scan down her shivering body.

Jane gasped seeing her wet chemise, sheerly cling to her skin. Frantically, she peeled the garment off her legs. She covered her chest with her hands, grateful her corset covered most of her bodice. *But where is my dress?!*

As if someone had knocked sense into her, her head snapped towards the gentleman standing in front of her. Warmth spread to her cheeks as she stood uncomfortably close to an unnervingly handsome man in nothing but her undergarments. She swallowed as her mouth became unbearably dry. Realizing it was a frock the other gentleman had placed on her shoulders, she quickly grabbed the lapels, closing any gap exposing what little she had on. Taking a step out of the man's grip, she hurried and surveyed the quiet pier, grateful they hadn't drawn a crowd. Unable to retain her mortified expression, she glanced between the two men standing before her.

Her eyes landed on the sopping wet gentleman, "Sir," she demanded. His shirt adhered against his body like an extra layer of skin. Broad shoulders widened when he pressed his hands to his narrow hips, the muscles of his defined arms becoming more prominent. Her anger wavered. *Great heavens, was he a blacksmith?* She bit her lip to concentrate on her anger. Shifting her gaze to focus only on his piercing-blue eyes, she inhaled a sharp breath. His intimidating gaze was so gentle and concerned that she shrunk inwardly. She tightened her hold and stuck her chin out for courage with what dignity she had remaining.

"What happened to my dress?"

His face reddened from his temples to his jaw. Muscles flexed in his smooth-shaven cheeks. Relaxing his stance, he nervously ran his hand through his dark, wavy hair. A drop of water rolled down his cheek as he stammered over his words, "I . . . if you beg my pardon, miss . . . I . . ." He took a deep breath, running his hand through his thick hair again, and glanced at the man at his side for support.

The man's brow arched, waiting for the answer, he too looked to him with the same horrorstruck look as she felt. Though, something about the man's pained expression made her begin to doubt he had the same feeling as she when she noticed his shoulders shaking. *Was he laughing?*

The gentleman cleared his throat. "I had to cut it off," he spoke more confidently, turning his shameful gaze back to her.

"Cut it off?" she shrieked.

"I'm sorry, miss, but it was weighing us down. What other choice did I have to keep us from drowning?"

Us? She stared up at him, allowing the revelation to seep in. Of course, the satin gown would have dragged them down. He could have easily left her in the harbor to save himself . . . but he didn't. He stayed. He risked his own life to save hers. How could she be so upset with him? Guilt tugged at her heart for having been more dismayed about her gown and immodesty, rather than showing the gentlemen gratitude for his chivalry.

"Please forgive me," Jane replied.

Both gentlemen gave her a perplexed expression as if they didn't seem to understand her apology. *This is so humiliating.* She hated being the center of attention, especially for all the wrong reasons. She rushed on, feeling the need to explain herself to these complete strangers, who had saved her life.

"Thank you, both, for rescuing me. Let me assure you, I'm never this clumsy, nor do I find myself walking sideways into the ocean."

Not wanting to prolong the uncomfortable moment any longer, she turned and stumbled forward to grasp Millie's arm. She paused as strong hands wrapped around her waist, anchoring her steady. Heat soared from his touch to her cheeks. Perturbed, she glanced down to see the man's large, weathered fingers encircled around her midriff. Her back only inches away from him, every nerve in her body shrieked in alarm, overly aware of his presence. Her head spun—*probably from my bump*—causing her to feel light-headed. Flustered, she twisted slightly and peered at him. Meeting his eyes, she raised a questionable brow and led his gaze down to where his hands held her.

Reddening, he quickly raised them in the air, awkwardly clasping her shoulders instead as though she was going to topple over at any moment. He seemed to think twice about that as he quickly removed them again—this time, as though she were revolting. Appearing conflicted on where to place his hands, he settled one on his hip, and the other nervously running through his dark strands.

"Miss," his voice lowered. "Please let me assist you on board." His striking eyes stared deeply into hers, making it impossible for her to think clearly. Feeling more vulnerable, she tightened her grip on the frock, afraid of being more exposed than a moment ago. "I would hate to have to dive in again to retrieve you both." His eyes pleaded, looking between her and Millie. "And it's not that I couldn't do it, I'd be more than happy to be of service." A slow smile followed, exposing a dimple on his right check. "I just think it wouldn't be a wise idea to walk without my help."

Jane held her head when she began to feel light-headed again. The idea of being in the water had her in knots. *He's probably right.* She groaned and looked at Millie, realizing if she fell this time, she'd accidentally drag Millie along with her. Millie shook her head as though she was terrified Jane would decline the offer. Not wanting to humiliate herself further, she gave a small, defeated nod. Keeping her eyes away from him and his sheer, soaked-through shirt, she slid her hand through the wide wool sleeve before tucking it through his offered arm. Her body grew rigid when she realized she hadn't accepted a gentleman's arm that she did not know. Usually her uncle or close colleagues escorted her. She bit her lip, feeling nervous being in his presence. Keeping her hand light on his arm, they walked frustratingly slow back towards the distressed ship. Millie followed on her other side, offering support when needed.

Her rescuer addressed the man behind them. "Thomas, will you inform everyone I'm finishing up at the dock and that I'll be there as soon as I can?"

Glancing over her shoulder, Jane studied Thomas. He appeared to be in his mid-twenties, probably close in age with the other man. He held a twinkle in his eyes as he gave the gentleman a small salute. "Aye, aye!"

"Miss, Miss." Thomas offered them a slight bow, then turned towards the town.

"Uh, Lieutenant," Jane called after him. She had noticed the epaulets on the shoulders of his frock, stating his rank. He paused to face her. Had she not been exposed to many of the militiamen in Bombay, his burly frame alone could have intimidated her but then again there was a gentleness in his light chocolate eyes, and his boyish smile that softened his daunting form.

"Thank you, for your frock. I'll be sure to return it, after we've had it cleaned." Heat spread to her cheeks as she felt self-conscious again. The large garment had been another reminder of her awkward circumstance.

"Thank you, miss. Take care of yourself." Giving a smile and a bow, he proceeded onto his destination.

Jane beheld the man who steadied her while they eased their way up the gangplank.

"How long have you been at sea?" he asked, his voice sounding rich and jovial.

Tiny bumps trickled up her arms. She tightened her grip on the lapels to calm the chill. "Six weeks. We were in the storm a couple nights back and I fear I've not been myself since. This is my first time off the ship since we docked yesterday."

"It sounds like you experienced land sickness."

"Land sickness?" Her brow perked with curiosity as they stepped around a pile of ropes on deck.

The gentleman went on with a little smile. "I've seen a few sailors experience it in my life. It occurs when you're on land after being at sea for a time and for some reason, you still feel the motion of the sea throwing you off balance. It can take days and sometimes weeks to recover."

"I certainly hope it won't last that long!" Jane looked up at him with surprise. She hated the idea of swaying back and forth wherever she went.

"I'm sure it won't." He gave her hand an encouraging squeeze, causing her stomach to take an unfamiliar dive.

She stopped and turned to the gentleman as they reached the stairs that led down to her quarters. "Sir, I must apologize if I delayed you from any prior engagement. I'm truly grateful for all that you have done for me." She wavered feeling unnerved by his gaze, her eyes flicked down to his distinguished jaw, trying to remember what more she wanted to say. "Thank you again. May I inquire what ship you're on, so that I may return the lieutenant's frock?"

The man held a crooked smile. "You did me a favor with this little excursion. I promise."

She examined him wearily. *What an odd thing to say. What could he possibly be facing that would be worse than almost drowning in an attempt to save someone?*

"We're stationed on the Ebony. It's the ship to the port side of the dock. Uh, by port I mean left side."

"I know the term," she replied freely. After all, she had spent most of her life around soldiers and sailors in Bombay, though he wouldn't know that about her.

His eyes brightened and the corner of his mouth lifted. "If you come in the morning, you'll be able to catch the lieutenant."

"Thank you."

He took her hand, slightly bowing to offer it a kiss. Warmth from his touch traveled through her hand like the morning sun, warming her cheeks. Jane caught herself staring at him with a strange desire. Many times her hand had been kissed, but never before had she noticed the touch of a gentleman's lips—so soft, warm, and surprisingly gentle coming from such a large-statured man. Her mouth parted, partly ashamed, the other aghast that she absentmindedly noticed his lips. Promptly, she pulled her hand away and gave him a small curtsy. "Sir." The absence of his touch immediately left her fingers cold.

With a final bow and a smile spreading across his well-defined cheeks, he departed towards the Ebony with water dripping off his clothes, trailing shamelessly behind. She enviously watched his swift steady movements as he walked down to the dock with ease. *What did he say his name was?*

"Miss Jane? Shall we?"

Startled, Jane jumped. She inhaled a deep breath, avoiding Millie's playful smile.

"Yes, let's try this again," she murmured, feeling somewhat guilty at being caught staring at the dashing gentleman.

Chapter Three

$\mathcal{H}$anding his bifold hat to a footman, James strolled confidently into the overcrowded pink reception room of Governor Keaton's home. Wearing fresh, dry attire, his arms and shoulders shifted uncomfortably in his jacket. His shoulders failed to loosen from the stiffness caused from the event at the pier. He surveyed the mingling crowd and noticed a few unfamiliar gentlemen among others who were his neighbors and friends.

A young-looking lieutenant with a very obnoxious laugh caught his eye. The gentleman stood by a large, white-trimmed, open window, socializing with Miss Elaine Keaton who seemed to take to him quite fondly—if the gleeful flick of her hand was any indication. A sparkle in Miss Keaton's eyes flashed while she studied the lieutenant. James winced when she released a high, musical giggle—*probably telling him the latest gossip.* Her blonde curls twisted loosely on her head and bounced joyfully with delight whenever she spoke.

James clasped his hands behind his back, hiding the small trembling of his tired muscles. Fortunately, no one was around the harbor when Miss Jane had had her mishap. Particularly, Miss Keaton. Miss Keaton would be certain to tell everyone she knew, and didn't know, about the incident for months. He tugged at his gold-threaded sleeves, agitated at the thought of Miss Jane being the target of someone else's malice. If anyone caught wind of what happened, he'd be sure to put an end to it.

His gaze shifted across the room and spotted the gentleman he needed to greet, Governor Keaton. Peppered-gray hair circled the shiny head of the governor. The governor bellowed out in laughter, his plump stomach convulsing merrily with what he heard. Stepping to the side to get a better glimpse of whom he conversed with, James spotted a slender gentleman with a full head of charcoal gray hair and small round spectacles resting above his stubby nose. They appeared to be in light conversation, smiling and laughing in an easy manner with each other. Being certain to stay on the opposite side of the room as Miss Keaton, James made his way over to the host, shaking hands with friends, making bows towards the ladies, and exchanging a knowing smile with Thomas along the way.

"There you are!" exclaimed Governor Keaton, grasping James's hand in a firm handshake.

"Please excuse my tardiness, Governor Keaton. I was delayed at the dock."

"No need to apologize, captain." Governor Keaton smiled up at James. His round, rosy cheeks pushed his twinkling, blue eyes into slants. "I want you to meet a very dear friend of mine." Governor Keaton turned to the gentleman on his right and placed his hand on his shoulder. James saw the admiration in the governor's eyes as he proceeded, "Captain James McCannon, may I introduce you to the finest surgeon that not only Her Majesty's army has ever seen, but all of England: Doctor Duncan Brown."

It was an honor indeed, for he had heard discussions of Doctor Brown's work circulate through the port as many soldiers and sailors bragged how the man had saved their lives from their battle wounds. The gentleman was extremely skillful with his surgeries and rarely relied on the techniques of other surgeons, who were quick to amputate the limb, if the lead balls didn't go through.

"And Doctor Duncan Brown, may I introduce you to one of Her Majesty's most honorable naval captains, as well as Jamestown's finest citizens, Captain James McCannon."

James shook the legendary surgeon's hand. "Sir, it is truly an honor."

"From what Governor Keaton has mentioned of you, the honor is all mine, captain." Neatly trimmed brows weighed heavy above his observing eyes. Confidence wavering, James tugged on his jacket sleeves, feeling it vital to appear his best under the doctor's discerning stare.

"Doctor Brown is just passing through as he's on his way to teach at Oxford University," Governor Keaton proudly stated.

"What an honor it is for them to have you, sir."

"Thank you, captain." The gentleman's soft green eyes continued to watch him through his spectacles.

"How long do you intend to teach at Oxford?" James clasped his unsettled hands behind his back. The doctor gave a pleasant smile.

"Until they tire of me telling them of my personal experiences with the Mysore Wars." Doctor Brown and Governor Keaton chuckled. James smiled at the man's lightheartedness.

"Well, they may never tire, Duncan," Governor Keaton teased, as his glass in his hand waved carelessly sloshing wine high up on the edges. "You'd best be sticking with the two years they offered you."

Doctor Brown chuckled. "I suppose you're right."

"May I inquire how you two met?" James couldn't help but observe how the two easily conversed with each other.

Governor Keaton grinned with the question. "Of course! Doctor Brown and I go way back. How long has it been, Duncan? Thirty plus years?" Governor Keaton proceeded before giving the doctor a chance to answer. Doctor Brown took it in stride and smiled amiably at his friend.

"It was in Bombay, during the First Anglo-Mysore War. We had just overtaken part of the Mysore Kingdom in an attempt to dismantle the French ally, in hopes of expanding the British East India Company. The Mysore were furious, ruthlessly sending men on suicidal missions, attacking the British soldiers at random day and night. Such callousness." Governor Keaton stared at the wall behind James with a haunted gleam in his eyes. He blinked as if to be rid of the nightmare. "Well, my battalion and I were advancing during one of the many battles, when I was shot. I found myself going in and out of consciousness. When I awoke, I heard this arrogant doctor call for his saws. He was going to amputate this leg!" Governor Keaton exclaimed, patting his right thigh. "I had calmly insisted that the doctor try and remove the lead ball before doing anything hastily—"

"Calmly?" Doctor Brown chuckled, cutting in. He peered at his friend through his spectacles.

"Yes, Duncan, I was calm." The governor's rosy cheeks darkened in hue.

Doctor Brown gave a low chuckle, throwing his head to the side with a genuine smile. "The man was a lunatic. He was screaming orders and obscenities at the doctor and nurse. Though," he began with sympathy in his voice. "I truly don't blame you, Terry. That must have been very terrifying for you."

"Well luckily you walked by the surgery when you did, otherwise I would have lost my leg." Governor Keaton took a long drink of his wine.

James's curiosity piqued. "How did you convince the other doctor to step aside?"

With another chuckle, Doctor Brown responded, "I didn't have to persuade the chief surgeon at the time to let me try to save his patient's leg. Governor Keaton did that by his own doing. Every object he had within his reach he started throwing at Chief Thorpe, causing the doctor to storm out of the room. I'll never forget his face. He was unusually red, just ready to explode." Doctor Brown laughed along with Governor Keaton at their shared memory. "Of course, as a newly trained associate, I was excited to do my first surgery on my own."

Governor Keaton lowered his glass from his wet lips. "Just a moment," he interjected abruptly with an intent stare. "Duncan, I was your first surgery? How did I not know this?"

"You never asked," Doctor Brown casually replied with a shrug, obviously sensing the shift in his friend's mood. "I remember spending four hours on his surgery, removing shrapnel and the lead ball. Thanks to the experience, it gave me the confidence to continue to perform the same kind of surgeries with others."

James held back a smile as Doctor Brown gave the stunned governor a friendly smack on his shoulder. Bluish-violet wine swished back and forth in the cup of the remarkably still hand.

"Duncan," Governor Keaton barely managed to whisper with surprise. He licked the wine off his lips. With his free hand, he began rubbing at the shadow of stubble on his chin in a nervous manner. "I didn't know I was your first surgery."

He blinked, still trying to process the little bit of new information when Lady Mary Keaton gracefully floated up to her husband's side in a red, satin evening gown. Every piece of her pulled into perfection. Her brown hair pinned finely above her long, narrow face, not a wisp of dark strands out of place. Her smooth, drawn out nose broadened when she smiled sweetly at him.

"Captain McCannon, so glad you could make it." She offered her hand to James, which he clasped, bowing over it. "Lady Keaton. Thank you for having me."

She gave him a satisfied smile then turned to her husband and spoke in a hushed tone.

"Dearest, it's getting late. Why don't you announce dinner?" Her hand rested on his arm in a delicate manner.

Governor Keaton cleared his throat as if it helped surface him from his troubling thoughts. "Yes, of course, my love."

"Doctor Brown," Lady Keaton turned to him, her blue eyes sparkling. "Will your niece be joining us for dinner?"

"I'm afraid she's still recovering. She'll be with us later this evening."

Her thin bottom lip pushed out with concern. "The poor dear. She must have been miserable during that storm,"

Doctor Brown stared at the governor's stilled glass with apprehension. "Yes, she was very miserable. I'm starting to have my doubts about having her on this journey."

"None of that now. I'm certain once she gets to Oxford, she'll forget all about your voyage. Why, there will be balls almost every night, the theater to attend, and as pretty as she is, she'll have plenty of callers. What more could a young lady want?" Lady Keaton perked up at this last sentence.

The line between the doctor's brows eased slightly but his eyes tightened with more apprehension. He didn't appear convinced. More than anything, he seemed unsettled by it.

"Ladies and Gentleman!" Governor Keaton rang out, "Let us all proceed to the dining room for tonight's meal."

The crowd continued their chatter, casually making their way into the dining hall. James followed behind Doctor Brown and Governor Keaton, fascinated by the gentleman's friendship. He knew better than to eavesdrop, but after witnessing Doctor Brown's revelation to the governor that he was his first surgery, he couldn't keep himself from following close behind to hear the rest of their conversation.

"Why cheer up, Terry, nothing bad happened." Giving his friend an encouraging smile, Doctor Brown peered down at his friend's leg. "You're both still with us."

Governor Keaton's face grew ghastly white. "I could have lost my leg, Duncan. Or worse, died on that surgery table. You probably had no idea what you were doing."

Doctor Brown let out a low laugh. "I had to start somewhere. I honorably couldn't have picked a better friend than you to practice on."

Governor Keaton gasped. Doctor Brown chuckled and threw his arm around his friend, offering him a quick reassuring hug. The doctor seemed to thoroughly enjoy himself and the harmless torment he'd brought to his friend. All these years Governor Keaton thought he had been in the hands of an expert, not a new, fresh apprentice. James smiled, observing the exchange between these two friends. Of course, Governor Keaton would eventually overcome his state of shock from the situation, but James could tell by the governor's expression, he would be unusually quiet this evening.

On the far, orange-colored wall, three paneled drapes framed large windows. The center of the windows were French doors leading out to the pavilion. In between the heavy drapes were gold candle holders, each holding three, white, dimly flamed candles. A large chandelier hung low above the long, white linen clothed table. The center pieces consisted of sugar-glazed fruit and short vases of wildflowers. Eight hand-carved chairs lined each side of the table, along with one at each end. Judging by the amount of people in the parlor, they'd fill all eighteen chairs. Now to be fortunate enough to find a seat quickly, before a certain young woman caught up to him. He felt a tug on his sleeve. *Too late,* he groaned to himself. He peered over his shoulder expecting to see Miss Keaton. He released his breath as Thomas strolled up to his side with a mischievous smile.

"How's our fair lady friend?" He spoke in a low secretive tone, being certain no one else could hear.

James gripped the lapels of his jacket at the sudden dip his stomach made from his friend's question. Eyeing the fruit, he took them as hunger pangs.

"She'll be fine. She had experienced land sickness, *not* a barrel of rum," he glanced at him with disapproval.

Thomas laughed. "Well at least we know she won't have to replace the rum." He offered a cheeky smile and scooted his chair next to James. James chuckled in agreement.

What felt to be the first meal in months at the governor's home, James's stomach was more than pleasantly full after he ate the delicious quail and boiled potatoes in peace. On occasion he would hear Miss Keaton giggle at the other end of the table while chatting with the same young officer. *Perhaps, the tables have turned and my evening will be pleasant after all.* James smiled to himself and took a long sip from his glass.

As if the stars were in her favor, Jane and Millie managed to scamper down the hall to their room before Private Whitby or any other sailor on duty could question Jane's sopping state, let alone the lieutenant's frock wrapped around her body. There would be too many speculating looks and presumptions from the men she had never become acquainted with over their journey. She couldn't possibly face the humiliating scrutiny now nor its lingering rumors during the rest of their voyage to England.

Discovering their trunks to be nowhere in sight, she asked Millie to inform Private Whitby that she had . . . *oh, what would she say?* The idea of coming up with an outrageous fib to what happened did seem humorous, but she didn't want to lie to the gentleman, not with his devotion to them. Her teeth began to clatter against each other while she stood in her cold, wet garments. A puddle formed at her sopping, stocking-covered feet. All the shivering and chattering made it difficult for her to think.

"J-j-j-ust inf-f-orm himmm," she tightened her muscles in her face and body in an attempt to control her unsteady voice. "That my gown had encountered salt water from off the p-p-ier and that it's too s-s-s-oiled for me to p-p-resent myself to my hosts."

Never did she like the phrase "less is more," but in this particular circumstance she couldn't agree more. If he were to decipher that she encountered salt water, then he'd probably assume the helm of her skirts were dampened, not her whole gown. A curve of a faint smile spread across Millie's young face.

"Very clever, Miss Jane. I shall inform him of that, but after I change you out of those wet garments. The last thing you'd want is to catch a cold during your time on land."

"V-v-alid p-p-point."

Shivering, Jane curled up into a ball on her firm bed, wrapped in a scratchy wool blanket. Even with her wet stays and shift removed, the shaking continued. A glimpse of sinking into the cold, dark abyss flashed before her mind as if she were staring into the depth of a frigid, deep portrait. Every part of her body tensed under the chilled blanket, her lungs still ached and burned from choking on the salt water. *How long was I unconscious?* Little bumps covered her flesh. Her teeth clattered like the wooden chimes hanging on the back pavilion of her home in India, clicking together from a gust of wind.

Staring across the room, the cabin's locked, thin door appeared to begin to tilt to its side. Knowing the harbor was steady, she curled her hold on the blanket, pressing it deeper to her chest and squeezed her eyes shut with hopes to feel more stable. The blackness behind her lids filled with the gentleman's pale blue eyes, staring at her with concern. The lingering memory of his warm touch began to spread a balmy feeling through her, calming the trembles. *How long had I been under water? Where did he come from?* She hadn't seen him on the tilting pier. Her heart sped with curiosity from the thought of him. He had to be a sailor, especially after he mentioned that "we are stationed on the Ebony."

Jane felt the heaviness of exhaustion sweep over her. Fortunately, the chances of seeing him again was unlikely. She'd have the governor's footman handle the delivery of the lieutenant's frock to eliminate any humiliating opportunity to converse with him again.

Pleased with her plan, she sighed and faded into a peaceful sleep.

"Miss Jane, Miss Jane." Jane awoke to Millie shaking her shoulder. The girl stood above her holding a lantern. The short wax candle flickered orange, illuminating the anxious expression on Millie's face. "Miss Jane, you better wake up. It's getting late."

Jane's eyes darted across the darkened room to see the silvery moon shining through their small port window. Frantically, she sat up, clutching the wool blanket to her bare skin. Had she slept most of the night? Her heart sprinted in her chest with an uneasy stir of panic. "How long have I been asleep?"

"You've been passed out for an hour, miss. You looked so peaceful, I waited for as long as I could before I woke you. I knew you were looking forward to getting off the ship and seeing the Keatons."

Jane sank back down on the straw mattress, relieved it wasn't later in the evening.

"Thank you, Millie, I am." She appreciated Millie's thoughtfulness. The idea of seeing her friend Miss Elaine and meeting the others raised her spirits. Surprisingly, feeling more rested than she had in the past few days, she grew more eager to depart from the ship.

Millie assisted Jane into her blue muslin evening gown. Once again, she carefully pinned up Jane's curls, being certain to avoid touching the bump that Jane had received from her fall. She decided it was caused by debris in the water, as no other object could have inflicted such a wound. When Millie finished, she stepped back, approving her work.

"You look beautiful, Miss Jane," Millie admired.

Jane smiled up at her, taking her hand. "Thank you, Millie. I couldn't have done this without you." Millie blushed with shyness and turned to give Jane her cream-colored eyelet-laced wrap.

Alerting Private Whitby who guarded the door of their departure, he hurried in the room to grab the trunk.

"Are you better, Miss Sawyer?" Private Whitby's brows furrowed with concern.

"Much, thank you."

"Would you like me to escort you out," he stood with their trunk in hand.

"I'll be fine, but thank you."

Private Whitby nodded, "I'll go fetch the carriage driver. I bet he's waiting for you at the pub."

Feeling a bit flustered that he knew what had happened, she delayed after he left the room with her belongings.

"Millie?" Jane looked at her handmaid with suspicion. "What exactly did you tell Private Whitby?"

"Everything you asked of me. Your dress got salt water on it and while you waited for the trunk, you decided to take another short nap. Nothing more."

Jane relaxed her shoulders. "Splendid. Thank you, Millie."

The two ladies headed outside towards the carriage. The cool night air felt refreshing on Jane's face while she walked confidently in a fine straight line. Other than a minor headache, she felt wonderful. She smiled as the last few miserable and humiliating hours were now behind her.

Chapter Four

The gentlemen of the dinner party had finished their time in the parlor discussing the latest attack from the French when their host announced it was time for them to join the ladies.

Entering the drawing room, James groaned as he mistakenly locked eyes with Miss Keaton.

"Captain James!" she squealed and bounded towards him with a gleeful hop in her step. "When did you arrive? How did I miss you at dinner?"

A few heads had turned to watch her greeting. Enthusiasm burst from her blonde, bouncing curls down her curvy body to the hem of her floral dress. Miss Keaton looped her arm through his and looked up with blue adoring eyes.

James forced a halfhearted smile as the woman's latest endeavor had apparently failed to keep her captivated.

"Why, Miss Keaton, I've been here all night."

"Come now, captain. You've known me since our youth, please call me Elaine."

James would never do such a thing. He wanted nothing more than to keep their relationship proper and at arm's reach. If he ever slipped and called her Elaine, who knows what she may spread.

"I believe 'Miss Keaton' has a nicer ring to it. I shall stick with that."

She raised a brow, but to his surprise, she simply said, "Well, I insist you join me for a game of chess. I don't know how I missed seeing you earlier. Come, there's a table over in the corner."

He didn't get a chance to object. She pursed her pink lips and, with her hand still linked through his arm, led the way.

While being dragged toward the remote table in the crowded room, James caught Thomas shooting him a wicked smile. James huffed a breath of irritation as Thomas leisurely sat at a table where he was desperate to be, playing cards.

"Now that I have your undivided attention, I have a proposition for you." Her bright, lively voice rang out almost in song. He had a sudden urge to pull at his cravat that tightened around his neck. *Just as long as she doesn't sing it,* James muttered to himself. Knowing Miss Keaton, he wouldn't put it past her.

She clapped her hands together then laid them in her lap. "I'm in need of your expertise. A dear friend of mine has arrived from Bombay, terribly sick. I'm afraid they were caught in the tropical storm and almost capsized twice! At least that's what Lieutenant Howard told me. He's the one playing cards with Lieutenant Thomas, over there." She pointed her dainty finger in the direction of the young officer. "Well, apparently during their voyage a lot of the men became sick and injured while the seas were choppy . . ."

The woman began to ramble on about the sailors' experience. James found himself tuning her out halfway through. He couldn't overlook, however, her shiny, blonde hair bouncing with every tilt of her head or wave of her hand. His thoughts wandered, *Maybe she got her color from her father's side of the family, her mom is more of a brunette. Governor Keaton's hair is grey making it hard to discern. It must be from the governor's side,* he concluded. *She also has his blue eyes though hers are rounder due to her slender, pink cheeks. They are nothing like Miss Jane's big hazel eyes.* All evening, his thoughts hadn't stopped turning towards the captivating blue-green eyed woman he had earlier encountered. *Could she be sailing through? Of course, she was sailing on, why would she stay?* The island was a stopping point for most people. *How long would she be staying?* Suddenly, he noticed Miss Keaton had changed her tune.

". . . They'll be here for at least another month and I want to make sure she sees all the best kept secrets that Saint Helena has to offer. So, will you help me?"

Slowly fluttering her blonde lashes, she started to draw circles on his hand that rested on the table. Pulling his tainted hand away, he moved a pawn forward.

"What did you need me to do?"

She scrunched her mousy nose, appearing annoyed at having to repeat herself. She moved her bishop across the black and white marble board and collected his castle in one swift motion. James looked up with surprise, *How could she pay attention to the board with all her jabbering?*

"I was asking if you could give us a tour of some of the springs. I don't know nearly as much as you about such things, and Lieutenant Thomas could join us." She smiled brightly. *A perfect scheme for them to pair off.*

He frowned. He would be trapped. And alone with her. He cleared his throat. "With the recent attacks, our fleet has been assigned to more patrols. I'm afraid I can't commit." James stared down at his knight, bracing for her response. After a rare moment of silence on her part, he glanced up. She beamed with excitement, peering towards the now crowded doorway. He hadn't noticed the small gathering.

"She's here!" Miss Keaton exclaimed, leaping to her feet then hurrying towards the group.

Relieved of her departure, James stood and walked to the table that now only occupied Lieutenant Howard and Thomas.

"James, take a seat." Thomas pointed at one of the two empty chairs that faced the doorway of the room. "The lieutenant and I are just finishing up and then we can start a new round of poker." James looked around noting very few people sat at their tables playing cards. The majority now congregated at the doorway welcoming the newcomer. "Did Miss Keaton's queen beat your king?" Thomas asked as he stared at his hand of cards. "Queens can be quite treacherous moving around the board . . . forcing the king into a corner."

"If I had my knight to protect my king, he wouldn't have been trapped," James rebuked.

Lieutenant Howard held a sly smile while observing the gentlemen's banter. "I must say, captain, that queen of yours is very high spirited. I can see her defeating every pawn, including the knight to get to your king."

James shot the lieutenant with a look of warning.

"I'm afraid, Lieutenant, you're right," Thomas remarked off-handedly. Ignoring the taunting, James skimmed through the cards that were abandoned in front of him. "The queen would do just that to get to the king." Thomas looked up from his cards towards the doorway. His eyes brightened with recognition then quickly resumed to a disinterested manner. "But forget about the pawns and the knight fellas." He laid his cards face down and casually rubbed his square chin. "He needs a queen—not just any queen, but one that isn't afraid to *dive* into action," he smirked at James who gave him a bored stare. Resting his jaw on his palm, James waited for his friend to be done with his dull chatter.

"One who is the fairest in all the land and that can be revived back to life. A queen," he paused, leaning back in his chair, "that perhaps looks a little like that lady over there."

James looked in the direction Thomas was indicating. Peering through the parting sea of people, stood the woman from the pier. James's hand dropped from his chin. *Was she the friend that Miss Keaton talked about?* He straightened his posture. His cravat tightened uncomfortably around his neck, but he was too taken to do anything about it. Unable to tear his eyes off her, he watched her make her way through with introductions.

This was not the same woman he saw at the harbor. Compared to how she had been earlier in the day, there was a drastic change in how she was now walking and carrying herself. Her complexion was less pale with more natural coloring in her cheeks. Certainly, the most beautiful woman he had ever seen, and unexpectedly graceful.

"I'm afraid that queen is not an option," Lieutenant Howard responded in a cool, somewhat bitter tone. He caught both men's attention. James's heart began to sink. He leaned back in his chair, studying the gentleman.

"Has she a fiancé?" Thomas inquired.

"No, just a very protective uncle," he sneered. James looked back at the crowd with dawning understanding. *Miss Jane is Doctor Brown's niece! That would explain the close friendship Miss Keaton has with her.* "He made it very clear to us officers that if he found any of us taking notice of Miss Sawyer, he'd make our life difficult, especially if we were ever wounded. Since that day, news spread like fire, and all the men aboard our ship have avoided Miss Sawyer like the plague. It seems everyone wants to be in the doctor's good graces."

"As they should be," James retorted. He didn't appreciate the lieutenant's disrespectful tone. The lieutenant raised his glass to James and nodded before drinking it empty.

James studied the auburn-haired man. His sharp angular features made him appear harsh, especially with the distasteful scowl on his face. An unsettling feeling brewed in James's stomach. The young man appeared to be around Thomas's height, though a lot leaner than any officer on James's ship. James looked down to where the lieutenant held his cup. His hand was smooth and not calloused like all the other hardworking sailors. In fact, judging by the man's stature, he doubted the man had ever done any hard labor in his life. The thought repulsed James. All the officers on James's ship were required to work alongside the other sailors as they kept up with the demands of the sea. Her Majesty's Navy did not allow room for idleness in any of her officers. Nor did he.

Governor Keaton was certainly adamant that Jane meet everyone in attendance. Having attended many social events with her uncle in India, she made her way through introductions at ease with graceful curtsies and a pleasant smile to the numerous eager guests.

One table to go and I'll be able to sit and enjoy a few gam—she felt the blood drain from her face. Standing before her were the men from the dock. The same gentlemen who were part of her humiliating catastrophe. Feeling exposed to the gentlemen once again, Jane unfurled her fan that dangled around her wrist and nervously waved the silk material to calm the sudden heat in her cheeks. From the corner of her eye, she peeked at the particular gentleman who had rescued her.

Goodness, why did he have to look so dashing in his officer uniform? Officer uniform! Her eyes flicked to the epaulets on his shoulders. *Captain? Could he be the same captain that Elaine had written about? Or was that a different captain? There had been too many gentlemen she had written about that Jane had lost interest in keeping tabs on all their names.*

Every fiber in her body awoke with a startling jolt when she locked eyes with him. He gazed at her without a hint of a smile but it was his eyes, those ridiculous light blue eyes that caused her to flush as they looked at her with such warmth. Fervently she fanned herself, swiftly looking towards Lieutenant Thomas who held a broad boyish smile and tipped his head.

"Miss Sawyer, may I introduce you to Captain James McCannon, Lieutenant Thomas Fletch, and of course you know Lieutenant Stephen Howard." Standing by her side, Governor Keaton's voice seemed to resonate from a distance. "Gentlemen, Miss Jane Sawyer." Jane dipped into a small curtsy. Avoiding the officers' eyes, she stared at the table as they bowed.

"Miss Sawyer?" Lieutenant Fletch inquired. "We were about to start another round of pontoon. Would you care to join us?" Jane opened her mouth to decline when Elaine came up from behind.

"Jane loves that game! Come, Jane, let's play." Wanting to be anywhere but there, her stomach sank. Squeezing the fan shut, she uncomfortably twisted it in her hand and forced a curt nod.

"I'll let you to it," Governor Keaton remarked delightedly. He smiled at Jane before wandering over to a table where her uncle was playing a hand of cards. Swiftly, Lieutenant Fletch grabbed a chair from an adjacent table, offering it to Jane as Elaine had already seated herself next to the captain. Hesitantly she sat, having to take her place between Elaine and the dreadful Lieutenant Stephen. Not hiding her disdain, she scooted her chair closer to Elaine.

Her first day on their voyage had been unsettling to say the least. A shiver ran up Jane's back as she reflected on it.

After convincing her lady's maid to stay in their quarter's—as she needed a moment in private, Jane stood alone at the stern of the ship, distraught, watching her beloved Bombay disappear into the horizon. Wiping away a few escaping tears, she swallowed the lump in her throat. The intended two years away from home already felt like a miserably long time.

To escape the reality of their departure, she closed her eyes and pictured the day like it was any other. It started out greeting her childhood friend Sophie and together they walked through the town's market smelling the aromatic spices and studying the vibrant stamped fabrics. Merchants yelled out prices while buyers negotiated them down. Hand carved beads organized into different trays were being sold next to fruit stands. Then after buying her fruit and her favorite jasmine, citrus soap, she'd walk home chatting with Sophie about their latest adventure in town followed with wishing one another a good day until they saw each other that evening for a social dance.

Slowly, Jane opened her watery eyes. A dull ache spread from her stomach to her heart. She didn't wish to leave her treasured home. With her uncle's new position at Oxford, he had begun adding pressure on her to find a suitable husband while in England. Jane couldn't deny there would be far more prospects there than in India, but unlike most young ladies she knew, such as her friend Elaine Keaton, she was candidly fine with the idea of waiting for a time before settling down. She loved the independence her uncle bestowed upon her and feared that no other gentleman would allow her the same. Jane dabbed at another tear trickling down her cheek.

"Beautiful . . . isn't it?"

She turned to see a familiar young officer staring at her with a sly smile. A couple hours prior, the same man had stood with another sailor watching her walk up the gangway with a wicked gleam in their eyes. Standing at the rail, their heads close together, they appeared as if they were plotting with quiet tones and smirks. The lieutenant's squinty eyes lingered over her bodice, like any young woman would if the gown she wore had been on display in the window of the fabric shop. From the corner of her eye the lieutenant nodded with approval to the sailor and chuckled. She rolled her eyes with disgust.

A shudder ran through her as he continued to stare at her with the same attention he had earlier.

"I love watching the land disappear, exposing nothing but a naked canvas."

The lieutenant slowly strode to Jane's side. He placed his hand on the rail, pressing it against hers. She stiffened from the warmth of his breath on her neck. Refusing to give him any of her attention, she stepped away from the man's advancements and continued to stare at the horizon. The jagged outline of the city had disappeared into a straight line separating the bright blue sky and the dark water.

An involuntary shiver ran up her spine as she could feel his eyes surveying over her while he got close to her again.

"I know how hard it is to leave your home behind, Miss Sawyer." She started to feel queasy when his finger traced up her neck, to catch an innocent curl. He twirled it around his finger. "If you were in need of any comfort or a shoulder to cry on, I'm here for you. It's a small ship." He gave her a frightening smile. "You wouldn't have to search far to find me."

Jane swatted his hand away, giving him the most menacing glare she could muster. "What I need, sir, is for you to keep your distance."

She was impressed that her voice stayed steady, unlike her trembling hands. She clenched her fist and took a deep breath to calm her heart and tried to relax her stomach. The man glared at her with an unnerving glint. He didn't appear like he would back down.

"Jane!" her uncle roared. She looked over to see him standing at the top of the steps with fire in his eyes. "Get back to your cabin," he ordered. "Lieutenant Howard and I have a few things we need to discuss."

Not giving the lieutenant a second glance, Jane gratefully obeyed her uncle's command, hurrying away from the ghastly man. Her uncle squeezed her arm in a loving manner as she passed him towards the stairs. Relief lifted her spirits within his comforting touch. She knew from her uncle's furious expression, Lieutenant Howard was about to receive his wrath—and unfortunately, she was going to get lectured for leaving her ship's quarters unchaperoned.

"I'm afraid I'm going to have to call it a night," Lieutenant Howard spoke, interrupting Jane's recollection. He awkwardly stood, refusing to take the two cards from Captain McCannon.

"But we've yet to begin! Won't you join us for one round, Lieutenant Howard, please?" Elaine was looking up at the Lieutenant with a pouty expression. Jane eased her hand under the table and tapped twice on her friend's knee, then gave one subtle shake with her head. Elaine's eyes darted to Jane for a mere second but maintained her same pouty expression. Discreetly she squeezed Jane's hand letting her know she acknowledged the sign. An exchange they had mastered during years of table talking. Thanks to stuffy parlors and dinner parties together, they creatively found a way to say which bachelor would best suit each other—particularly for Elaine. One tap and an arch of the brow meant the gentleman was available. Fluttering of lashes with the tilt of the head meant he was taken. Two taps, one shake meant the gentleman was trouble. That gesture was rarely used.

Lieutenant Howard appeared apprehensive when he gazed across the room. Jane's eyes followed his, landing on her uncle. Uncle Duncan flashed a threatening scowl at the lieutenant.

"I'm afraid I must. Captain McCannon, Lieutenant Fletch, ladies, it's been a pleasure." The Lieutenant delivered a quick bow before scurrying off to say his good-byes to the hostesses.

Her chest swelled with admiration towards her uncle. There had been times when she didn't appreciate his protective manner, but tonight, she was ever grateful. She released her breath as the lieutenant departed the room.

Elaine shifted in her chair to adjust her skirts. Leaning towards Jane, she muttered softly, "Later."

Jane gave a slight nod. She would be certain to explain it all to her.

As relieved as she felt that the lieutenant was gone, she still had to deal with the dilemma of being in the presence of the other two gentlemen. Slowly she relaxed her shoulders and eased her hands into her lap. Under her heavy weight of humiliation, deep down she felt safe in their presence. Holding onto that feeling of certainty, she allowed the embarrassment to dissolve—at least as much as she could muster, for she still felt flustered in Captain McCannon's presence.

"Well, shall we?" Lieutenant Fletch scooted himself closer to the table. He began to shuffle the deck then stopped. "I'm afraid having an extra chair will throw off my rhythm with my deal. I fear I may accidentally deal to that spot."

The captain eyed the lieutenant suspiciously. "You're dealing two cards per person."

"Yes, but look. This seating arrangement is all wrong. The rule of the game is there needs to be a gentleman seated between each of the ladies."

The captain raised a questionable brow. Elaine began to giggle. And Jane looked to the empty chair beside her. There was no such rule to this game. She began to understand the captain's questionable stare. What were the lieutenant's intentions? Elaine was already seated next to her captain.

"Yes, Miss Keaton, would you be so kind as to switch seats with our captain while I remove the extra chair? I do believe he prefers to sit on that particular *throne.*"

Jane observed Captain McCannon giving his friend a hard stare. His irritation by the notion was as clear as the crystal glass in front of her. Already feeling self-conscious with the two men, she questioned if the captain preferred to avoid her as much as she preferred to avoid him.

Oblivious to the gentlemen's exchange, Elaine grinned, eager to oblige. "Oh, this is just like musical chairs."

"Yes, but without the music," the captain muttered.

Smiling at the captain's glower, the lieutenant sat himself closer to Jane. "Minor detail."

Elaine giggled some more. "We'll make our own music!"

"No, no," the captain eagerly got to his feet.

Unnerved by his nearness, Jane stared at the grain of the wood table.

The captain situated himself with his arms in front of him. "Miss Sawyer," his voice was low, almost to a whisper.

"Captain." She cleared her throat, attempting to rid the submissive voice she didn't recognize.

"Splendid! Now, let the game begin!" Lieutenant Fletch exclaimed, speedily passing out two cards to each player.

James wished he could say Miss Sawyer was glad to see them as he was with her, but disappointedly she seemed a bit resentful. Under the candlelight her beautiful eyes glowed with uncertainty while taking in the scene before her. She appeared very uneasy next to Lieutenant Howard. When she had shifted her body away from him, he began to doubt that Miss Sawyer's discomfort was solely due to being in his and Thomas's presence.

James looked over at Thomas who made a questioning look toward him. He had caught the look of hesitancy as well. Feeling protective, James was about to request a stroll around the room with her but changed his mind when Lieutenant Howard bid his good-byes.

"Jane, Captain James here has agreed to take us around the island! Isn't that exciting?" exclaimed Miss Keaton.

"Oh, has he now?" Thomas asked, giving him a questionable smirk. He knew his friend would never have agreed to the chore of calling on Miss Elaine Keaton. Though unbeknownst to Thomas, now that Miss Sawyer had entered the picture, James had had a change of heart.

"I have," James confidently stated. He looked over at Miss Sawyer who studied her cards very closely.

"When are we going on this grand adventure?" she asked, still peering at her hand. James ran his hand across the evening stubble that had started to grow on his cheek. The idea of seeing her again made it hard to focus on the game.

"Tomorrow morning too soon?" he asked, noticing she bit one side of her full bottom lip as she concentrated. The game had moved onto gin rummy and he got the impression Miss Sawyer didn't play it very often.

"Tomorrow?" Miss Keaton squealed. "Why that's perfect! And you must join us too, lieutenant."

Thomas smirked at his friend. "I'd be delighted. Perhaps we could ride up to the falls and have a picnic. I know with all the rain we've received the falls will be coming back to life."

Miss Keaton clapped with excitement. "What a wonderful idea!"

Miss Sawyer, on the other hand, appeared lost in her own world. Scrutinizing her cards, her head tilted to the side exposing a short brown curl tucked behind her ear. Her long fingers softly drummed the table. James averted his stare and attempted to look at his hand.

"What are your thoughts, Miss Sawyer?" he asked, hoping to shift her attention towards him. She had been avoiding his gaze ever since they started playing.

"Hmm?" She moved a card up and placed it down in a different section of her hand. "Oh yes, sounds lovely." She smiled up at Miss Keaton, not him.

Feeling desperate, he cleared his throat for his next attempt. "Do you enjoy riding, Miss Sawyer?"

She switched around another card. "I do."

"Jane's an excellent rider!" Miss Keaton gushed. "We've been riding many times together while I was in India."

Miss Sawyer smiled up at Miss Keaton. "Thank you, and may I add you're quite a splendid rider as well."

Miss Keaton beamed at her friend and then towards James with the hope he heard the compliment. He nodded politely at her.

"How long have you been acquainted?" Thomas asked, grabbing a card from the deck. Miss Keaton tapped the table and arched her brow at Miss Sawyer, motioning with her eyes towards Thomas. *Did she not know how to answer the question?* James wondered by the way she kept trying to get Miss Sawyer's attention.

"Eleven years." Miss Sawyer smiled at Thomas. Her cheeks slightly flushed. "Through the years, Elaine and her parents have visited me and my uncle in India."

James jumped on the chance to ask her a question. "So, is this your first time on this island, Miss Sawyer?" Perhaps she'd flash him a smile? His stomach sank with disappointment.

"It is," she replied. She was back to focusing on her hand and reorganizing her cards. Clearly avoiding him. Somewhat amused, James shifted in his chair, to draw closer to her.

"You'll love the ride to the falls, Jane! You can actually relax and enjoy the forest instead of keeping your eyes peeled for wildlife." Miss Keaton scrunched her face from a repulsive memory.

"Well, I certainly look forward to it," Miss Sawyer chuckled at her friend and drew a card.

Once again, she had smiled at someone other than him. James straightened in the uncomfortable wooden chair. He was convinced if he were to be struck down and dragged out of the room by French mercenaries, she'd continue to look elsewhere. An idea came to his mind that could ruin any chance of her speaking to him ever again. He rubbed his neck as he contemplated it. Considering how things were already going, he had nothing to lose. Keeping his face impassive, he stared at his cards and addressed the group.

"The rocks are a little slippery by the bottom of the falls. As a preliminary caution might I suggest we bring extra blankets?" He drew a card and candidly added, "In case someone falls in, of course."

Thomas stared wide-eyed at his friend. Just as he hoped, Miss Sawyer's eyes darted towards him. He swallowed and held his breath, refusing to feel any regret from his bold statement.

"That's a brilliant idea, captain," she revived, the corner of her mouth twitching. "I'll be sure not to wear my favorite dress, in case it gets cut up by any infuriating branches."

Confounded! He released his breath. Of course, that was her favorite gown. How was he supposed to know? In his defense, the weighted drapes acted as ballasts. They were going to drown for pity's sake. But if he'd learned anything from Miss Keaton's jabbering, a woman's dress is not to be taken lightly. He wiped his palm on his thigh. Despite feeling perturbed, he carried on calmly.

"Yes, I'm afraid the branches up there can be infuriating. But they do serve a great purpose as they protect the delicate fauna from falling in the river and drowning."

Miss Sawyer bit her cheeks, appearing to fight a smile.

"And may I add, there are other places to explore if you're looking for beautiful *green* vegetation. I'd be happy to oblige you in your quest, as it's truly hard to love just one specific area." James was hopeful with his offer. Courtesy of Miss Keaton, he'd heard of one seamstress in town that often-imported exquisite fabric from India.

"I suppose you're right, Captain McCannon." She smiled up at him, causing his stomach to churn like a riptide. *Yes, there it was.* She offered him a radiant smile.

"Though, I must say, once I find an area I love, I stay devoted to it and I have a hard time branching out." She bit on her bottom lip, doing her best to hold her somber façade. James smiled, trying not to laugh at the amused gleam in her eyes.

"That's not true," Miss Keaton interrupted. "You love to explore! That's one of the reasons why I asked Captain James to take us."

"What's the other reason?" Thomas implored, knowing quite well what the other reason would be. Miss Keaton flushed.

Wonderful, Thomas, thanks for that. "It's settled," he stated before Miss Keaton got a word in. "Since it's over an hour's ride each way, we'll leave tomorrow morning by nine."

"Nine?" Miss Keaton whined, but thankfully thought better than to press it.

"Nine, it is. I'll be sure to wear my shabbiest dress." Miss Sawyer gave him a teasing smile that he knew would be impossible to forget.

He laid down his hand, earning him a total of a hundred points for his first win of the night. With a triumph, he declared, "Gin."

Thomas threw his hand down on the table. "Of course, you won. I just needed one more card," he muttered under his breath.

James chortled, "Better luck next time, my friend." Thomas rolled his eyes as James flashed him a crooked smile.

"Ladies, I'm afraid dawn will be upon us soon. I bid you all a good night," he stated, taking to his feet.

He gave each lady a kiss on their hand, perhaps lingering longer on Miss Sawyer's.

"This has been a very entertaining evening indeed." Thomas stood. "Till tomorrow." He gave them each a bow.

Chapter Five

James and Thomas bounced on their benches as their carriage rolled over rocks on the dirt road. "So, you're finally surrendering your heart to Miss Elaine Keaton," Thomas spoke casually in his usual taunting manner. "Good for you. Though I must say, I did have higher expectations from you. But I assume many years at sea will cause a man to settle."

"I'm not settling and definitely not with Miss Keaton," James stated casually to his friend's jab. "I just want Miss Sawyer to enjoy the next few weeks while she's here. She deserves to, especially considering how their voyage has been so far."

"That's very considerate of you." Thomas eyed his friend. "'Tis a shame she's just passing through."

James flinched. It was a shame. The coach creaked along the dirt road while the men fell silent. Everything within him sank with anguish from a memory that surfaced.

It had been a few years prior, when James was in Bombay and Thomas sailed patrolling Saint Helena island. A merchant ship had ported in their harbor for three weeks, carrying swindles of fabric, exquisite jewelry and a few militiamen heading home to England from their assignments in Africa.

Jenny, Thomas's cousin, being too trusting at the time, fell for one of those scoundrels on the merchant ship. He promised the world to her and spent every chance they had together. When the day came for him to leave, she had opened her eyes a moment too late . . . their time together could never be plausible. Considering over four thousand miles of ocean separating her in Jamestown and he in England, how could it work?

James clenched his gloves uncomfortably, his jaw tightened, *'Tis a shame how false hopes and infatuation can deceive a person.* He closed his eyes in frustration as the scars of guilt that were-engraved within him surfaced.

If only he or Thomas had been there. They would have told her to steer away from him, or they could have exchanged a few words with the fellow that gave him no choice but to stay far from her.

The day the blasted swindler sailed off was the day he stole a piece of Jenny's heart. When he and Thomas came back, they found their joyous Jenny bitter and broken. Crying whenever she thought they weren't looking. Making snide remarks about sailors and their lack of propriety—coming to port for a short period only to sail, leaving behind their love affair stranded in the sand. It took months if not a year for her to recover from the incident. After that time, she stopped talking about it—about him. He became a haunting memory to her; one she refused to ever acknowledge. James and Thomas knew it deeply wounded her and after witnessing such anguish, James would always remember the heartache it caused his dear friend. Since that time, he managed to do his best to avoid misleading any lady, especially those passing through.

He sat quietly, letting the resolution of the matter sink in. Avoiding Miss Sawyer for four weeks would be an impossible task. Mainly due to the fact she was staying at the Keaton's plantation. When not patrolling, he often called upon Governor Keaton to report on the island's security. He'd just have to take extra precautions to avoid her. *It shouldn't be that difficult,* he mumbled grudgingly to himself.

He pictured the woman's beautiful eyes glistening under the candlelight. She stared at him with amusement. An unexpected dip of excitement consumed his stomach. He rubbed his forehead, uncertain what to make of it.

"I thought for certain the only time I'd see her again was when she returned my coat. That was quite a pleasant surprise for the evening."

James tugged at his constricting jacket when he thought of her teasing smile. "Yes, it was."

"So, tell me, how do you propose tomorrow will go?" Thomas sounded too excited with his question and then continued on, "You see, the way I picture the day unfolding is Miss Keaton will strategize a way to get you two alone. Graciously leaving me in the company of Miss Sawyer."

James chuckled at his friend's wishful thinking. Miss Keaton may have been strategizing a way for them to be alone, but he was already two steps ahead of her.

"Not to put a damper on your plans, but we're going to recruit a few people to join us on our picnic. There's one person I specifically have in mind for the job."

Thomas leaned forward, broadening his shoulders while he rested his arms on his thighs. "Who might that be?"

"Captain Richard Norton."

"He would be perfect!" His enthusiasm dropped. "If only he were here in time for the picnic."

"Well, as luck would have it, he arrived shortly before I left for dinner tonight."

"You're joking!"

James wouldn't have believed it himself if he hadn't seen his friend at the dock with his own eyes. "Not at all. I spotted him in the harbor on my way to the governor's. We talked briefly before I had to leave."

"Well, I'll be. What are the odds?" Thomas laughed with approval. Normally James would never pawn his friends off to a lady like Miss Keaton, but knowing Richard, he'd do just fine.

James had an early meeting with the city's commissioner, Gordon Harrlow, at the Town Hall regarding the port's security. They had just concluded their discussion when the gentleman's daughter, Miss Catherine Harrlow, entered the commissioner's office.

Gliding through the door like a ray of sunshine through a foggy morning, Miss Harrlow announced brightly, "Good morning, Father!" Her golden hair resembled the color of a wheat field on a clear blue day and was pinned carefully under a blue-ribbon hat. "Oh, Captain McCannon, good morning!" She offered him a charming smile. Her deep blue eyes twinkled above her rouge apple cheeks. "I'm terribly sorry, I didn't realize you two had a meeting!"

"Good morning, Miss Harrlow." James gave her a bow before she could turn to leave. "You couldn't have picked a better time. We just finished up."

James always thought Miss Harrlow to be an attractive young lady with her dazzling smile. She had been very pleasant towards him in all the five years she and her parents had been living in Jamestown.

"Catherine, I thought I mentioned I was meeting the captain last night." The commissioner gave a thoughtful shrug with his broad shoulders. "Doesn't matter, what can I do for you, my dear?"

"I was out riding and thought I'd come by to see if you had plans for lunch later today?"

"I'm sorry, my dear, but I'm afraid I've already made plans."

Miss Harrlow pressed her heart-shaped lips with disappointment. The middle-aged commissioner furrowed his bushy gray brows with slight irritation. "Didn't I tell you my schedule last night?"

"Yes, I was hoping you'd have a break somewhere in between." She let out a sigh and looked over at James with disappointment. For some odd reason he felt compelled to take it upon himself to ease her burden.

"Miss Harrlow, a few of us are riding to the falls this morning. Would you care to join us?"

"I would love to! Are you certain I wouldn't be imposing?" she eagerly asked.

"Not at all. We plan to leave within the hour. Lieutenant Fletch and I can meet you at home before we gather at the governor's plantation."

Her smile faltered with the mention of the governor's plantation but she quickly composed herself when she replied, "Sounds wonderful! I'll be ready."

Satisfied with solving both his and Miss Harrlow's dilemmas, James walked out of the town hall towards the misty harbor. Now on to the one man who will make this expedition successful: Captain Richard. From a letter he'd received a couple days ago, he knew his friend would be arriving anytime that week. He hadn't seen Richard since they'd both been stationed in Bombay for extensive training the year prior. Keeping themselves entertained, they'd notoriously pulled pranks on each other. Unfortunately for Richard, the admiral became the victim of one of their very clever pranks with the consequence that Richard was reassigned to Kingston, Jamaica. James let out a chuckle from the memory, then with little time, jumped out of the way of the tavern's swinging door.

"I don't care who you are! No one makes advances on my daughter. This is not that type of establishment." Rob Harris, the tavern keeper, boomed with fury as he threw out a very intoxicated lieutenant. James grabbed the unstable man's arm firmly to steady him. A misconduct like that was not tolerated and was strictly enforced on the island, especially if he was military personnel.

"I'll take it from here, Mister Harris. I'll be sure he's no longer allowed in your tavern."

"See that you do, Captain McCannon. That man is no gentleman."

James nodded then forced the half-conscious man towards High Knoll Fort. Every now and then they would run across a scoundrel that was passing through.

"Do you understand the penalty for your drunken behavior, lieutenant?" James spoke sternly to the man. He couldn't see his face as his head slumped with his stringy hair masking it. "You can't touch me," the man slurred.

"That's captain to you. You represent Her Majesty's Royal Navy and that inappropriate behavior is not tolerated, especially here in Jamestown."

"My uncle won't allow it."

The man was irritating. "Your uncle's not here."

The lieutenant sneered. "I believe . . ." he paused to look up towards James. "Ahh, Captain James. You see, I'm untouchable. My uncle is none other than Sir William Howard, Duke of Brandon." The hair parted on the man's face revealing none other than Lieutenant Howard.

"I'm sure the duke would be very disappointed in your actions of disgracing the family's name, Lieutenant Howard. Infraction is infraction and you're not getting away with it."

The man was ridiculous. To be bullied into being intimidated by the lieutenant's uncle's title was completely absurd. If needed, he too had connections and wouldn't hesitate to use them to put this despicable man in his place.

They reached the fort and James instructed the guards to put the lieutenant in a holding cell until he had a chance to speak with the man's commanding officer.

Lieutenant Howard scoffed at James. "We shall see, captain."

James turned towards the guards and gave an order, "Gentlemen, make sure he gets the brightest quarters." Unphased by Lieutenant Howard's scowl, he left the fort.

This already started out to be quite an eventful morning. Advancing towards the pier, his thoughts were lighthearted. He felt no hurry to find Lieutenant Howard's commanding officer. In fact, confinement would do the lieutenant good for James was certain he needed some alone time. He smiled to himself at the thought, the lieutenant's hangover in the brightly lit room would be just the right touch.

"James," Thomas yelled, hurrying through the thick fog from the direction of their ship. "I thought you should know that I recruited Lieutenant Nathanial to our little excursion."

"Didn't he just finish the night shift?"

"That he did," Thomas grinned. "But after a little persuasion and a short nap, he'll meet us within one hour."

James smiled with approval. They knew Nathanial from when they were young lads.

"But no time to chat," Thomas quickly exclaimed, "I must be off to enlist my cousin, wish me luck."

"You know Jenny would be more than thrilled to have an excuse to leave the orchard."

"Yes, but somehow she'll manage to ploy me into doing her a favor." Thomas shook his head. "I don't know how she does it."

James laughed at the truthfulness of the statement. Just three years younger than them, Thomas's cousin, Jenny, was the little sister neither of them ever had. Since birth, she managed to coerce Thomas to accommodate any of her needs, especially now with the chores. Her family did employ a few servants as they were successful exporting fruit from their orchards, but her parents insisted that each of their children learn the true value of hard work. Jenny just happened to merit the skill of bargaining in the process, thanks to her interactions with Thomas.

"Hopefully she doesn't get you to wash her stockings again," James jested with a hearty smile.

"Yes, that was a horrid bet I lost with her." Thomas scrunched his nose in a childish manner. "I'm quite certain she walked through manure to prove her point." He scratched behind his head of sandy colored hair. "Perhaps she best be staying—"

"Go," James laughed, shaking his head.

Thomas let out an exasperated breath. "Whatever she comes up with, I'll be certain you get to be the one carrying it out," he yelled over his shoulder, setting out in a brisk walk.

"I look forward to it," James hurried in the opposite direction to the piers.

"Good morning, sleepyhead!" James barged into Captain Richard's cabin and flung open his heavy red drapes.

"Ugh, if you've come to short sheet my bed again, you're too late," Richard groaned. Lifting his hand, he gestured that he was already under the covers. James smiled at his friend.

"That does complicate things. Well, until another day."

"How did you get aboard my ship? I gave my men distinct orders to keep you away until I came on deck."

"Come now, that's not how you treat an old friend."

"Ha! Who knows what mischief you have planned."

"Well, I do have some exciting plans today involving only the most beautiful women on the island. Would you care to join?" All James had to mention was women and Richard was quick to follow. The man could be the biggest flirt.

"Just tell me when and where."

"You have ten minutes. I'll meet you on deck." James threw Richard his pants and headed towards the door. "Oh, and Richard. The governor's daughter, Miss Keaton? She fancies me, do try to keep your distance." He hid his smile until he got in the hallway. That's all it would take for Richard to go after the young lady. He was a competitor and, when he saw a challenge, he couldn't resist.

"Jane, I'm so happy you've finally met the honorable Captain James. He's the one I told you about a few months back. Isn't he so handsome?" Elaine gushed as she stood on her toes to brush her horse's mane—for the hundredth time. She had been carrying on about him since breakfast that morning.

"How long have you known the captain and lieutenant?" She never heard a lady talk about men the way Elaine did and usually she found her mind wandering with such chatter, but not at this moment. This particular time, curiosity piqued her interest.

"Since we were children. Captain James moved to the island with his parents when he was five. His father was an admiral in Her Majesty's Navy, but he retired over a year ago. His parents moved back to England to be closer to his mother's parents. The captain still lives in the cottage two miles north of us, by the orchard."

"And Lieutenant Fletch?" Jane whisked a curl off her ear.

"He has lived here his whole life. His parents and siblings live in the orchards too, just a mile away from the captain. Those two have been inseparable since they were children." Jane started adjusting her stirrups when Elaine added, "You'll like Lieutenant Thomas. He's very witty and can be quite charming. Not to mention he's very handsome, if you haven't noticed already. You two would make a handsome pair," she declared encouragingly. Jane forced a small smile; she wasn't too keen about the idea. She hated the feeling of being forced into a situation when she'd rather have it come naturally. Nothing against Lieutenant Fletch. Of course, he was a charming gentleman, but she didn't want someone else to decide that for her.

The sound of horses trotting up the cobblestone drive caught their attention.

"They're here!" Elaine squealed, squeezing both Jane's hands. Elaine grabbed her reins and strolled out of the stables with her horse trailing behind. The thought of riding to the falls with the intentions of being left to pair off was making Jane feel confined. Truth of the matter, she had never experienced courting, let alone having such freedom to be alone with a gentleman. She blew out an anxious breath. *Is this a small taste of how England's going to be?*

She recalled the chancellor had informed her uncle that his wife would love to introduce Jane into society, especially with her many connections.

Jane moaned, remembering her uncle's lit-up expression. The idea of matchmaking didn't compel her and he knew it.

She rubbed at the sudden tightness in her shoulders. If she felt uneasy now, then how would she fare in England? Dread would have her knotted like a constrictor knot—which was impossible to undo. *Take a deep breath and take little steps,* she encouraged herself as she loosened her clenched grip on the reins. Sooner or later she'll have to face society and today is a perfect day for practice. Besides, there's no commitment tied to any of this. Not while she's just visiting.

Flexing her stiff fingers, she straightened her shoulders and gave herself an encouraging nod. *Time to make the most of it.* Gaining more confidence, she smoothed out her navy riding skirt and took the reins.

Chapter Six

Out of the stables the dimly lit fog enveloped Jane and her horse. She shuddered as it cast an eerie sensation into the heavy air.

Stepping up on the rider's mount, she sat on her side saddle and arranged her navy-blue habit. Adjusting the pins to her hat, she secured them to her thick hair. Satisfied, she gave the horse named Chestnut a flick with the reins and rode towards the sound of voices. The fog thinned exposing not three but *seven* other riders.

"Good morning, Miss Sawyer!" Lieutenant Fletch called out to her.

"Good morning, lieutenant." He seemed enthusiastic about her arrival and appeared even less intimidating in his civilian clothes.

"Ah, Miss Sawyer," Captain McCannon quipped, "It's good to see you riding Chestnut. He's a fine steady horse."

Jane peered at the captain. He sat poised in his riding attire, refreshed and alert with his dimpled smile. Steady horse? Was he still bantering with her? She leaned down and patted her stallion's neck.

"Indeed, he is a fine horse, captain. As for his steadiness, I dare say I have yet to discover, but thank you for your reassurance."

She looked up from her stallion, meeting his gaze. Irritated with how unnerved he made her, she quickly glanced away. At times she had her doubts with Elaine's preference in gentlemen but with the captain . . . he certainly wasn't what she expected—*not that she had any expectations of the gentleman.*

"Miss Sawyer," the captain pressed, "May I introduce you to some of our friends?" Everything came back to focus as she looked around the group. "To my left we have Miss Jenny Oakley of the Silverado Orchards." The woman smiled warmly at Jane. Her slightly bronzed face hinted she was often outside in the sun.

"Lieutenant Nathanial Woods of the Ebony." The gentleman was clean cut with coal-black hair that matched the coloring of his long, fluffy side-burns. Compared to the other gentlemen in the group, he appeared half their size and a few years younger. He gave her an assertive nod.

"Miss Catherine Harrlow, daughter of Commissioner Gordon Harrlow, of Saint Helena." The petite young lady appeared to be around Jane's age with golden hair and dark blue eyes. She sat stiffly on her English saddle with her chin held high. She gave Jane a slight smile which faded fast when her eyes fell on Elaine.

"And Captain Richard Norton of Her Majesty's naval ship, the Sphinx. He arrived here yesterday from Jamaica." The captain held an air of confidence. He and Captain McCannon sat in their saddles with the same broad shoulders and height. If they stood next to each other on foot, Jane guessed they would be the same height and similar build in frame. Tipping his hat, he smiled charmingly at her. His black, pencil thin mustache stretched across above his lip while he raised a friendly brow.

"Everyone, this is Miss Jane Sawyer, Doctor Duncan Brown's niece. They're visiting for a few weeks until they sail on to London."

She grew excited with the new development. Apparently, Elaine's plans of matchmaking were put to a halt with the welcoming sight. "It's a pleasure to meet you all," Jane responded. Daring to look at Elaine, she was surprised to find no sign of disappointment. Instead, she was ogling the attractive Captain Richard Norton. *How could she be so erratic?* Jane held a laugh that was ready to escape.

"We'd best be off," Captain McCannon announced as he straightened in his saddle. "We have over an hour's ride to get to the falls."

Captain McCannon took the lead, guiding them towards an open field. Jane became aware of the beautiful views. She savored the scenery, locking them away until she could retrieve them for a dreary day in England. There grew to be a vast change in the landscape the further inland they rode. The beginning of their ride started out in open orchards, surrounded by rolling hills covered with luscious vegetation. Ascending deeper towards the center of the island, tall yellow grass waved in their path. The volcanic terrain made its appearance with rugged rocks, scattered plains, and plateau formations. In the distance, over the island's cliff's edge, the sapphire ocean glistened in the sunlight, it stretched into the distance until it met the pale blue sky.

Pulling on her horse's reins to be alongside her, Miss Oakley smiled at Jane. "Miss Sawyer, where have you traveled from?"

In the broad field, the group had become divided as the gentleman drew close to each other while conversing amongst themselves.

"My uncle and I have traveled from Bombay."

Miss Harrlow rode up to her other side. "I've heard India's very dangerous for young ladies, especially with all the militiamen." Through her pale lashes, she peered down her short nose at her with condescension.

"It can be dangerous for a young lady wherever she goes, not just in India," Jane stated calmly, not appreciating the lady's implication. "I felt very safe in Bombay. We were far enough away from the attacks to not worry—"

"Oh, Jane had plenty of militiamen to protect her from any scandals," Elaine sweetly proclaimed. "If that was what you were implying." She jeered patronizingly over her shoulder at Miss Harrlow. The lady's blue eyes darkened as she glared back.

"Elaine," Jane whispered with alarm. She knew what she had implied, but worried others may interpret it as her being promiscuous. Particularly Miss Harrlow who then tsked with scorn.

"There's no harm with having many friends, Jane," Elaine assured, still riding in front of them. She waved her hand to displace any despair. "Especially when many of your gentlemen friends made certain you didn't have to worry about any unruly fellows who looked your way." Elaine smirked at Jane.

Miss Harrlow feigned a smile. "How noble."

"It certainly was," Elaine continued, not willing to let the subject drop. "You see as soon as the gentlemen found out Jane's name, they retreated like they were discovering a crocodile at the watering hole." Elaine giggled. "Oh, if only you could have seen it." She turned towards Miss Oakley who smiled amiably. Jane closed her eyes, wishing she didn't have to hear Elaine tell the story.

"It's not that great of a tale," Jane rebutted, arching her brow at Elaine. Her horse's ears flicked back from her low tone of warning.

"It certainly was!" Elaine exclaimed, slowing her horse to squeeze in between her and Miss Oakley.

"Last I visited with Jane there was a new officer who insisted on escorting us back to her townhome from the marketplace. Oh, he was handsome with dark dreamy eyes," she gushed to Miss Oakley. Miss Oakley smiled, appreciating Elaine's enthusiasm. "Was he not handsome, Jane?" Jane looked up at the cheerful blue sky, wishing it to be over.

"Well, he certainly had an interest in Jane. Our friend, Miss Sophie could attest to it, if she were here. She was with us when it happened." Jane adjusted herself on the saddle. Her friend, from Bombay would have made the pink of her cheeks turn crimson while she encouraged Elaine to embellish the story. Elaine carried on with delight, "He kept insisting on helping her carry her packages of things which she flatly denied him from doing." She tsked again at Jane and laughed from the painful glare she gave her.

"He only offered once," she muttered. Elaine shushed her and proceeded.

"We didn't even make it out of the marketplace when Jane started to talk about her uncle—her excuse every time she wanted the gentleman to leave." Elaine slowly shook her head with disappointment. Miss Harrlow remained silent at her other side, fixed on staring ahead. Jane leaned forward to address Miss Oakley.

"I find it's best to be up front than to allow things to carry on," she stated. Miss Oakley smiled and nodded with understanding.

"So, after the gentleman inquired about her uncle, she simply smiled—which, may I add, made the poor fellow swoon harder and informed him that he was none other, than *the* Doctor Duncan Brown."

"What did he do?" Miss Harrlow asked, suddenly interested in the conversation. Elaine brought her petite nose up in a snobbish manner. Ignoring her, she looked at Miss Oakley to finish the story.

"The man paled. He stopped walking and began retreating a few steps back as though she carried the plague."

Jane covered her mouth when a giggle escaped. "We did try to warn him—"

"But he wouldn't listen or couldn't with his state of shock. The poor gent," Elaine laughed.

"What happened?" Miss Oakley exclaimed.

"The gentleman backed into a basket that held not one, but two cobras!" Elaine screeched.

Jane shook her head. "It was awful. The snake charmer was in the middle of his song so the snakes were halfway out of their basket when he stepped into them."

"No," Miss Oakley covered her mouth.

"I've never heard a grown man scream before." Elaine burst into laughter. "It was the highest pitch I've ever heard." She covered her ear as if she could still hear his shrill cry. "Like a screaming rabbit."

"He did escape unharmed," Jane assured them through suppressed giggles. "Fortunately."

"Except for his pride," Elaine laughed. "He sulked away like a troubled puppy."

Jane closed her eyes. Whatever her friends had mentioned to the other gentleman to keep him away from her, had been extremely effective.

Miss Oakley giggled. "What would I have done to witness such a scene! How did you gain all those men's loyalty?"

Jane bit her lip. Being away from it all suddenly made it become foreign, and yet, how strange that it was only a couple months prior that she was roaming the streets of Bombay. A piece of her felt empty as though it were a lifetime ago.

"When I was a girl, I'd visit the wounded soldiers in the hospital while waiting for my uncle to finish his surgeries. Many of the gentlemen accepted me as though I were a younger sister and continued to treat me as such through the years."

"Which only entitled them to scaring the life out of all the gentlemen who looked your way." Elaine laughed.

"Evidently," Jane muttered. Especially over the past two years, when she blossomed and became of age to enter into society. The soldiers that she came to know from when she was a girl protectively took her under their charge and scared any suitor away from speaking to her. Some of her friends voiced how bothered they were that they hindered her from having a chance with a potential suitor, but Jane never minded. She was too focused on her uncle's work to take notice of the gentlemen anyway.

The open fields drew to an end as trees began to enclose their group closer together. The men rode closer, still engaged in their conversation.

"Tell me more about India," Miss Oakley implored. "I've only traveled to England, so the idea of being somewhere like India is intriguing."

Jane nodded, but before she could respond, Elaine excitedly whirled towards her.

"Tell them about the elephants! Oh, and the jungle cruise that we went on last time we visited. That was exciting!" Jane smiled and watched her friend ride ahead to Captain Richard Norton's side as they entered a narrow, lusciously green ravine. Banana trees and white flowers were scattered all around. Their horses began to bicker, sensing their new surroundings.

"A jungle cruise?" Lieutenant Fletch curiously asked. He and Lieutenant Woods trailed behind them.

"We had taken a boat along the Dahisar River just a few miles down from Bombay, through the jungle. It was a quick excursion, but an exciting one as we witnessed a crocodile fight."

"It was petrifying!" Elaine appeared frightened with her hand resting on Captain Norton's forearm as though she were trying to include him in the conversation. "I hadn't seen anything like it. I was afraid our boat would sink, leaving us at their mercy." He gave her a polite smile.

"Yes, you definitely don't want to swim in the Dahisar River," Jane emphasized. "It's notorious for crocodiles."

"Do you swim, Miss Sawyer?"

She glanced over to see Captain McCannon riding at Miss Harrlow's side. He appeared to be studying her. She would have suspected him to be baiting her again had not his expression and tone seem too sincere.

"Of course. It was a requirement when I was a little girl as we swam to escape the summer's heat."

"Sounds indecent," remarked Miss Harrlow. Her nostrils flared with disgust. Jane raised her brow. She was beginning to understand Elaine's shortness towards the haughty lady.

"Well, I think it's essential that everyone knows how to swim," Captain McCannon added. "Especially when they live close to the water. You never know when the occasion calls for it." He gave Jane a wink, causing her to flush. She ignored him and looked to Miss Harrlow.

"I can assure you, Miss Harrlow, you'd never find the men and women swimming in the same watering area."

Miss Harrlow held a stubborn expression. She didn't seem satisfied by either Jane's or Captain McCannon's answer.

Elaine looked over her shoulder at Jane. "What's the name of that dreadful bird that sounds similar to a peacock?"

"That would be the Asian Koel," Jane replied, relieved her friend changed the topic.

"Yes! I despise those birds. They always kept me awake at night with their never-ending songs."

"Were there any waterfalls?" Lieutenant Fletch inquired, everyone in the group had now focused their attention on her.

"Yes, there are quite a few, especially during the monsoon season."

"I hope you're not too disappointed by Heart Shaped Falls," Captain McCannon commented. "She's not as impressive as some of your falls in India."

This perked Jane's interest. "Have you been to India, captain?"

"I have . . . a few times. That's where Captain Richard and I met. We were stationed together in the harbor for a few weeks."

"That wasn't long," Miss Harrlow sounded more polite with the gentleman than she had with Jane.

"They had to separate us." Captain Norton let out a loud laugh.

"Separate you two? For what?" Miss Harrlow pried.

Captain McCannon smiled at his friend. "Let's just say there was a little mishap as someone else took the brunt of a prank."

"What happened?" Elaine's curiosity piqued. Both the captains remained silent, exchanging looks with one another. A horse's neigh filled the silence. "Oh, won't you please tell us?" Elaine persisted. Captain Norton gave an approving nod.

"Richard, would you like the honor, or should I?"

"I'll have the honor," Captain Norton said confidently. "It was a brisk afternoon and I invited James over for a drink. You see, earlier in the week he had pulled a joke on me, and—"

"Oh?" Elaine interrupted. "What did he do?"

"Yes, Richard, do tell," the captain encouraged with a grin. The gentleman's face scrunched with hesitation. After a moment of uncertainty, he yielded.

"He outlined my spyglass with soot," he surrendered. "Later that week I—"

Elaine cut him off before he could continue. "Was it to prevent you from seeing out of the glass?" She didn't understand the prank which made Jane giggle harder as the captain had to explain further. He cleared his throat.

"You see, Miss Keaton, when I held the spyglass to my eye it left a dark ring around it."

"Oh!" Her brows raised high and she burst into laughter. Jane watched from behind and caught the exasperated look he gave Elaine before turning away.

"Later that week—" he tried to continue but was interrupted again.

"Just a moment." This time it was Captain McCannon. "You failed to mention how long you had the black ring around your eye."

"That's irrelevant, James. Nobody wants to—"

"How long did you have it for?" Elaine peered up at the gentleman with an amused expression. He cleared his throat.

"Until one of my men, who *wasn't* bribed by James, informed me."

"Which was?" Captain McCannon pressed.

The gentleman shifted in his saddle. "A few hours."

Everyone was in fits of laughter. Everyone, except for the gentleman who was the brunt of the joke. He only shook his head and smiled. "Yes, bravo. You had me on that one." Clearing his throat, Captain Norton called out as the laughter died down. "Back to the story. There was a trick I learned as a boy that my siblings and I used to do to each other. If you pour ink into tea and drink it, it will stain your teeth for days." He gave a satisfied smile as he appeared to reminisce his childhood.

"That's horrid! Couldn't you taste it in the tea?" Miss Harrlow asked, appalled.

"Not at all." It was Lieutenant Woods who had spoken up. Everyone turned to look at the quiet gentleman with the fluffy sideburns. "Not that I've ever experienced drinking it," he quickly added.

"Uh-huh." Lieutenant Fletch smirked at the lieutenant who shifted uncomfortably in his saddle.

Captain Norton proceeded. "Well, I had everything in motion, the tea was set out, complete with ink, when who should arrive at my ship? But Admiral Kensington! We sat discussing some of the attacks when James arrived. I didn't notice the admiral taking a sip of the tea until it was too late."

"I'll never forget the startling black smile the Admiral gave me when I stepped into the room," Captain McCannon boomed. "It took everything I had to maintain my composure." More laughter erupted.

"So, that's what happened!" Jane exclaimed aghast, letting out another giggle.

Both captains paused to look at her. Silence filled the air as their horses' hooves clicked over rocks and dirt.

"You know Admiral Kensington?" Captain Norton asked. His freshly trimmed brows rose high on his forehead.

"I do, he and his family are friends of ours. Looking back, I had always thought he had a toothache by the way he kept his mouth covered with his handkerchief." Jane let out another laugh. "Captain Norton, no wonder you were reassigned!"

Jane reflected on the day the admiral had come to their home. His pleasant, warm demeanor had shifted that day. The admiral was in a panic when he had burst in her uncle's home. She thought there had been an attack, but then while he held his mouth, he grunted an unusual greeting towards her. After that, she had concluded it was a toothache. Behind closed doors of her uncle's study, Jane could hear the admiral on the verge of hysterics. He demanded her uncle to fix it. At the time she thought it was her imagination, for she could have sworn she heard her uncle laugh. She remembered thinking he would never laugh at such turmoil but now, now it made perfect sense.

"Fortunately, I've returned to his good graces as I'm being reassigned back to India."

"How long will you be at port, Captain Norton?" Elaine asked through a forced smile.

"Until we can restock on our water and supplies. My guess it will be by the end of the week."

"That's not long at all," Elaine fussed, not hiding her disappointment. The gentleman appeared surprised by her dismay and watched her with a keen eye.

"Do you hear that?" Captain McCannon asked. Everyone quieted. He managed to take the lead again. In the distance, Jane heard a roar of tumbling water. The air thinned and cooled making it easier to draw a breath. "We're close, it's just around the bend," he said, raising his voice so all could hear.

⇛ Chapter Seven ⇚

They continued their ride in silence with an occasional neigh or snort from their horses. Anticipation grew with every step. The noise of the falls increased to the thunderous crash of water. They reached the bend and turned to behold a majestic sight. Falling from the high cliffs, water showered down crashing onto large boulders of rocks below. A rippled pool laid before the continual downpour. To the left of the pool, a steady stream trickled out and burbled down the ravine towards the town. Vegetation and trees scattered around them, climbing up the wet rocks to the top of the cliff's edge. The sun's rays broke their way through some of the branches. Jane leaned back and stared, getting lost in the mystical beauty.

Overcome with such tranquility, she didn't realize everyone had already dismounted from their horses. Blinking, she broke the trance the falls had cast on her and glanced down to find Captain McCannon standing with his reins in hand. He brought his fist to his mouth in what appeared to be an attempt to clear his throat. He spoke but she could barely make out what he said over the thunderous falls. She leaned closer to hear his words.

"May I assist you down, Miss Sawyer?"

"Yes, thank you!"

She placed her hands on his broad shoulders. His strong hands gripped her waist, and with little effort, lifted her off her saddle, bringing her to the ground in front of him. Her breath staggered as she stood inches from him. An intoxicating citrusy aroma of his fragrance filled her nose. Her thoughts were hazy from the mixture of the dampened air and his presence. The thunderous roar faded into the luscious green background. Her eyes stared ahead at the rapid rise and fall of his chest, that matched her own breathing.

"Are you two coming?" a low voice called.

The falls began to thunder back within her ears. She barely heard Lieutenant Fletch's yell that resounded from the other side of her horse. Captain McCannon's hands dropped to his side and he took a step back. She released a staggered breath and quickly took hold of her horse's reins, being sure to avoid looking in his direction. Concentrating on catching up to the group, neither exchanged glances. The thunder of the falls became less deafening the further they distanced themselves from it. They released their horse's reins, allowing them to graze with the other horses and strolled towards the group that walked ahead.

Her steps slowed as a large, floral meadow sprawled out beneath their feet. The joyous field stretched far towards a heavily vegetated tree line. In the treetops, birds chirped cheerfully, soaring through the cloudless sky. Jane stared in awe, taking in the radiant scene. The waterfall, humidity, warm sunshine, birds singing, and the beautiful flowers—each gave her such peace and familiarity. For the first time in weeks, she felt she found a piece of home. She smiled and plucked one of the unique flowers. Twisting it in her fingers, she admired the five, silky wide petals. At the center of the unique flower were stamens that formed a distinctive star.

"Captain?" She whirled around to find he stood closer to her than expected. Her breath caught. His posture was stiff as he held his hands behind his back, staring ahead like he was on duty. Or could he be in pain? She couldn't decide. His jaw flexed and he met her stare. Startled to be caught studying him, she looked down at the petals. "What type of flower is this?"

"It's called an Ebony. They're rare flowers that can only be found here on Saint Helena."

"Is this what you named your ship after?" Jane held the delicate flower up before them.

"Actually," his dimple deepened exposing a captivating smile, "I named it after the Ebony trees here on the island. The tree is unique since the core is dense, making the wood extremely strong."

She looked up at him. He watched her cautiously. It was as though she had become a threat. Her stomach sank. *Perhaps I misinterpreted it?* Though, it wouldn't be the first time a gentleman has looked at her that way.

"Ah," she spoke, ignoring the unsettling thought. She briefly glanced at the pale blue sky as though to ponder. "I can see how being named after something strong would be more fitting for a frigate." She casually peered at him. "Though, I'm confident a beautiful, rare flower such as this could be intimidating as well."

The corner of his lips lifted. "If you only knew, Miss Sawyer." The implication in his voice caught her off guard.

"I believe the others took this trail to get a better view of the falls." He pointed towards an overgrown trail in front of them. "Shall we?" He offered his arm.

She accepted, taken aback by the solid muscle she felt under her gloved hand. He certainly was no stranger to physical work. Not that she was feeling! She lightened her hold. An intriguing thought seeped through her mind. What would it have been like if she were conscious when he saved her? He would have had to wrap his arms around her waist while he pulled her out of the water and she would have had her arms wrapped around his neck for support. A sense of thrill bolted through her veins. Suddenly she was feeling very flustered and out of her element. Once again, she found herself being escorted by him, but this time they were alone, and her thoughts were getting too obscene. Slowly she peered at him from the corner of her eye. He caught her gaze and offered a half smile. She flushed, darting her eyes forward. His muscles flexed under her hand when he adjusted his footing from an unbalanced step. Warmth rushed through her whole body. She closed her eyes, desperate to control her thoughts. She should count sheep. *What? That only works if you can't sleep.* A gentle breeze blew in her direction enveloping her in the captain's aroma. She inhaled a sharp breath. *ONE, TWO, THREE, FOUR!*

"I'm afraid it's too narrow of a path for us. It's just at the head of the trail. I'll take the lead, if you don't mind?"

"Five!" Jane exhaled.

"Five?" The captain looked at her confused.

"Fine," she clasped her gloved hands together. "I mean that's fine."

She gave him a reassuring nod and he stepped in front of her on the path. They walked single file through the overgrown shaded trail. Her hands calmed and she relaxed as the distance between them grew.

"Are you feeling better today, Miss Sawyer?"

Better? She assumed he thought she was still dealing with land sickness by the way she was handling herself.

"Yes, thank you."

"I'm glad to hear it." He gave her a sincere smile. She met his bright blue eyes before he abruptly looked away. "What brings you and your uncle to England?" He tugged on his cravat as though it constricted his neck.

"My uncle received an opportunity to teach at Oxford University."

"I can only imagine how elated the University will be to have England's most skilled surgeon teach their students." He sounded impressed.

Dipping under a branch, she looked up at him. "You've heard of my uncle?"

"I believe every militiaman has heard of Doctor Duncan Brown. Rumor of his work has spread through every port like a torrent." The side of his mouth raised, briefly exposing a crooked smile. Meeting his gaze, she watched his smile fall.

"That certainly is impressive," she stated and she walked past him.

"The University's chancellor sailed to Bombay himself to offer my uncle the position. When my uncle agreed, the chancellor was thrilled to say the least." She chuckled at the memory. The chancellor had fervently shaken her uncle's hand, not letting it go for what felt to be a full minute while expressing how honored he was to have him.

"Are you thrilled about Oxford?"

For an odd reason, the question caught her off guard. Oxford, the university that she yearned to be a part of, but that wanted nothing to do with her. Her greatest dream to become a surgeon would never happen. She had always known that, but that didn't keep her from hoping. It had brightened the day when the chancellor came and had turned his attention towards her. What she only dreamed of being an invitation to attend the university, turned instead to talk of London's fashion, operas, and balls. Her hope shattered into specs of dust that day, leaving her dull and empty inside.

Her uncle had advised her that there were too many closed-minded people to accept women to participate in a gentleman's profession. Then, after he had encouraged her to turn her focus elsewhere, with a twinkle in his eye, he always made time to teach her his tricks of the trade. She would even find his textbooks of human anatomy and medical procedures on her bed after she had asked him a million questions. He was always supporting her with her passion.

Jane ran her hand across her heart as an emptiness formed there. Going to Oxford only made her feelings raw and her future dim. Her uncle's time and focus would be spent teaching others and accompanying her to social gatherings with hopes of finding her a suitable husband. It was nothing that she hoped for, but it was a wonderful opportunity in his career. After all that he had done for her, she wanted nothing more than to be supportive to him. She forced a smile and answered the captain. "Yes, of course. It will only be for two years and then we'll sail back to Bombay."

"Will this be your first time in England?" Strolling to her side, he studied her from the corner of his eye.

"I used to live there when I was a little girl, though I remember very little about the area."

Captain McCannon held a tree branch high so she could pass under it. She stopped, allowing him to take the lead again, but he waited for her as the path widened for them to walk side by side.

"What took you to India?" He clasped his hands behind his back. He appeared calm and unflustered compared to how she was feeling inside. He unnerved her and she couldn't figure out why. She had conversed with many militiamen and naval officers in her life. And a few of them were just as handsome. She bit her lip. At least she thinks they were. She's never paid attention to truly notice.

"My uncle," she declared, ignoring the peculiar, ruffled feeling within, "my parents passed away from influenza when I was eight. As soon as he heard the sad news, he sent for me."

Compassion filled the captain's eyes. "I'm so sorry to hear about your loss."

She caught her breath at the sincerity in his rich velvety voice. Was it always so deep? Most people skittered uncomfortably around the topic. "Thank you, captain."

"Your uncle sounds like he really cares about you to have you live with him in India."

She let out a soft chuckle. "Some viewed it that way." He raised a questionable brow, only to encourage her to proceed. "By the time I had left England, the war with the Mysore had intensified. Bombay was receiving a lot of sporadic attacks that killed many of its civilians. Before my departure, many of my parents' friends had voiced their disapproving opinions to our housekeeper. They worried he was removing me from the safety of England to the perils in Bombay. But I was only a child and didn't know about the dangers, at least not until a week before my voyage." Jane stepped over a rock that was on the path.

"The week before?"

As if a long-lost door from her past was opened, she continued, "Our housekeeper had a habit of muttering under her breath when she was uneasy about anything. The day she helped me pack was when I learned about the war in India. The usual talk of how the cook found another mouse in the pantry was replaced with that particular topic." Startled by her own openness, Jane glanced over at Captain McCannon's bewildered expression. She had never told anyone of the day she was preparing to leave England. Not even her uncle.

He stared at her with dismay. "Don't worry, captain," Jane assured, while attempting to make light of the conversation. "My parents had bought a cat. The mice were kept at bay."

He scoffed. "It wasn't the mouse that concerned me, Miss Sawyer." His eyes were soft as he studied her. "A child should never hear such things, especially after experiencing such a loss."

Fidgeting at a button on her glove, she bit her bottom lip. She felt vulnerable having exposed a part of her that had been stored away. She pulled the tailored jacket of her riding habit, trying to further cover herself up, though there was nothing left to cover. She was fully clothed up to the base of her neck with her white riding handkerchief trimming the lapel of her navy jacket. Forcing a smile, she continued to make light of the conversation.

"At eight I didn't fully understand what she talked about," she shrugged. Though she had understood the fear behind her housekeeper's words. "I was too excited to be with my uncle to be deterred from leaving," she spoke truthfully. "And it sounded more adventurous than a boarding school in London."

As much as she had been excited to live with him, she had been extremely nervous. She had only one memory of him. Jane had been five when she had last seen him. She and her parents met him at the train station heading for the shipping yard on his voyage to Bombay. She'd never forget how he had picked her up and embraced her in his loving arms, swinging her back and forth to make her giggle. His countenance was so calm and kind, like how her mother—his sister—treated her. Which she witnessed on rare occasions whenever she was free to visit with her. Desperately wanting a piece of her mother back in her life, she had been very eager to see her uncle.

She stared up at the captain. "I've never known such a virtuous person. He's raised me as if I were his own." Adoration warmed her heart from the truth of the matter.

He gave her a soft smile. "From what I've observed, he's a very noble man." Jane grinned. "Yes, very."

"While in Oxford, do you have plans on visiting London? I believe it's less than a day's ride."

Afraid so. Jane gathered her skirts and stared ahead. Any single young woman visiting London was usually there on a pursuit to find a husband. Often, they were matched with a suitor by relatives, or perhaps in her case, the chancellor's wife. The chancellor informed her uncle that it had already been discussed with his wife and she would take great pleasure in introducing Jane to many of the eligible suitors of England. Jane grimaced at the thought of the unacquainted lady making a forced union but quickly relaxed feeling confident her uncle would never agree to such an alliance—unless it was something she wanted.

"Afraid?" The captain looked at her with a perplexed expression. *Did I say that out loud?*

"I mean, yes! Yes, we are." Jane tried her best to be convincing.

"Do you not want to go to London, Miss Sawyer?" the captain raised a questioning brow.

"Of course!" She's been trying to convince herself that she did ever since her uncle presented her with his plans. "Every young lady wants to go to London." *Don't they?* "Why do you ask?"

"Forgive me, I was only wondering." He appeared deep in thought. He tugged at his cravat and she was beginning to suspect he or his footman had tied it too tight.

"One can only hope it's as wonderful as others say." She had to see the positive in this, it only made her feel better.

As if sensing the shift in mood, he changed the subject. "Tell me, Miss Sawyer, what do you enjoy doing?"

Learning about surgeries and techniques on how to remove shrapnel. Though, she would never tell him any such secret. She decided to tell him the next best thing.

"This. I love exploring." She smiled at him as they continued up the path. "What do you enjoy?"

"I enjoy sailing."

"Sailing?" Jane couldn't disagree more.

"What do you have against sailing?"

"Everything." She gave him a nervous smile. "I've never been so sick in my life. I'm afraid our trip from Bombay was far from enjoyable. I also don't like being at the mercy of the open water. It makes me feel vulnerable."

The captain lifted another low-hanging branch to allow Jane through. She could feel the warmth of his body in the cool shade. Hesitantly, she glanced up at him while she passed. He stared down at her with his half-dimpled smile.

"That's where we're different, Miss Sawyer. The ocean can be very temperamental, but I feel a sense of freedom and empowerment as I sail through its unpredictable water. The sensation I get when the ship soars up a wave then crashes down is invigorating."

"It's nauseating." Jane let out a chuckle from their apparent differences. She started feeling queasy from his description of the ship's movements. "I'm afraid the last storm may still be fresh on my mind."

He nodded. "From what I've gathered, you certainly experienced a rough voyage. Hopefully for your next trip, the weather will cooperate and the water won't be as choppy."

"One can only pray." Jane was already praying every night that it would. "Tell me, captain, is that why you joined the Navy? For the love of sailing?"

"Surprisingly, no. I haven't told too many people this, but I used to be terrified of the ocean."

"You were? Please tell me you entered the Navy after you had overcome your fear." Jane looked at him perplexed. Why enter a career that surrounded him with his fear? He laughed.

"That is a story for another time. Come, the others are just beyond that ledge." He pointed towards the top of the hill. They continued onward, discussing more of his career, until they made it to the top. The trail opened up to a thirty-foot ridgeline where the group was peering over the cliff's edge. Elaine clung to Captain Norton's arm while she observed something far below. Jane held in a laugh as she pictured her friend feigning the object just to be near him. Lieutenant Fletch walked towards them.

"There you are. We might have sent a search party had we not been so distracted by the views." He held an impish expression and continued on. "I hope you don't have a fear of heights, Miss Sawyer."

Jane enjoyed Lieutenant Fletch's jaunty demeanor. "I don't."

Miss Harrow took notice of them. "There you two are." She strolled over, her hips swaying with every step.

"The view is just breathtaking. Come, Miss Sawyer, let me show you," Miss Harrow held out her hand for her. Jane got the impression she wasn't doing it out of the kindness of her heart. Reluctantly, she accepted.

The woman looped her arm with hers and led them to the edge. Captain McCannon and Lieutenant Fletch trailed behind, talking with each other in low murmurs. Jane gaped at the view before her. The trail had taken them around to the front of the falls. She peered out at the magnificent waterfall pouring over a rocky cliff.

Captain McCannon approached her other side. "Do you notice how the cliffs dip down towards the top of the falls?" Jane followed his finger that pointed towards its direction.

"I do."

"We would have to be further back to fully see it, but that's the top point of the heart. The green vegetation along the sides trickle inward towards the ground forming the curve of the heart. Which is how it received the name, Heart Shaped Falls."

"Isn't that fascinating, Miss Sawyer? I've never heard that before," Miss Harrlow exclaimed, appearing to be surprised. Captain McCannon gave her a side glance.

"It is," she replied. "Tell me, captain." Avoiding the lady, she turned her attention towards him. "Does this waterfall run throughout the year?"

"Unfortunately, it doesn't. The monsoon season is what keeps it running. It dries up during the warm summer months. Being that it's fall, we've experienced an unusual amount of storms that overfilled the reservoir above."

Jane wanted to laugh at the irony. Meeting her eye, the captain began to smile as though he knew what she thought about the abnormal rainfall.

"There's a ball held at the beginning of September," Miss Harrlow exclaimed, her blue eyes tightened slightly. "It's in celebration of the abundance the falls have given to the crops and orchards. 'Tis a shame you won't be here." She feigned a sympathetic smile.

"Mmm," Jane ignored the offhand remark. She would probably be in London, attending a ball of her own. She gazed down to the large trees below. *Are they ebonies?* As she turned towards the captain to ask, Miss Harrlow quickly spoke. "These falls have been the main source of water for the town during the season."

"Is that so?" Jane offered politely.

"I'm not sure about the rest of you, but I'm famished," Lieutenant Fletch called out, holding his stomach. "Shall we attend our picnic?"

There were a lot of cheers, mainly from the gentlemen, as they made their way to the trailhead. Jane was about to follow the captain when Miss Harrow lightly grabbed her elbow.

"Miss Sawyer, I'm so glad you were able to see our falls. I do hope you'll continue to enjoy your time while you're here."

"Thank you."

With a small smile, the woman then slid between her and Captain McCannon to speak with him. Lieutenant Fletch strolled to her side. "Is it as impressive as the falls in India?"

She smiled at the lieutenant, grateful for his company. "It is."

"Now, Miss Sawyer. If you had to choose between here and India for the most exquisite scenery, which one would you choose?"

"That's a tough question." She smiled up at him. "Each place has its own majestic appeal, it's hard to compare. From all I've seen in India, I would have to choose there."

"Well, I'll have to take your word for it."

"Were you not stationed there with Captain McCannon and Captain Norton?"

"No, unfortunately, I had to miss out on all their mischief as I stayed here."

"Is Jamestown where you grew up?" Jane already knew the answer, as Elaine had mentioned it earlier, but for conversation's sake, she thought she'd like to hear it from him.

"My whole life. Believe it or not."

"That's a long time to stay in one place."

"That it is, but sailing the open sea gives me a sense of freedom that I love."

"Captain McCannon mentioned the same thing about sailing. That it gives him a sense of freedom."

He nodded. "Many men join for that reason. Isn't that right, lieutenant?" The lieutenant called over his shoulder at Lieutenant Woods who had been talking with Miss Oakley. The lieutenant looked up at him.

"What's that, Thomas?"

"You joined the Navy for a sense of freedom."

"That's correct."

"See?" He flashed her an all-knowing grin. Naturally, Jane returned the smile. Lieutenant Fletch had a way about him that made a person feel at ease.

Chapter Eight

The walk down the trail was brief compared to the amount of time it took with the captain. She followed the group towards a shaded area of the meadow. Miss Oakley, Elaine, and she spread out a cream-colored blanket over the tall grass.

Plates of chicken, scones, cheese, crackers, and fruit were all spread before them.

"This looks wonderful!" Jane remarked, taking a seat next to Elaine. Elaine smiled, then continued to tell Captain Norton all the details of her new tailored dress she was going to wear to a certain festival. Jane couldn't help but notice how patiently he listened with a polite, yet tight expression.

Across from her, Lieutenant Fletch made a comment to Miss Oakley, which made her laugh. Lieutenant Woods was on Miss Oakley's other side smiling at the two. To her left, Miss Harrlow sat stiffly. She settled far enough away from Jane that another person could have sat between them in their circle. She must have realized that when she saw the captain approach from the horses.

"Captain McCannon, please come join me," Miss Harrlow warmly offered. "Let me serve your plate. Here, have a seat." She stood and pointed to where she sat. "I'll only be a moment."

"I can serve myself, Miss Harrlow," he objected, but she waved him off.

"None of that now. I insist. I have to pull together my plate anyway."

Jane caught the captain flash Lieutenant Fletch a bewildered expression when Miss Harrlow's back faced him. Lieutenant Fletch pressed his lips, appearing to be holding back laughter.

"Thank you, Miss Harrlow," he mumbled, when she handed him his plate full of meat, cheese, and scones. She flashed him an audacious smile, then sat strategically between Jane and him. Clearly, she was marking her territory. Jane glanced at Elaine. She knew she would be upset by the lady's bluntness, but Elaine was still lost in her own conversation with Captain Norton. She hadn't even noticed! Suddenly, Elaine's lip turned downward into a pout. *Good gracious, here it comes.*

"Captain McCannon, please tell Captain Norton that he must stay at least one week longer than scheduled. He's going to miss our town's festival."

Jane bit into a strawberry and winced from Elaine's whiny tone. She could be a little melodramatic when she was trying to get her way.

"Of course," Captain McCannon encouraged. "Captain Norton, you must delay your trip for at least another week." The gentleman flashed his friend a murderous glare before forcing a polite smile for Elaine when she gazed his way.

"I almost forgot it was happening in the next couple weeks," Miss Oakley exclaimed, setting down a piece of chicken to her plate.

"A town festival?" Jane couldn't think of any special holiday during that time.

Covering her mouth to hide her small bite of cheese, Elaine exclaimed, "Oh, I can't believe I haven't told you yet! Saint Helena was discovered May 3rd of 1602, so on that day, we celebrate, every year."

"For tradition," Miss Oakley jumped in. "There's a festival that's held at St. James's churchyard. They hold contests and competitions."

"Yes, being one of the commissioners, my father is in charge of the race up Jacob's ladder this year," Miss Harrlow boasted, dabbing the corners of her mouth with her napkin. "Are you fine gentlemen participating? I'd be curious to see who wins. If I were a betting woman, which I'm most certainly not, my bet would go towards you, captain." She held a flirtatious smile, then continued, "You won last year. Didn't you?"

Jane watched, amused, as Captain McCannon adjusted his legs from under him. He was clearly uncomfortable by Miss Harrlow's directness.

"Just a minute," Lieutenant Fletch interjected, reaching for the napkin and wiping his fingers. "That race was a tie! James and I both took home an award that day. It's a good thing you're not a betting woman, Miss Harrlow, because I'm confident there will only be one winner this year and that award will be given to me."

Jane's eyes widened. Taking a bite of a scone, she chewed slowly, watching the entertaining exchange.

"Now let's not get too hasty, Thomas," the captain intervened. "The only reason we tied was because I intentionally slowed to keep from losing the pie I ate earlier. Which was delicious, Miss Jenny."

Miss Oakley's tan face lit up with a radiant smile.

"Are you talking about that mango fruit pie?" Miss Harrlow questioned patronizingly. She crinkled her nose at the woman.

"What of it, Miss Harrlow?" Elaine challenged. "Weren't you the one who made the passion fruit pie that made poor Mister Matthew Harris sick for days?"

"Please," Miss Harrlow rolled her eyes. "If anyone fell sick, it was Mister Tucker Bryson. Your little mix up with salt and sugar had him guzzling the whole water pail."

The two ladies glared at each other. Jane choked back a laugh. The poor fellow. Knowing how Elaine easily gets distracted, she could picture her making that honest mistake. Jane made herself a mental note. *Don't eat the pies.*

"Well, as enticing as it all sounds," Captain Norton's serious tone was laced with humor, "I'm afraid we're still going to have to leave before the festivities."

He took a bite of a chicken thigh and chewed as though he didn't want to discuss the matter. His thin black mustache moved up and down, keeping up with the grinding of his teeth. Elaine went to press the matter, but he took another large bite. Jane dabbed her lips to hide her smile. *The captain was clearly keeping his mouth full to avoid conversing further.*

"Oh! But we've only skimmed the surface, captain," Elaine urged. "There are egg races, shooting competitions, and then my favorite part of the day, the picnic basket auction. All the proceeds go towards the town's orphanage." Taking advantage of his thoughtful expression, she carried on. "The baskets are provided by some of Jamestown's finest ladies. The gentleman that buys the basket, gets to take that lady on a picnic." She leaned towards the captain as he held cautiously still. His chewing ceased while he stared at her. "Later that evening the town has a dance. Please, consider it. It will be a wonderful time."

Her eyes shone bright with determination. She wasn't going to give up the fight. Peering at her with a relinquishing smile, Captain Norton swallowed. "Very well, I'll consider it. But I can't promise anything."

She let out a squeal. "You're going to love it!"

"I'd hate to dampen the mood," Lieutenant Woods quietly cut in. He rubbed at his long sideburns. "But aren't we scheduled to patrol that day?"

Everyone fell silent, anxiously waiting to hear Captain McCannon's response.

"I don't know how I let that slip my mind, but you're right, lieutenant. Usually, we're scheduled back at the harbor by that time. We won't return till the following week."

The muscles in Captain McCannon's neck tightened. His piercing blue eyes intently fixed towards the tree line, as he appeared lost in his thoughts. He held very still, reminding Jane of a roman sculpture she'd seen at the mayor's home in Bombay. Realizing she was foolishly staring, she looked to her plate.

"When do you leave?" Miss Harrlow asked, disappointment seeping through her voice. The pink of her pouty lips matched the rouge on her cheeks.

"Tomorrow morning."

The ambience had taken a gloomy turn of silence. Lieutenant Woods certainly did put a damper on things. In an effort to cheer the gentlemen up, Jane offered the first thing that came to her mind. "Not to worry, I'm sure there will be plenty of leftover pie." She gave them a reassuring smile, but it immediately turned into a giggle as everyone else humorously cheered and laughed. Everyone except for Miss Harrlow, who scowled at her.

The early afternoon sun blazed down on them, thickening the air with humidity while they packed up their picnic. It was a warm fall day on the island. James adjusted his cravat, hoping it would alleviate the heat building underneath. He had just finished packing one of the baskets when he heard Nathanial holler, "Lieutenant Thomas, will you pass me a mango?"

"Didn't get enough to eat?" Thomas jested, throwing a mango to the lieutenant. Catching it, he gave a shrug, "Nah, it just sounds refreshing in this heat." Pulling a knife from the sheath in his boot, he cut into the fruit.

"Captain, would you be a dear and step off the blanket?" Jenny asked, as a piece of her auburn hair fell across her cheek. "We need to shake it out." She and Miss Sawyer stood by its corners waiting for him to move.

"Yes, ma'am!" James teased. Jenny scowled at him, causing him to chuckle. She hated it when he and Thomas called her that. Jenny's mother, Thomas's aunt, preferred to be called ma'am by her children as a sign of respect. Jenny on the other hand firmly disagreed. She felt it was a way for her to show authority over them. Ever since she had confessed her disapproval to Thomas and him, they made certain to call her ma'am whenever she asked them to do something. Particularly, when she was being bossy.

He moved off the blanket, allowing Jenny and Miss Sawyer to proceed. As the ladies gave a quick flick, a large spider flew off the blanket, landing directly on Miss Keaton's bodice.

A startling, bloodcurdling scream rang out from the petite woman. Whimpering, she frantically brushed off her dress, pulled out her bodice and hopped about wildly. *Heaven help the little fella—should he survive,* he chuckled to himself.

"Miss Keaton, I'm confident with a piercing shriek like that, you killed the petrified spider," Captain Norton agitatedly declared. His finger dug into his ear, trying to alleviate his pain.

"Agh! Mmm!" Nathanial bit his lip as he cried out in agony. James's heart skipped a beat as he glanced his way. Drops of blood fell from Nathanial's hand, staining the white flower petals below. Next to the flowers laid a bloody knife and a split open mango. It appeared Captain Richard wasn't the only one harmed by Miss Keaton's terror.

"You alright there, lieutenant?" James asked apprehensively.

Nathanial clasped his bloody hand. Through gritted teeth, he spoke, "I didn't even get to enjoy a bite. This feels like a deep one, captain."

He hurried over to Nathanial to examine him. The man bled profusely, making it impossible to see where his cut ran.

"Thomas, see if there are any clean napkins in the baskets," James ordered, pointing to the wicker-woven containers. "Nathanial, keep the pressure on your wound."

"Ah, I get faint with the sight of blood," Miss Harrlow groaned. She turned her shockingly paler face towards the opposite end of the field. James looked at Jenny who was a shade of green. Of course, the ladies shouldn't see this. Miss Keaton was too preoccupied with Captain Norton's ear to notice the lieutenant, and then there was Miss Sawyer. Miss Sawyer who oddly appeared to be holding herself back from coming over to the lieutenant. Her color was intact and her large eyes eager, as though assessing the gent.

"I'm not seeing any clean cloths," Thomas hollered over. James looked down at his shirt and was debating whether or not to remove it in front of the ladies and sacrifice it for the man's hand. He glanced up at the lieutenant who was now ghostly white. He needed to stop the bleeding fast. Settling on tearing a section off his shirt, he started to uunbutton his waistcoat but paused when Miss Sawyer approached them from the corner of his eye. She lifted up the bottom of her dress and tore off a strip of white cloth from her petticoat. She grabbed the lieutenant's hand and applied the wadded-up fabric.

"Hold this here, lieutenant—that's it. Now I need you to slowly sit. Captain McCannon, can you assist him to lay on the ground?"

James stalled, surprised by the lady's orders and confidence. She stood by the lieutenant's side, clasping his bleeding hand.

"Captain?" She looked over her shoulder at him. Her countenance was calm.

"Yes," James stammered, helping Nathanial to the ground. The lieutenant appeared ready to pass out with his sickly pale skin.

He gaped at Miss Sawyer as she tore another piece of fabric from her petticoat. She applied it to the already-soaked-through fabric.

"Lieutenant Fletch, would you be so kind as to retrieve my bag. It's tucked under the backside of my saddle."

Thomas didn't ask questions. Knowing the urgency, he ran over to her horse.

"Captain," she whispered. "He's about to pass out, can you grab a basket that's large enough to elevate his legs?"

James nodded and went over towards the ladies to retrieve a basket by their feet. Uncomfortably they shifted farther from the scene as the lieutenant moaned in pain. James shook his head, completely aghast by the drastic contrast Miss Sawyer illustrated. Swiftly, he returned and lifted the lieutenant's feet and carefully placed them on it. Miss Sawyer retrieved what appeared to be a small medical bag from Thomas and pulled out a tonic. Still conscious, Nathanial closed his eyes. Miss Sawyer lifted up the fabric to observe the wound. It was a deep gouge that sliced from one side of his palm to the other. Blood pooled immediately around the laceration.

"None of your tendons were sliced but I'm afraid your cut is going to require stitches."

The young man gave a faint nod.

"This is going to sting . . . a lot."

She poured the tonic over his wound and swiftly applied a new piece of fabric to stop the bleeding. Nathanial grimaced and groaned in agony through his clenched teeth. Calmly, she looked up at the closest person to her. Determination mixed with excitement filled her eyes.

"Captain, will you hold this in place for me, please?"

James obediently knelt by her side, holding the cloth on the lieutenant's hand as directed. A waft of sweet jasmine mixed with vanilla consumed his senses. *Great heavens, she smelled amazing.* He released an unsteady breath. She steadily pulled out a curved needle and thread from her bag. Her soft skin brushing against his arm in the process. His hold tightened as he battled to concentrate his attention solely on the lieutenant and not the bewitching woman beside him.

"My uncle always insists I carry this bag with me whenever I go on excursions," she whispered, almost to herself.

Her confidence suddenly appeared to falter. Why? Surely, not by the wound. She bit her lip, and her hands began to tremble. Instinctively he gently placed his hand on her arm wanting to calm any sudden uncertainty.

"It's a good thing he did."

Her big blue-green eyes met his. Staring longer than intended, he blinked and briefly looked away. Color raised to her soft cheeks. Offering him a small smile of gratitude, and her confidence regained, she made her first poke. Thread trailed behind as she swiftly stitched. She became focused and at ease, with a steady rhythm. It was as though she had been practicing the technique for years. Poke, poke, knot, then cut. Every stitch tied evenly spaced apart. He watched, astonished by her expertise. Apparently, he wasn't the only one who was observing her skills. He leaned back on his boots and caught Richard and Thomas hovering over their shoulders, transfixed by her every move. The other ladies kept their distance from fear of becoming faint.

Miss Sawyer examined her work after she cut the last piece of thread. Pouring more tonic on a clean fabric, she proceeded to gently clean his hand. Once satisfied, she tore a few strips of fabric then wrapped his hand with firm pressure.

Richard leaned over and began to whisper to him, "I bet you're wishing that was you in the lieutenant's place right now." They watched as she tenderly cradled Lieutenant Woods's hand in hers. "You'd be a fool not to."

James nodded in agreement with his friend. Never in his life, nor in his days of service, had he ever seen a young lady clean and suture a wound like Miss Sawyer had just done. Being so gentle and efficient without ever being affected by the sight of blood, Miss Sawyer perfectly applied what appeared to be an impeccable work of sutures. She did better work than any doctor he'd ever seen.

"I'm all done. You'll want to keep the wound dry for the next two days or so and then in about two weeks you can have your sutures removed."

"Yes, miss," Nathanial weakly replied. He laid perfectly still, though James noted a curve of a smile on the man's pale face.

"Where did you learn to do that?" Thomas gawked.

Miss Sawyer's eyes widened, taking in the gentlemen who hovered around her. She gracefully stood.

"Needlework," she sweetly spoke without hesitation. "I've given enough hours of embroidery to know how to sew a straight line, lieutenant," she teased as she offered him a small smile. "If you'll excuse me a moment, I need to wash my hands."

All the men stood awestruck, gazing after her as she departed towards the water. Each one of them appeared to hold a new level of respect for Miss Sawyer.

"Gentlemen," Richard stared off longingly, clasping his heart, "I think I'm in love."

James and Thomas smirked at each other. Miss Sawyer had certainly been entrancing. Any man would be blind to not take notice.

Chapter Nine

Restless, Jane finally settled in her tangled sheets before a form caught her attention. A gentleman on a surgery table rolled back and forth in pain. His excruciating cries grew louder when she approached. The muscles on his neck tightened as he let out another anguished cry. His flushed face glistened from perspiration streaking across his forehead down into his long black sideburns. She grabbed a cloth and attempted to dab his dampened skin. Immediately his cries ceased, and he held disturbingly still. His face became deathly gray. Her heart stopped as everything around them became an eerie silence. She leaned closer to make out his familiar face. Large green eyes opened with a start, staring at her with fury. Startled, she jumped back, immediately recognizing him.

"You—you did this to me!" he yelled, his hand quivering in the air. Yellow pus from the infection seeped between the stitches that *she* had administered.

Jane gasped. Every limb frozen with fright; her heart pounded against her chest. Catching her breath, she stared into the heavy darkness of her bedchamber.

"Well, that certainly was disturbing," she whispered to herself. She squeezed her eyes shut to block the memory from her nightmare. Could this be a premonition? *It couldn't be. I followed everything I was taught.* She wiped at her damp face and shook out the chemise that clung to her skin. *What hour is it?* The drapes in her quarters hung over the large window, shielding any light from seeping into the darkened room.

She felt along her comforter and threw off the covers. Crawling to the edge of her bed, she stepped onto the bench that sat at its foot. Hurrying to the drapes and she threw them open.

A thin white mist tucked over dark green fields, like a soft blanket protecting them from the cool morning. The stars in the heavens were dimming. The black sky had drifted into a gray-blue backdrop with a wisp of orange painted across the horizon.

Still shaking from the disturbing dream, she rushed to be rid of the vivid feeling and dressed herself in a cream muslin overlay dress. Tying a purple ribbon around her waist, she slipped into her walking shoes and eagerly set for her escape.

The brisk morning air sent a chill through her as she quickened her pace. She tightened her floral wool shawl across her chest, becoming distracted by her thoughts.

He couldn't get an infection, she repeated to herself. Never in her life had she had the privilege to work on a person. Without a doubt she was certain she had done precisely what her uncle had taught her. Following his instructions, she shouldn't have any fear of the lieutenant getting an infection. There's nothing to fret over.

She strolled aimlessly through a dampened field. *Oh, it was exhilarating,* she smiled, reminiscing over the ordeal. *To be able to close the wound all by myself.* She shrieked with glee and took a few little skips. Years of practicing her sutures by way of needlework was finally beneficial. She spread her arms to let her shawl sail behind her like a kite catching wind. *My first surgical procedure!* She joyously raised her shawl higher, enjoying how the warmth of the rising sun began to softly caress her skin. *Uncle Duncan would be proud... wouldn't he?* Her smile faltered. *Or would he be more concerned that my reputation would be tarnished? Which could happen.* Lowering her arms, she slowed her pace.

"Miss Sawyer," a deep voice called from behind. Her heart stopped with recognition. She whirled around in the waist-high grass and faced her rescuer striding towards her in his officer's uniform. "And what are you doing up at this hour?"

She struggled to gather her thoughts as he gave her a striking smile. Removing his bifold hat, he tucked it under his arm. His chestnut wavy hair was unkempt from where the hat had laid. She dipped into a quick curtsy trying not to focus on how becoming he appeared with his disheveled appearance.

"Captain McCannon." Controlling the startled feeling within, she maintained her gaze on his distinguished jaw. "I couldn't sleep."

"Ah," he strolled to her side, carrying a large burlap sack over his shoulder. "Was skipping through the grass supposed to help you tire?"

Her cheeks flushed. His eyes brightened with amusement. She gripped her shawl and whisked it over her shoulders while giving him a stern look. His smile broadened in a playful manner.

Feigning annoyance to hide her embarrassment, she tossed her loose braid over her shoulder and began to walk towards the manor. He rushed to her side, keeping pace.

"It's customary in India for one to skip, when they're in need of dire sleep," she candidly replied as a quick giggle from the absurdity of her words squeaked through her tightly pressed lips.

His eyes humorously gazed on her. "Is that so?" he asked, maintaining a curious expression. "Is it effective?"

She lifted her chin high and proud. "That, sir, is something you should discover for yourself."

An image of a large-statured man skipping on his ship came into her mind. She bit her lip, struggling to maintain her serious composure.

"Do tell how you've fared, after you've attempted it," her voice quivered as she held in more laughter.

He chuckled. "You have my word."

"Splendid." Jane couldn't contain her smile anymore. She brushed her hand across the grass, letting its pointed edges tickle her fingers. "And may I ask what are you doing on the governor's ground at this time in the morning?"

Captain McCannon adjusted the heavy looking sack on his shoulder.

"I'm passing through. Governor Keaton has granted me access to cut across his fields, should I ever need to shorten my journey to the harbor."

"That was very considerate of the governor. And here I thought I had the field to myself," she teased.

His bright gaze continued to shine on her. "Don't let me stop you from performing your sleep ritual," he stated as his dimple deepened. "Your secret is safe with me."

She chuckled. "You know, I do believe you would keep that secret." *Or any for that matter*, she thought to herself. Like the one at the pier. She was relieved beyond measure that no rumor had surfaced about her incident. Elaine even kept an ear out for such talk, though she had reassured Jane on a few occasions that Captain James McCannon and Lieutenant Thomas Fletch were too respectful and would never spread such a tale.

She glanced up and caught him studying her from the corner of his eye. She detected a flicker of conflict in them before he darted his attention back in front of them. His knuckles whitened, clinging on the sack that hung over his back. She had never recalled them being so pale against his weathered hands. Something clearly unsettled him. Could he be anxious?

"Tell me, captain, are you still afraid of the ocean?"

He gave a halfhearted smile. "Not anymore."

If not the fear of sailing, then what else caused such distress? She tugged at the tall grass and twisted it in her hands.

"I'm glad to hear that." She threw the grass stem and clasped her hands behind her back. They walked along in silence. She had to be a mile away from the house now.

"Captain McCannon, since our conversation yesterday, I've been eager to know if you entered the Navy still having a fear of the ocean?"

He chuckled, adjusting the sack on his broad shoulder. "I did."

"But whatever for? Couldn't you have chosen a different profession? One that didn't require sailing for long periods of time?"

She clenched her jaw, hoping she didn't come off too presumptuous. Subtly, she glanced at him only to abruptly look away as warmth spread through her cheeks—again. He was staring at her with a humored gleam in his eye. Irritated, she brushed away a curl that fell across her face. It was becoming extremely vexing that he could have such an effect on her.

"Of course I could have. But I decided I'd rather face my fear than avoid it. And before you think I'm half-witted, let me explain."

She peered at him, smiling to herself with how easily he had set himself up to be taunted. "Please do," she challenged. "I was beginning to have my doubts."

His irritating, absurdly blue eyes brightened with amusement. "Come now, Miss Sawyer," he grinned with a taunting smile. "I may sound a little foolish, but at least I have other ways to catch a person's attention rather than throwing myself into the water."

Touché, she laughed to herself. Avoiding giving him the satisfaction of a smile, she pressed her betraying lips together.

"Is that what I did?" She plucked a flower as they began to pass.

"All I'm saying is, if you wanted my attention, you only had to say hello, or offer a smile."

Pretending to smell the flower's sweet aroma, she hid a laugh.

"I'll be sure to remember that, captain. Next time I'm at port and I happen to see you, I'll refrain from jumping off the pier." She exerted a heavy sigh. "One can only do so much to get a gentleman's attention these days. My gowns and I are extremely grateful for your honesty."

He laughed—a low husky laugh that defeated her fight to refrain from smiling.

"You're most welcome, Miss Sawyer." In an instant, he shook his head. His face fell into a more serious manner. The air between them grew thick with an unspoken barrier as they strolled through the grass in silence. Jane couldn't help but notice that his leisurely strides had turned into a stiff stalk. Even the way his brows furrowed, heavy above his confused daze, revealed he was experiencing an internal battle—a battle that he appeared to be losing. What caused him such troublesome thoughts? Could it be about his assignment to patrol the island?

She was contemplating inquiring about what weighed heavy on his mind but thought better of it. If it was regarding the war, then he may not want to discuss the matter. From what she's learned while being in the hospital, light conversation was more welcoming for the militiamen—not a heavy topic such as the French and war.

"I hope I'm not taking you away from your endeavors," his soft voice broke the silence. He kept his gaze ahead. A sudden urge to ease whatever could be troubling him swept over her.

"Not at all, if you don't mind, I'll walk with you until the field meets the road. I've been needing to stretch my legs."

She watched him, carefully trying to observe if he'd be fine with the prospect. He nodded, never looking her way. The corner of his lip turned upward—hinting of a smile.

"Of course," his pace slowed, and he briefly peered at her.

"Captain, forgive me if I'm prying, but how did you overcome your fear after you joined the Navy?"

"Not at all," he offered a small smile. "When I was a young lad, I used to love sailing across the ocean. My father was an admiral on a ship called the Infinity. I used to beg him to allow me to sail with him on his ship. So, after my ninth birthday, he allowed me to join him and his crew as there was no threat of war. At the age of twelve, we were caught in a storm. I had remembered some of the sailors mentioning monstrous waves that would get so high they could engulf an entire ship. Being my first storm on board, I had never witnessed such a sight. My father had told me to stay in his cabin but naturally curiosity got the best of me and I headed to the deck."

"Mmm, naturally," Jane repeated, unaware that she had spoken the words. She had become lost in his story, thinking how she'd never dare venture on deck in the middle of a storm. Noticing his silence, she glanced up.

He was observing her with a humorous gleam in his eyes. "Are you mocking me, Miss Sawyer?"

"Not at all." She bit her lip, holding back any sign of irony. She didn't mean to tease.

"Are you certain?" he challenged, the corner of his lip lifting.

"I would never." Jane looked at him appalled. She plucked another flower and hid her amusement behind its petals. "Though, out of my own *curiosity*, did the thought of being swept off the deck and drowning in the merciless waves ever cross your mind?"

Captain McCannon let out a heartfelt laugh that caused an exhilarating wave of excitement to flood through her veins. Her breath caught in her throat. Surprised by the feeling, she held the flower tighter. "Believe it or not, that's exactly what happened, minus the drowning."

A soft gasp escaped her lips. "How did you survive?"

"I had tied a rope around my waist."

"Is that what the crew taught you to do?"

"No, they didn't . . . I learned to do that on my first day of sailing." The captain appeared hesitant before he proceeded. "I was five and my mother had insisted I had a rope tied around my waist whenever I went on deck without her."

"Dear me," she exclaimed as she did her best to stifle a laugh. She could only imagine how twisted and tangled he would get with the crew and masts. "Did you go on deck very often?"

"Only when I felt claustrophobic in our cabin, which happened frequently."

"I know the feeling well."

Jane reflected on her voyage to the island. She felt trapped many times due to her seasickness. When she wasn't sick, she mostly avoided the deck from any chance of seeing Lieutenant Howard.

"How long were you overboard?" She tossed the flower into the grass. Their steps became easier as they were now walking on pebbles that trailed through the manicured gardens of the plantation. The manor stood far in the distance on the hillside with the sun reflecting off a few windows.

"Not very long. One of the sailors saw what had happened and with the help of a few crew members, they pulled me out of the water onto the deck."

She fell silent, letting his words sink in. "My goodness, captain, your father must have been so upset."

"I'd never seen him so distraught." He turned solemn; his gaze stared off towards the blue horizon. "I learned a very valuable lesson that day. From that point on I did my best to obey my father's orders."

"Is that when you became afraid of the ocean?"

"It was. The ocean could have swallowed me in that storm. Rope or no rope. I learned to respect her with its sovereignty. When the time came for me to join Her Majesty's Navy, I did it without hesitation. Knowing I'd not only be battling the French, but I'd also be wrestling with my fear. Now, I embrace sailing and enjoy every minute I'm out on the water."

"That's very courageous of you. I'm most certain I will never overcome mine. Nor do I want to face it." She paused before adding, "Though I must say, I'm not sure if going on deck during a storm would convince me of your sound state of mind." She walked ahead of him at a faster pace.

"Ha! Fair enough." He had a broad grin when she looked over her shoulder. Disappointingly, it disappeared quickly as she caught a glimpse of it.

"Do tell me, Miss Sawyer, what is your fear?"

She slowed to his side. Her eyes widened as she cautiously searched the tall grass that they entered again. "Snakes." The word squeaked from her lips. She glanced up and saw the dimple on his cheek deepen.

"Snakes? Even the little garden ones?"

"All snakes. Of every form." Feeling determined to have him understand her fear, she added, "Here's my story for you, captain."

He stopped, standing at ease in the tall waving grass, giving her his full attention.

"Shortly after I moved to India, there was a night that I shall never forget. I had drifted off to sleep but was soon startled awake with the sound of hissing near my ear."

He involuntarily rubbed his shoulder against the side of his head. "I'm certain I would have bolted for the door."

She nodded with a chuckle. "Fortunately, I didn't, otherwise there may have been very bad consequences." She wrapped her arms around her body to contain the haunting reminder. "Not knowing what else to do, I laid there as still as I could. I could hear the echo of my heart beating, while it slowly slithered its long thin body over my shoulders, under my blanket, across my body, and towards my feet."

The captain grimaced. "I can tolerate snakes but that, I'm certain I couldn't."

"Believe me, I was struggling. It had curled its body at my feet." She shook her shoulders to rid herself of the unnerving feeling.

His eyes widened. "How did you manage to get out?"

"I didn't. I laid there for a few hours before I fell back to sleep." Jane held her breath and humorously watched the captain's mouth drop dumbfoundedly. She paused dramatically and raised her brow. "I'm teasing you."

His dimple deepened, as he scoffed.

"I couldn't resist." She bit her lip.

His eyes danced while studying her. "Of course you couldn't."

She chuckled and continued to walk in the direction towards the dirt road with him by her side.

"All teasing aside, I slowly inched myself up and slid out from under the covers. Once out, I hurried to my uncle's study to tell him what had happened. He had the snake killed immediately. Turns out, it was a hump-nosed pit viper."

"What was a poisonous snake like him doing in your home?" he asked, perplexed. "Aren't they found in dense jungles?"

"Yes, but they also like to lay in coffee plantations and one happened to be near our home. We concluded that he made his way up the tree next to my balcony and dropped in."

"That's very plausible. Sounds like we both came close to near death experiences."

"Yes, it does." Grabbing her braid, she combed her restless fingers through the curls at the end.

As they continued in silence, an odd feeling of uncertainty began to cloud over her. When she glanced over at Captain McCannon, his face appeared pained. His eyes filled with conflict particularly whenever he glanced her way. Her stomach sank. This wasn't about the French. After witnessing many gentlemen scurrying away from her, she knew the look too well. But she was confused as there was no one on the island to threaten him—not like the other gentlemen were in Bombay. Feelings of doubt rushed through her. Perhaps the men didn't run from her because of the threats. Perhaps, all this time it was her. She inhaled a sharp breath.

He looked down at her briefly and eased his way to the side, withdrawing himself further from her as they nearly brushed arms. That was to be a kind gesture, right? Swallowing the sour taste of bitterness, she settled the matter. It was her. It only made sense for there was no other reason to explain his behavior. Why else did he try to draw away from her? He's just trying to be polite, probably out of obligation for saving her life. She cursed at herself. How could she have been naive? Most perplexing, why did his reaction bother her so?

"I fear I may have overexerted myself this morning." She forced the lie in a breathless manner. "I best be turning around."

They stopped. The muscles tightened in his clean-shaven cheeks. His dark brows furrowed when he looked at her, as though he were at odds with himself.

"Miss Sawyer," his voice strained. He placed his sack to the ground, then ran his hand through the loose waves of his brown locks, disheveling them more. His face was disgruntled, like the day he had rescued her—when he was uncertain on where to place his hands.

"Yes?" She couldn't fathom what he would say. Did she say too much?

He gripped the back of his neck as though whatever it was nagged at him. Letting go he gave her a nod.

"I hope you enjoy your time at the festival."

Jane forced a smile, hiding her confusion. The festival?

"Thank you, captain. I bid you smooth sailing."

The corner of his mouth lifted. He bent down and grabbed his sack. Placing his bifold cap on his head he tipped it towards her and continued on his way. Jane's mind raced as she tried to decode his meaning. The festival was mentioned yesterday. The waterfall, the picnic, oh . . . her heart sank. Lieutenant Woods.

"Captain McCannon?" she softly called.

He stopped. His shoulders tightened before he turned to take a few strides towards her. She swallowed, building courage for what she wanted to ask. Straightening her skirt, she stepped forward. Her throat tightened by the intensity of his stare. Regret for ever calling his name began to gnaw at her—but she had to know. For some reason his opinion mattered. More than anyone else's. Her heart quickened. She'd only push him away—farther than he already grew during their walk, but the desire for his thoughts became more and more unbearable the longer he studied her.

"What are your thoughts of a lady ever performing a surgical procedure?" she rushed.

Her hands began to slightly tremble as he watched her. His eyes softened with understanding. Slowly he removed his hat and brought it to his broad chest. Jane held her breath. Her legs became unmovable, as she stared deep into his intimidating eyes, searching for his answer. He took a step forward, drawing intimately close.

"If any woman embroidered the way you do, Miss Sawyer," the corner of his mouth lifted, deepening his dimple. "Then my answer is simple," his voice softened "Her patient would be the most fortunate person to be performed on."

She drew in a sharp breath.

"Truly?" her voice softened, desperately hoping he meant every word.

"Yes," his voice lowered.

Relief washed over her. Her actions at the picnic didn't appall him after all. "Thank you, captain."

Respectfully, he nodded and placed his hat back on his head, tipping her a farewell.

She felt elated to have such a compliment but at the same time she felt frustratingly more confused. She stood a moment watching him depart. The sack bumped against his solid back with his every step.

If suturing the lieutenant's hand didn't bother him, then what else could be amiss? Surely there was something bothering him, and yet she couldn't help but feel it had something to do with her.

Chapter Ten

In the sun lit parlor, Jane stared at the green satin stitch she had sewed into the cream-colored linen. She decided to embroider a wreath of jasmine flowers, to give herself a piece of home as the white petaled flower had grown in a shrubbery below her balcony. She closed her eyes and slowly inhaled. If she concentrated hard enough, she could almost catch the memory of the sharp, sweet aroma.

Across from her, Elaine spread herself on a wingback chair next to the window, her foot tucked under her. The other swayed back and forth mindlessly above the hardwood floor. She coiled a blonde curl around her finger as she read her novel.

"Uh, hmm," a deep voice cleared, calling for their attention. Jane's head whirled to the door, where the elegantly tall butler, Mister Gibbs, stood. Elaine quickly sat up. Straightening into a proper lady's stance. She closed her book strategically with her finger in between the pages.

"There's a Miss Jenny Oakley here to see you ladies."

"Send her in please." Elaine relaxed her stance and smiled over at Jane as Miss Oakley entered the purple parlor. Dressed in a pale-yellow damask gown, Miss Oakley hurried in with the vibrant enthusiasm of a mynah bird.

"Well, it's just as we suspected. It's all over town," Miss Oakley exclaimed, never pausing to give a proper greeting. Her manner was bright though she held no smile on her elegantly long face.

"Oh?" Elaine clapped giddily. Miss Oakley shook her head when she caught Elaine's eye. Elaine slouched with defeat. "I assume it wasn't by the lieutenant's doing."

Unpinning her straw hat, Miss Oakley removed her laced gloves and sat in the adjacent wing back chair.

"Before he departed, he gloated his part beautifully, but as soon as she caught wind, she countered it, making it sound repulsive and improper."

Feeling unsettled with what they could be discussing, Jane cautiously watched the two ladies.

"Drat that woman. She always twists gossip for her own gain. She never likes having anyone outshine her." Elaine scowled with irritation. "But no worries, we'll correct that." She threw herself back against the chair and resumed her position. Miss Oakley nodded and turned her attention to Jane.

"You'll have to forgive us, Miss Sawyer," she spoke warmly. "We were hoping your skills on Lieutenant Woods would have a more positive effect in town."

Jane's mouth dropped. "My skills?" A cold sweat broke out across her back. Just as she feared. How could she have been so careless? Stitching a gentleman's hand was a doctor's task, not other's, let alone a woman. Not caring about her reputation, she looked at her friend Elaine who sat casually twirling her finger in her hair. What of the Keaton's? Boarding such a woman? How could she do that to them? She should have let the gentlemen help the lieutenant—but that would have been too gruesome as they appeared to not know what to do. It wasn't in her nature to not help those who were in desperate need. Let alone ones who were bleeding profusely—and that gentleman certainly was in a grave state.

"Jane," Elaine interrupted her thoughts. A curl was wrapped around her motionless finger. "Don't start regretting what you did. I can see it in your face," she reprimanded.

"Oh goodness, please don't," Miss Oakley urged, staring at her with repentant eyes. She straightened, holding the brim of her hat on her lap. "I didn't say that to worry you. On the contrary, what you did was admirable."

"Quite," Elaine giggled. "I get faint with the sight of blood but you—"

"Took charge with such boldness. The men obeyed you like you were their admiral—which between the lieutenant and the captain, never happens, unless they were orders from me." She winked, her tan face brightening with a beautiful smile.

"Don't forget, you also saved Lieutenant Woods from bleeding out," Elaine added, twisting her curl again.

Jane gazed at her clenched hands. Surprised with how tense she had gripped the tambour hoop, she nervously tugged at the partially embroidered fabric to smooth the wrinkles.

"Well, I certainly didn't mean to cause a stir, especially to gain any attention." Certainly, not for the rumors. She dreaded the thought.

"Oh, we know," Elaine smiled at her. "You're too modest. Which is a shame. A lady with such skills is refreshing—and quite scandalous." Jane's eyes widened. "But nevertheless, refreshing." Elaine tapped her fingers across the book in her lap. "Though, I should have known you knew all the medical procedures with all the time you spent at the hospital. Here I was envying you, assuming you were scouring for potential suitors."

Jane's mouth fell by such an accusation.

"You would think that," she retorted.

Elaine flashed her a shameless smile.

Miss Oakley laughed, sinking further in her chair and fanning herself with her hat. Yellow ribbons waved gracefully in the air, trailing behind the brim. "You may not have been hunting, Miss Sawyer, but Elaine certainly would have, had she the chance."

"It's true. All those handsome men needing to be comforted." She released a heavy sigh. Jane shook her head. Life in the hospital wasn't dreamy at all, especially after an attack. She adjusted herself on the couch to hide her emotions as the memories of the times she had spent in the recovery wing flooded her thoughts.

There were fond memories of laughter, card playing, and sharing stories among the men. All which was to help keep each other's spirits up. Then there were the soul-crippling sounds of once unbroken men, screaming in pain, crying and praying for relief. Rusted smell of iron mixed with bitter taint of laudanum, lemon cleaners, and linens. She often felt helpless whenever there was an attack. She was always being whisked away from the hospital, solely due to her uncle's protective orders. He's never wanted her to witness anything too traumatizing.

She played with the satin edging at the bottom of her bodice. No, she won't tell Elaine the nightmares laced with the pleasantries.

Jane mustered a smile and added to her friend's passion-filled heart. "You indeed would be a sight for sore eyes."

Elaine smiled at her and glanced back to the window. Suddenly, she scrambled to sit up. "Oh! Captain Norton is riding up the drive."

"Captain Norton now?" Miss Oakley baited. "Whatever happened to Captain James?" she gave her a questionable brow.

Elaine stuck her petite nose in the air and waved off the comment with her dainty hand.

"There's a time when a lady needs to accept defeat." She tossed her book onto the coffee table between her and Jane. "And my time has flown by months ago—after I made my intentions clear," she laughed. "Besides, I believe someone's finally tripped the captain's stubborn anchor."

Jane half listened to Miss Oakley and Elaine. If the townspeople were talking, would her uncle be ashamed? It only happened yesterday, but she had yet to tell him, as he was fishing with Governor Keaton all afternoon. Even this morning she had missed him when he had left to see the coast. She'll be certain to inform him as soon as he comes back to the plantation. Although, if he'd pass through town, he would have already heard the news. Her stomach knotted with cold pricks of dread.

Across the way, Miss Oakley chuckled. "Yes," she smiled. "What with the wind howling in from the east, I suppose his sails can't resist. They'll likely surrender, itching to let the breeze guide him wherever it goes."

Still processing the unsettling gossip, Jane only caught part of the conversation between the two and didn't quite follow where the howling wind would lead him. Were they speaking of Captain McCannon or Captain Norton?

"And where do you suppose that is?" she questioned, resting her needle work to the side of her.

Elaine flicked her hand at Jane. "And ruin all the fun? Honestly Jane, you've spent years in Bombay, sailing around with a crew at your command. Who've also fought valiantly to protect you from any sea monsters and storms." Her face brightened with excitement. "It's time for you to sail the uncharted waters by yourself and discover the magic within those seas."

"Elaine." She held her composure from the surprising jab of having her own crew to command. Knowing how courtship was such a serious matter to her friend, she attempted to keep the humor hidden from her face. "I shall explore the uncharted waters, once I'm in England. Perhaps if I'm lucky, I may catch a few fish." Considering she had no other choice.

"You'd best be catching one of those large, bluefish tuna, then." Elaine smiled knowingly at Miss Oakley and back to her. "Blue is such a fetching color on a gentleman." Miss Oakley smirked at Elaine and nodded.

Jane picked up her needlework again. She straightened in her chair, thoroughly enjoying the crypted messages.

"Blue is a fetching color, but I'm afraid a nobleman would steer his course away from my title-less ship." She shook her head and chuckled by all the metaphors.

"Not that shade of blue—" Miss Oakley started but Elaine cut in with a huff.

"Oh Jane, laugh now but you'll soon find that without those gentlemen friends in Bombay, you're going to experience life as a terrifying yet thrilling adventure. Just wait. Soon enough you'll find out."

"Yes, but there's no urgency in the matter. Why fret when England's almost two months away? Until then I shall be carefree without having to worry about all those sea monsters." She gave Elaine a wink. She wasn't a lost cause to the prospect of courting. Many of the gentlemen warned her how to tell the bad fish from the good. The idea of trying to discern it herself did have her a little unsettled though.

Elaine sighed hopelessly, shrugging at Miss Oakley.

"Well, keep an eye out for the jellyfish," Oakley piped. "They're such mystical creatures but leave a nasty sting."

Jane tilted her head with curiosity. What jellyfish had she encountered?

"Or the blowfish!" Elaine giggled through her words. "They're too pompous." She burst out in laughter with Miss Oakley and Jane, until Gibbs entered the room and interrupted.

"There's a Captain Richard Norton here to see—"

"Thank you, Gibbs! Carry on," Elaine exclaimed, hopping to her feet.

"Careful, Elaine," Miss Oakley warned. "He may be appealing now, but he'll leave you with a dreadful mark that could scar."

"Oh, he's harmless. Besides, I know exactly what I'm doing. With a few outings, he'll be as good as mush."

"Is that what you thought of Captain James?" Miss Oakley teased.

"No, that gent's eyes needed to be opened by someone more . . ." She bit her lip then grinned as if she found the right word. "Exotic."

She exchanged a knowing smile with Miss Oakley. Exotic? Jane felt completely lost. Unless—her eyes widened. She was hinting at someone foreign and if she had meant her, why she was mistaken. The captain only opened his eyes to her out of obligation. She forced him to see her the moment she fell in the water. He even hinted at it when he teased her how she could have just said hello. And there was nothing more between them except a wedge he placed earlier that morning.

"Jane, I'll see you later this afternoon." Elaine called out. Her muslin gown rustled behind her when she departed.

Miss Oakley stared at her with a smile. "Miss Sawyer, I'm so glad you're here in Jamestown." Jane eased in her presence. She found the lady's countenance quite endearing.

It was a bright, beautiful morning. Three days since they left the harbor. The white sails fiercely protruded against the blue sky and turquoise water. Sailors scattered abroad the deck seeing to their tasks while the officers yelled orders. Being their captain, James always believed in being prepared for an attack or a storm, so he held drills frequently. The crew respected him for it, keeping them organized and alert. Stationed at the wheel, James guided the ship through the open waters.

Earlier that morning, merchant ships they had crossed reported seeing two French battleships. One was close to the island and another further south in the Atlantic. They only had a few days to patrol around the island before they had to report back to monitor the harbor. His goal was to cross their path. He wanted to be done with them once and for all. His thoughts were quickly interrupted when Thomas joined him on deck.

"With all the drills you've been ordering, I almost forgot to mention to you that I saw our pal Lieutenant Howard before we departed."

The last person James wanted to think about was that wretched man.

"He was being released from confinement, swearing up a storm and making threats to each of the guards."

"They should have thrown that ungrateful scoundrel back in for his obscene behavior." James tightened his fists, infuriated with the lieutenant and his commander. After the picnic, James located Lieutenant Howard's commanding officer, Captain Charles Lucas. He was in the pub drinking with a couple other officers. When he had pulled him aside to inform him of the lieutenant's circumstance, the officer demanded that he'd be released. James was appalled and held firm to their rules regarding infraction. After arguing, they settled with the lieutenant staying one night in confinement instead of two—as long as Captain Lucas followed through with his punishment on his own ship. *Which was highly unlikely.* He had warned the captain that if he saw or heard of any other misdeed committed by the lieutenant, he would arrange with the governor to have him shipped off the island, immediately. The captain snorted at James, clearly not taking him seriously . . . big mistake.

"One could only wish." Thomas rubbed his square chin with deep contemplation. "I was conversing with a few of the merchants from the lieutenant's ship this morning. What I gathered was due to the death of the lieutenant's father, his uncle had been raising him since he was a lad. His mother passed away while giving birth to him. After boarding school, his uncle quickly enlisted the gent, due to his obscene conduct with the ton. It sounds as though his uncle is hoping the few years in the navy would earn him a respectable reputation in society. Which is why he would do anything to keep him where he's at."

James scoffed, thinking back at Captain Lucas's frantic reaction to the lieutenant's confinement. "Bribing or threatening an officer is a high offense and could be court-martialed."

"True, but if one were to have friends in high places, many of those scoundrels slip through the system."

"I suppose we'll have to deal with matters ourselves."

Thomas nodded in agreement. The lieutenant already had a blackened reputation. He certainly wasn't showing any penitents for his previous life. Instead, he walked around with entitlement as he pleased. The thought seethed James's blood. How he'd do anything to catch the impudent opponent.

A moment of silence passed through them. Thomas's brows began to furrow. He stared at his palm, running his finger down the center.

"I can't stop thinking about the picnic," his voice lowered. "I've never seen anything like it. She was swift with her movements. Like it was as easy as tying a reef knot." He paused, rubbing his jaw. "She was even better than our ship's doctor, Doctor Bentley, who's the best surgeon on our island. There's no way she learned all that from embroidery."

James smiled at the comment. She had surprised him—and not just him, all of them. She didn't turn from the sight of blood but instead she faced it with stride. Of course, she didn't learn how to skillfully suture a wound from embroidery.

"You do remember who her uncle is—Doctor Duncan Brown? England's *finest* surgeon? He's obviously taught her the ways of the trade."

"Do you think he'd risk her reputation by teaching her those skills?"

Risk her reputation? James grip tightened at the wheel. More than anything it added to her character. The woman was captivating.

"I'm sure he didn't see any harm from her learning without anyone else's knowledge. She's not flaunting it nor is she saying she wants to get into the field of medicine. She just . . . embroiders, perfectly straight lines."

"On people?"

James chuckled, "Just one." *That we know of.* He smiled to himself. A figure on deck caught his eye.

"Lieutenant Woods!" James yelled out to the gentleman below them. "How's your hand?"

Lieutenant Woods held his gauze wrapped hand over his heart and smiled broadly.

"Never been better! Feels like it's been saved by a Goddess Divine!"

The men laughed. Thomas shook his head. "Mark that as another admirer of Miss Sawyer. I get the impression she's oblivious to it."

James nodded grudgingly. How to stay clear from such rarity? Everything about her lured him in, like a siren's melody. He pulled on his cravat. He had every reason to avoid talking with her before his patrol, but couldn't. No matter how hard he fought it, his heart had pulsed fiercely, refusing to listen to what his thoughts kept repeating over and over. *Remember. Stay clear. She's only passing through.* Though, ever since his first encounter with Miss Sawyer, he'd been certain he'd be the one heartbroken should anything ever happen between them.

He took off his hat and raked his hand through his hair with frustration. He shouldn't have agreed to have her walk with him towards the road. But the idea of refusing such an offer gnawed at him and would have left him full of regret.

He tried, oh how he tried, not to get tangled up with her conversation, but she was so blasted enchanting. Spending time with her only made it more difficult for him to ever want to avoid her.

Slapping his hat back on his head, he returned to manning the wheel. Cursing himself for clouding his thoughts of her. He shook his shoulders, relaxing the tension that built.

"I imagine Captain Richard will attempt to win her affection in the next few days, while he's docked."

A mischievous laugh rumbled through James's chest. He was aware of how Richard meddled with ladies' hearts and he wasn't going to allow Miss

Sawyer to become a victim to his charm. She deserved more than that. Any lady deserved more than that. He laughed to himself. But only one lady in particular could avoid any such charm by frightening the gent away with her babble. So he did what needed to be done.

"Not anymore," James rubbed the back of his neck, pleased with his scheme.

Thomas smirked. "Go on."

"After our picnic, I managed to pull Miss Keaton aside. I told her how Richard made mention that he fancied her. Then I proceeded to tell her if he ever came to visit, she should be sure to take a stroll in the gardens with him or read him poetry, as he desired the two."

Thomas roared with laughter. "Considering how persistent she is, he's never going to venture out of the harbor for fear she'll cling to him."

"That's the idea," James laughed.

"He's going to get you for this, just you wait!"

"As long as he doesn't know it was me, I'll rest easy. Till then, at least I'll be at ease knowing Miss Sawyer won't be seeing the captain anytime soon."

Both men laughed and carried on with their duties.

Chapter Eleven

Jane stood against a dark wall of a golden ballroom lined with elegant candelabras. People mingled all around her as though she didn't exist. Her shoulders slumped with disappointment when suddenly, a tall shadow of a man held out his hand and asked her to dance. Out of habit, she glanced around to see if any of her gentlemen friends would object and motion the gentleman away, but they were nowhere to be found. She stood alone, able to make the decision herself. She accepted it freely, as if unchained. Candles flickered with the butterflies in her stomach. He reached for her waist to pull her closer. Her heart quickened by his touch. Could this feeling of peace and excitement be love? Soft angles of his nose and lips began to be crisp and clear, to reveal the gentleman. She held her breath, waiting to see who he was, the dark hair lightened under the candlelight, and then— the disturbing sound of drapes being thrown across a metal bar caused the whole scene to slip away. Jane groaned and threw her pillow over her face in an attempt to recapture him.

"It's time to wake up, Miss Jane."

Why did Millie have to sound so chipper this early? She groaned. She needed to know what was going to happen next.

"It looks like a perfect day for you and Miss Oakley to do your shopping."

Shopping? Jane threw off her pillow and rolled to her back. How could she have forgotten about her and Jenny's plans? Excited, she quickly sat against her pillows as Millie headed towards the armoire and pulled out a lavender gown. Jane smiled from the brightness of the delightful sunshine illuminating her room. For the first time in over a week, the sun made its appearance, exposing a gorgeous blue sky. Millie was right, a perfect day was ahead of them. She scrambled out of the covers, leaving behind her mystery man. *Until another dream,* she sighed wistfully.

"Do you know what you're going to make for your basket?" Jane wobbled as Millie pulled on the strings of her corset. "Will it be some of the Indian dishes back home?"

She tightened another row of laces on Jane's dress.

"No," she breathed. Her voice was unsteady with the tugs. "It has an acquired taste. I'm afraid to make more of a spectacle out of myself than I already have." Her hands ran down the soft cotton fabric. "I decided to do something simple and more local."

Since suturing Lieutenant Woods's hand, Miss Harrlow had gone ahead and told everyone how peculiarly she'd behaved. The gossip spread like wildfire and thankfully, Miss Jenny, Elaine, and unexpectedly Captain Norton were quick to defend, defusing the flames the foul woman set.

Evidently, Miss Harrlow was to blame for most rumors that were spread and had the impertinence to pin them on Elaine. No wonder Elaine despised the woman.

"I think what you did to the lieutenant's hand was brave, Miss Jane. I faint with the sight of blood."

Millie's round face appeared from behind her. Her freckles on her small nose lifted up and fell back down as she gave her a reassuring nod. Jane bestowed a lighthearted smile, "Thank you, Millie."

Millie ducked her head down and led her to the stool in front of her vanity. She sat staring at her reflection, while Millie pulled from a drawer pins and a comb.

She had thought she'd disappoint her uncle with her rash decision, but she was mistaken. He was very proud of her, especially since the gentleman was in dire need of assistance. Thankfully, with the preparation and excitement for the festival, everyone had moved on from the gossip.

The festival. She drew restless with the thought of it. Her head began to tilt with each stroke of the comb. She had never attended any festivals in Bombay. The risks were too high due to public attacks by the Mysore.

Ouch. She bit her lip; Millie unknowingly poked her scalp with a hair pin. Her handmaiden's pale brows drew together in concentration. She took charge of Jane's curls, pinning and twisting them loosely in a fashionable style.

Tapping her slipper against the soft carpet, Jane shifted her attention back to her reflection. The circles under her eyes from the first few days on the island had disappeared. She even had a pinker hue in her less-gaunt cheeks, giving her a healthier appearance.

"Finished," Millie declared, stepping back to admire her work.

"It looks wonderful, Millie, thank you." She gave her a quick hug and then rushed downstairs towards the breakfast parlor. She was the first to arrive. The buffet filled the breakfast bar with fresh fruit, toast, poached eggs, and sausage. The delicious smells made her mouth water and her stomach rumbled with a sharp pain. Obeying its plea, she grabbed a plate and filled it with a scoop of fruit medley, a piece of toast, one poached egg, and two sausage links.

Once sat, Elaine, dressed in her riding habit, entered the room, clearly out of breath.

"Good morning, Elaine." Jane smiled at her and, as always, was excited to hear what her high-spirited friend would delve into.

"Oh . . ." Elaine straightened, attempting to catch her breath. "Good morning." She offered Jane a lively smile and headed to the buffet.

"What are your plans for today?" Jane poured herself tea from the kettle in front of her plate. "Is the captain calling on you this morning?"

Elaine brightened with the mention of him.

"He is, he's taking me riding! Well, more like I'm taking him, so I can show him around the island. I'm so excited, I don't know how I'm going to eat."

Elaine appeared conflicted when she sat down and stared at her plate full of eggs and fruit. She and Captain Norton had been seeing a lot of each other the past two weeks. When he had called on them the day after the picnic, Elaine had whisked him away to show him the gardens. The next day she read him poetry and then the next he took her into town to show her around his ship. They seemed inseparable as he called on her almost every day. He even extended his trip another week so "his men" could be a part of the festivities before heading off to India. Jane smiled at the sweet courtship that was forming between the two.

"At least take a bite of your eggs," she advised, looking out for her friend's wellbeing.

"Will you and Jenny be in town this morning?" Elaine poked at an egg but failed to bring her fork to her mouth.

"We will. We're going to buy supplies to pull together our baskets tomorrow." She took a sip of her tea. "Have you an idea of what you'll be putting in yours?"

Elaine laid down her fork and folded her hands in her lap.

"I'll be putting slices of ham, cheese, baked potatoes, grapes, rice pudding, and wafers. All of Rich—Captain Richard's favorite foods." A triumphant smile spread across her face.

"I thought the gentlemen weren't supposed to know whose baskets were whose?" Jane teased. Elaine shrugged guiltlessly.

"They're not," she stated, shifting in her chair. A slow smile spread across her porcelain face. Her nose turned up in the air with defiance. "But the captain wanted to be certain he knew which one to bid on. So naturally I asked him what his favorite foods were."

"Of course," Jane taunted. She was enjoying how Elaine found herself a gentleman that was as smitten with her as she was with him. The butler entered the parlor and gave a bow.

"Captain Richard Norton has arrived," he announced with a rather boorish tone.

Elaine could barely refrain herself as she practically jumped out of her chair.

"Thank you, Gibbs! Tell him I'll be right there . . . Right, right, deep breaths." Elaine fanned her flushed face with her napkin.

"Would you like some water?" This Jane could relate to. Only one gentleman had made her flush uncomfortably. Then it was usually followed with parchedness as she found herself at times lost for words. It was rather annoying.

Elaine giggled. "I'll be fine. I just need a moment." The color began to calm down in her face. "Hmm. See?"

Swiftly heading towards the doorway, she paused. "Jane, have a great time in town. Give my regards to Jenny."

"I shall."

Cedar and oak trees lined the grassy hills on either side of the dirt road. A warm breeze drifted by, shaking their leaves joyously. Songs from birds merrily chirped in the sky, enhancing the delightful enchantment. It was a glorious fall day. Jane sighed to herself. She pleasantly leaned against the leather bench. The open carriage turned onto a short gravel drive, pulled by two grey horses. They cantered over the tiny rocks to the front steps of a two-story, white stucco cottage. Eight large windows faced the drive, framed with dark blue shutters. Two stone pillars stood on either side of the entrance's blue double doors, with a large stone carved pediment resting on top. It was charming.

With Elaine being preoccupied with Captain Norton, Jenny and Jane found themselves enjoying each other's company immensely. Their friendship built over the past couple weeks to where they began to do everything together, such as shopping for their baskets.

The blue door of the cottage flew open. Jenny walked out with a broad smile, her light brown eyes sparkling in the sunlight. Every step she took, her pink muslin dress flowed effortlessly around her feet, and a small wicker basket swung carelessly in her hand.

"Jane! Don't you look lovely," she beamed, always full of compliments. Jane smiled. Her charismatic personality always brightened any circumstance.

"Jenny, I was just about to say the same about you. Pink is such a fetching color on you."

"Thank you, my friend."

Their driver, Samuel, assisted Jenny into the carriage.

"What a morning!" she sighed. "Our servant, Anne, had to stay home to tend to her ill father. The poor man's suffering from gout and hasn't been able to walk for days. So, in addition to washing the linens, I have to dust the whole downstairs and I'm not even halfway done! I don't know how she does it."

Stressful as it sounded, somehow Jenny's upbeat personality still managed to make it just a little hiccup in her busy, unconventional schedule. It's unique for a woman coming from a well to do orchard to have to perform such tasks. Jenny had explained that her parents grew up poor before their success with the orchard and learned the value of work. They carried out their lesson with their children, and expected them to follow suit, even though they had the means to hire servants.

Jane would never say this aloud but with all the help on their property, she found Jenny's parents a bit peculiar with how they raised their children. Then again, many people would say the same with her uncle, having allowed her to venture in the hospital with all the wounded men.

"Do you know how he's treating the condition?"

"I'm not certain but my assumption would be willow bark tea and rest. That's what the local doctor recommended for my pa a couple years ago."

"I see," Jane bit her lip, determining how to best correct the doctor's recommendation without being condescending.

"What is it?" Jenny asked, studying her with a smirk.

"Well for the sake of the gentleman and your chores, may I suggest a few things in addition?"

"Anything to help my chores." Jenny magnified her loath with a heavy groan. "As well as her pa, of course," she assured.

"Of course," Jane smiled, knowing Jenny did have good intentions for Anne.

"Does the island grow any ginger root?"

"No, but we get it imported from India."

"Splendid," she clapped with excitement. "What he'll need to do is boil finely chopped ginger for a few minutes. Soak a cloth in the ginger water. Once cooled, wrap the area of gout for twenty minutes, only once a day. It may irritate the skin so if he sees any redness and bumps then he's to stop."

Jenny leaned back on her bench and stared at her with awe. "Did your uncle teach you to do that too or did you figure it out on your own? Like you figured out how to stitch wounds through embroidery?" she teased with a knowing gleam in her eye. After hours of interrogation with thousands of questions regarding her life, Jenny knew almost everything there was to know about herself and her time in India.

"Neither," Jane laughed. "A native doctor taught me while I watched him treat my uncle."

Jenny's brow perked. "Your uncle? But wouldn't he know how to treat it himself?"

"He specializes in wounds and surgeries. When it comes to illnesses and diseases, he's not as educated, so he called on the locals to learn of their remedies."

She tilted her head to the side and studied Jane. "Fascinating."

"It was. Now to further help the inflammation from the gout, her father needs to drink lemon water mixed with a spice called turmeric. Have him ease if not stop the willow bark tea. The willow bark may make the condition worse."

Jenny shook her head and laughed. "You'll never cease to amaze me, Jane. Have you ever considered midwifery? With your knowledge you would be outstanding."

Jane fidgeted with the ribbon on her gown. She's thought about it . . . a lot. She compared all the good and the bad to determine if that's what she should do but she never fully decided.

With limits of what she can practice, midwifery appeared to be her only option for helping people. Some members of the ton may disapprove of such a career for a young woman like herself. Most midwives were older with years of knowledge and practice. Never having the opportunity of delivering a baby before, she would have to start as an apprentice. Could she balance such a task in England and attend social events or would it be frowned upon? There were many midwives who were married and varied in their stations. Couldn't she have the same luxury? Most importantly, would she enjoy it? She readjusted her straw hat on her dark curls. She had been trying to distract herself from the thoughts of midwifery, but they had been churning in her mind since the chancellor spoke about England and its luxuries.

"I've contemplated it," she responded. "But becoming a midwife would be complicated."

"How so?" Jenny challenged.

She hesitated but proceeded knowing Jenny wouldn't think ill of her. "I fear I'd live a life of solitude."

"For goodness sake, being a midwife would not cause you to live a life of solitude. Why our midwife here on the island has been happily married for many, many years with children and grandchildren."

Jane shook her head. "Did she decide to become a midwife before she was to wed?"

"I don't suppose she did but—" Jenny stopped, seeming to have better understanding. "You're afraid you won't be accepted."

Jane remained silent, processing the word "accepted." Is that what she truly wanted? Being an orphan living with her uncle, she always felt unique given the circumstances of spending most of her free time away from her studies, and at the hospital. Many of the folks accepted her in Bombay and never thought her odd. Though, she had rarely expressed her love for medicine.

"Oh Jane, believe me, there are gentlemen out there who would adore you with your knowledge and passion. You just have to weed out the foul ones from the *ton*."

Jane then smiled. "Yes, I appreciate you saying that. It's just been a thought. Nothing more. Midwifery may not even appease me. I've never attended a birth, nor have I had the strong desire to. I suppose I've been more fascinated with learning and absorbing every drop of knowledge I can when it comes to my uncle's profession."

"You'll never know until you try." Jenny watched her as though she were processing the information. She held her hat as the carriage rolled over a rock. "You know, I'm quite the opposite. I have often found myself bored in school. But if one were to teach painting or embroidery, my attention is captured. Which reminds me," she wiped away a strand of auburn hair off her shoulder, "I need to have you teach me some of your stitches. Your jasmine flowers are turning out beautifully."

Jane smiled with the compliment. "Thank you, I would love too."

"Perhaps, after the festival? I have too much to do from now till then."

"Of course." Jane stared out at a tall grassy field that lay outside of town and faced her friend. "Jenny, you're doing me such a service with helping me and my basket, let me assist you with your chores. I would love to return the favor."

Daunting as it sounded, she's never done the wash, but she wanted to try—at least for her friend and the experience.

"Jane, you're such a dear. If this were an ordinary day, I'd be quick to deny you but given the festival is less than two days away with much more to do, I would love your help."

"Splendid. Now what stores do we need to stop at?"

"Well, Brickstore Smokehouse for cheese and sausage. Jamestown General Store—for our auctioned baskets. Cushman Fabrics—ribbon to decorate the baskets. And then we need to go down to the harbor to buy tuna for your fish cakes. The other ingredients I have at the cottage."

It was going to be a busy day indeed.

"Jenny, why don't you go buy the ribbons while I go down to the harbor to buy tuna?" Jane offered after they stepped out of the carriage.

"Are you sure?"

"Of course! As you mentioned earlier, we are on a tight schedule. Here are two shillings. If it's more, then I'll pay the difference. We can meet at the General Store within the hour. How does that sound?"

"Wonderful." Jenny gave Jane's hand an encouraging squeeze then handed her the small basket for the fish. "You'll want to find Mister Paul Rutkin. He's who I buy my fish from. His prices are reasonable as well as top quality."

"I will, thank you. I'll meet you back here soon!" Jane hurried down a side street on her mission to find Mister Rutkin. She was excited and relieved that Jenny was so willing to let her use her grandmother's recipe for fish cakes. She was even being gracious to take the time to teach her how to make them. It was the custom on the island that regardless of the lady's rank, she would be putting together her own basket for the festival.

Towards the harbor, a ship's bell rang in the distance. With the buildings blocking her view, she grew anxious to see the docks. She hastened her steps while walking along a quiet narrow cobblestoned street positioned between the small shops and the steep slope of the valley wall. She smiled a greeting at an older woman carrying a basket of fish. Perhaps she had visited Mister Rutkin? Her pulse skipped a beat. If she had, by the look of her heavy basket, she began to doubt there would be any tuna left. With a sense of urgency, Jane walked as fast as her long legs could carry her. Being the quickest route to the harbor, away from the hustle and bustle of townsfolk and merchants on main, she was hoping to shorten her course. The narrow street drew closer to the large steep cliff, chilling the air from the magnificent cool gray surface. Tightening her grip on the basket, she rounded a corner of the stone wall when suddenly she collided with someone.

"Oomph!" Bony hands grabbed her arms to steady himself and her.

"Oh, pardon me!" Jane glanced up. Her eyes widened, taking in the man whose hands clenched her. Squinty, glossy eyes glared back at her. His thin pointed nose angled slightly to the side as if it had been broken—quite recently. Stringy, auburn hair draped across his forehead, appearing as though he hadn't bathed in days. Blood drained from Jane's face. Instantly she regretted putting herself in a vulnerable situation by taking the fastest course.

"Why, if it isn't the beautiful Miss Jane Sawyer," he slurred. Liquor poured off Lieutenant Howard's breath. She stepped back, causing his hold to tighten with more force. "Where are you off to in such a hurry?" His frigid fingers dug further into her skin.

She looked around, hoping to see others in shop windows. Her stomach dropped. There were only a few white, vacant shops to her left. Beyond the lieutenant she caught a glimpse of a rope rail lining the edge of the harbor. She was so close yet they were still too far from the piers. Her fingers started to tingle from his grip.

"I'm on my way to see my uncle," she lied, attempting to keep her voice steady. "He assured me he would meet here."

He stumbled, bringing her towards him as he looked around. "Lucky for me," he sneered, his upper lip curled. "He's not here."

An involuntary shiver ran through her spine as he scanned over her with a wicked gleam. In the distance, seagulls cawed, gliding high through the sky above them. If only she too had wings to escape this swine.

"I really need to be going." She clenched her teeth to keep from letting a whimper escape.

He ignored her remark, maintaining his grip. "I know all about you, Miss Jane Sawyer," he slurred, staring into her face with a vicious smile. "The fairest, yet untouchable woman in Bombay. 'Tis a shame you don't have your entourage of soldiers here to protect you. The prized doe suddenly becomes," he paused, to lick his lips, "unprotected." Her eyes widened. She went to scream for help, but a frail squeak escaped her self-constricted throat. She couldn't move, her limbs drained of any hope, frozen with fright. Her body shamefully failed her, giving up before she could muster a fight.

"I can see why the men watched over you. All trying to keep you to themselves." He tsked, scanning over her body again. "You are the most alluring woman I have ever encountered—and I've encountered many— many who've never turned me down." He bitterly spat while taking a step closer and bringing his thin lips to her ear. "You see, I've been told I'm a man of good judgement. By the way your body curves perfectly in your gown, I know you'd put Aphrodite of Knidos to shame." She sucked in a sharp breath, awakening her limbs. She wrenched her body to free herself from his talons.

He gave a menacing laugh. She gasped as he abruptly pulled her against him. Breathing heavily on her, her stomach soured from the taste of the sickly, stale brine oozing off his breath. She grimaced as his whiskers grossly tickled the side of her neck as he inhaled her scent.

"Why is it when you're told you can't have something, it becomes more desirable?" he purred in her ear, sending a terrifying shudder through her. He stared down at her lips with lust clouding his eyes. Her heart pounded in her dizzy head, screaming out an alarm, demanding for her to do something!

She shunned away from him, drawing any form of distance. His fingers dug deeper into her arms, forcing out a whimper from her trembling lips. The intense ache from his claws sent an excruciating pain into her shoulders. Her arms uncontrollably shook. The basket slid from her hold, dropping to the ground along with any hope of courage she had. She tried to not focus on the pain as her mind turned for a chance to escape. He sneered at her, drawing his fowl lips towards hers.

Quickly, Jane peered over his shoulder.

"Uncle!" she forced with all the enthusiasm her voice allowed.

The lieutenant loosened his hold, looking in the direction she indicated. Remembering what she had been taught by one of the soldiers at the hospital, she stomped on the man's foot with her heel and kneed him towards his gut.

He released his hands, grunting in pain. Jane broke free, sprinting across the street towards the vacant shops, choosing the most promising building with red curtains covering the bottom half of the windows. She raced through the door, grateful it opened and slammed it behind her. The windowpane on the wall rattled from the force. Her hands shook as she fervently felt around the door for a lock. Her heart sprinted, striking hard against her chest then skipped a beat with terror, when the door yielded no such latch.

She breathed heavily, peeking under the curtain of the window. Dressed in his disheveled uniform, his greasy hair tossed, he stood across the street staring at her with a devilish grin. Slowly, like a tiger inching towards its prey, he stalked towards the building. Her head spun from her shortening breaths. Every limb shook from her escape, but the danger was far from over. How was she going to get out? Maybe the store had a backdoor? She whirled around to scour the shop for her exit when a large figure stepped forward. The blood drained from her body, her heart faltered in her chest. A blood-curdling scream rang through her ears before blackness consumed her mind like the still of the night.

Chapter Twelve

"Miss Sawyer? Miss Sawyer?" A deep rumbling voice was drawing her back to consciousness.

"The poor dear," came a cry from an elderly woman. "Should we fetch a doctor?"

"Don't you worry yourself, Mrs. Kimble. She just had a dizzy spell. She'll wake up soon." The deep velvet voice sounded familiar. Where had she heard it before? The room grew bright while she attempted to open her eyes.

"Mrs. Kimble, would you mind fetching her a glass of water?" The gentleman gently spoke. She could get lost by his soothing, low hummed voice. Comfortably she nudged her head against her extremely firm pillow, curious to see where her dream would take her.

"Oh, I should have thought of that. Of course, dear, I'll be right back."

Footsteps pitter-pattered across the floor. *Just a moment.* She turned her head away from her pillow towards the fading steps. A door squeaked open and gently closed shut. *This isn't a dream!* Jane fluttered her eyes open. In front of her, ropes of drastic sizes hung on the wall. To her left, red curtains covered the bottom half of the windows. She continued her gaze down to the floor and onto herself. Her feet and legs were weak, resting on the floor, but her upper body comfortably cradled across someone's arm and lap. *This is no pillow.* She snapped her head up to see whose arms she awkwardly laid so intimately in. Appearing as handsome as ever, was the man who had been entertaining her thoughts since the day she came to the island. He gave her a half-dimpled smile, causing her heart to pound hard against her chest. Gazing at her, his crystal blue eyes brightened against his tan skin. She cringed shamefully to herself. *I even nuzzled into him!*

"Captain McCannon." Flustered, Jane bashfully looked away. She didn't realize how much she missed him the past two weeks until this awkward moment. *Wasn't he on duty for at least another week?*

"Miss Sawyer. You know, I never thought I'd see the day when you would swoon over me." He offered a teasing smile that made her want to laugh all the embarrassment away. His strong facial features softened as he watched her with ease.

"Is that what I did?" She began to push herself up off the ground and—him. Captain McCannon immediately assisted her to her feet. *How this felt familiar,* she self-consciously moaned to herself, bringing her shawl over her shoulders.

"I'm most certain it was." He grinned, his hands balancing her by her throbbing arms. She bit her lip to keep from grimacing. *Why were they so tender?*

"Well, I must confess, captain, I've never swooned in my life. This will have to be marked as my first."

His dimple deepened but his eyes grew cautious as he studied her. She enjoyed teasing him yet truthfully never in her life had she ever passed out—not even while watching a surgery or assisting with her uncle with a procedure at home. Never. Startled by being in Captain McCannon's arms—again—she forgot why she had blacked out in the first place.

"Here you are, my dear. Drink this slowly." An elderly woman with gray hair and white streaks pulled into a bun, came into the room carrying a glass of water. A head shorter than Jane, the woman had a sweet countenance as she looked over her with a gentle smile.

"Thank you . . ."

"Mrs. Kimble, dear," the woman's kind eyes squinted with her smile.

"Mrs. Kimble." Jane smiled at the woman and took what she meant to be a small sip but thirst took over as the warm water poured down her throat. Realizing how parched she was, she clasped the glass and swallowed every last drop. Surprised by her ill manners, she lowered the glass and slowly licked the remnants off her lips. Captain McCannon studied her, the muscles in his cheeks flexed. Mrs. Kimble gently removed the empty glass from Jane's hands.

"I'll only be just a moment while I return this dear."

Jane numbly nodded. Giving a loving pat on Captain McCannon's arm, the woman left the room.

Jane's legs shook, being on the verge of collapse. "I think I need to sit," she whispered. Captain McCannon swiftly took her elbow and guided her to a wicker chair that sat next to a table in the corner of the room. She observed the shop as they walked. There were two rows of shelves with various types of supplies and tools. At the far end of the room was a large merchant's desk.

"Where am I?" she asked, feeling dazed.

"This used to be the shipyard's supply shop, but a few years ago Mrs. Kimble's son took over when her husband passed. His shop is on the other side of the harbor. She stays open for the locals to sell odds and ends."

"I see." That would explain why there was hardly anyone around.

Helping her to her seat, the captain addressed her, "Now, Miss Sawyer," his voice held a gentle yet concerned tone. He pulled the adjacent chair close to her and sat, studying her like she was a fragile vase about to tip over. "May I ask what had happened before you ran into the shop?"

Jane trembled uncontrollably. Her eyes began to sting with tears. Quickly, she looked away and blinked, trying to keep them at bay.

"Is he still out there?" Her words trembled with a soft whisper as her face grew cold. Captain McCannon stood, nearly knocking his chair over from his abruptness and rushed to the window.

"I'm not seeing anyone." He spoke gently but his fierce expression was far from. His head shifted back and forth while he scanned the area. "Who am I looking for?" He stepped away from the window with determination in his eyes. Jane quickly wiped away a tear that had escaped.

"Lieutenant," She was about to choke out a sob. She swallowed it down to keep her composure. "Lieutenant Howard." Her voice felt weak and unrecognizable.

The captain's face lost expression but his eyes filled with fury. The muscles in his thick neck tightened.

"Did he hurt you?" he demanded, attempting to be calm but struggled to control the anger in his voice. Fear shook throughout her. Fortunately, she'd escaped before he could. Her hands began to tremble.

"No." Jane's voice cracked as she choked back another sob. She started to rub her arms in an effort to control her quivering. They felt so tender to the touch. Why do they ache so bad? She lowered her shawl and held out an arm to investigate. A gasp escaped her lips. Forming against her unusually blotchy skin, were small little bruises of the heinous man's fingerprints. *No, no, no, no! Get them off!* She wanted to cry, but she couldn't, not in front of him. Not in front of anyone. Biting her lip to keep the emotions from springing out, she rubbed her arm harder to rid of his markings. Extending the other arm, the exact same circular purple spots developed against her cream-colored skin. She choked out a sob, sucking in sharp breaths to bury what happened only moments before. Her eyes blurred. *No. Stop!* She didn't want any reminders of their encounter. Nothing to show he ever touched her. *Please!* She whimpered to herself, rubbing harder.

In one swift motion, Captain McCannon crouched down to her side, his expression alarmed. Vulnerable, she quickly covered her arms with her shawl, staring shamefully down at her trembling hands. Soft callused fingers gently brushed away a tear that rolled down her cheek. The motion felt so soothing to her troubled heart. His fingers clasped her chin. Gently he lifted it so she looked directly into his eyes. His light blue eyes that were usually bright, had clouded over and were now dark and stormy. She shuddered from their intensity.

"May I?" his hoarse voice was thick with compassion. He stared into her eyes, pleading to her in a solemn manner. Reluctantly, she lowered the shawl. Refusing to see the marks again, she stared at the wall while his gentle hands lifted her arm. Focusing on calming her breaths, she felt him lower her arm with care. Self-consciously, she pulled her shawl tightly back around her shoulders.

"Miss Sawyer," his voice rumbled, sounding deeper than before. Shame filled her as she continued to stare at the wall. *This was just a dream, no, not just a dream, a nightmare. Wake up, Jane.* She blinked hard, hoping she'd awake in the safety of her room. His deep voice broke her yearning desire. "This doesn't have to be now, but when you're ready. I need to know exactly what happened. I need to report this so he can be held accountable for his crime."

She already felt exposed to the captain, but the thought of telling him more—what would he think of her? Thankfully, nothing had happened, but it could have if she hadn't escaped. A shiver ran up her spine, shaking her to the center of her core. She had encountered her worst fear, and that venomous snake needed to be caught. *Take courage, Jane, this is going to be very difficult.* Nodding, she looked at him. To her relief, he didn't appear appalled with her having been nearly tainted. She closed her eyes with gratitude. Of course, from what she knew of his character, he would never be the kind to look down on any woman should any occurrence ever occur. She inhaled a breath for courage.

"I'll tell you now." Staring at her lilac dress, she began to twist a thin ribbon in her hands. "Or I fear I may never speak the words again." She breathed in deeply then slowly released her breath to help soothe her nerves. Captain McCannon scooted his wicker chair closer and angled it to her side.

"Since I've boarded the merchant ship in Bombay, he's always had his eyes on me. Giving subtle hints about offering comfort if I should need it. Though his offers heavily indicated more physical touch, than emotional." Her hand grasped her neck from the memory of his breath on her skin. "And his eyes, scanning over me as if I were a stallion to be bought."

She wiped away a tear and stared off to the opposite end of the room, too abashed to look at him. He quickly pulled out a handkerchief from his coat and offered it to her. Glancing at the white material, she gratefully accepted and dabbed her damp cheek.

"Thank you," she whispered, staring at her lap again. "On the first day, my uncle saw his forward behavior and demanded that he would be released of his duties and reassigned to a different ship. But the captain refused. Instead, he settled with having a guard stationed with me at all times." She paused when she noticed Mrs. Kimble walking into the room. The woman smiled warmly at her then went to her counter and took out a large leather-bound book and began to write in it. Relieved the woman had no interest in the conversation, she continued. "After the first day he continued to watch me from afar with his sneering smile. Blowing me appalling kisses when my uncle wasn't looking. I did my best to avoid him during the journey by staying in my quarters. Other than today, the closest encounter we ever came to was the night of the dinner party. Governor Keaton didn't know of the situation, otherwise he wouldn't have invited some of the officers of our ship to supper."

He would have been mortified to have done such a thing. Nervously, she peered over at Captain McCannon who leaned forward in his chair, staring out the window with a distant look in his eyes. His tightened fist loosened when he caught her studying him. Subconsciously she held her wounded arms.

"Can you tell me what happened today?" he spoke quietly, with a rough edge in his voice. The gentleness of his eyes stared into hers, bringing her calmness.

"I was walking to the harbor when we collided with each other." Unexpected tears pooled around her eyes. She dabbed at the escaping drops. "He grabbed my arms to steady us but then he wouldn't release them." Her hands continued to tremble uncontrollably. She stared at the handkerchief she clasped. "His words were obscene, he attempted to—" She choked out a sob into the square fabric. Taking a deep breath, she continued. "I tried to run . . ." Her body shuddered. "But he tightened his hold. He wouldn't let me go . . . he only got closer." Her voice grew faint as it cracked, breaking her words. "I felt weak. Helpless. Too enervated to scream." She twisted the handkerchief in her hand with frustration. "Had I not distracted him—I could only imagine what he—" Her voice rose into a high pitch as a sob formed in her throat. She wiped a tear, clearing her throat. "But he didn't." She confirmed aloud, trying to calm the quiver that rattled her body and thoughts. She needed to remind herself that nothing worse came from their encounter. Nothing. "I escaped and ran into this shop."

Solace threaded her veins as she began to feel strengthened by admitting what happened. Apprehensively she glanced over at Captain McCannon who remained silent. His face was still expressionless, his broad jaw tight. He released a staggered breath and loosened his fist.

"Thank you for opening up to me." His strong hands clasped hers, cradling them in a genuine manner. Warmth of comfort spread throughout her body. The shivering within her, began to soften. "I promise, I'll do all within my power to see that he'll face the consequences of his actions."

Relief washed over her as the last of her shuddering subsided. The thought of the lieutenant's actions from their voyage had been weighing on her for weeks. She felt her hands had been tied in the matter and wasn't looking forward to the rest of their journey to England. Not with the vicious man on her ship.

"Thank you, captain. I believe you will."

His eyes widened when their gazes fell upon each other. Everything began to fade around them. The gentleman who stared back had not only witnessed the most mortifying experiences in her life, but had stayed by her side genuinely giving her support. The chivalrous gentleman truly was unlike any other gentleman that she had ever met. Blinking, he broke their stare and released her hands. He drew back, rubbing his neck as though it were sore.

"Now, you mentioned earlier that you were heading to the harbor. May I accompany you?"

Jenny!

"What time is it?" Pushing aside all that had transpired, Jane anxiously began to smooth any detached strands of hair and repined her loosened hat. *Please don't let it be too late.*

He pulled out his pocket watch. "It's fifteen past eleven."

Blast! Poor Jenny, I'm late. Jane rose to her feet. He swiftly followed suit.

"Captain, I'm afraid it's too late for me to go. I promised Miss Jenny I'd meet her at the General Store." She dabbed her cheeks with his handkerchief for good measure. Not wanting to chance another encounter with the wretched lieutenant, she paused and faced the captain. Resting her hand on his arm, she looked to him. "Would you mind accompanying me there?"

Immediately his pressed expression melted into a soft smile. "It would be my pleasure."

She smiled up at him with ease. "Thank you."

Mrs. Kimble came into the room carrying a tray of biscuits and cookies. Jane hadn't noticed her leave from behind the counter. "I thought you two would like a little snack before you venture out."

"You're too kind, Mrs. Kimble, but we need to be going." Captain McCannon spoke on their behalf. The shopkeeper's smile fell with disappointment before he quickly added, "I'd love to take a few of these delicious cookies with me, if you don't mind?"

The genuine woman regained her smile and held the tray up towards him. "Help yourself. Miss Sawyer, I insist you take a few for yourself as well."

How could she say no to her kindness? "Thank you, Mrs. Kimble."

"James, dear, I'll be sure to have your part ready by the end of the day. Now, you two have a good rest of the day, you hear?"

Jane exchanged a smile with her. If she had a nana, this was how she pictured her. A sweet woman who brightened one's spirit with her cheerful demeanor.

He stepped forward and gave the woman a quick embrace and accompanied Jane out of the shop.

"Just a moment." Motioning for him to wait, she hurried across the cobblestone street and collected Jenny's basket. When she looked up, she was startled to see Captain McCannon walking towards her. She drew back, surprised by the dark, threatening stare he held towards the ground where her basket laid. As soon as he looked at her, his face softened.

"Please, allow me," he held out his hand for the basket.

"Thank you." Jane's hand shook as she handed it to him. She didn't realize how vulnerable she would feel being in the street where she had her encounter.

"She has such a loving countenance," she stated, attempting to distract the fear that surfaced. "Mrs. Kimble."

"That she has," he remarked. He offered his arm to which she gratefully accepted. "I used to play in her shop as a boy when my father had to get supplies. When he didn't need any more supplies, Thomas and I would sneak over for cookies. With her son off to school, she enjoyed having us around."

They strolled through an alley towards main street. His hand laid protectively over hers as it rested on his arm.

"I can only imagine how you two filled her void. From the few minutes of being in her present, I found her very endearing. I would have loved her company as a child."

"I'm certain she would have loved yours as well."

Why this made Jane blush, she did not know. She stared ahead, trying to appear composed.

"Captain, when did you and your crew get back from your assignment? I thought you wouldn't be back in time for the festival." The excitement of the festival magnified with hopes of his attendance.

"As luck would have it, the commissioner pulled me aside the morning we were to leave and asked that we'd be back in time for the festival. We're here for extra security purposes." He smiled warmly at her. "Fortunately, we're also allowed to participate in the activities."

"Extra security purposes? Are they expecting any attacks or do things get out of hand at the festival?"

Surely, the French wouldn't be foolish and attack the heavily guarded harbor.

"It's just a precaution. In all the years I've been a part of the festival, I've never seen it get out of hand . . . though, there was a time when a fight broke out."

Jane glanced his way. "Oh? Was it over a pie?" she jested. He gave a hearty laugh, making her smile.

"Actually," he drew his head closer to her as he spoke quietly for her ears only. She ignored the stammer it caused her heart. "It was over a basket."

"A basket?" Jane didn't want to pry, but there had to be an interesting story if it regarded a young lady's basket.

"It happened years ago when the baskets weren't anonymous. A couple lads were trying to outbid each other for a certain young lady. Things took a turn for the worse as they began to fight. Unfortunately for them, the only thing they won that day were a few bruises and a night in confinement. After that incident, the governor at the time changed the rule that until the bid was final, the baskets were to be anonymous."

Anonymous. Jane smiled, reflecting on earlier that morning with Elaine. There was nothing secretive with Captain Norton and her basket.

"Well, I can see how that avoids hostility."

"Indeed." He paused, appearing to ponder, before he spoke again. "On a rare occasion, there's a certain exception to this rule, especially when a gentleman is seeking out a certain young lady." A crooked smile formed across his face. "That is, he'll usually discover which one is hers before the bidding starts."

"Is that so?" Did he intend to inquire about her basket? Her heart quickened.

"It is. We have our ways." He confidently flashed her a heart-stopping smile that muddled her thoughts.

Doing her best to hide the disarray, she confidently uttered her finest retort that came to mind.

"Mm hmm?"

Mm hmm? Great heavens, Jane, all because of a smile. She bit her lip, mystified she couldn't think straight.

"Tell me, Miss Sawyer, what is it that you plan on winning the gentlemen over with, in your basket?"

"Ha." *Is this how he was going to play?* Wanting to give him a challenge, she glanced at him slyly. "Well, if you must know . . ."

"Indeed, I must." His attempt to sound serious failed as he couldn't contain his smile. "I'll be certain only the most charming of gentlemen will bid on your basket."

"And will you be among them, sir?"

"Of course! That is, assuming you find me charming." The gentleman's eyes danced with amusement. He offered her an endearing smile.

"That may be debatable," she giggled. His face scrunched in pain, pretending to be wounded from her words.

Giving a little sigh in defeat, she shrugged her shoulders. She enjoyed this lighthearted side of him.

"Very well. As long as you promise only the most honorable and the most charming of gentlemen will bid, then I shall tell you."

"I promise," his voice lowered with intensity.

Ignoring the warm glow that kindled through her, she began to whisper. "In my basket," He leaned his head closer to hers, as though eager to catch her every word. "I'll be adding cheese . . . a little bit of delicious fruit and . . . meat." She held a proud smile as he looked at her with a raised brow and an expectant stare. Pressing her lips, she refused to offer him any more clues.

He chuckled, shaking his head. "I'll be sure to keep my eye out for it." He gave her a wink which recaptured any thoughts she had.

"Jane!" Jenny rushed from the shade of the general store. Jane released her hold on the captain as her friend threw her arms around her. "I was so worried! I just saw Mister Rutkin a moment ago buying more salt for his fish. I asked if he met with you and he stated you never came. I had this horrible feeling and I was about to send for your uncle. I'm so glad you're here, where have you been?"

Jane took a startled step back from her friend's embrace. The time with Captain McCannon had passed so quickly that she hadn't noticed her surroundings.

"James! When did you get back?"

Jenny gave him a quick embrace. An uneasy feeling draped over Jane as she watched their exchange. *Were there feelings between them?* Jenny never spoke about Captain McCannon. At least not the way Elaine had gushed about him before Captain Norton entered the picture. She knew they were childhood friends but from what she had witnessed with a few of her friends, there's usually a deep regard for one or the other. The kindle inside blew out, leaving nothing but smoke, to hide her feelings. She hoped that wasn't the case between them, but she'd be happy for Jenny if it was. She was remarkable and they would make a fine match.

"Good to see you too," he chuckled. "We sailed in early this morning. How's the family?"

Perhaps they were related? They looked nothing alike. Her brown eyes to his blue eyes, and she was a lot shorter than him. Hadn't Elaine mentioned he was an only child? *Think Jane.*

"They're doing well. Pa could use your height with pruning some of our apple and mango trees."

"I have a few items to take care of now and as soon as I'm done, I'll head over."

"Forgive me for asking but are you two of relations?" How could she not have known? She should have paid closer attention to Elaine's ramblings.

Jenny laughed. "Heavens no. Though, he certainly treats me as though I were his younger sister. I don't think I've ever told you this, but Lieutenant Thomas Fletch is my cousin."

"I didn't know!" Jane was surprised, though she could see *their* resemblance. The strong chins, brown eyes, similar facial features.

"The three of us grew up together, which apparently entitled them to act as my older brothers. Unfortunately for me, no gentleman bothers to court me unless they want to face the wrath of Thomas and James."

"Someone needs to keep an eye out for you." He gave her a playful nudge.

"I'm going to end up a spinster if you two keep it up," Jenny groaned.

If anyone could relate to that feeling it was Jane. "You have my sympathy, Jenny."

"Thank you, Jane."

Captain McCannon gave an unapologetic smile at both of them.

"Jane, I hope you don't mind but I took the liberty of picking up the basket that you ordered. It's in the carriage."

"That was very kind, thank you. I'm sorry I didn't get the fish and I know we're short on time. How about I retrieve it tomorrow before I come to your home?"

"That's fine. Come, let's hurry. There's much to do."

"Just a moment." Captain McCannon softly took hold of Jane's hand before she was whisked away with Jenny. Startled by the warmth of his touch, she looked up to find the smile in his eyes clouded over. "I still need to track down Lieutenant Howard. Miss Sawyer, will you be at Jenny's home the rest of the afternoon?"

She had felt so safe with him that the only reminder of what happened earlier were her sore arms. She pulled her wrap tighter around her bruises.

"I will, until supper time."

"Lieutenant Howard?" Jenny looked at him perplexed. "If you're looking for him, I saw him walk towards the pub."

"Miss Sawyer, will you wait for me at Jenny's, until I can escort you home?" A shiver ran up her spine, as she gazed into his concerned eyes.

"Yes, of course," her voice grew weak again.

"I'll be with you shortly." He handed Jane her basket and offered the ladies a bow. Jane followed Jenny to the carriage while keeping an eye on the captain. She watched him storm towards the pub, collecting two soldiers who were patrolling nearby.

"That was strange. I've never seen him so perturbed." Jenny gave Jane a questioning look as they settled into the carriage.

"I've never felt so frightened." Jane spoke quietly to her friend.

"My goodness, Jane, what happened?" Jenny placed herself next to her. Swiftly she took hold of her shaking hands while they rode out of town.

"I bumped into Lieutenant Howard on the way to the harbor. We were alone and he attempted to," Jane swallowed, building the courage to admit it, "make advances on me."

"No," Jenny gasped, squeezing Jane's hands.

"I managed to escape into Mrs. Kimble's store before anything could happen," she assured quickly.

"Oh Jane, I'm so sorry. Are you alright?" Jenny's lips tightened. Her thin brows lowered with anguish.

Nodding, Jane dabbed her eyes with Captain McCannon's handkerchief.

"Fortunately, Captain McCannon was there for an order." She inhaled deeply, trying to calm the shuddering in her body. "To make matters worse, I didn't recognize it was him, so I fainted from fright." She shook her head at the memory. Oh, what he must have thought at that moment, especially when she thought he was her pillow! Her cheeks uncomfortably warmed. "When I awoke, I found myself in the captain's arms." Jane buried her face in her hands. "I've never fainted in my life, Jenny. Why did it happen in front of him, of all people?"

"I don't see why that's a problem," she chuckled. "I know plenty of ladies who would love to find themselves in his arms."

Jane rolled her eyes at her.

Grinning, Jenny wrapped her arm around her and gave her a loving squeeze. Jane inhaled sharply as she felt the stabbing ache in her arms.

"Jane!" she whispered in alarm. Gently she brushed her fingers down the vast black and blue stains painted against her milky white skin. "Did James see these?"

Jane choked back a cry that was crawling to escape and nodded. She hated them. Hated that she had to see his finger marks linger on her as a constant reminder of his disgusting behavior.

"That despicable man," Jenny's voice shook, "will be lucky to make it off the island alive. Mark my words, Jane. James will do all that he can to see the lieutenant gets what he deserves. When we get back to the house, I have just the salve to apply to this. You're in no condition to help me with my chores today. I insist you rest!"

Jane swallowed the sob. "I'll be fine, I promise."

"No, Jane," she spoke in a more nurturing tone. "Please, rest. I won't be long. My sisters will help me finish if they haven't already."

A nap did sound enticing after the whirlwind of emotions she experienced. Normally, she preferred to keep her mind busy with a project, but with the sun's draining rays, perhaps a little rest would be rejuvenating.

"Only if you promise to let me help after I'm rested."

"I promise." Softly smiling, she added, "First, before you do, we'll apply my miracle salve. It will help calm those marks."

Jane leaned into her friend's kind embrace. "That sounds wonderful."

Chapter Thirteen

James set his quill on his papers when a knock resounded from his cabin door. *Perfect timing.* He had just finished his letter to Admiral Kensington regarding all of Lieutenant Stephen Howard's infractions. Before he could stand to answer, Thomas barged in excitedly.

"It's all settled! That brute will be sent off the island first thing in the morning." He plopped himself down on a chair. "Captain Paul was more than gracious about having him aboard his merchant ship. Turns out," he leaned back and kicked his boots on the desk, "the captain fancies the tavernkeeper's daughter. So, he knows all about the lieutenant's behavior. This should make for an interesting voyage for Howard, wouldn't you say?"

James nodded, rubbing the soreness in his fist.

"I couldn't be more pleased. Now, I just need the governor to co-sign my papers for approval of the lieutenant's banishment and then I'll give them to Captain Paul to deliver to the admiral. The admiral will see to the scoundrel's fate from there."

"Are you worried the admiral will lighten the consequences because of Stephen's uncle, the Duke of Brandon?"

"I don't," James said confidently. "The admiral has a close relationship with the Prince of Wales. Once it's in the admiral's hands, I doubt the duke will even attempt to threaten any of us involved. If he's wise, he'd steer clear from any of it."

"I'm happy to hear that. He deserves every bit that's coming for him." Thomas paused then looked at James's swollen hand. "How's the fist?"

"Couldn't be better!" James grinned broadly. "Words can't express how pleased I am that that man charged me."

When James had walked into the pub, he'd approached Stephen and told him he was to be put in confinement. He left out Miss Sawyer's name intentionally to avoid any chance of her reputation being tarnished. The man grew angry and hastily charged James with a bottle in hand. With one solid punch, he knocked Stephen to the ground. No charges would be pressed as too many witnesses were there to testify it was self-defense.

"The man's a fool! You're twice his size," Thomas laughed.

"A fool indeed," he smirked in agreement. "Come, I need to stop by Jenny's on my way to the governor's plantation."

The two men departed the Ebony. They retrieved their horses from the town stables and rode to Jenny's cottage.

"How did it go?" Jenny approached their horses from the clothesline that hung freshly cleaned linen. She didn't bother with greetings, appearing too eager for the news.

"Please, tell me that barbarian is leaving the island."

James and Thomas jumped off their horses.

"He's leaving tomorrow morning with a battered jaw," Thomas replied, giving his cousin a quick embrace.

"I'm so relieved to hear. I'm sure Jane will be too." Jenny sighed as she ran her hands down the front of her apron.

James earnestly stepped forward. "Where is she?"

"In the house. I made her rest." She paused, shaking her head with disgust. "I've never seen a lady's arms so black and blue."

His jaw clenched with fury. They must've been worse than what he'd seen earlier. He'd done everything in his power to control his anger when Miss Sawyer had told him what had happened. Then when he saw the brute's fingerprints on her delicate arms, he knew she'd escaped from something far more menacing.

"Her arms?" Thomas fumed. "James, you assured me he didn't touch her."

Agitated, James rubbed his swollen hand in his palm. He hadn't mentioned the bruises to Thomas because it took every piece of dignity to keep himself from doing further damage to Stephen. Thomas would have only added gunpowder to his fire, and he feared he'd have nothing left to refrain himself.

"He gripped her arms. Nothing else," he retorted, rubbing the back of his tightened neck. He'd only meant to reassure, but his anger scoured his thoughts, reflecting in his tone. He inhaled deep breaths through his nose, letting them out slowly. He needed to think about something else before temptation took over and he rode back to confinement where the lieutenant was being held. Thomas took a look at James's expression with understanding.

"Say, Jenny, do you have any more of that salve? James's fist could use a little bit of it."

He gave James a reassuring pat on his back as they headed into the house towards the parlor. Jenny handed James the salve and he applied it to his throbbing hand. There came a tingling sensation as the salve calmed his pain. He flexed his hand open and shut. It wasn't broken but it would take a few days before it felt back to normal.

"Jenny, I believe you mentioned your pa needed help in the orchard." James removed his officer coat and draped it over the parlor chair. He rolled up his sleeves and gave a look of expectation to his friend. Hesitantly, Thomas stood from his chair, and letting out an exasperated groan, he followed suit.

From the kitchen door, Jenny hollered after them. "You should find him by the mango trees. I'll let you know when Jane's ready."

Drops of sweat ran down James's forehead while he focused on his work. To keep his mind distracted from Lieutenant Stephen, he kept his thoughts on their latest patrol. The only vessels they'd come across were of merchants. They flagged each of them down to see if there had been any sightings of the French battalion but were disappointed when there were none. A prickling sensation grew within his bones. He knew they were out there, somewhere, waiting for their next attack. He let out a grunt while he reached high to trim a branch.

Gradually, thoughts from earlier trickled through his mind. Gratitude filled him for being at Mrs. Kimble's shop at that precise moment. It certainly wasn't a coincidence. If only he crossed paths with Miss Sawyer before Stephen had. Perhaps, he should have encouraged Richard to pursue *her*. He didn't like the idea but at least she would have had his protection, as he doubted he'd ever want to part from her.

He hewed away with frustration on a thicker futile branch. Beads of sweat rolled down his back. He didn't expect to see Miss Sawyer there, as very few people visited that section of town. He gripped his shears with anger as her face flashed before his eyes. Her skin was ashen, her captivating eyes that watched him cautiously were wide with fright. Her hat had hung loosely to the side of her head. He forcefully snipped another branch. She was terrified. Even approaching to see if she needed help had caused her to faint. He grunted, cutting another branch. Heat scorched through his body. The despicable man made his blood boil. James climbed higher up the ladder, poking through low-hanging leaves and branches.

Luckily, he rushed to catch her before her head could hit the ground. He stalled on a branch as he reflected how peacefully she had stirred in his arms. Her dark, thick lashes fanned above her pale cheeks. Her full lips, softly parted. His stomach tightened. Somehow, she had become even more beautiful than when he last saw her.

He shook his head and watched the freshly cut branch fall to the ground. When she opened her eyes and had looked up at him, he thought time had stopped ticking. Her eyes were so bright as she had recognized him. Was she excited to see him? His stomach twisted into knots while he continued to snip away at the branches.

"James!"

Thomas hollered down his row. He motioned with his arms to come back to the house. Wasn't he just in the tree next to him? James finished the last branch before climbing down his ladder.

Then seeing her tears—he threw his sheers by the ladder. He had used all the dignity he had not to wrap her in his arms to console her until each of those drops ceased. He kicked at a mango that laid on the ground and watched it bounce over twigs and branches, landing in front of a lilac gown.

"Miss Sawyer," he stammered. *Stammered?* She stood poised and beautiful as ever. Her brown curls neatly pinned half up while the rest of her hair beautifully fell over her shoulder. The warmth from her green-blue eyes stirred a longing that he had never felt before. Realizing he was staring, he quickly regained his composure and gave a curt bow.

"Captain McCannon. Lieutenant Fletch told me I'd find you here."

Tightening her shawl around her shoulders, she took in his untidy appearance. James promptly ran his hand through his disheveled hair and swiftly unrolled the sleeves of his shirt.

"I just finished up. Are you ready to leave for the plantation?"

"I am." Miss Sawyer appeared flustered as she quickly gazed up at a mango tree. Running his hand through his hair once more, he buttoned his shirt sleeves in an attempt to appear more respectable.

"I, uh, wanted to return your handkerchief." She stared to her side then peeked through her lashes at him, to see if he was done. He must have appeared extremely disheveled by the way she kept turning her eyes away from him.

"I appreciate that." Smiling, he accepted the freshly pressed fabric. His fingers brushed hers. He stood still, surprised by the unfamiliar churn it caused. Her eyes widened and darted away from him staring towards the trees. The color in her cheeks deepened. Refraining from reaching out to touch the alluring hue, he tugged on his sleeves and walked forward.

"Did you know that there are over two hundred and eighty-three different types of mangoes in India?" he asked, looking at her as she eased to his side.

"What would you say if I admitted I did?" she challenged.

"Then I would be impressed," he admitted.

"I've learned a lot about mangoes from a few of the street merchants. A couple of them cultivated mangoes and told me of its origins. Did you know it's seen as a symbol of good luck and prosperity?" Her brow arched in an extremely engaging manner.

"What would you say if I admitted I did?"

"I may be only slightly impressed," she teased.

"Well then, by all means be impressed, Miss Sawyer." He grinned down at her. "Then perhaps," James continued. "You knew the 'king of fruit' in India is none other than the mango? And might I add, India is the top producer in the world for mangoes?"

"Now I'm very impressed, captain." She flashed him a radiant smile.

"I may have learned a thing or two while I was assigned there," he stated in a collected manner.

"Aside from playing practical jokes on Captain Norton and the admiral?" She held an innocent expression.

"May I remind you, Miss Sawyer, I was not part of that joke with the admiral. My hands are clean, as I was just an innocent bystander."

Miss Sawyer giggled. "That's right. I must have forgotten."

They stopped walking as they reached the back of the house.

He began to be immersed in the joy resonating from her smile. His gaze trailed down from her dark curls to her expressive eyes and lingered longer than intended. Her cheeks flushed, intensifying the brightness of their color. It was stunning. She was stunning. His hand raised towards her face. He longed to feel the warmth of her soft skin. She didn't move as she stared back with anticipation. *Could she feel the same way?* He began to feel desperate that she did. *Wait.* He clinched his hand and drew a staggered breath. *What was he doing?* Stepping back, he shook his head, needing to clear his thoughts.

This was far from appropriate. After her traumatic experience, the last thing she needed was for him to make his own advances. Shame pricked his heart as he tried to find the right words to say. His head spun and he began to mutter out words that he hoped sounded logical.

"I . . . I just need to . . . my coat then we go."

Confused disappointment crossed her face as he hurried around her towards the kitchen door. Jenny and Thomas sat snapping beans at the table as he rushed by.

"I guess that means we're leaving?" Thomas called after him.

James didn't respond. Once in the parlor, he felt the tightness in his chest ease as he drew a few deep breaths. He never recalled when his heart pounded so hard around a young woman. He gripped a side table to regain his emotions. *This can't be right.*

"Are you alright James?" Jenny strolled into the room holding his hat.

Hastily he stood, composing himself. "Fine. Fine. Just needed to clear my head." He straightened the front of his shirt and grabbed for his coat that hung on a chair. The side of Jenny's mouth tugged upward. She handed him his hat and brushed off the shoulders of his officer coat.

"Now I'm going to say this as your devoted friend, as I dislike seeing you torture yourself—and especially since I'm in need of your wonderful help with my tasks tomorrow."

James smirked. "Is that so?"

Jenny always had a way with bargaining to get what she wanted. What information did she have that would make it worth it for him to miss his own duties at home and do hers instead? His curiosity was piqued.

"Tuna," she casually replied.

Tuna?

"What?" He brought his hand to the back of his neck. Was she being cryptic now? This was a horrible bargain.

"That's what Jane was going to get today at the harbor. I figured you may want to assist her tomorrow by retrieving it."

Completely taken back, he studied her. Was she encouraging him to pursue Miss Sawyer? Jenny gave him a sly smirk with a knowing gleam in her eyes. Never would he have expected such a thing. She has never approved of any sailor courting a woman who passed through—especially if it were to come from Thomas or him. Did she suspect something good would come of it? She must have otherwise she would never have allowed it. Having the highest respect for her opinion, James suddenly felt he could breathe again. It was as though the burden he carried the past few weeks was lifted. How daft he was. He was just holding himself back from a rare opportunity. An opportunity that he was willing to give anything to take a chance on.

"Tuna, you say? She wouldn't happen to be making the Oakley family's fish cakes for her basket, would she?"

She gave him a slight shrug. "Perhaps," she responded, as she absentmindedly peered out the window.

He chuckled. "Jenny, you are something else. I owe you one."

"Owe her for what?" Thomas asked as he and Miss Sawyer stepped into the parlor.

"I agreed to help James mend his shirts." She didn't miss a beat and surprisingly sounded so casual. James smiled at her. She had definitely picked up a thing or two from Thomas and him.

"I believe tomorrow morning will suffice. I'll need to be in the kitchen, assisting with a certain dish for a picnic." She gave him a wink. He shook his head with a chuckle.

The horses' hooves clopped against the dirt road while James and Thomas rode silently behind the opened-roof carriage. They turned onto the stone drive lined with mango trees reminding James of his and Miss Sawyer's pleasantries earlier.

"What are you smiling about?" Thomas asked, eyeing him quizzically. James drew his smile into a more serious manner. He didn't realize he'd been smiling.

"It's nothing," he cleared his throat.

"Uh-huh." Thomas flashed him a mischievous smile. "You don't just smile about nothing. What's going through that thick head of yours?"

James shrugged.

"Uh huh," he mused.

Riding close behind Miss Sawyer, James quickened his horse to a trot, ignoring his friend's bothersome grin. He didn't want to chance her overhearing Thomas's taunting.

Outside the governor's home, James jumped down from his horse, and handed the reins to the stablemaster. With great haste, he made his way to the carriage to assist Miss Sawyer. She tightened her shawl around her shoulders before gracefully placing her delicate hand in his gloved one. She remained silent as he escorted her towards the doors. He patted her hand with soft reassurance as she was concentrating on the door handles.

"Everything will be alright,"

She swallowed and gave him a feeble smile. "Thank you, captain." Sincerity shone through her gaze. A perfect brown curl escaped over her cheek. He had a strong urge to tuck it behind her ear but refrained.

Clearing his throat, he managed to say, "You're welcome."

They entered the foyer as her uncle descended the stairs, his demeanor brightened when he saw her.

"Jane, my darling girl. I feel I haven't seen you in days. Captain McCannon. Oh, and Lieutenant Fletch. A pleasure to see you two back from your assignment."

James and Thomas gave a bow as Doctor Brown took the last step to the foyer floor.

"What impeccable timing. I was just about to head to the gardens. Would you care to join me?" The doctor grabbed his niece's arms to extend a kiss on her cheek. She flinched from his grasp, biting her lip in pain.

"Why Jane, are you alright?" He slowly released her arm and peered down to where his hands were.

"I'm fine uncle. I promise," she rushed, tightening her shawl. "I would love to join you in the gardens if you give me a moment to change."

"Why Jane, what's the matter? Come now, is it your arms? Let me see." She bit the corner of her quivering lip and looked to the floor.

"If you would excuse me, sir." James took a step towards the doctor. "I was wondering if I could have a moment of yours and Governor Keaton's time. It's a matter of great urgency."

"My time?" The doctor looked perplexed between the three of them. Understanding dawned on him as his expression tightened and his face turned a shade of red.

"What happened?" Fury appeared to be building behind the doctor's eyes. "Jane," he softly spoke. "Come with me to the parlor."

"It's alright, uncle. Captain McCannon and Lieutenant Fletch know everything, I'd rather discuss it with them present."

James felt a sense of pride as she expressed trust towards them with her uncle.

"Very well." His voice was calm and steady. "Let us go find Governor Keaton. He should be in his study."

Echoes of their footsteps rang down the marble hall with their steady pace. Governor Keaton sat at his desk when they all entered the room.

"Why, it's great to see you, Captain McCannon, Lieutenant Fletch." His pleasantry turned into concern as he took in everyone's solemn expression. "Was there another attack?"

He didn't want to answer. Not in front of her. She didn't deserve to relive this. But as much as he wanted to remain silent, he knew he needed to get the point across in order to succeed in banishing the man. He needed to be direct. "More like an attempted attack." James stood calm, despite how he felt like he was seething inside. "It wasn't by the French; this fellow is far more corrupt."

All eyes fell on Miss Sawyer who blanched in the doorway.

"Jane, oh my dear, dear, girl. Please have a seat." The governor frantically waved his hand, motioning her to sit in the chair in front of his desk. Straightening her shoulders, she did as she was told.

"I assure you, governor, I'm fine, but I would like to see the man charged." She proceeded to tell her story as the governor, her uncle, and Thomas watched her with clamped jaws and pinched brows. James couldn't listen as he felt the raw anger stir. He studied the books on the governor's shelf to keep himself distracted. *Interesting.* They were all lined up in alphabetical order except for one. *Othello* by William Shakespeare was placed with the R's. Someone must have not noticed the order. It couldn't have been Miss Sawyer, for she's far too observant to do such a thing. Perhaps it was Miss Keaton.

"Jane dear, were there any witnesses?" the governor pressed.

"I'm afraid there weren't." Her voice lowered with disappointment.

"I'm sorry, captain." Governor Keaton grew discouraged. He rubbed the shiny smooth surface at the top of his head. "This case isn't strong enough. It will turn into his word against hers."

James clenched his hand, his nails digging hard into his skin. There had to be a way. The man couldn't get away with what he did to her.

"I witnessed his first advancement," Doctor Brown spoke eagerly. He pushed his round spectacles higher above his nose.

"Yes, but we need more proof from this morning." The governor looked remorseful at Miss Sawyer and the doctor. James rubbed his jaw. His mind raced on how they could charge the brute. If only he saw him. Even if it were for a moment in the street after she fainted.

"Would physical markings be proof enough?" Miss Sawyer sat straighter in her chair. Her full lips pressed with determination.

James lifted his head out of his hand. Yes, of course it would. He ground his teeth. That blasted swine.

"I suppose they would. If someone saw you without them prior and then after between the time you were with him, then yes! Yes, it would." The governor's enthusiasm faltered as his face fell. "Oh, dear Jane. Did he leave markings on you?"

With a curt nod, she lowered her shawl. The bruises drastically loomed on her slender arms. Four purple and blue smudges overshadowed a red patch of skin on the back of her arms. A light blue patch stained the opposite sides.

Alarmed, James stood defensively with the rest of the men in the room, their faces stern and tight. He took in deep, slow, steady breaths to control the rage that sprung in him. Her arms were marked as though he branded her with each of his fingers. James opened and closed his sore fist to alleviate his frustration. Her uncle gently lifted her arm for a closer inspection.

"Jane. My dear sweet girl." He knelt down in front of her face, on the verge of tears. "Do you promise that he hasn't done anything more to you?"

She nodded, and softly placed her hand on his cheek. "I promise, Uncle. I was very fortunate." She shrank back into her chair, covering her bruises with the shawl.

Wanting to draw attention away from her, James took off his gloves and eagerly pulled papers from his pouch. "Governor Keaton, can I get your signature to these orders to Admiral Kensington requiring Lieutenant Howard to be shipped off the island tomorrow morning? I've listed all his misconduct including an attempted assault on an officer."

"I'm disgusted by this man's behavior. He assaulted an officer as well?" Governor Keaton roared, hitting his desk. Loose papers fell to the floor from the rattle.

"He attempted," James answered calmly, not going into further detail in front of Miss Sawyer.

"But he didn't stand a chance against the captain's right hook," Thomas proudly stated, smacking James on his shoulder.

Doctor Brown held out his hand, his eyes glistening with unshed tears. "I couldn't be more pleased, captain. I only wished I was given the same opportunity."

James held back a grimace as he shook the doctor's sturdy hand with his sore hand.

"Likewise," Thomas rang out.

Miss Sawyer gave James a relieved smile as she tightened her shawl closer to her body. How he wanted to take away her pain, but the smile she extended helped calm his fury. He returned the smile and noticed the doctor observing him more closely, catching their exchange.

Pleased, Governor Keaton added, "That should do, gentlemen," as he finished signing the papers.

James collected them from him and tucked them back into the pouch. "I'll see that these are taken care of immediately."

The men shook hands and Miss Sawyer rose to her feet.

"I'll see the gentlemen to the door," she spoke softly and gave her uncle a peck on his cheek as she passed.

"Come back when you're done, Jane."

"Yes, Uncle."

James held the door open, allowing Miss Sawyer to walk past him. She led them down the bright hallway towards the foyer. Once there, she paused to face Thomas and him.

"You two gentlemen have miraculously appeared at the most vulnerable, and may I add, less graceful times of my life." She laughed lightheartedly. "I feel I'm forever indebted to you two."

James fought the urge to wrap her in his arms. Her light laughter and cheerful demeanor brightened the troublesome memories.

"To be honest, Miss Sawyer," Thomas patted James across the shoulder, "I just aided Captain James. He's the one you should be indebted to." He gave her a wink.

"Since you mentioned it, I know just the thing to settle the debt." James grinned with his brilliant idea.

"You do?" She eyed him suspiciously, causing him to broaden his smile more. "And what is that, captain?"

"Your debt will be repaid, if you tell me what will be in your basket at the festival."

Thomas's mouth fell as he briefly stared at him with disbelief. It didn't take long before his lips stretched into a smug smile. He couldn't blame his friend. Had he been told weeks, months, or even a year ago that he'd ever utter such a request, his answer would have been no. In all his life, James had never been so forward with a woman nor had he ever wanted to be.

Miss Sawyer relaxed her stance and stared at the ceiling, pretending to ponder.

"If I recall, captain, I believe I've already told you."

He smiled. "I seem to lack the memory. Pray tell what kind of fruit and cheese do you intend to put in?"

With adoration, she bit her bottom lip trying to hide her smile. He already knew she was making fish cakes. All he needed was a few more pieces to this code and he would be able to decipher it, earning him a picnic with the lovely woman.

Her face lit up when she spoke. "I've yet to decide between the Gloucester and Colwick cheese." Taunting him she added, "The fruit will definitely be mangoes. I may end up with a total stranger so it's only appropriate to add a little luck."

James chuckled at her remark. "That's very wise, Miss Sawyer. Well, we'd best be off."

Having watched their exchange, Thomas offered her a bow.

"Miss Sawyer, it has been a pleasure."

James took a step towards the lady. His heart leaped as he lifted her delicate hand towards his face. He bent down and kissed it. Her eyes were wide as she stared intently at him. He stood, clearing his throat.

"Miss Sawyer." The hoarseness in his voice exposed the effect she had on him. Quickly, he left the home with Thomas at his heels.

Let the interrogation begin.

James shifted uncomfortably in his saddle as his friend scrutinized him while displaying a foolish grin. As they silently rode back to the fort, Thomas continued to stare annoyingly back and forth between James and the road.

James knew better than to yield to his senseless tactic. He focused on the road and to a long grassy field. He followed the grass towards an orchard of trees in the distance. Mango trees. Promptly he stared ahead. The silence began to gnaw at him as he felt his facade begin to crumble. Sensing victory, Thomas began to whistle an obnoxious tune. The high-pitched song caused James's upper lip to twitch with exasperation. He shifted again in his saddle. One more mile to the fort. If he could endure months of Miss Keaton's ramblings, surely, he could put up with his friend's absurdity. Thomas changed his tune to a song they used to sing as children. They strategically sang it to annoy their classmates as the song stayed in their head for hours, sometimes even days. James began to hum a tune of his own to fade out Thomas's loathsome song. By the time they reached the fort, both men were laughing and belting out their own songs, trying to one up each other.

Chapter Fourteen

James hurried off the hazy dock heading towards Mister Rutkin's stand. The cool mist greeted many of the fishermen who came back from their fishing trip. To be certain he intercepted Miss Sawyer before she made her way to the harbor, he had slept on the Ebony that night.

"Mornin', Cap'n James! How goes ye?" The cheerful Paul Rutkin called out. The seasoned fisherman's dark weathered skin wrinkled around his face when he offered James his greeting. The gentleman's grey beard held traces of his morning toast.

"Mister Rutkin! I'm doing fine."

"Any news on tose Frenchies?"

"Nothing yet. I hope we catch them before their next attack."

Mister Rutkin nodded, rubbing his beard thoughtfully. Little specs of crumbs fell onto his sweater.

"T'aire like 'em tiger sharks. T'ay stalk ta waters and only make their appearance when t'ay strike. I hope ye find 'em before t'ay do ye."

"As do I. As do I." James nodded in agreement. "Say, do you happen to have any tuna available?"

Finishing her last bite of porridge, Jane looked up at her uncle who was still eating. As everyone else chose to sleep in, Jane and her uncle were the only people in the dining area. She wiped her mouth with her napkin before placing it on top of her bowl.

"Uncle, may I be excused?"

He set his spoon down and wiped the corners of his mouth. "Are you heading to the harbor?"

"I am. I'm hoping to get there early so I don't miss out on Mister Rutkin's tuna. I've heard he sells out before noon and with the festival tomorrow, I can only imagine what he'll have left by the time I get there." Anxious for his answer, she rubbed the ribbon on the bottom of her bodice.

"Very well," he placed his napkin next to his bowl. "I'll join you."

"But you haven't finished your porridge. I'd hate to take you away from your breakfast."

"No, it's fine," he held his hand up decisively as though it was final.

Not wanting her uncle to go hungry, she leaned back in her chair.

"I'll wait. Please, go ahead and finish."

Ever since he heard about Lieutenant Howard, he'd been extra attentive. He hadn't left her side all evening. When she left supper, he followed her to the library. They played a game of checkers instead of his usual nightly read. When she told him of her schedule the following day, he insisted he accompany her. That included riding in the carriage with her to see her off at Jenny's home later that afternoon. She dreaded to see what the festival would bring the next day. What if he was the only one to bid on her basket?! Thank heavens it's anonymous. She'd have to be cautious to take extra measures to hide it from him.

"Excuse me, Miss Sawyer." Mister Gibbs, the butler entered the dining room. "Captain James McCannon is here to see you."

"Thank you, Gibbs," her uncle announced, wiping his mouth. "Let him know I'll meet with him first, in the parlor."

No! What's he going to say? She stood to her feet and hurried to his side. She's never had a gentleman call on her before, at least none that successfully entered their home.

"Uncle, why don't you finish your porridge? I'm certain I'll be just a moment."

A smile stretched across his face in a loving manner while he patted her hand, his subtle way of saying he'd take care of it.

"I'll only be a few minutes. Why don't you head to your room and gather your shawl and parasol? We should be done by then."

Considering her uncle's suggestion, she left feeling heavyhearted. To avoid any hope of seeing the captain, she took the back stairs.

She wasn't used to her uncle being the one to speak with any gentleman who attempted to call on her. Not that they ever did. He was too busy at the hospital to converse with any of them. It was usually Major Humphrey,

Captain Withifer, or Captain Blythe, her uncle's previous patients. They were the ones who pulled aside any interested gentleman for a "discussion."

With her parasol in hand and feeling disheartened, Jane closed her bedroom door. She supposed now it was her uncle's turn to do the task that others had done before.

Captain McCannon wasn't like the other militiamen or gentlemen she'd met in Bombay. She knew that had the major and the captains become acquainted with him, they would see what she saw—a valiant, honorable, kind, thoughtful, and an extremely becoming gentleman, which increased the more she became further acquainted with him. They certainly would approve of him. Which means her uncle certainly would too, right?

Toting her parasol in hand, she took her time descending the stairs leading towards the foyer. It had been an unexpected surprise, indeed, to have the captain call on her this early in the morning. Was her uncle going to scare him away? She groaned to herself. Rolling her slump shoulders back, she took another step. If it was anything like how it had been in Bombay, then this might be their last encounter together, that is, if he was still downstairs.

She sighed, rubbing at her sore arms.

"Jane," her uncle called up to her from the front entryway. "Don't dawdle, dear, the captain is waiting."

With her heart leaping into her throat, her gaze jumped towards the bottom of the stairs, capturing the surprising sight before her. His hands tucked behind his back, Captain McCannon stood next to her uncle. A crooked smile spread across his face, favoring his right dimple. Warmth spread through her cheeks while his striking blue eyes illuminated, taking her in. Her uncle gave the captain a pat on his arm before he turned to her.

"Jane, the captain has offered to take you into town for me." He gave her a kiss on her cheek. "Now, I'd better go finish my breakfast."

Jane looked incredulously at her uncle. As he passed her, he whispered loud enough for the captain to hear, "Close your mouth, dear."

She quickly snapped it shut as he gave her a wink. Baffled, she stared back at the captain who broadened his smile.

She hurried towards him and spoke in a hushed tone, "What did you say to him?"

Bowing, the corner of his mouth rose in a humorous manner. "Well, a pleasant morning to you too, Miss Sawyer."

"I'm so sorry James— *Captain*!" Heat rushed through her cheeks again. "Captain McCannon, where are my manners."

"James is fine." His eyes danced with amusement at her unnerved state. She scoffed as she walked around him towards the—*where am I going?* She paused, trying to gather her thoughts. *The stables!* Yes, she was going to ride to town. She proceeded to head towards the door.

"Miss Sawyer," Captain McCannon rang out. "I hope you don't mind, but since you weren't able to get your fish yesterday, I took the liberty of bringing it to you." Casually, he brought out a brown paper package from behind his back. "May I present to you, your tuna."

"My tuna?" Her brows rose with surprise. "Why, how did you know?"

"I have my ways." He held a serious expression while his eyes depicted amusement.

"Jenny," she breathed. It wasn't a question, since she knew her friend's relationship with the captain. At least he didn't know how she was preparing it. Or did he?

"A gentleman never discloses his informer." He held the package out for her to take.

"Thank you, captain." She stepped forward to retrieve his offering. Her fingers brushed his, sending instant flutters through her stomach. No, not the cheeks! She exhaled slowly, trying to calm the warmth in her face.

"How much do I owe you?" she asked coolly, turning her back towards him. She took a few steps away. Distance felt like the best idea at the moment.

"Please," his voice lowered. He adjusted his cravat while clearing his throat. "It's a gift. I insist. Besides," his serious tone shifted to one of a tease, "Tuna is my favorite fish. I look forward to eating it tomorrow."

"Mm-hmm." Facing him, she raised her brow. "That is if you can guess which one's mine."

"Oh, but Miss Sawyer, I have my ways. I'll find out."

"We shall see." She tried her best to keep a straight face as his smile was contagious. "Thank you for the gift. I shall deliver it to the kitchen. I'll only be a moment."

Stepping towards her, he rushed, "I'm afraid I must be going."

"Oh." She couldn't hide the disappointment that she felt. Quickly, she lightened her mood, not wanting him to sense it. "Well, until tomorrow then."

"Tomorrow." Taking a step forward, he gently took her free hand and lifted it towards the warmth of his breath. She held impossibly still as she desired to feel his firm lips on her hand again. He slowly leaned down, then swiftly gave her a peck. He didn't linger like yesterday, but she could still feel the excitement spread from her hand throughout her body. Softly he spoke while gazing into her eyes. "Good day, Miss Sawyer."

"Good day, Ja—Captain."

He flashed her an encouraging smile then left.

"Jenny?" Jane called from over her shoulder. In front of her, a fish cake was sizzling and browning in the hot frying pan on the hearth's warm ashes. "Does this appear to be done?"

"It's perfect." Jenny smiled over Jane's shoulder. "Now let us dive in and take a bite. Shall we?" She held up two forks excitedly in her hands.

Holding the pan with a towel, Jane slid the cake onto a plate.

"It looks and smells delicious, Jane."

Jane smiled while wiping her hands on the towel.

"I couldn't have done any of this without your assistance."

"Do you feel confident to make these on your own tomorrow?" Jenny took a bite.

"As long as I have my notes and instructions, I should be fine." Jane replied before slipping a piece of fish cake into her mouth. "Mmm," she covered her lips with surprise, "this is absolutely delicious."

Jenny beamed and took another bite. "If I do say so myself, I think you did a wonderful job."

"Mmm, thank you," she laughed with delight. It certainly was delicious. Never had she made something so simple, yet scrumptious.

Jane jumped as the kitchen door swung open, hitting against the wall with a loud thud. Lieutenant Fletch rushed in the room, flushed with drops of sweat rolling down his temples. "Jenny, we need a bucket of clean water and rags, Poppy's in labor!"

Jane's lips parted. "Labor?" She quickly pushed from her chair. "I should fetch the doctor."

Jenny laughed and stood. "No, Jane," she calmly exclaimed. "It's our goat, Poppy. Thomas gets a little overzealous whenever an animal is about to deliver. He has yet to get over where babies come from."

She smirked when he gave her a pointed look. "Water and rags," he repeated. "I've been told she's been at this for a while." He whirled around and closed the door.

"Well Jane, shall we go?"

Jane clamped her mouth and forced herself to nod. A birth. She's never witnessed such a miraculous event.

"Jane," Jenny called from the stone well behind the house. Jane closed the door to the kitchen and approached Jenny and Thomas who both held an empty bucket in each hand.

"Would you mind taking these rags to the barn for me? Thomas is going to help me bring fresh water for Poppy's trough, and such."

A short pile of linens lay neatly in a basket at Jenny's feet.

"Of course." She whisked the basket away, anxiously strolling past a few workers carrying sheers towards the orchard. Large wispy trees trailed the path to the large whitewashed barn. Eagerly she entered the dimly sunlit building. Her nose twitched by the greeting of hay mixed with leather and manure.

A goat bleated in the last stall.

"Here we go," murmured a deep voice.

Jane tiptoed to the stall's door, not wanting to disturb the stablemaster. The pen's window opened wide to allow a fresh breeze and sunlight in. A brown spotted goat lay on a fresh hay floor, alone, in the middle of the enclosure. She panted fervently, appearing exhausted. *Where was the stablemaster?*

Abruptly, Poppy's stomach dropped and lifted in one area as her baby moved inside her. Jane gaped, fascinated by the rolling motion.

"Alright Poppy, here comes another one," the voice whispered gently.

Startled, Jane took a step back. *What is he doing here? Where's the stable hand?* The doe let out another bleat, swishing her tail as every muscle on her hips and stomach tightened.

"That's it," Captain McCannon coaxed, stepping out of hiding from the corner of the stable. He strode through the hay in black knee-high boots, his civilian jacket off, and his white sleeves rolled up past his elbows exposing his well-toned arms. She stilled, astounded to see him so strikingly disheveled. His head darted up with the same surprise when he noticed her standing in front of the stall. Dread spread through her with this uncomfortable encounter. She stood tongue-tied, uncertain of what to say.

"Miss Sawyer." He offered her a small nod, his gaze bright. "Please come in." He trod through the hay and lifted the latch. Opening the gate, he removed the basket of linens from her hands. "Have you ever attended a birth?"

She swallowed and shook her head, too surprised to say a word. Poppy grunted and began to get up, only to lay back down.

"She's been pushing for almost forty minutes," he whispered, standing close to her as they watched.

"How do you know it's been that long?" she whispered back, peering at him from the corner of her eye. A strand of his brown wavy hair laid across his forehead. She twisted a ribbon around her fingers, unnerved that they stood alone in the stall together. *Where was Jenny and Lieutenant Fletch? They should be here by now.* Flustered, she dared not turn his way for fear she'd expose how truly rattled he made her feel.

"I'm an expert with time," he gave her a playful smile, "though truth be known, I checked my pocket watch before I saw you." He pointed to his watch dangling from the pocket of his jacket, which hung on a peg in the corner of the stall.

She gently clasped her hands in front of her. "I see."

"Here we go." He knelt down by Poppy's side. His burly stature next to the small goat seemed so out of place in the stall. Jane covered her mouth with surprise when he began to examine the goat. "I apologize if this seems, undignified," he looked repentant at her. "But it's been too long since Poppy's been in labor. I need to check to see if the baby's hooves are together and if it's head is in its proper place."

She nodded, and with curiosity, knelt down by his side. She began to focus on steadying her breaths when they became shallow and short from being so close to him.

"As I suspected, the head was tilted back," he continued in a hushed tone. He pulled away and leaned back on his heels, his shoulder gently brushing hers in the process.

"Tilted back?" she swallowed, her heart pounding fervently against her chest.

"It was maneuvered back towards its hind legs, but not anymore." He smiled and wiped his hands on a rag. "You see, the kid is supposed to come through the passageway like it's taking a dive, with its head forward."

She chuckled when he lifted his arms toward his head as though he were going to dive into water.

"If only it were that simple, captain." Her eyes widened, mortified by her thoughtless remark.

He laughed, shaking his head. "If only." Color rose to his tan cheeks.

The goat bleated and heaved, interrupting the uncomfortable silence. A white sac covered two legs and the head of the baby. Poppy panted, completely exhausted with the baby halfway out.

Captain McCannon leaned forward and tore the sac the baby was enclosed in.

"This will help ease her labor," he said softly.

Panic prickled up Jane's back as she saw the kid motionless.

"It doesn't appear to be breathing."

He scrunched his brows. "Miss Sawyer, could you hand me a rag please."

Immediately she retrieved the cloth. He gently wiped the baby goat's face and swiped through its mouth. Poppy pushed again and the precious tiny goat fell into his hands.

Jane looked to him as he began rubbing the little goat. "Is it breathing?" He shook his head, attempting for it to gain its breath.

"Miss Sawyer," he calmly spoke. "Can you listen to Poppy's stomach for another heartbeat?"

Jane crawled through the hay to Poppy's side, while he focused on the kid. Her pulse raced through her veins as she pressed her ear to the goat's warm, furry stomach. Poppy fervently panted making the task extremely difficult.

She sat back defeated. "She's breathing too hard. I can't keep my ear on her." Jane pressed her hand to Poppy's belly uncertain to what she should be feeling. She waited a moment. Right when she thought it was all in vain, Poppy's belly rolled like a wave.

Jane squealed with delight from the movement under her hand. Never had she felt such exhilarating motion like that. She grinned at Captain McCannon who kneeled at Poppy's head with the baby goat, breathing rapid in his hands.

He smiled at her, the strange mix of admiration, desire, and tenderness she saw in his eyes locking her gaze to his. She felt seen in a way she never had before.

Abruptly, the goat's hips and stomach tightened. Jane broke from James's stare and scooted back to give Poppy room, enthralled watching the contraction expose half of another baby in a white sac.

"Jane," he spoke softly. He held the other baby close to Poppy's mouth, encouraging her to clean it as it shivered. "If you see a white film, I need you to tear it for me."

She nodded. Eager to help, she did as he asked and exposed the baby goat. Seeing that it wasn't breathing she crawled to the basket nearby and grabbed a rag to repeat the process she had watched him perform. She wiped its face, and swiped through its mouth, but still no breath.

Poor Poppy panted with exhaustion and let out a low moan.

"Alright, now, Jane." A shiver ran up her arms when she just realized he called her by her given name. "I need you to wrap your rag around its legs, when you see a contraction, gently pull the kid down, one leg at a time. Poppy's too worn out to do this on her own."

She took in a breath and nodded, feeling privileged to carry out such a great responsibility. She wrapped the cloth around the baby's slippery legs and looked at James. He offered her an encouraging nod. Poppy's hips and stomach tightened with a contraction. Holding her breath, she gently tugged on the baby's legs one at a time. In one swooshing motion the baby was freed and bleated, taking its first breath.

She marveled at the precious life before her. The kid feebly crawled towards its mother like it instinctively knew who she was. Poppy responded, looking behind her. She mumbled a bleat before laying her head down, exhausted. Sensing the goat was desperate to see her child, Jane helped the kid get to its mother's face, next to its sibling. Poppy licked her kid's head for a moment then rested again. Jane's vision blurred as her eyes welled with tears from the enriching experience. Even the love Poppy showed for her kids was natural as they shared a beautiful bond with each other.

James scooted around Jane, feeling Poppy's belly and pressed his ear to her stomach for a moment. Her heart sped as she watched with admiration.

"It's just these two," he whispered. She darted her eyes from him to Poppy when he caught her staring.

"Will she be alright?" she asked anxiously.

He gave her a gentle smile. "Yes, she's just exhausted. Thomas should be by any moment with her molasses water, it will help build her spirits." He studied her then held out the rag in his hands.

"Would you like to wipe off the kid?" His voice was raspy. "She's too tired to clean him."

Excitedly she grabbed the cloth and gently dried the sweet little goat.

"How do you know so much about deliveries?"

The kid nudged towards his mother, causing Poppy to lick him. Jane leaned back on her heels as Poppy eagerly took over.

James smiled, wiping his hands on a new rag. "I grew up helping out with this orchard. Whenever there was an animal to be born, I attended, while Thomas floundered his way out of it." He chuckled and shook his head.

"Where's the other help? Isn't there a stablemaster to assist?" Jane accepted his hand as he assisted her to her feet.

"That would be Mister Perry." He smiled easily at her. "He's at the pasture with the horses. Poppy tends to get skittish if there's too many people around so he left me in charge to be certain the delivery went smoothly. I'm rather grateful for the opportunity. I'd rather be here than shoveling manu—" he hesitated with the word and stopped himself from finishing. His face pinched. Jane held back a laugh. Did he think that was indecent to mention it in front of her?

"I would have to agree with you, captain." She smiled at him as they approached a water bucket and bar of soap in the corner. "I would rather attend a birth than shovel horse droppings."

He smiled broadly at her, warming her heart and unfortunately her cheeks. She bent down quickly, hoping he wouldn't see the color rise in her face. She scrubbed her hands then handed him the bar.

She marveled, reflecting on the enriching experience. Poppy sat up more alert, licking each of her kids.

"I can't believe how gratifying that was," she wiped her hands dry, watching the baby goats, "to deliver precious little babies." She shook her head and took a deep breath in. "There's such passion behind it, I can't find the right word to describe it." She smiled blissfully and turned to Captain James. "It was beautiful."

Her smile faltered. His rag stilled in his wet hands, where water dripped off them into the bucket. He gazed at her with such intensity she forgot how to breath. The muscles in his cheeks flexed as his jaw tightened. He leaned towards her, ever so slightly.

Boots squished with heavy steps towards their stall. He blinked, giving her a slight smile and began to study his hands as he quickly finished drying them.

Jane clasped her lips, realizing she had leaned towards him as well. Her heart soared, blurring her thoughts. Swiftly as she could, she departed the stall, hoping not only to clear her head but to catch her breath. She stopped, startled from the sight before her.

Thomas fumed, as he held two buckets of water. His hair was disheveled and his clothes muddy from the top of his shirt down to his pants. Jenny came from behind with a look of annoyance.

"What happened?!" James joined Jane's side. His mouth dropped then quickly clenched closed as to hold in laughter.

"Jenny," Lieutenant Fletch exclaimed in exasperation. Placing his buckets down, pieces of mud fell onto the barn floor as he shook out the front of his soiled shirt. "She carelessly dropped her buckets of water on the dirt, *not* the grass, the dirt. When I went to assist her, she had the audacity to kick a bucket at my feet."

Jenny set her buckets down and placed her hands over her hips.

"I didn't kick the bucket! I tripped into the bucket," she scorned. "My apologies, Thomas, but I didn't expect you to," a giggle erupted from her lips but quickly she refrained, "fall on your face."

"Is that so?" he challenged.

Jenny pressed her lips tighter. Her cheeks raised, squinting her eyes while she held in another laugh. Jane began to giggle from their exchange, but quickly cleared her throat when Lieutenant Thomas glanced at her.

"How dreadful." She suppressed her smile and shook her head. The captain chuckled next to her.

Lieutenant Fletch threw his hands in the air. "So excuse our delay, but Jenny somehow found a way to empty our buckets which I had to refill."

Jane caught Jenny giving James an unforgiving shrug before she rolled her amused eyes at the lieutenant.

"Well, now that that's over with, did Poppy deliver?" She smiled at Jane.

"Oh, it was wonderful! She delivered two boys," she gushed.

"Splendid!" Giving Lieutenant Fletch a side glance, Jenny clasped Jane's hand. "Shall we?"

"Yes, but don't you want to see them? They're so precious." Jane smiled thinking about their sweet, little bodies.

Jenny waved her hand in the air. "I've seen plenty of baby animals to last me a lifetime. I'll see them later. Come, Jane, there's much to do with our baskets still."

Feeling the urgency to end any talk of baskets in front of Captain McCannon, she quickly nodded. "Of course. This has been one of the most memorable moments I have had the pleasure to witness. Captain McCannon," she faced him, not daring to look into his eyes. "Thank you, for letting me be a part of it."

"My pleasure," he gave her a smile that deepened his ridiculous dimple. She sucked in her breath and whirled back to the lieutenant.

"Lieutenant Fletch." He gave her his boyish grin and, with a dip of a curtsy, Jane walked away feeling slightly unnerved.

Jenny hurried to her side cheerfully. "Shall we finish with our baskets?"

"Let's," Jane laughed at her friend's demeanor. "After I clean myself up."

It had been a glorious afternoon indeed. Curiously, it gave her lots to ponder. Many thanks to Jenny, whom she suspected had played a big part.

Chapter Fifteen

"Millie, can you help me find a dress that will cover my arms?" Jane frantically searched through her wardrobe, attempting to find the perfect dress to wear for the festival. The yellow one she had picked out days before barely covered her bruises. She had been so wrapped up in preparing her basket that she'd forgotten all about her attire. Millie stood beside her, contemplating as they dug through the different dress fabrics.

"Oh, I have it," Millie exclaimed excitedly. She pulled out a white cotton dress with tiny pink floral prints scattered broadly around the fabric. Jane had nearly forgotten about the gown, as she had bought it right before they left Bombay. While standing in front of the mirror, she held it against her body. Millie held the sleeve against Jane's arm.

"Why, it covers the bruises beautifully, Miss Jane!"

Jane ran her fingers across the lace trim of the square neck. The pearl necklace her uncle gave her for her sixteenth birthday would go splendidly with the dress. He loved seeing her wear the necklace.

"It's perfect! Thank you, Millie."

Millie beamed from the compliment. With Millie's help, she was dressed and ready for the festival. During the morning tasks, she kept taking deep breaths to soothe the flutters that increased with anticipation of the basket bidding. She only wished she had given Captain McCannon more clues so she was certain he'd bid correctly.

The light fog enclosed the huddled men on the valley floor of Jamestown. Low murmurs and laughter echoed off the stone ravine that held the morning dew. Cheers rang out from the spectators lined at the top of Ladder Hill along with the small crowd gathered in town as they watched a pair of competitors race to the finish line. With the stairs only wide enough for two to run at a time, the runners had to wait one-minute intervals before the next pair of competitors raced up the daunting, steep stairs. Some men stretched, leaning down in an attempt to touch their toes, others clasped their hands, rubbing them together in a nervous manner, waiting for their turn. Unable to hold still, James paced back and forth aimlessly in a small section next to Thomas, who stood with ease. Spectators lined the top of Ladder Hill. Thomas and James were in the middle of thirty men waiting their turn to race up the seven hundred steps.

"How about we have a wager?" Thomas mischievously glanced at him. James wiped his clammy hands on his thighs.

He didn't trust the gleam in his friend's eyes. "And what are we wagering?"

"There's a certain basket I've got my eye on. It has my favorite fish cakes, colwick cheese, and mango phirni."

"She put mango phirni in it? Did Jenny tell her to?" It was one of James's favorite puddings. He was first introduced to it when stationed in India. But the way she turned his stomach upside down, he doubted he could eat it.

"I may have overheard them talking in the kitchen yesterday."

James laughed, rubbing the back of his neck. This just made it easier.

"If I win, I get the basket. And if you win, you get the basket."

He snorted at his friend's challenge. It would be a close match. But his confidence of winning grew as he felt his heart pumping to awaken every fiber of his body.

"I hope you have another basket in mind, because you're about to lose some delicious fish cakes."

Thomas grinned at James. "We'll see. Just know when you lose, I plan on taking her out by the pond. You know the place by the willow tree. The mango phirni will be so refreshing after our run."

"Ha! Yes, it will." James rolled up his sleeves and shook his shoulders and his legs loose. He wasn't going to let Thomas have a taste of his pudding. The pair of men in front of them raced up the stairs when the race official had yelled, "Go!" Just one more minute until it was their turn. Thomas gave a sly smile towards James when they stepped up to the line drawn into the dirt. James's heart continued to anxiously pound in his chest. His breathing came in short breaths while he focused on the stairs ahead of him.

Last year Thomas and he tied for first place with a time of five minutes and forty-eight seconds. This year, he had no choice, he needed to beat that time.

"On your mark," the man called. James took a step forward, bent both knees, and hunched down.

"Get set."

A drop of sweat rolled down his back as he brought his arms up angled by his side.

"Go!"

He dashed forward with Thomas by his side. Cheers broke out all around the valley as they climbed each step at a rhythmic pace. One, two, one, two, one, two. His feet pounded against the concrete steps with Thomas keeping pace. One, two, one, two. Their breathing became heavy as they broke through the fog towards the bright blue sky. The sun beamed down on them, intensifying the heat he felt radiating from his body. As James pushed harder, his legs burned, begging him to stop.

Fish cakes, he grunted. One, two, one, two. *Colwick cheese*. One, two, one, two. He could hear Thomas's heavy breathing next to him. He knew they were nearing the top as the incline steepened. His lungs were on fire as he gasped for air. *Pudding*. One, two, one, two. *Come on, James!* Cheers began to filter in through the sound of his pounding heart. Sweat dripped into his eyes, causing him to blink multiple times. *Stay focused, James. Keep the pace.* One, two. His legs grew more and more heavy with every step. His shirt no longer allowed air through as it clung to his back. Just a few more steps. *Come on. Push through.* His heart throbbed ready to burst. ONE, TWO . . . ONE!

"Time!"

James collapsed to the ground gasping for air. He laid there for a moment with his eyes closed. Fish cakes . . . pudding . . . Jane Sawyer. He breathed out heavily.

"And time!"

He opened his eyes as Thomas collapsed next to him, panting. James smiled at his friend.

"You . . ." Thomas gasped. "Just . . . proved . . . my theory correct."

"What theory is that?"

Before Thomas answered, a race official ran up to James. "James! You just beat the town's record by three seconds!"

He stared with disbelief. The record was five minutes and thirty-four seconds. He glanced at Thomas who raised his brows, shaking his head to say *I told you so.* Rolling his eyes, James let out a snort.

"Come," he grunted as he stood to help Thomas to his feet. "Let's go clean up. I've got a basket to win." He flashed Thomas a victory smile.

Freshened up and only minutes to spare, James and Thomas rushed to the churchyard before the bidding began. The churchyard looked like a Sunday afternoon filled with women holding their parasols and fanning their faces, and gentlemen dressed in their Sunday best. James and Thomas weaved through the crowd towards the front row. He had yet to see Miss Sawyer. Commissioner Gordon Harrlow stood behind a podium banging his gavel loudly.

"People of Jamestown!" His voice boomed. "It is my greatest honor to be hosting this year's 'Baskets for Charity' event. These lovely baskets," he turned and pointed at the table full of colorful ribbon-tied baskets, "have been donated by Jamestown's finest ladies. In order to earn a picnic with one of these ladies, you must bid on their basket. The lady who owns the basket will remain anonymous until the end of the bidding. There are a few rules with this auction. As chaperones are required, we have assigned areas where you are allowed to take the young lady. These areas are Heartspring Pond, Castle Gardens, and Ebony Park. All proceeds will go to the orphanage at Jamestown. Let the bidding begin!"

A loud resounding echo darted into the crowd as he hit the gavel against the wood. His assistant brought up a bright pink ribbon basket.

"In this basket there are hard boiled eggs, fried chicken, slices of pineapple, cornbread and mixed berry fruit tarts. Let's start the bid at one shilling. Do I hear one shilling?!"

Murmurs rippled through the crowd like a pen full of chickens. Men began raising their hands, shouting out their numbers in an orderly conduct. In nervousness, James wiped his hands on his thighs as the baskets were being auctioned. After what felt like an eternity, there were six baskets left. He adjusted his stance for the hundredth time and tugged at his collar. Thomas chuckled at his unusual behavior.

"This lovely basket has ham, cheddar cheese, baked potatoes, grapes, rice pudding, and wafers. Do I hear one shilling?"

"Two crowns!" A familiar voice rang out. Gasps erupted in the crowd. James joined the wave of heads turning towards the voice. There, with his thin black mustache above a chivalrous smile stood his friend Captain Richard.

Thomas's brow arched with confusion as he whispered to James, "I thought he left last week,"

"So did I." James squinted his eyes to see who Richard was smiling at. "Whose basket did he just bid on?"

"And for ten shillings?!" Thomas exclaimed.

"Sold!" roared Commissioner Harrlow, banging the gavel. Applause arose from the audience.

"Up next, we have fish cakes, colwick cheese, rolls, and mango phirni. Do I have two shillings?"

"Two shillings!" James called with a lump forming in his throat. A few heads turned in his direction with surprised expressions. Most of the townsfolk knew James, and were aware of the fact that he had never before bid on a basket.

"Three shillings!" a man called.

"Four!" yelled another.

James nervously rubbed his hands together.

"One crown and two shillings!" he offered, swallowing down the lump. Ladies began to whisper behind their fans.

"Going once, going twice," the pause caused James's limbs to grow weak. "Sold! To Captain McCannon."

He tightened his fist in a subtle triumph. People began to applaud, and he even heard a few cheers. He smiled broadly as relief and excitement rushed over him. The feeling felt better than the win from his race that morning.

"Bravo, James." Thomas clapped his hand across James's shoulder. He couldn't contain his grin. The nervousness from the auction began to dissipate as Commissioner Harrlow continued on.

"Alright folks, we have here our last basket! Let's see. I see a parfait with mangoes and berries, Gloucester cheese, slices of bread, and fish cakes."

James's stomach slightly dropped as doubt began to fill his mind. Miss Sawyer had been debating between the two cheeses and she stated she would put in mangoes.

"Thomas, are you certain you heard Miss Sawyer say she was going to put in mango phirni?" He asked calmly, trying not to show the panic that was building.

"I know it wasn't Jenny who mentioned it."

"Could it have been someone else who was there, other than Miss Sawyer?"

Thomas grew quiet for a moment as he thought. "I honestly haven't the faintest idea who else would have been there."

"Sold! To Lieutenant Woods." Applause broke out.

"Thank you everyone for attending! Now, we ask all the young ladies to find the gentlemen who bid on their baskets."

The crowd began to shift as people maneuvered to find each other. Many of the bidders already knew whose basket they were bidding on. James clutched the lapel of his jacket as a prickly sensation consumed his fingers and toes. *What if I bid on the wrong basket?*

"I don't believe it! James, look!" Thomas gripped James's arm and pointed towards Captain Richard. The man beamed as he smiled down at Miss Keaton. She clung to his arm, devotedly staring up at him with doe eyes.

"Well, I'll be." James laughed. "Never in a million years would I have guessed the two of them together."

"That explains why he'd delayed his trip," Thomas smugly remarked.

"It certainly does." James scratched at his head. Whenever they were reassigned to a different location, they were often given a month's worth of leeway, due to weather or a battle. Richard must be using that time for her.

"Captain McCannon?" a sweet voice called amidst the commotion. His stomach tightened. This was it! He turned and felt as if someone had knocked the air out of him.

"Miss Harrlow." He offered a slight bow.

"I believe you bid on my basket." She smiled sweetly at him. Her blonde hair pinned elegantly under a pink feathered hat.

"Your basket?" Keeping his smile in check, he felt the words take another blow to his gut.

"Yes, that's correct," her dark blue eyes glistened as her full pink lips spread pleasingly towards her rosy cheeks.

From the corner of his eye, he saw Thomas's shocked expression tighten as he was fighting back fits of laughter. *No, no, no. How could this be? If this was hers then the other one would have been Miss Sawyer's. Where's Lieutenant Woods?!* He cleared his throat.

Attempting to appear composed, he extended his arm to her. "Well Miss Harrlow, shall we?"

"Thank you, captain." The feather on her hat bobbed across his face. He grimaced as it tickled his nose. *How could his afternoon have come to this?* He felt completely empty inside when she wrapped her arm through his. Nothing compared to the jittery feeling Miss Sawyer inflicted on him. James flashed Thomas a scowl, who in return offered him a repentant smile. He led his undesirable companion towards the direction of Lieutenant Woods's voice.

Jane's chin dipped to her chest. Her hand clutched her elbow that held her parasol feebly in the air. *Not only did Captain McCannon bid on the wrong basket, but it was Miss Catherine Harrlow's basket.* She took a deep breath in trying to avoid scolding herself for not being forthright with him.

"Miss Sawyer!" She turned to see Lieutenant Woods smiling excitedly at her while carefully removing his hat from his head. His black hair slicked neatly back and his sideburns trimmed shorter than the last time she had seen him.

"Why, Lieutenant Woods, I was just on my way to find you."

He didn't appear surprised by her remark. *Did he know that basket was hers?* she wondered. Only two people knew what was in her basket, besides Captain McCannon—*who had been so close to figuring it out.* Lieutenant Woods stared down at the ground, nervously, fidgeting with his hat clasped in his hands.

"I have a confession. I may have asked a certain someone to check out your basket to see what you had."

Ah, of course! It all made sense now. Timidly, he looked at her. The corner of her mouth raised into a half-smile. "Let me guess." She tilted her head to the side. "Miss Harrlow?"

He nodded.

The previous day, Catherine had unexpectedly called on Jenny while she and Jane were decorating their baskets. Jane thought it was peculiar that when she shared what she was putting in her basket, Catherine piped up and exclaimed how ironic it was that she too would be putting similar things in hers. She even declared her items were added specifically for a gentleman who had his eye on her for a time. *Did she really mean James?*

"I hope you don't think it impertinent of me, but after what you've done for my hand, well," he hesitated to find the right words. "I thought it would be enjoyable to have this picnic together."

"How very thoughtful of you, lieutenant, thank you," she spoke with sincerity.

His face brightened. "I can't take all the credit." He twisted his hat in his hands. "It was Miss Harrlow who inspired the idea. I really have her to thank."

Normally, Jane didn't have any ill feelings towards others, but Miss Catherine certainly left an unpleasant taste in her mouth. Swallowing her irritation, she looked up at the lieutenant and smiled. Miss Catherine may have intervened, but that didn't mean she couldn't make the most of it.

"Have you been to Heartfelt Pond?" he asked.

"I haven't. But I hear it's lovely."

Tall grass, wispy trees, bright flowers of many colors scattered around the edges of the clear pond. Jane was surprised that the large body of water could be called a pond as it appeared to be more like a lake. Keeping cool under a large ebony tree, Jane and Lieutenant Woods, quietly ate by the water's edge. Across the smooth surface of the pond, couples sat in row boats chatting and laughing under the afternoon sun.

Jane rested against her hand, her knees bent, legs to one side, enjoying the majestic scenery. Lieutenant Woods leaned closer to her side.

"You can't see from here but beyond that line of trees, there is a bend in the pond that leads to another little pond." He pointed across the water. She held her hand above her eyes peering towards the direction he indicated but couldn't see past the sun's glare.

"It appears there are a few boats left, would you care to see it?" His emerald eyes beamed with anticipation.

She smiled warmly. "I'd like that."

Together they put away their basket, which disappointedly still had a few leftover fish cakes. Oddly, they not only tasted different from the one's she had made the day prior but they appeared crispier than when she had made them that morning. Brushing aside the suspicion that Miss Catherine would stoop so low as to switch fish cakes, she helped fold the blanket and placed it in the container.

Accepting his hand, she stepped into a small boat that sat on the water's edge. Sitting at the stern of the wooden boat, she quickly adjusted her skirt to fan comfortably around her before the lieutenant pushed the vessel into the water from the shore. She watched with excitement as water splashed around his boots and legs while he ran. When he jumped into the bow, she bit her lip from the rocking he caused, briefly reminding her of the horrible storm that resulted in her experiencing this wonderful delay in Jamestown. Taking the oars, he offered Jane a genuine smile, and turned their boat in the direction of the little pond he had mentioned. With long swift pulls, they were gliding across the satin smooth surface.

As much as she wished she were sitting with Captain McCannon, she felt content with Lieutenant Woods's enjoyable company. Not only was he quiet, but he didn't cause her heart to beat recklessly, making her lose focus with all her thoughts. She opened her parasol, blocking the warm rays of the sun. Nor did he make her stomach flutter uncontrollably. She smiled to herself. Instead, she felt comfortable and content. She released a pleased sigh. The rhythmic harmony of the oars sloshing through the water's surface put her in a pleasant frame of mind. She leaned back on her hand, and while staring up at the cloudless sky, she soaked in the tranquility feelings that overcame her. Birds soared across the blue canvas as they chased each other towards the thicket of trees in the distance. Jane's eyes followed a dragonfly that zigzagged up and down, keeping pace by her side before darting off into another direction.

Suddenly, their boat began to sway unsteadily. Startled, she looked around. The once smooth water was now rippling from under their boat. Her eyes darted to Lieutenant Woods. His hands shifted awkwardly on the oars, struggling to hold his grip.

"Lieutenant, are you alright?"

His cheeks were reddened by her observation.

"Fine, fine. Just trying to adjust my hand."

She peered over at his bandage-free hand. It had been a few weeks since she sewed the gash in his hand, and if he hadn't taken proper care of the wound, it would be very tender to the touch and may even open back up.

"How is your wound?"

"It's fine. I'm just struggling to get a firm grip on this . . ." His breaths came out in pants as he flexed his hand. He tried rowing with only his good hand, but in doing so, had to release the other oar. As he released the one oar, he failed to secure it into the oarlock. Jane bit her lip as she predicted what would happen next.

"Oh! Lieutenant!"

Abandoning the oar, he frantically turned back to the other oar to prevent it from falling into the water but was too late. It had already slipped out of the rowlock, landing with a soft splash, while the boat continued to glide forward.

"Oh, no!" she helplessly leaned forward after noticing the other oar sliding out of its rowlock and into the water. He jerked his body towards the last oar, but all in vain, for it too, became a lost cause. Jane's hand flew up to her mouth, stifling a giggle that begged to escape. The oars floated freely behind them like two lone ducks on the water. Steadily they drifted along the pond . . . oar-less.

The poor lieutenant turned a crimson red as he stood staring longingly at the floating oars. His hands gripped his coat as he appeared to be debating whether he should jump in after them. Jane peered around to see if anyone was nearby to assist them. Her heart sank. No one was in sight. They were alone floating around a wide bend that took them out of sight from the other boats on the pond. He slowly shrugged his coat off his shoulders.

"Lieutenant," she rushed. The last thing she wanted for him was to be a target for the town's gossip. "I'm certain there will be another boat that can give us assistance."

He paused and appeared to be contemplating. Defeated, he collapsed back down on his bench, resting his face in his hands. Silently they sat, slowly drifting around the bend. Water sloshed along the side of their boat as a breeze picked up. Jane twisted her parasol in her hand, watching the shadows from the lace dance across the boat's bottom. She didn't feel at a loss with the oars, more so the opposite. She enjoyed the peaceful chirps of the birds and the humming of bees. Nothing terrible could come of this, it was just a little hiccup in their day. She glanced up at Lieutenant Woods.

The poor gent held his face with his scar free palm. He didn't appear to feel the same. He looked so distraught as he picked at the side of the boat with his free hand. Their boat drew closer to the bend of the tall grassy and heavily vegetated shoreline.

"Would you mind if I looked at your hand?" she asked, breaking the uncomfortable silence.

Disheartened, Lieutenant Woods glanced over at her. She ached for him. His plans of showing her the other pond hadn't turned out as he had hoped, and it certainly put a damper on his mood. He nodded and held it out. She scooted towards him to get a closer look, then rested herself on the heels of her slippers.

The red scar on his hand peeled and appeared inflamed from the oar rubbing against it. With her free hand, she clasped his hand while still holding the parasol. She angled his palm back and forth to see if there were any signs of openings or infection.

"It doesn't appear to be infected. May I suggest you keep it covered to add cushion while you use your hand? Just until it's no longer tender to the touch."

He nodded and his eyes began to brighten. "Thank you, Miss Sawyer. I'll be sure to do that."

She smiled as his spirits appeared to be lifting.

"Ahoy there!" A deep smooth voice called out to them.

Jane stilled with recognition. That morning's race flashed across her mind as she pictured Captain McCannon sprinting up the stairs. He was fast, determined, and so fierce. She exhaled slowly, with hopes to control her quickening pulse.

"Oh!" A feminine voice rang out. "I hope we're not interrupting anything."

Jane cringed. She didn't dare glance their way. She could only imagine what they assumed as she was still holding the lieutenant's hand. Gracefully as she could, she scooted back onto her bench.

"Not at all," Lieutenant Woods rang out. "Miss Sawyer was inquiring about the healing of my hand."

Gratitude filled her as Lieutenant Woods appeared to clear any assumptions of intimacy between them. Though, it could add to the assumption that she was being forward with the gentleman. Oh dear. Warmth spread to her cheeks.

"I saw a couple of oars floating by, they wouldn't happen to belong to you would they, lieutenant?"

She glanced over at Captain McCannon. His broad jaw clenched. Not expecting him to look her way, they locked eyes. She loosened her grip on the parasol, causing the handle to slide down her hand. Quickly she regained her hold. She bit her cheek, trying to control her disheveled emotions. Drawing in a sharp breath, she swiftly looked back at Lieutenant Woods.

"I'm afraid they do." He laughed, rubbing his sore hand. He appeared more at ease with their presence.

"That is a shame," Catherine stated, with pouty lips. "Perhaps the captain and I can flag someone down to tow you back."

Jane scoffed, staring at her lap. *What an absurd thing to say. Clearly, Miss Catherine has her own agenda and wants to be on their way.*

"What a fine idea, Miss Harrlow," Captain McCannon resounded. Jane's mouth dropped. *Surely, he was joking. He would never leave them stranded. Would he? Perhaps, he did fancy Miss Catherine?* Slowly she dragged her feet back and tucked them under her bench. From the corner of her eye, Jane could see Miss Catherine raise a brow, and while smiling smugly at her, shifted herself comfortably in the boat, like a snobby cat. The ill feelings Jane felt earlier that afternoon thickened like the muck the chef had called stew during her voyage to the island.

"Lieutenant," the captain called. "Catch!" He threw a rope toward Lieutenant Woods. Jane straightened, her wide eyes swiftly fell onto Captain McCannon. Relief turned into a jolt of exhilaration as he winked at her. Catherine leaned forward with her mouth parted in protest, but quickly drew back and smiled when Captain McCannon glanced her way.

"The best way to tow you is for you to tie the rope at the stern," he directed to Lieutenant Woods. Lieutenant Woods peered around Jane as she was sitting where he needed to be.

"Allow me, lieutenant." She closed her parasol and removed her laced gloves. He scrunched his brows with uncertainty.

"Are you sure, Miss Sawyer? Perhaps we could switch places."

"I'm quite certain. I'd hate for any of us to fall in while attempting to maneuver."

Shrugging, he handed her the rope. She stood hunched over while rotating around ever so carefully until her body faced the stern. Once situated, she released a staggered breath that she had been holding. Looking at the rope in her hands, she began to twist it around the hook while the captain positioned the bow of his boat towards her. *A rabbit comes up through the hole, around the tree, back down the hole. Done! Impeccable timing if I say so myself.* She looked up, startled to see *him* in front of her. A section of rope dangled in one hand as he stared at her, astonished with a half-crooked smile.

"Where did you learn how to tie a bowline, Miss Sawyer?" His voice was low and husky sounding.

Her mind whirled for the answer. "At the hospital, in Bombay."

His head tilted to the side with a blank expression.

"Some of the militiamen taught me a few knots while I visited them in the hospital. It was actually very entertaining, as we would all race each other to see who could tie it the fastest." She smiled at the memory while putting on her gloves.

He continued to gape but quickly jumped when Catherine's honeyed voice interrupted.

"I'm excited to see the fireworks tonight. Aren't you, captain? My father announced there will be more than last year."

His brow furrowed in a serious manner as he tied his end of the knot with his back towards the lady.

"Uh, yes. Yes, I am." He sat back down on his bench still facing Jane and grabbed the oars.

"I do beg your pardon, Miss Harrlow," he called over his broad shoulder, "But I'm afraid I'm going to have to have my back towards you until we return to the dock."

Jane could only picture Catherine's face now. Shaking her head, she stood to turn back around, but quickly wobbled down to her seat as their boat lurched forward. She glanced ahead with surprise. Captain McCannon flashed her a smile then pulled back on the oars again.

She shook her head with disapproval, which made him chuckle. Attempting to appear unphased by his motive, she opened her parasol and gazed across the water. She felt confident the lieutenant wouldn't mind that her back was to him.

Her eyes drifted to the rope that held their boats closely taut together. He certainly had left no room between their vessels. With each pull he made, her boat thrust forward, barely skimming his boat. Heat spread through her as her boat wasn't the only thing swaying towards the captain.

Tightening her posture, she swiftly fanned her face to cool the warmth of her flushed cheeks. Aimlessly taking in the views around the pond, her eyes fell back onto him. Astonished, she watched how his jacket stretched across the flexed muscles in his arms, as they pulled the weight of the two boats. She didn't realize she had stopped fanning herself until he flashed her an impish smile. Mortified that he caught her staring at his arms, she promptly lowered her fruitless accessory and peered across the pond. Twisting the fan in her hands, she tried to focus on anything that wasn't in front of her. She observed that there were very few boats in the water since many couples had already departed to get ready for the evening's ball.

As she continued to search for a diversion, she noticed that Captain McCannon was staring at her. Peering from the corner of her eye, she watched him give her a half smile. She began to shift in her seat as his stare continued to bear down on her. Feeling out of sorts under his gaze, she faced him to break the awkward silence between them. "I can't tell you how much we appreciate your willingness to tow us back to shore, captain."

"It's my pleasure, Miss Sawyer." His smile broadened as the thick muscles from his neck down to his shoulders and arms flexed with another pull. He looked over his shoulder towards the open water of the pond.

Jane began fanning feverishly, glancing away from him and watching the oars dip into the water. She couldn't think of anything to say. Even though the captain's large stature blocked Miss Catherine, Jane was still very much aware of her presence, as well as Lieutenant Woods's.

"I hear congratulations are in order, captain," she began again. "First place running up Jacob's ladder and defeating the town's record. That's very impressive."

He beamed with pride at her acknowledgement.

"Yes! That was impressive indeed!" Miss Catherine called over his shoulder.

"Thank you," his smile faltered as he focused back on his rowing.

"Did you not attend, Miss Sawyer?" he asked thoughtfully. With the sun shining down on him, his blue eyes became all the more piercing as he stared at her.

"Perhaps." Her breathing grew rapidly as one side of his mouth turned up. Oh, she was there. She remembered how her heart raced as she watched him take the lead. It was exhilarating to see him power through the way he did. She blew out a staggered breath towards her flushed cheeks.

"Perhaps?" he challenged as he pulled again at the oars. Jane's eyes traced up his arms to his half smile. He was studying her again. She inhaled sharply, feeling ever so flustered. She didn't want to admit to him that she had watched him, well, more like gawked at him. She and over half the ladies around her. It was too embarrassing to reflect on. He again looked over his shoulder towards the water's surface. Hastily, securing an oar to the oarlock of the boat, he let go. Twisting his body to the port side, he plucked a stranded oar that was still floating on the water's surface. The oar dripped across his leg as he tucked it to his side.

"Lieutenant!" he hollered. "Retrieve the oar on the starboard side."

"Aye, captain."

Jane heard a splash from behind her. The lieutenant must have flung the oar across their boat as she watched drops of water fling past her. She gasped, straightening her spine from the shocking coolness of the spray splattering across her neck and arms. Apparently, the lieutenant was oblivious to the mishap as he remained silent behind her.

Across from her, Captain McCannon's eyes danced with amusement and he chuckled. She bit the corner of her mouth, refusing to smile back at his ridiculous enjoyment. That caused him to chuckle more as his oars gripped the water and his muscles strained to heave them forward. She tightened her grip on both her fan and parasol, avoiding the temptation to regard Captain McCannon's arms flexing in his jacket. He heaved as he continued to pull the boats with a rhythmic motion. The sound of his throat clearing caught her attention.

"Perhaps?" He repeated quietly, as he leaned farther forward with his stroke, so only her ears could hear. Through a long pause, he continued to stare intently at her.

"Perhaps, captain?" Jane raised her brow at him, pretending he was asking her a new question. He chuckled as he leaned away with another pull. Her body swayed forward with the pull.

"Perhaps you did attend the race, Miss Sawyer," he stated as a matter of fact, releasing another breath of air as he pulled back.

Jane smiled. "And if I had?" she challenged, staring into his stunning eyes.

"Then you made my run worthwhile," Captain McCannon remarked sincerely. She stared at him, astounded. The captain peered back over his shoulder, breaking away from her.

Steadily he glided their boats to the dock. He and Lieutenant Woods jumped out to tie them to the posts then assisted the young ladies out. Miss Catherine didn't appear as chipper as she had been earlier. As she stepped out of the boat, her nose was held high in the air, and her lips tightly pursed together.

"Thanks, captain. I'm glad you were out on the water." Lieutenant Woods clamped Captain McCannon's shoulder.

"I suppose you could say luck was on your side, lieutenant." He caught Jane's eye when he said it and smiled, a knowing smile. She bit her lip, understanding he referred to her mango parfait.

A silence fell between the group as they made their way back towards the carriages.

Before Jane and Lieutenant Woods parted ways, she quickly turned to Captain McCannon.

"Captain," she rushed.

"Miss Sawyer?" Eagerly he offered her his attention.

Demurely, she gazed up at him. "I'm glad to hear your run was worthwhile."

His eyes danced as he stared into hers. "Me too." He flashed her a smile before he and Miss Catherine climbed into their separate carriage.

Chapter Sixteen

James felt claustrophobic while he adjusted his cravat. Making his way into the dance hall of the governor's plantation, Miss Harrlow clung to his side. Not only did he get cornered by her mother after he saw Miss Harrlow home, he had been pressed into accompanying her to the ball. The orchestra's melody rang through the hall as couples took to the dance floor. James scanned the room. Somewhere in the sea of ballgowns was Miss Sawyer. He tugged at the sleeves of his jacket. He double checked inside the front of his suit pocket for the calculated note. Miss Harrlow beamed up at him as she held tightly to his arm. Feigning a smile, he politely lifted the corner of his mouth.

"There you two are!" cried her mother, Lady Harrlow. Hurrying over to them, her cream muslin gown swished back and forth while the plump feathers in her hair bobbed up and down. "Why, don't you two make a handsome pair."

James groaned inside as he bowed over Lady Harrlow's hand. Miss Harrlow beamed at her mother with a hopeful expression.

"Catherine, darling. That color red is most becoming on you," the lady gushed. "Do you not agree, captain?" The eyes of the two ladies fell upon him with expectations of his approval. He stared back with no emotion.

"Of course, Lady Harrlow. Miss Harrlow, you do look lovely."

Lady Harrlow smiled with approval. "Oh look, Lady Thompson." She waved over one of her friends. "Come see my daughter and Captain McCannon."

James tugged at his sleeve again. He was beginning to feel all the more trapped while discussing earlier festivities—particularly the auction. Suddenly, he began to feel like he became the rooster in the hen house. He smiled on cue when their audience began to grow with more of Lady's

Harrlow's friends. He just needed to put up with it a little longer before his plan went into motion.

"Excuse me, Captain McCannon?" He turned to a woman's voice.

"Miss Oakley," James smiled at his friend. She smiled back, standing firm against the looks of scrutiny around them.

"I believe you promised to save me this dance." She lifted her brow, beautifully performing her role. The orchestra began playing a minuet.

"I did promise that earlier this morning, didn't I?"

Whispers began to float around them when he turned to a somewhat disappointed Miss Harrlow. He took her hand in his and gave a bow, then bowed to the circle of women.

"Ladies, it's been a pleasure, but I believe I must keep to my prior commitment."

Fanning her face, Lady Harrlow gave him a tightlipped smile. Miss Harrlow also feigned a smile at James, and, as he turned with Jenny at his side, he caught the young lady giving Jenny a menacing glare. He was going to owe Jenny big for this.

Jenny grinned and batted her lashes while making their way to the dance floor. For the first time all evening he felt himself able to breath. He guided Jenny in front of him, standing next to another couple in the dance lineup.

"Is everything in place?" he asked, stepping towards her to the rhythm of the song. Following the dancers, Jenny stepped back then forward.

"Yes, I spoke with him and he approved of it."

James smiled before they switched partners. From the corner of his eye, he saw Miss Harrlow glaring in Jenny's direction. The woman was a true spitfire. He looked at Jenny with her bright countenance. He winced at the predicament he put her in.

A few turns with other dancers, and he was back in front of Jenny. She smiled at his worried expression.

"I'll be fine," she casually spoke, as she looked in the direction of Miss Harrlow. James must have shown the uncertainty he felt because she was inclined to say, "Trust me. I've put out many fires like hers."

"I'll be sure to assist you if any are created."

The song ended and he took a bow.

"I'll see you soon." She smiled up at him, and briskly walked away. After her departure, Miss Harrlow immediately came to his side displaying a sweet smile.

"Miss Harrlow," he offered a polite bow. "I'm sorry Miss Oakley was unable to stay to converse with us. Being the sister I never had, I've always made certain to dance with her."

Miss Harrlow's smile relaxed when she looked in the direction Jenny departed from. "I see. That is a shame she couldn't stay."

James offered his arm, uncertain how long he had until the next ploy came into action. He couldn't leave Miss Harrlow's side. Not yet. Seeing her glare at Miss Sawyer after his attempt to capture her attention, he feared what she would do next. He had heard that she attempted to tarnish her reputation from suturing the lieutenant's hand. If she saw him dance with her tonight, she would make the rest of her journey miserable. He was not about to let that happen. Nor was he going to allow the lady to ruin his night to dance with her. Miss Harrlow gazed at him while possessively holding his arm. When she realized he was leading them off the dance floor, her smile began to fade.

"Captain McCannon?" Thomas hurried over to him.

Relieved to avoid the henhouse, James gave him his full attention.

"Lieutenant Thomas?"

"You're wanted at the dock. There's been a disturbance with a few of the men."

James gave a nod to his friend. "Thank you, lieutenant." He turned to the distraught Miss Harrlow, while Thomas lingered by his side. Her flushed cheeks caused her eyes to darken even more. It was an unbecoming look on her. Nothing compared to the coloring on Miss Sawyer's cheeks, whose hazel eyes tended to brighten against the hue.

"Miss Harrlow, I'm afraid I must depart."

"Will you be back in time for the fireworks?" Her eyes pleaded as she looked up at him, but not before flashing a disapproving glare at Thomas. Did she blame Thomas for the men's behavior? Not that there was any obscene behavior. Thomas agreed to playing along to his plan hours before the ball commenced.

"I highly doubt I will. I have my duties to attend to." She pouted her lips. How he had found her attractive was beyond him. "I hope you have an enjoyable evening, Miss Harrlow," He offered a curt bow, then turned with Thomas, who weaved them through the crowd towards his endeavor.

James adjusted the gloves on his trembling hands. He reached into his pocket and pulled out the note and hid it in his palm. With Thomas in front of him, they made their way towards the opposite corner of the ballroom. Thomas flashed James a mischievous smile over his shoulder before he heard him say, "Miss Sawyer! Doctor Brown! What a delight it is to see you." Thomas took a sidestep as he shook hands with the doctor.

James's heart faltered to a staggering halt as he was enraptured by the most captivating woman he had ever laid eyes on. He barely noticed her blue gown as her pinned curls and pink lips lured his eyes towards her enchanting face. His heart yearned with desire. He was delighted seeing that her face brightened as she stared warmly back into his gaze. They stood for a moment until James heard Thomas clear his throat.

"Miss Sawyer," James softly spoke as if on cue. He lifted her gloved hand up to his lips and there placed a gentle kiss. His hopes soared when she bashfully looked to her side, but not before he caught a glimpse of her smile. She didn't say a word as he subtly slid the note into her palm before turning to Doctor Brown. The doctor had a twinkle in his eye when they shook hands.

"It's great to see you again, captain."

"You as well, Doctor Brown." He smiled at the gentleman. Their conversation earlier had gone smoother than James had hoped. "I hate to cut this short, but I must be off to the docks." Miss Sawyer remained quiet, carefully studying him. "I hope you two have an enjoyable evening."

"You as well, captain," Doctor Brown carried a serious tone. "Please, don't make it a late evening." Miss Sawyer's head tilted to her side and she looked up at her uncle with a confused expression. Her uncle gave James a knowing smile before bowing to him. A corner of James's mouth curved up. He returned the bow and met with Thomas to head towards the harbor.

Jane looked up to her uncle, holding the note in her hand. There had been an odd exchange with the captain and him, and she wasn't sure what to make of it.

"Jane, dear." Her uncle's eyes sparkled as he spoke in a hushed tone. "Why don't you go read that upstairs in your room?"

He noticed their exchange?

"My room, uncle?"

"That's right, dear."

He grabbed her hand that held the note and gave it a loving pat. Kissing her cheek, he then stated aloud, "I do hope your head feels better soon. Why don't you go upstairs and rest?"

A few people turned and gave Jane a sympathetic look. She offered them a pained smile. She'd never faked a headache before, so she wasn't certain how to act.

"Thank you, uncle." She coated her words with forced anguish.

"I'll be up after midnight to check on you." His eyes danced merrily. Jane's brows drew together. She felt ignorant as to what he could have meant. She gave him a nod then hurried away. *What was this all about?* Her ears perked up as she heard a couple of older ladies holding a boisterous conversation.

"Of course, he'll be expecting her hand in marriage. Captain McCannon has never bid on a basket before," the older woman's feather fluttered in her hair as she spoke to the other woman.

"Why didn't Miss Harrlow look divine standing next to him? They do make a perfect match. Did you notice that he escorted her here tonight? I thought—"

"Miss Sawyer," a woman sweetly called from behind. Jane turned to see Catherine standing in the middle of three young ladies looking intently at Jane. Jane groaned inwardly to herself, Miss Catherine was the last person she wanted to see.

"Do you have a moment? I have some friends I'd like to introduce you to."

The older woman's gossip continued to play in her mind. *Was any of it true?* Too distracted by their conversation, Jane reluctantly walked towards the conniving woman and her friends. Miss Catherine held a deceiving smile that made her appear even less inviting. *What was she up to?*

"Miss Sawyer, it's so nice to see you this evening," she continued with a pleasant tone.

"Thank you, Miss Harrlow," Jane offered her a smile but refused to provide her with the same compliment. She was not happy to see her. More than anything she felt confused at the moment. Miss Catherine's lip began to curl with annoyance but quickly spread into a smile.

"May I introduce you to Miss Margret Fletcher, Miss Lydia Coy, and Miss Jessica Swan."

Jane gave them a slight nod.

"Ladies, this is Miss Jane Sawyer . . . *the* Miss Sawyer," her voice lowered as she looked at her friends.

The audacity! Jane never felt so disgusted by a woman's ill-mannered behavior. Each of the women stared at Jane with contempt. Their eyes scoured over as they scrutinized every piece of her, as though they wanted to trample upon any dignity she owned. Silence filled the air between them until Jane could bear no more of their catty behavior.

"Yes, how lovely," she maintained a pleasant tone. "Miss Harrlow, I only wish you had introduced me to your delightful friends sooner." She smiled politely at each of the ladies that sneered back at her. *Now that you all had the pleasure of meeting the one and only Miss Sawyer,* she astutely thought. "I must carry on in my endeavors."

"Oh, Miss Sawyer, there's something I wish to discuss with you." Miss Catherine turned to her friends and gave them a knowing look. "Ladies, if you'll excuse us." Each returned a sly smile. Without a mention of a good-bye, they clustered together, buzzing like a hive of bees as they glided away.

"Pay no attention to them. They've never met a woman who's quite so . . . diverse." She offered Jane a smug smile that she fought hard not to return.

"Miss Harrlow, do you enjoy the theatre?" Jane asked, as they walked away from the dancers.

"Of course," she looked at her confused.

"And the arts?"

"Yes." She continued to stare at her trying to discern where she was trying to lead her.

"And your fine friends, I assume they have the same wonderful tastes as you?"

"For the most part," she answered smugly.

"Mm," Jane paused, as though she were deep in thought. "There are so many *diverse* composers, artists, and people that bring such beauty to this world. Do you not agree?"

"I suppose."

"Yes, to be blessed with such talents to share with others." Jane gave a wistful look and turned back to Miss Catherine. "That is such a marvelous rarity." Jane offered her a smile. "I thank you for the sweet compliment, Miss Catherine. I shall always treasure it. Now if you'd please excuse me."

Catherine's cheeks reddened and her nostrils flared.

"Just a moment if you please."

Jane paused, clamping her lips together. Miss Catherine boldly stood beside her. *What did she want now?*

Lacing her arm through Jane's, Miss Catherine continued to speak to her in a hushed tone.

"Earlier I didn't get a chance to tell you, but I was so excited when I heard Lieutenant Woods bid on your basket." She led Jane towards the entryway of the dance hall. "I knew he had his eyes on you since the picnic."

Jane politely offered a halfhearted smile when Miss Catherine glanced her way.

"I'm just excited this worked out for the both of us. I know it's not going to be long until James asks for my hand." Catherine peered at her through her lashes.

Had she not heard the ladies speaking in passing, she wouldn't have believed it. Did he ask to see what was in her basket to avoid bidding on it? Jane maintained a pleasant expression, though her heart was heavy in remorse thinking she had betrayed herself by falling for a gentleman that was almost engaged.

"He's been extremely busy with his assignments that he hasn't had time for us lately."

Jane glanced down at the hidden note in her hand, attempting to process this new information.

"You see, he has a history with ladies who sail through Jamestown, leading them to believe he has feelings for them." She released a heavy sigh. "That's where his kindness and service is often distorted." She let out a soft chuckle. "Oh James, my dear, sweet captain. Will he ever understand how charming he is? I guess he can't help himself. Why, a few weeks ago we went riding together and he stopped his horse to help a struggling woman with two children in tow. He carried her heavy basket to the front steps of her home. He'd do anything to help a woman in distress. That's what I admire about him."

Jane stared hard at the dancers, elegantly floating across the room. She certainly made it easy for him to feel obligated to help her. *How could she have been so foolish?*

"And silly me! I can't believe I actually was beginning to fear that perhaps you were falling into the same category as those other simpleminded ladies." She let out another laugh then shook her head.

"No, I'm just diverse." Jane raised her brow in a challenging manner. Miss Catherine lips curled before she let out a laugh.

"Yes, well, seeing you with Lieutenant Woods and the sparks flying between you two were undeniable. Rest assured, I know now, that's not the case with you."

Catherine gazed at her through her thin lashes. A conniving smile spread across her powdered face. Jane slowly let out the breath she held. She mustered a polite smile to hide the disappointment.

"I do wish you all the best. Well, I must be off. My uncle gave me strict instructions to rest before you stopped me."

"Are you unwell?" Catherine feigned a concerned look and pressed her hand over her chest.

"Yes, a headache," Jane held her temple with her fingers. "I'm afraid the high pitch of your voice made it worse."

Of course, she didn't say that last part. Though it was rather tempting! Jane bit her tongue to keep from stooping down to Miss Catherine's level. "Excuse me," she stated instead.

Catherine feigned a smile, "Do get better."

The weight of the unpleasant news squeezed her tight, making it difficult to breath. She didn't know he had brought Miss Catherine to the dance, nor did she know he was wanting her hand in marriage. *Was it really true?* She peered down at the note again, which now weighed heavy in her hand. *Was he trying to be polite by writing about his feelings towards Miss Catherine?* Her heart sank. The taste of bitterness soured from within her gut. This was why she was protected from the militiamen in Bombay. All their flattery hid their deceit.

She had no desire to become a victim of Captain McCannon's heart revealing note. If she didn't read it, it never happened, she decided with pride. She rubbed the ache in her chest. She could play as though she never had an interest in him. Her steps were heavy as she climbed the stairs that led towards her room. *Of course,* she slowed her pace with dawning. *It makes perfect sense.* He was so guarded with his emotions while at the falls and then afterwards in the field. It wasn't until she had become a victim to Lieutenant Howard that he really softened and showed her sympathy. She clenched the note in her hand. That's all this was, she looked up with a new understanding. *He pitied me.* The word spread through her like poison. Resentful tears began to build and stung the brim of her eyes. The valiant gentleman felt sorry for her. She hurried onward to her room, infuriatingly blinking the tears away. Perhaps she had a headache after all.

Jane burst through her bedroom door, ready to alleviate her tears of frustration when she was startled by not just Millie's presence but . . . Jenny's? Jenny was clothed in a less formal gown, grinning at her.

"Jenny? Millie? What's going on?" Both ladies looked to her with alarm. Not wanting them to witness a betraying tear, Jane quickly wiped it away.

"What's wrong?" Jenny hurried to her side and assisted her over to her vanity. "Is it your arms?"

Occasionally she felt the bruises throb, but it disappeared whenever she distracted herself with others, specifically a certain, unavailable someone.

"No, it's silly." Though the ache within her heart hurt more than her bruises. "I'm not even sure why I'm upset," Jane lied, dabbing at her eyes. Jenny gave her a warm embrace.

"Did you not read the note?" she asked softly.

She shook her head. She didn't want to feel the anguish behind his words.

"Jane dear, get dressed." Jenny sounded less compassionate than before. Confused, Jane looked up at her. Her friend stuck her chin out with determination.

"Come on. Stand up. We're changing you out of this get-up and putting you in something more suitable."

"I don't understand."

"Millie, help me unlace her back," she ordered.

Millie rushed over to Jenny and the two of them began unlacing Jane's gown. Jane gripped the vanity to keep from falling off balance with all the pulling and tugging of her dress.

"Honestly, you two," she huffed from all the jerking they did. "I'll be more content going to bed."

"Jane dear, will you read the note? You'll have a better understanding of his intentions."

Millie and Jenny helped Jane out of the heavy gown. Millie rushed back to Jane's wardrobe and pulled out Jane's second favorite green dress, as the first one laid helplessly lost at the bottom of the harbor. Tears sprang to her eyes again as she thought about Captain McCannon. *Why did I allow myself to fall for him?*

"No, none of that." Jenny grew impatient as she handed Jane a handkerchief. "I did not face the wrath of the Harrlow's and their entourage to have you sulk over a misunderstanding."

She whirled to face Jenny with hope brightening inside. "A misunderstanding?"

Is all of this a misunderstanding? Jenny pointed impatiently at the crinkled note, which was placed on her vanity. She hurried to un-wrinkle the letter. Long graceful calligraphy curved over the paper. Unaware of her own actions, she allowed Jenny and Millie to dress her while she focused on his words.

Jane,

> *It was your basket I wanted. Please ignore any scrutiny*
> *that came from it. Meet me at Saint James's churchyard*
> *for a proper Jamestown celebration.*

Sincerely, The most honorable and the most charming gentleman
you'll ever know,

Captain James McCannon

She bit back a smile, but it quickly faded as she recalled Miss Catherine's condescending words.

"So, he doesn't intend on marrying Miss Harrlow?" She squeezed the paper into her chest.

Jenny popped from behind Jane with a silky green string in hand.

"Heaven's no! Oh, how dreadful. A woman like that would never be worthy of James."

A whirlwind of emotions swept through Jane while she reread his note, now with an open heart. She found herself breathing more easily. Everything that Miss Catherine said was a lie but she couldn't fight the doubt that lingered in the back of her mind. Miss Catherine may not be worthy of him, but that didn't mean it would stop him from pursuing her. Pushing aside her insecurity, she reread his note. He wouldn't be going out of his way to do this if he fancied Miss Catherine, she assured herself.

"Finished!" Jenny called out breathless. "Jane, if you were ever wanting to be rid of your gowns, by all means, please let me know."

Jane smiled as Jenny admiringly ran her hand down the muslin skirt.

"You will be the first I'll inform." She clasped her friend's hand. "Thank you, Jenny. And Millie. I truly appreciate you two."

Once they had settled into their carriage, many questions filled Jane's mind.

"Jenny, how did you manage to pull this together?"

"It all started after today's festivities. I was at home and was heading towards my bedchamber so I could get ready for the ball when James came over with Thomas in tow. Poor James looked so distraught as everything had gone from bad to worse."

"How do you mean?" Jane asked, desperate to hear every word.

"Thomas had told him what was in Miss Catherine's basket when he thought he overheard you talking in the kitchen, yesterday. Then after the picnic, when James brought Miss Catherine home, her mother coerced James into taking her daughter to the ball, eliminating any chance of you two ever dancing."

"Was my uncle aware of any of this?" Jane considered his odd exchange with the captain.

Jenny's hands flew up. "Just a moment, I'm getting to that part," she excitedly exclaimed. "James and I came to the plantation right before the ball, to speak with him. He told him all of his plans, including this little adventure with me accompanying you to town."

"He did that?" Jane stared at her friend, astonished. "And my uncle was fine with it?"

"Of course, he agreed to it. It doesn't take much for James to earn some-one's trust. Besides, he's proven himself to be a virtuous gentleman on many occasions since you've both met him."

"Indeed, he's certainly shown himself more than respectable." A smile crept across her face. She stared out the dark window, reflecting on Captain McCannon's clever plan.

Music floated through the street as their carriage made its way along the joyous crowd. Jane fidgeted with the lace on her shawl, refraining from pressing her face to the glass to take in the scene of the festivities. The carriage door opened and their driver, Samuel, extended his hand into the darkness to assist Jane and Jenny out onto the crowded street. Cheers and laughter rang all around them while they weaved their way to the church-yard. Excitement flooded the air as crowds rallied around couples who were merrily dancing to a high-spirited folk song. Fiddles quickened the tune and the flute and the tambourine followed their lead. Jenny and Jane joined the crowd, clapping to its rhythm. The dancers commenced to interlaced arms and danced to a joyous country dance. Jane grinned at the exhilarating sight.

Ovations erupted all around them when the song ended. Her heart raced with anticipation as the ambience became stimulating with the com-motion. After a short pause, the musicians picked up their instruments and readied themselves to play the next tune. A tap on Jane's shoulder caused her to turn around. Surprised, she faced a young, skinny, freckle-cheeked militiaman.

"Would you care to dance, miss?" he yelled over the loud chatter that surrounded them. Jane smiled at his bravery as he timidly played with the cuff of his jacket. With all the laughing and chipper faces on the dance floor, she couldn't resist the opportunity to join the fun.

"I'd love to!" she loudly exclaimed.

He brightened and pointed to himself. "I'm Timothy!"

"Miss Sawyer!"

Jane grinned at Jenny as the young lad led her to the center of the dance floor. Within a moment, Jenny joined them with her partner. They exchanged grins of excitement and the music began. Timothy held Jane's hand while she carried her skirt with her other hand. Raising it high enough to prevent herself from tripping. They were off! Jane and Timothy hastily skipped around the churchyard with the other couples, weaving in and out of each other. She couldn't contain a giggle that erupted as Timothy turned them into Jenny and her partner.

"Timothy! You clumsy man. Watch where you're going!" Jenny's partner called over his shoulder turning her in another direction. Jane caught Jenny pressing her lips to keep from laughing.

Crimson red, Timothy continued to lead them along the buoyant dance. By the time the song ended, Jane was breathless, and thoroughly enjoying herself. She joined the applause along with everyone around her.

"Mister Timothy," she took a breath. "Thank you for the dance." Timothy's freckled face brightened. She curtsied and turned to leave before the eager lad would ask her for another, when a different militiaman tapped her on her shoulder. He stood taller and appeared older than Timothy. His black hair was shiny under the flickering flames of the lanterns, and his eyes were dark against his sun-weathered skin. Timothy's shoulders dropped with discouragement. He bowed to Jane and with a slouch, he disappointedly trudged off the dance floor.

"Miss? Would you care to dance?" The dark-haired man thundered. His stern expression and size intimidated Jane, but she saw a softness in his squinty eyes.

"Yes," she offered in a small voice. They took their positions. The musicians commenced another lively song. She and the gentleman bound across the dance floor. Couples made room when they saw the large gentleman skitter in their direction. He twirled them around with the rhythm of the vivacious song. She was enjoying his high-spirited pace, but as the twirling continued, Jane felt pings of pain in her stomach. The roasted chicken she had eaten earlier began to swirl, sloshing its way up her throat. Tiny, cool drops of sweat trickled down her back. When the song ended, she could barely applaud, as she concentrated on refocusing her vision. The vigorous gent held out his hand. Jane blinked as she saw three of his hands in place of his one. A lump formed in her throat. She was going to be sick.

"Would you care for another?"

She managed a polite smile but before she could answer, a richly deep voice called into the boisterous mass of people all around her.

"I'm afraid she's taken for this one, Paul." Her heart leaped into her throat. The nausea worsened from the fluttering in her stomach. She fanned herself with her hand in an attempt to cool herself down.

"Captain McCannon!" The man gave a respectable bow. "Of course, sir." He turned to Jane and bowed. "Miss."

Jane gave a small curtsy before she returned to fanning herself. She turned to face the captain. "I hope I interrupted in time, Paul's notorious for making his dance partner sick." His face illuminated when she glanced up at him. A cold sweat formed across her face and chest. She fervently fanned herself as heat rushed to her cheeks and stomach. She needed to depart from the crowd, quickly.

"Are you alright?" He hovered his hand over her arm, as though he knew better than to touch it.

"I'm feeling a little unwell from all the spinning," she whispered, breathless.

His face calmed with understanding. "Come with me."

Swiftly, he grabbed her hand and led her through the masses towards the calm of the dim lit street. Behind them, music drifted through the air again and the people clapped joyously. They ambled along the quiet cobblestone road. Jane welcomed the cool night breeze as it refreshingly calmed her skin and stomach.

"Did this help?"

Her stomach tightened again by the sound of his voice. She peered over at him through her lashes, his tan face glowed in the lamp light.

"Yes, thank you." She smiled from his genuineness.

The captain came to a stop in front of a tavern. Chatter and laughter floated out of the open, lit door into the street.

"Rob Harris, the owner of this tavern, received a shipment of one of my favorite drinks. He promised to save me some before it sold out. Would you care to try it?"

"What is it?"

The corner of his mouth raised. "You'll have to see." He took her hand and led her into the tavern. "It's also a great remedy for an unsettled stomach," he resounded over the loud chatter.

Chapter Seventeen

"Hot chocolate." Jane tightened her eyes, doubtfully peering at the cup of creamy warm chocolate. "This calms the stomach?"

Sitting across from her in the dimly lit tavern, Captain McCannon took a long sip. "It's an ancient remedy. It's used for medicinal purposes to soothe a troubled stomach."

"How could something so delicious be used as medicine?" she asked while stirring the thick, dark chocolate with a dainty spoon. "Wouldn't the sweetness upset it more?" Not that her stomach was hurting her anymore from all the spinning. All that bothered her were the fluttering knots and those weren't going away any time soon.

He laughed. "Let me assure you, Miss Sawyer. I've heard about this from a few of my men, who learned it while stationed in South America. They would never lie to me."

"Never?" Jane's brow arched while she studied the captain.

"Never," he spoke confidently. She didn't realize how close they sat to each other until he leaned towards her, inches from her face. The boisterous tavern quieted around them as they seemed to be the only ones in the large room.

"Are you certain?" she asked in a low hushed tone.

He stared into her eyes before they traced down to her lips. The muscles in his cheek clenched. He quickly blinked and leaned away. "Of course!" He took a sip of his hot chocolate, leaving a hint of a chocolate mustache above his clean-shaven lip. She suppressed a smile.

"Not even while you were in Bombay and Captain Norton played pranks on you?" she challenged. A candle sitting in an old wine bottle flickered next to them.

"Not once." He gave her a smile that boasted his confidence. She sipped more of the creamy chocolate with hopes to settle the dip her stomach made. "My men are loyal. You even had the honor of dancing with one of them."

"Mister Paul?" She held her stomach with the thought of twirling with him again.

"No, Timothy Brighton."

"Ah, yes. He did seem to be the loyal kind." Jane smiled, reflecting how he delayed his departure after their dance. He appeared to want to keep dancing before Mister Paul cut in. *Just a moment,* she rested her cup on the well-worn table.

"Captain McCannon. You saw me dance with Mister Brighton?"

"I did."

She leaned against the wooden bench, perplexed. "Why didn't you ask me to dance before Mister Paul?" If only he had!

He stared intently at her. The candle's flame flicked and reflected off his glazed blue eyes. "Were you wanting to dance with me, Miss Sawyer?" The corner of his mouth slowly raised, exposing his dimple.

"I . . ." She didn't know what to say. Of course, she wanted him to, but she wasn't going to freely give out that information. She took a sip of the smooth hot chocolate, hoping to delay a quick answer. His eyes intensified with interest from her loss of words. Thankfully, the note he had written had flooded her memory.

"In your note, you did mention a proper Jamestown celebration. It's only a proper celebration if it includes dancing."

"This is true. Are you feeling well enough to join me for a dance?"

"Now you want to dance with me?" she teased. She brought her warm cup filled with the soothing drink back up to her lips.

"Miss Jane." He spoke her name with such reverence that she didn't dare move. "I've been looking forward to dancing with you all evening. I just couldn't get to you in time."

He sounded so sure and sincere. "You couldn't?" she heard herself ask. She was in disbelief that she could say anything at all with how empty minded she suddenly felt.

He shook his head no. "I was delayed with greetings from a few of my crew and their families."

"That does sound to be a probable excuse," she managed to say in a teasing manner. The corner of his mouth turned upward. She quickly took the last sip of the "medicine," then placed it down on its saucer. "Shall we?" she asked, feeling eager to escape the uncomfortable yet pleasing feeling that filled the air—particularly between them.

Captain McCannon grinned at her and took to his feet, holding out his hand.

Jane clasped his warm hand and stood. "Oh, captain." Before heading towards the door, she whispered quietly towards his ear. "You have chocolate above your lip." She tapped her lip, then grinned at his stunned expression. With poise, she started towards the door.

James slowly exhaled the trance she bestowed upon him. He thought his heart had stopped for a moment. He took a deep breath to clear the haze.

Licking his chocolatey lips, he wiped off the remaining traces with a napkin. Enraptured, he couldn't contain his high spirits as he made his way out the door towards the endearing lady.

She stood by the doorway looking towards the crowded churchyard down the road. A man with a painted face walked past, juggling three lit torches. He nodded with a smile at Miss Sawyer. A few giggling children followed behind the gentleman, waving their ribbon wands through the air. James nodded a greeting to the group while feeling the torches' flames briefly warm the side of his face as they passed. The evening chilled as it grew late but the crowd grew livelier. He held out his arm to Miss Sawyer and together they made their way toward the celebration. She joyously laughed with the animated crowd. It was captivating to see. The song ended by the time they reached the dance floor. Joining the other couples in the line, he cradled her hand in his, tenderly enveloping his fingers around her soft skin.

His chest rose quickly with short, shallow breaths. Her cheeks flushed when he pressed his other hand against the small of her back and drew her closer. Under the lamp light he noticed goosebumps spread up her arm.

"Are you cold, Miss Sawyer?" His voice was hoarse.

"No," she answered as though breathless.

The music commenced. Together, they capered across the dance floor, stepping to the lively beat. Her steps effortlessly kept with his. He avoided twirling them as much as possible, in spite of the fast rhythm. By the end of the song, both of them were breathless. He gazed down at her. In the dim-lit night, the blue-green hues of her eyes darkened to blend into a hazel color. She refused to look up as she stared wide eyed at his chin, drawing in sharp breaths. Applause broke out, alerting him to step back from their close proximity.

"Excuse me, miss? Would you like to dance?" A young, red-haired lieutenant had summoned the courage to ask Miss Sawyer. She hesitated and from the corner of her beautiful eyes, looked at James. He offered her a knowing nod. Confidently, stepping forward before she could answer.

"Sorry, lieutenant. I promised the lady the next dance."

The gent nodded with understanding and walked away.

"What if I wanted to dance with him?"

"I just did you a favor," he spoke quietly.

"You did?" she mused.

"Not only is this the last dance of the evening, but I believe the lieutenant has two left feet."

Miss Sawyer laughed. "Considering how right you were with the last gentleman I danced with, my feet are eternally grateful, sir."

"As they should be." He smiled, causing her to quickly look elsewhere. How he enjoyed vexing her.

James managed to control his composure as he held her in his arms once more. The music began, this time the instruments played into a slow waltz. He drew her nearer to him while they promenaded across the crowded dance floor.

"Captain," she whispered. "Did you know this was going to be a waltz?" She almost had a look of panic in her large eyes.

"I did." He paused, taking in her unsettled expression. The last dance of the festival always ends with a waltz. "Do they not waltz in India?" Slowly he held her further away from him to study her face.

"Rarely." She furrowed her brows, concentrating on his movements.

"Miss Sawyer, have you ever waltzed before?"

She glanced up at him with a bashful expression. "Aside from attempting it with Millie? This is my first time. Though, we did end up making up our own waltz, as neither of us had any idea of what the steps were."

He smiled. "Well, you're doing splendid." He was impressed indeed, as she gracefully kept with him. "Here," he whispered. "Mirror my steps. As my left foot goes forward your right goes back. Then I'll step to my right as you step to your left."

Her steps quickened while she remained focused down at his feet.

"One-two-three-four-five . . . six. One-two—" she muttered under her breath. After a few more counts, she gazed into his eyes with confidence. She had figured it out. Drawing closer to him, he glided them around with the other couples. When the music died, he hesitantly let her out of his embrace. She beamed up at him.

"Thank you for the lesson."

"Perhaps next time you'll teach me your version of the waltz?"

She let out a laugh and shook her head.

"I can assure you, it's not as refined as this version."

"I have my doubts. Everything you do is graceful, Miss Sawyer," All the conversations around them began to muffle. He cleared his throat in hopes of clearing his head. "Except, of course, walking on piers," Giving a crooked smile, he straightened his jacket, breaking from his stupor of thought. "I have yet to see you successfully cross one."

"I would have to disagree with you." Her eyes gleamed with laughter. "I gracefully fell into the water. It was my most successful endeavor, as I clearly captured your attention."

James chuckled in remembrance of the jab he made to her. "I stand corrected. You gracefully succeeded at capturing my attention."

She captured more than my attention, he thought as his heart beat against his chest.

"I thought I might find you two here!" Jenny maneuvered around a few people to face him and Miss Sawyer. The cheerful Toby Humphrey joined her side. James felt a protective twinge in the pit of his stomach. Jenny flashed him a stern look of warning as she made her introductions.

"This is Toby Humphrey, our town's blacksmith. Mister Humphrey, may I introduce you to my friend, Miss Jane Sawyer?"

He offered Miss Sawyer an inept bow as she elegantly offered a quick curtsy.

"How do you do, Mister Humphrey."

"And Mister Humphrey, you already know Captain James McCannon." Jenny eyed him closely. Of course, he was going to keep his promise. The two of them shook hands on it.

"James."

"Toby. Good to see you." He held nothing against Toby. He was very skilled with his forging tools as he'd helped James on many occasions, but with Jenny? She deserved someone with a higher education.

Jenny flared another warning, and he relaxed his disapproving stare. She had made him promise in exchange to help him that he wouldn't interfere with any of the gentlemen callers. He knew she would have helped him regardless of their deal solely due to her friendship with Miss Sawyer. Jenny thought the world of her. As did he.

A deep voice yelled out across the crowd.

"TEN! NINE! EIGHT!"

Everyone joined in.

"SEVEN!"

Jane glanced around with a confused expression.

"SIX!"

"It's the countdown for the fireworks!" He spoke loud enough for her to hear. Understanding drew across her face. She smiled at him then joined in the count.

"TWO!"

"ONE!"

Cheers broke out for a moment before they turned into silence. Everyone gawked as the first mortar spun into the night sky above them. The flame disappeared on the mortar, filling the crowd with silent anticipation. A loud explosion erupted into the sky, followed by crackling. Orange sparks shattered against the starry night, drizzling down into the black sea below. The mass cheered with excitement except for Miss Jane, who jumped by James's side. He looked at her, surprised to see her eyes were wide with uncertainty. She offered a reassuring smile to Jenny who regarded her quizzically on her other side.

The fireworks continued to shoot rapidly from the fort at the top of the hill. Bright colors of red, blue, and orange, whirled, spiraled, and scattered across the firmament like glistening specs of paint. The gunpowder from the mortars crackled and twinkled into the darkness as a cascading waterfall. Each explosion vibrated through James's body. His chest tightened as the explosions resembled cannon fire. He scanned the crowd and saw the uneasiness of some of the soldiers with their companions unphased by the effect. The last of the booms rumbled through the air. Cheers erupted but were less fervent from some of the men. The crowd began to disperse from the courtyard. Jamestown's festival was officially over.

"Wasn't that wonderful?" Jenny exclaimed.

Miss Sawyer quietly looked at the people around them. "Yes, it was," she replied somberly. James studied her wavering behavior. She appeared to understand the negative effects of war as she compassionately watched the soldiers from afar. Bombay was known for sporadic attacks by French allies, the Mysore. She had probably not only heard explosions throughout her years in India, but from visiting the hospital with her uncle, she would have seen the effects of war and what they did to a person both physically and mentally.

He escorted Jane towards her carriage, following behind Jenny and Toby.

"Did you enjoy your evening, Miss Sawyer?" he lightheartedly asked, despite the solemn mood. She gazed up at him.

"I've never experienced such a delightful night as I have tonight." She stopped outside the carriage and regarded him. "Thank you, captain."

"Thank you, Miss Sawyer."

"Oh, James?" Jenny called out from the carriage to him. He was so consumed with Miss Sawyer he hadn't noticed Jenny and Toby part ways. "Will you and Thomas be coming out to the orchards tomorrow?"

He broke his gaze from Miss Sawyer to address Jenny. "We're shipping out again tomorrow morning,"

"How long will you be gone for?" Miss Sawyer stared up at him with a mixture of hope and sadness.

"A little over a week. Since we had to come back early for the festival, we're finishing our original assignment."

Disappointment filled her face.

"Then, if all goes well, I'll see you before we leave." She offered a small smile. James's heart felt it was being ripped into pieces with the dawning that Miss Jane had approximately two more weeks on the island before she made her way to London. His smile didn't reach his eyes as the weight of her departure grew heavy on him.

"I'll make certain to see you before you leave." He stepped forward and held her hand in his, gently lifting it up to his lips. Softly, he kissed her warm skin. His heart quickened when he heard her catch her breath. She gaped at him with her beautiful blue-green eyes. Those eyes that he'd ingrained into his memory to be certain he'd never forget. Not that he ever could, not with the warmth they carried.

"Miss Jane." He held her hand in his. With a crooked smile he spoke. "I'm forever grateful for your rash decision on the pier."

The corner of her full lips raised into a radiant smile. "Until I see you again, captain."

He helped her into the carriage and closed the door. The latch duly clamped shut. His hands clasped tight behind his back. He struggled thinking he may never see her again. He took a hard swallow, and disappointedly watched the carriage roll away into the darkness. Disheartened, he trudged his way to the docks where the Ebony devotedly awaited him.

James sat at his ebony carved desk studying his map. He had a few minutes to spare to review their route before they left the harbor. A knock sounded at his door.

"Enter," he called, his forehead resting against his hand.

"Captain, sir." The young sergeant set foot in his cabin.

"Yes, Clifford?"

"I've been instructed to give this to you, sir."

James looked up to see the sergeant hand him a box tied with a green ribbon. His eyes tightened as he stared at the carefully wrapped package.

"Who's it from?"

The young sergeant turned a shade of red as he shifted from foot to foot. "She didn't give me her name, sir." He fidgeted with the buttons on his jacket.

James wasn't sure what to make of the young sergeant's discomposure. He's never yelled at Clifford for not knowing a person's name. Nor had he ever condemned the poor fellow. What could possibly be the cause of his— it struck him.

"Did the woman have brown hair, blue-green eyes that transfixes you, and a radiant smile?" *Leaving you feel disheveled inside?* James thought to himself.

The sergeant brightened. "That's her!"

He let out a hearty laugh. He understood exactly how the young man felt. Promptly he untied the green ribbon. *Of course she chose green,* James chortled. Opening the box to reveal what was inside, he began to chuckle with amusement. Clifford peered around him to see what could be humorous. He squinted his eyes with confusion.

"A mango, sir?"

James grinned and picked up the mango, reading the note underneath to himself.

For good luck.
Sincerely, The most graceful woman you've ever known,
Jane Sawyer

He foolishly smiled.

"Clifford," James set the mango on the desk in front of them. "This is more than just a mango." He grinned at the sergeant. "This here is our lucky mango."

James let out a hearty laugh at Clifford's muddled expression.

Jane sat dazed under the shade of a large tree out in the yard. Birds were singing as they flew merrily around her. The overcast clouds dimmed the sun's radiance. She fanned herself from the day's heat. It was going to be a hot day for it had yet to be noon. The unopened book sat on her lap as she became consumed with her thoughts. It had been seven days since she saw Captain McCannon last. The anticipation of seeing him before her trip gnawed at her. The mast of their ship had been repaired and the sails were close to being sewn. Their captain told her uncle the day prior that they hoped to make way in another six days. Six! To be precise, five now.

"I thought I'd find you out here." Her uncle eased his way in front of her. His charcoal hair lightened in the sunlight. He propped his cane down and leaned his weight onto it, studying her thoughtfully. "Jane, you've been quiet all week. What's been on your mind?"

She pulled a piece of grass out of the ground. Twisting it in her fingers, she leaned back against the cool bark of the tree's trunk and gazed up at him. There had been two things on her mind, the delivery at the orchard and Captain McCannon.

"I can't stop reflecting on Poppy's delivery," she decided to say. The other topic, she felt uncertain how to address.

"Poppy, the goat?" he asked, resting against a large rock on the side of her. She twisted her body to face him.

"Yes," Jane grabbed another piece of grass, "I thoroughly enjoyed myself. I found it gratifying in a rewarding way."

Her uncle brought his cane in front of his hands and leaned on it as he listened.

"You see, if I could feel that with a goat's delivery, how do you suppose I'd feel with people?" she pondered aloud, while twisting the grass.

He twisted his cane as he mused. "That is a lot to consider."

"I suppose," she moved her legs to her side, "if I can't be a surgeon and save lives then what if I helped bring life into this world? Wouldn't that be just as gratifying?" she smiled.

"I believe it may even be more gratifying." His green eyes twinkled proudly, behind his spectacles. "I think you would make an exceptional midwife."

"I was hoping you'd say that." She smiled and leaned against the tree's trunk, pleased with his approval.

"Now if I may be bold and offer you a conflicting predicament?"

She straightened, "Of course."

He gave a curt nod. "We're in London, you're attending a ball, dancing with a dashing gentleman and let's say he asks you what your passions are in life."

Jane smiled confidently; she knew where he led with the question.

"What do you say?"

"By then I would hope my answer is being a midwife."

He nodded. "How do you suppose he'll respond?"

"Uncle, if the gentleman should be dismayed by my passion, he clearly isn't the gentleman for me."

"Very wise." He leaned back and peered down at her with his eyes full of years of wisdom. "But suppose you're madly in love with him and he doesn't want you to pursue it, what would you do?"

"Oh, I pray that never happens."

She didn't know what she'd do. There was only one gentleman that she dared ask his thoughts regarding one of her greatest desires. If she had waited to ask him the question now, and he disregarded it—she inhaled a sharp breath. It would be more than devastating.

"There's a chance your suitor will try to persuade you to change your mind. There will be many crossroads that you'll face in life. When the time comes to decide, you must be true to yourself and with the gentleman you court." He leaned towards her. "Now, I want you to be mindful of these next few things. The gentleman you court may want his wife at home, tending to their children instead of leaving frequently at odd hours to aid in a delivery. Or he may find the profession perfectly fine and embrace it." He took a heavy breath and wiped his forehead with a handkerchief. "Be honest to him and most importantly with yourself regarding what's in your heart." He tucked the handkerchief back into his pocket. "By doing so, you shall succeed in discovering a well-suited husband."

She knew that was the only way she could sift the wheat from the tares. "I'll be forthright, Uncle."

He nodded his approval. "I'll always support, you Jane, with whatever you choose to do." His face drew down. "After your parents' death, you came to me broken. You were so distraught, you hardly ate, always wanting to sleep and you cried every time I left. It was as if your light had burnt out. Days turned into weeks. Weeks turned into months and I slowly saw the light within begin to glow. There was hope." His eyes began to glisten as he gazed at her. "Through the years, that spark began to grow until one day it ignited into a lovely bright, warm blaze. I absolutely love that fire within you, Jane. After experiencing that with you, I vowed that when the day came for you to find a husband, I would make certain you found a gentleman who not only kept your fire burning but continued to help it grow. I vowed to protect you from anyone who'd dare put out the flames . . ." He looked down at his cane then stared into her eyes. "Which is why I had Major Humphrey, Captain Withifer, Captain Blythe, and a few others, keep tabs on you while I was preoccupied at the hospital." He let out a heavy sigh as though the truth of the matter had weighed on him.

Swallowing the shock, she managed to speak. "You did?" Jane leaned back and blinked dumbfounded. "Why, all this time, I thought it was because they took me in as if I were family."

"They did indeed, very much so," he nodded assertively. "Which is why they were eager to fulfill my wishes."

She took to her feet. She paced in front of him, trying to understand how she didn't see his part in any of it.

"But why? Forgive me for asking—but didn't you trust me?"

"Of course I trusted you, and I still do." He gazed into her eyes. "I just didn't trust them. It was very difficult for me to leave you alone, especially after the horrible rumors I had heard flowing through the hospital. Soldiers breaking young ladies' hearts. I felt helpless."

She knew exactly what he meant. She's heard the rumors and stories, which helped her steer clear from certain gentlemen at the dances, though she suspected they avoided her as well.

"You're not a plain young woman, Jane. You're a rare jewel that many of the gentlemen are lured too. After my recruitment of those fine gentlemen, I was finally able to sleep peacefully, knowing you'd be protected while I worked."

Her mouth dropped. She had no idea the worry and stress he carried regarding her. She knew he loved her, that he would do anything to make her happy, and safe, but not to that extent. She sat back down on the grass and stared at him. Too surprised to feel or say anything.

"I could easily do the same for you in England but it is time you do things on your own. Which is why I promise I'll do my best to let you act for yourself but only if I get to have a say with your final decision. If I find that he doesn't embrace all of you, then I won't hesitate to put an end to it."

She nodded, wiping a tear that fell down her cheek. "Agreed."

Her uncle huffed in a settled manner.

"I must say, you've been more of a light to me than you could ever know." She chuckled at her fragile state and wiped away another tear. "I appreciate you opening up to me,"

Her uncle watched her with glistening eyes. "When we get to England, we'll look into all the requirements for you to become a midwife."

"How did I get so fortunate to have you in my life?" She wrapped her arms around him. They embraced each other a moment before she pulled back. Her uncle dabbed his eyes.

"I'm the fortunate one." He gave her his loving smile that squinted his soft eyes. "I love you, my dear Jane."

"I love you, too." She gave him a peck on the top of his head.

Echo of horse hooves galloped up the cobblestone drive.

Excitement soared through her. "Are they back?" she exclaimed.

"Captain McCannon?" her uncle asked, watching her closely.

"Yes. They're due any day now." She swiftly grabbed her book and looped her arm through her uncle's.

"Come," she exclaimed with excitement.

Elaine scurried to them through the back door.

"There's been another attack!" she rushed. "One of the merchant ships heading for England was burned."

"And what of the people aboard?" her uncle pressed.

Elaine grew ghastly pale as the blood drained from her face. "They were killed." Her voice barely rose above a whisper. She stared past Jane with a distant harrowing gaze. Jane gasped. Her uncle bounded past them to Governor Keaton's study.

The ladies grasped each other's hands for support.

"Was there any news of Captain McCannon's ship?" Jane asked anxiously.

Elaine swallowed and nodded. "They were the ones that discovered it. They flagged down another merchant ship to send the news as they continued their search for the French vessel."

Her chest tightened.

"Richard's delaying his voyage so he can aid with any protection we need. The fort is on high alert. All the merchant ships are sitting ducks as the few ships we have are patrolling the island, unable to assist them. They have no protection until the fleet that Captain James requested arrives."

Her stomach grew queasy, as she understood the danger they'd be in if they continued their journey. The French frigates are hunting in the merciless waters and they could be next.

"I need to speak with my uncle." Fearing for their lives, Jane left Elaine and knocked on Governor Keaton's door.

"Come in," the governor's voice rang out.

"Excuse the interruption." She stepped into the solemn room as Governor Keaton, her uncle, and a soldier hovered over the governor's desk peering at a map. Her uncle glanced at her with a vexed expression. He stepped away from the desk and pulled her aside to the corner of the room.

"It's worse than what Elaine mentioned." He kept his voice low and calm as though they had been casually discussing their day. Jane knew he didn't want to frighten her but the alarm in his eyes told her of his distress.

"The French have attacked more than this merchant ship. It's been happening for a few months and it appears the attacks have been increasing." He paused to draw in a breath. "We're not going to England this week. Not under these circumstances. Oxford gave me five weeks to settle in before I start teaching. We'll use however much of that time needed here." Her uncle quickly added, "Governor Keaton has invited us to stay as long as we need until the fleet arrives to aid in our journey."

Jane numbly stared at him. Bobbing her head, she gave him a quick embrace.

"I just pray they catch the French vessels before any more lives are lost," she whispered, watching the governor continue his conversation with the soldier.

"As do I." Her uncle softly kissed her forehead and walked her to the door. "I'll speak further with you after supper."

She squeezed his hand and left the room, gently closing the door behind her. Standing in the empty hallway, she pressed her trembling hand to her chest. *Oh, please keep them safe,* she prayed.

Chapter Eighteen

"Are you ready, Jane?" Elaine called from outside the stables. Jane finished buckling her horse's reins and walked him out of the freshly swept barn into the sunshine. Jenny, Elaine, and Captain Norton already sat poised on their horses in their regular day apparel as the heat of the day would make their riding attire uncomfortable for their adventure. At least that's what Elaine had explained to her earlier that morning during breakfast. Jane adjusted her thin sole shoes before taking a step onto the mounting block. Once saddled, she shifted her skirts.

"We'll head south through the thicket," Elaine called, leading the way with Captain Norton by her side.

"Have you ever seen humpback whales before?" Jenny rode by her side.

"Never. Do you suppose we'll see any?"

"I hope so. This time of year, they migrate here to give birth to their calves before swimming off to who-knows-where. This beach is one of several on the island, but it leads up to a ledge that overlooks the ocean. The cliff is low enough for us to get a close-up view of any sea life."

"I hope we'll be fortunate enough to see them."

"If not today, then perhaps tomorrow or the day after that," Jenny offered, with a reassuring smile.

"I'll certainly have plenty of time now." She smiled back.

Jenny and Jane continued to converse as they trailed behind the couple in front.

"This is it," Elaine called over her shoulder. Captain Norton jumped from his horse to assist Elaine. They were completely smitten, giggling with each other regarding some sort of secret between them.

Jenny rolled her eyes at Jane, causing her to smirk. In an unladylike fashion, they hopped from their saddles and hung their horse's reins loosely on a nearby bush. Cautiously, stepping through thick vegetation, they pushed branches and leaves aside to make way. After a few minutes of their clothes and hair being snagged by the assailing, prickly limbs, they reached a black, rocky beach. Low rumble waves crashed against the boulders, spraying salt water into the air.

Jane stared in awe, scanning the dark jagged rocks. "I've never seen a black beach before."

"The island is an inactive volcano. This is all volcanic rock and sand," Elaine stated. "Across the beach is a path that will lead us up towards the ledge." She pointed across the treacherous surface towards a lush green hillside. It must have been overgrown with the flora as Jane couldn't see any signs of a dirt path.

Captain Norton held out his hand and led Elaine across the black terrain. Jenny and Jane followed in a slow steady manner, carefully watching their footing.

Jane pictured herself as a turtle awkwardly maneuvering over the rocks, lagging slowly behind. How she wished she had thicker soles. *Ouch!* She stepped on a pointed stone that shot a sharp pain through her foot like a dagger stabbing her heel. Why didn't Elaine mention wearing sturdier shoes for this "stroll along the beach"? She leaned against a boulder to examine her wound as it throbbed against her stocking. The leather soles of her shoes were far too thin for the perilous beach.

"Are you alright, Jane?" Jenny called. She had already made it across.

"I'm fine!" she called back. "I'll meet you up there!"

She slid off the slipper. *Surely, a rock had sliced through the material.* Holding her shoe in one hand, she balanced on her leg while raising her throbbing foot. As she went to examine the painful spot, a startling sound of crunching rocks came from behind. She straightened. Her heart leaped into her throat. The sound grew louder and faster as the mysterious creature approached. *Could it be a cheetah?* Her hand clutched her shoe against her chest. *Leopard, bear, hyena . . . crocodile?* Jane's heart pounded. *But they don't exist on the island!* Hastily she whirled around to see what predator it could be. Her shriek was muffled by the crashing waves resonating through the air.

Suddenly she was swept off her feet in one swift motion. Her head spun as she felt weightless. Cradled in strong arms, she was being carefully carried across the treacherous rocks. Tightly she clung to the man's broad shoulders in fear she'd fall onto the besieging stones. His stride was steady, easing over the uneven terrain. Taking courage, she relaxed her hold, daring to peek at the gentleman. Her breath caught as he stared adoringly at her.

"James," she breathed as her stomach came alive with tiny little flutters.

Calmness threaded her veins as they gazed into each other's eyes. His face brightened, flashing her a crooked smile. Instinctively, she reached her hand to his face and ran her thumb across his irresistible dimple. Tiny stumps of grain brushed against her thumb. The dimple began to disappear as his pace came to a slow-moving halt. His eyes flashed something that caused her heart to beat faster in her chest. The thumping in her head escalated as their stare intensified. Jane's breathing grew staggered. She attempted to swallow the burning that grew inside of her but failed as it magnified. With all the self-control she could muster, she hastily withdrew her hand. Dazed, she took a deep breath, and closed her eyes briefly, breaking away from his gaze. Gradually, he started to tread along the rocks again while her heart slowed back to its rhythm.

He began to chuckle. "Never in my life have I had the honor of smelling a lady's shoe," Captain McCannon said, his voice muffled.

Smelling a lady's shoe? Jane's head shot up with dawning. She completely forgot she still carried it in her hand. Mortified was an understatement to how she felt as it now angled in front of his nose! Promptly she grabbed it with her other hand and reached down to slide it back over her stocking-covered foot. Heat ignited from her chest to her cheeks.

"I hope it smelt as wonderful as you thought a lady's shoe ought," she teased, avoiding any more eye contact.

She stared out across the white foam that had formed from the rolling water. Her stomach mimicked the waves crashing and turning inside her while held in his remarkably strong arms. *Just a few more feet till I'm back on soft ground,* she breathed, trying to keep her focus from being so intimately close to him.

"You know, I must admit I've never taken the time to ponder the smell of a lady's shoe. Pray tell, what would I have thought?" Humor filled the captain's voice. Jane bit her lip to keep from smiling.

"Only of the sweet aroma of flowers, of course."

"Well, that was exactly what I smelled!" He held a cheeky smile.

She let out a chuckle. "I expect nothing else from my shoe." She smiled, locking eyes with him once more. He cleared his throat. The spark flashed before his eyes—again. Gently he lowered her on the sturdy ground. Facing each other, he steadied them with his hands on her waist. Jane held her breath from his touch. Footsteps scrunched on the rocks causing them both to take a step back from the pull between them.

She glimpsed towards the grinding of rocks. "Lieutenant Fletch!"

"Miss Sawyer!" He was breathing heavily. "I see . . . James has taken . . . the honor of carrying you across the beach." The lieutenant took a few more deep breaths.

She studied the slightly hunched lieutenant collecting his breath. "Are you alright?"

"Fine, fine." He straightened, clasping his hand on Captain McCannon's shoulder. "I just didn't get the epistle saying James and I were racing to get here."

Captain McCannon grinned broadly at Lieutenant Fletch and shrugged as they began to climb their way up the hillside. Her foot throbbed with every step. She strolled along, hiding her limp under her skirts.

"That's twice I've beat you this past month," the captain taunted.

Lieutenant Fletch rolled his eyes. "It's amazing what one can conquer with a certain chess piece." He flashed him a sly smile as he pressed forward.

Chess piece? "Captain, do you carry around a chess piece?" Jane asked.

Lieutenant Fletch barked out a laugh. The captain adjusted the sleeves of his frock and shot a look of warning to his friend.

"Something like that," he muttered.

"Miss Sawyer, you should ask him which piece he holds dearly," the lieutenant provoked.

Jane raised an expectant brow towards the captain. He shook his head at his friend.

"Are you not going to tell me, captain? Or do I have to guess?"

"Definitely guess! I'm curious to see what you would say," Lieutenant Fletch chimed.

Captain James ran his hand through his hair. His finely defined jaw shifted forward in a stubborn manner.

"Alright, then," Jane pressed. "Is it a knight?" A knight sounded fitting. A knight's courageous, faithful, brave, and . . . she glanced over at Captain McCannon . . . a bashful voice in the back of her mind spoke, *extremely becoming.*

The captain adjusted his cravat.

"Nope," Lieutenant Fletch beamed.

"A castle?" That could work. Castles are durable and protective.

"Wrong again!" Lieutenant Fletch was thoroughly enjoying the game. His steps came with a bounce after her answer. Captain McCannon now fidgeted with his sleeves and ran his hand through his hair nervously. His suntanned cheeks hinted a little pink hue. *Could he be embarrassed?* This piqued Jane's curiosity even more.

"Oh," she exclaimed excitedly. Both Captain McCannon and Lieutenant Fletch glanced her way with two opposite expressions. Lieutenant Fletch's eyes danced with laughter. His smile broadened while Captain McCannon's eyes darted down at the ground when her stare locked with his. He dragged his hand across his pink cheek to his chin.

"A king!" It had to be, a king was full of integrity and was extremely decisive. A natural leader.

"Getting warmer." Lieutenant Fletch laughed mischievously.

Really? Jane was certain that's what he'd carry.

"Jenny!" the captain hollered, breaking away from the interesting conversation.

What was he hiding?

"James! Thomas!" Jenny embraced each of them.

"It's good to see you, James. Thomas." Captain Norton clasped each of their hands. Elaine offered them a warm smile as she replaced her hold on Captain Norton's arm.

"How did you know to find us here?" Jenny asked.

"Doctor Duncan informed us," Lieutenant Fletch explained with a cheeky grin.

"We had some pressing matters that we needed to discuss with Governor Keaton, before crossing paths with the doctor," Captain McCannon eyed Captain Norton who exchanged a knowing nod.

"So, is it true? Have the whales arrived?" Lieutenant Fletch inquired, shifting the severity of the mood.

"I've heard from Mister Rutkin that he spotted some feeding east of the island early this morning. So far we've had no sightings," Captain Norton stated.

"This is the best spot, if any, to watch. It's one of their feeding grounds," Captain McCannon remarked.

"That's exactly what I told Richard earlier today," Elaine rang, ogling up at her captain. Captain McCannon's eyebrows shot up. Jane watched him give Captain Norton a questioning look from Elaine's informal use of his name. The captain shrugged and grinned down at the devoted woman by his side. The corner of Captain McCannon's mouth twitched as he glanced to Lieutenant Fletch who rocked on the heels of his feet and shook his head.

"Come, have a seat!" Jenny called from the ground. Everyone obliged, making themselves comfortable on the tall grass. They gazed across the twinkling vast, blue sea. The sound of waves crawling over the rocks and colliding into the barriers drifted up to where they sat on the cliff.

Jane could taste the salty air as a breeze blew tiny little droplets their way. She tried to recollect some of the drawings of humpback whales she's seen from her old study books. Never had she seen a whale in person.

She rotated her ankle as the bruise on her foot developed its own heartbeat. Leaning to her side to adjust her shoe, her hand landed on top of Captain McCannon's hand. Heat flushed through her, as she gaped up at him with surprise. His eyes bore down on her intently, making her cheeks burn even more fervently. She flicked her gaze away, quickly removing her hand from his. A tingling sensation lingered on the tips of her fingers from their touch.

"Look!" Jenny exclaimed.

Grateful for the distraction, Jane peered across the water in the direction Jenny pointed to. Over one hundred yards out into the ocean, a gray whale expelled mist forcefully from its hump high into the sky. A few feet away from it, another whale breached up out of the water, exposing its thick, white pleats on his underside. Crashing into the surface, water splashed and leapt, scattering far across the sea.

"Oooh," a few of them exclaimed.

Jane gawked at the sight. *They're enormous.* Their wing-like flippers alone had to be three times her height in length.

"Oh! There's another one," Elaine called with excitement.

Loud blows resounded as a third whale slapped its tail repetitively against the sea. Arching its body, it dove smoothly under the dark water. Its massive tail fin flung high into the air before swiftly sinking below.

"Wait for it," Lieutenant Fletch called. Everyone stared at the glistening sea with anticipation. Jane's breath quickened as she surveyed the choppy water. *What were they waiting for?* Then, in the blink of an eye, a whale leapt from the ocean's surface, soaring high into the air and twisted its torso back, throwing its body against the blue sea. Another loud blow sounded. Tremendous amounts of water darted and showered drops into the air and across the area from where he crashed.

Cheers rang out as they all applauded. They continued to gape at the eye-catching show with oohs and ahhs. The performance was soon over, as one by one the whales began to descend through the blue curtain. The last of the whales tarried before lifting its tail out of the water, waved its final goodbye and elegantly dipped into the ocean below to join the others.

"That had to have been one of the most magnificent phenomena I've ever seen," Jane breathed.

"Was this your first time whale watching, Miss Sawyer?" Captain McCannon studied her.

"It was." Her voice hitched in her throat under his stare as he studied her.

"How long do you gentlemen get to stay before you leave for patrol?" Jenny asked.

Disappointment cast over Captain McCannon's face.

"We leave tomorrow," Lieutenant Fletch replied, solemnly.

"But you've only just arrived today!" Elaine's startled tone matched Jane's unsettling feelings.

Disheartened, Captain McCannon looked to Captain Norton. "There are a few details we'll need to discuss before we leave tomorrow."

The hair on Jane's arms stood. He sounded so somber; she almost didn't recognize him without his lightheartedness.

"James, are the attacks getting worse?" Jenny asked with worry.

"They are," his voice was gruff.

"How so?" Elaine pressed.

"Well, the attacks are more frequent. Being out to sea for as long as they have, they've become more desperate in stealing from the merchants to replenish their own supplies and," he paused, taking a glimpse at Jane, he winced, and pressed his lips tightly together as though he didn't want to continue.

"And what?" Elaine inquired.

"Killing the passengers," Lieutenant Fletch added. Everyone solemnly cast their eyes towards the sea. A cool breeze blew through the group causing Jane to shudder by the chill of its salty touch. The thoughts of innocent lives being slaughtered, cut deep into her consciousness as she knew she and her uncle could easily be one of the victims had her uncle chosen not to stay. Captain McCannon peered at her, catching the motion. His brow furrowed with concern as if he knew what crossed her mind.

"It appears we have some strategizing to do," Captain Norton broke the grim silence. "Shall we?" he offered, helping Elaine to her feet. Jenny and Lieutenant Fletch were quick to follow behind. Captain McCannon stood, reaching for Jane's hand and assisted her off the matted grass. Standing, she shook the now dull pain in her heel.

"Miss Sawyer," he quietly spoke, watching the others trickle through the thick fern that led to the beach. "May I have a moment?" urgency heavily coated his words.

"Yes, of course." Jane couldn't help the unsettling feeling that stirred from his strained demeanor.

He began to pace in front of her with his hands behind his back, staring at the ground with concentration.

"I beg your pardon, captain, but am I supposed to offer you a salute at this given moment?" she teased, attempting to lighten his unusual manner.

"Miss Sawyer," his voice was low and rough as if it were constricted in his throat. His pacing ceased and he faced her, his brows drawn together like what he was about to confess tortured him. "I know how frightened you must feel with all the attacks," he proceeded, his hands wrung out in front of him, "but I promise, the day your ship leaves the harbor, my ship will be there. I can only escort you out as far as we're permitted, which is a short distance in comparison to your voyage. I'll do all that is in my power to protect you and your uncle. If I had my way, I'd escort you all the way to London just for the peace of mind of knowing that you were safe."

Jane blinked in surprise. His words, compiled with her heart echoing in her head, made it difficult for her to reply. "Captain." Wanting nothing more than to get rid of all his worries, she instinctively reached for his arm. "My uncle has insisted that we stay here at Jamestown until the reinforcements arrive."

She went to pull her hand away but he clasped it into his, enfolding it toward him while taking a step closer. Staring at her hand cradled tenderly in his, her breath quickened, matching the rise and fall of his chest.

"You mean," his voice lowered into a deep husk. "You'll be staying? For a few weeks?"

She felt the warmth that illuminated off his chest resonating in her heart. She turned her gaze to his collar, trying to maintain her composure. "Yes . . . Captain." Her voice felt unfamiliar as she spoke feebly in a hushed tone.

"It's James."

"What?" she breathed, her eyes flickering up to his. Fervently he stared back. The breeze whisked at the tall grass brushing against her dress. Waves rolled into the rocks below. All the noise faded into silence as time suddenly stood still. Her legs grew weak as he leaned closer to her.

"Just simply, James," he whispered, taking another step forward.

She tilted her head back, keeping her gaze locked with his. "James?" she breathed.

His eyes combed over her face, pausing on her lips. Her heart raced, eagerly responding to the same desire she felt raging within. Slowly he brought his hand up to her chin. Her skin felt soft, cradled in his well-worn fingers as he tenderly clasped it, tilting her head further back until it angled perfectly towards his slightly parted lips. She caught a staggered breath as he leaned forward, tilting his head ever so slightly to the side.

"You two are slower than molasses!" Lieutenant Fletch yelled somewhere from the bottom of the trail.

She took a step back, breaking from their daze. Her head spun. She clasped her dress in hopes to control the trembling feeling. Timidly she glanced back at him. His eyes fixed on her, appearing clouded over.

"James?" she asked. He blinked, taking in a deep breath.

"Yes," his voice hoarse. "Shall we?"

They eased their way down the trail with a peaceful feeling lingering between them. Reaching the treacherous beach, they discovered no one in sight. James offered his hand with a soft smile. She welcomed his support, shyly keeping her eyes away from him. After a few steps on the sharp-angled rocks, he gripped her hand, motioning her to stop.

"Jane?" Her heart raced from the gentle way he spoke her name. She looked up to see his half-dimple smile. "May I?" He raised his brows at her and held his hands up, indicating he wanted to carry her. She scanned the beach in front of them. They weren't even halfway across. She bit her bottom lip, contemplating what decision to make. Her cheeks flushed as his smile broadened, watching her decide. She pictured herself in his strong, sturdy arms. She felt weightless as he held her close. Even light-headed. She didn't trust herself with what she may do. Last time, she felt his irresistible dimple. Her breaths shortened and grew shallower.

"This is fine. We're almost there," she voiced indifferently. James let out a chuckle.

He began taking one step to her every two in an attempt to prove a point. She knew she was painfully slow but she was determined to get there on her own two feet. She eyed his smirk while he continued holding her hand, taking one long stride before pausing for his next.

"If you'd like to go on ahead without me, I can meet you there," she offered, peering at him from the corner of her eye.

He appeared to be thinking as he paused before his next big step. "As tempting as it sounds, I think it's best if I stayed by your side. I'd hate to see your pace without me."

She glared sideways at him, causing him to give a deep-hearted laugh.

Leaves rustled ahead and Lieutenant Fletch came out impatiently.

"We are on a tight schedule, James," he stated eagerly.

James grinned up at him.

"Impeccable timing, Thomas!" With a mischievous smile, he bent down and swooped Jane up into his arms, cradling her close to his body.

"What are you—" Jane began to protest.

"As Thomas reminded me, we are on a tight schedule." He winked at her, sending flutters from her stomach to her dazed head.

She had no rebuttal as she concentrated on a bush ahead of them. Anything, to help keep her mind distracted from being cradled in his arms.

Chapter Nineteen

Jane began tossing and turning in her bed, trying to get comfortable. How was she supposed to sleep with all the unnerving fluttering? *Honestly,* she puffed out a frustrated breath. *It was as if someone released little winged creatures from their cages—all at once.* Ever since Captain James effortlessly cradled her close to his body, the feeling hadn't ceased. On top of the disrupting feeling, she yearned to see him again. Just two more weeks until he came home. *Two* long, dreary weeks.

Rolling over on her side, she tucked the blankets between her legs. *Ugh!* That wasn't helping. Tossing to the opposite side, she pulled the blankets under her feet. She laid there for an uncomfortable moment. Lifting her head, she hit her lumpy feather pillow. She laid on her back and began to relax in her soft cottony sheets. The flapping wings settled in her stomach, as if they too were drifting off to sleep. Her mind settled, blurring the events of the day. A crisp image of a handsome tan face with a crooked dimple smile flashed before her mind's eye. Ever so slowly, he leaned down towards her lips. The flutters awoke, accelerating at full force, sending her stomach through a whirlwind. She squeezed her eyes tighter in hopes it would block the vision, but it only made it worse; for, as she did, his lighthearted laugh resounded through her mind. Her heart pounded against her chest, alerting her mind that sleep wasn't in the near future.

Jane flung the covers off and jumped out of bed. Tossing her braid over her shoulder, she slipped into her slippers and robe. Perhaps a warm cup of tea would do the trick, she hoped as she tiptoed to the servant's stairs that led to the kitchen.

Sitting in the candlelit kitchen, Jane took a sip of warm peppermint tea that she had brewed for herself. Inhaling the warm steam, her body slowly eased from the day's excitement. She felt the tea's calming aroma working, calming every flutter in her stomach. Everyone else in the house was peacefully asleep at the late hour and she desired nothing more than to be joining them soon.

Noises from the servant stairs echoed down to the kitchen. Padded steps creaked a wood plank. The steps grew faster and louder.

Whoever it could be was barreling down the steps at a rapid pace. Jane tightened her robe across her chest and held the dimly lit candle high in the air. Who on earth would be making such a ruckus at this hour? A dark figure stepped into Jane's candlelight. The hood of the dark cloak fell back revealing an anxious face. Her dark cloak draped over her pink muslin dress and her hair perfectly pinned on top of her head. Elaine walked further into the light, dressed as though she was going to church.

"There you are. We've been looking all over for you," she whispered. Startled, Jane drew back. Elaine took long strides and briskly blew out Jane's candle.

"Elaine," she protested. "I don't have any more matches." Elaine held her hand up in a commandeering way.

"Jane," she whispered hastily. "There's no time. Mama's about to come down any minute for her nightly snack. You'll need to go up the main stairway to your room. Hurry along and get dressed. They're all waiting for us by the stables."

"Who's waiting for us? Where are we—" the floor creaked above them. Elaine ran to the door that led to the grounds. Another creak sounded, this time it was a stair.

"Go," Elaine squealed.

Footsteps softly crept down the stairs towards Jane. Swiftly, she carefully placed her cup in the kitchen's dishpan and hurried out of the kitchen into the long dark hallway. She paused. There were no windows down the dreary hall, making it difficult for her to see what was in front of her. Blood rushed to her head, making her unbalanced in the darkness that consumed her. The eerie stillness of the night thickened the desolate corridor. She placed her hand on the wall for support and guidance as she adjusted her bearings. Her other hand still clung to the unfortunately blown-out candle. The wall had proved successful as she confidently quickened her steps while her eyes adjusted to the blackness. *The door to the study should be coming up about—now.* Jane's hand sloped down against the wood panel and brass knob. She proceeded, gently easing her hand along a picture frame then back to the wall. The coolness of the smooth wallpaper under her hand sent a chill up her spine.

I best wear a long-sleeved dress with the crisp night air, Jane thought to herself. She let out a shiver. She had yet to adjust to Saint Helena's chilly, fall evenings. Pressing her hand more firmly against the wall, she hurried along with anticipation of the next door. Ahead, branches swayed in front of a moonlit window towards the foyer. Her breath caught as its dark shadows crept across the marble floor. She slowed as a haunting feeling of someone lurking in the dark started to overcome her. *Too many novels,* she breathed to herself. A dish clattering to the floor in the kitchen echoed through the stillness. Jane jumped, pressing herself against the library door . . . *but the closed door was cracked open.*

She stumbled into the dark library. Strong hands came from behind, wrapping around her arms to catch her—or attack her! Her candle dropped to the rug with a thud. Her eyes widened in the moonlit room with a jolt of panic shooting through her body. Horrific memories of Lieutenant Howard flooded her mind as the hair on her neck stood on end. Jane attempted to scream, but it was useless as one of the mammoth hands quickly flew against her mouth, muffling her sounds. He held her firm against his warm body. Her heart hammered in her chest. She threw her hands to his in an attempt to remove the calloused, wide palm from her lips. He was strong! Her two hands didn't stand a chance against his brawny clutch. He was speaking to her but she couldn't make out what he muttered. All sense of reason had left her as she frightfully began to squirm in Lieutenant Howard's arms. His devilish grin flashed from her memory. *No!* She bit the man's hand. He let out a yelp.

"Jane!" he whispered hoarsely, keeping his hand to her mouth.

He was probably afraid she would scream for help. She puffed air through her nose. The fight wasn't over. Her blood pumped fiercely through her veins. Her heart accelerated as she screamed against his hand.

"Shush!" he breathed, pressing his hand firmly against her mouth.

Her nostrils flared as she continued to puff through her nose. Did he dare to shush her?! Furiously, she stomped on his foot with all her might, but it was hopeless. Her heel that was still tender from the rock now throbbed in her dainty slipper.

"Jane, easy there. It's me. It's me. It's alright," he husked. Recognition dawned on her. She froze in his arms.

"Jammm?" she muffled into his hand. Ever so slowly he lowered his hand.

"You have quite a fearsome bite," he whispered, rubbing his hand. Jane promptly turned toward him. Inches from his face, the moonlight exposed his apologetic expression. A quick shiver ran through her body, liberating her from the nightmare.

"Thank goodness it's you!" She threw her arms around his neck and sighed in relief. His body went rigid from her embrace. She had forgotten her manner of dress—or the lack there was. She hastily adjusted her loosened robe over her chemise.

"What are you doing here?"

Looking away, James cleared his throat. He opened his mouth to speak but quickly closed it as padded footsteps sounded down the hall. Swiftly, he grabbed her hand and moved the two of them behind the opened door. His back turned towards her, shielding them from whoever was about to enter. Tucked behind the door, she pressed her forehead against his back, trying to hide from her shame. Still holding her hand, James securely curled his fingers around hers, bringing her only the slightest of comfort. Had she been sitting in the gardens with him, in daylight, she would have cherished that his thumb was now caressing her skin as it ran back and forth. But her mind was more grounded than her heart as it screamed out warnings regarding their scandalous situation. She wasn't even modest as she was only in her nightgown! What would they assume? If they find the two of them together like this, her uncle would have his head!

"James," came a deep hoarse whisper. "James, are you in here?"

The muscles in her body relaxed; it was only Lieutenant Fletch. James pressed his fingers to his lips to warn her to remain quiet. Motioning her to stay, he stepped out from behind the door.

"There you are, you don't have to search any longer, Elaine found her. She'll be out soon. Come on."

Jane stood behind the door, breathing unsteadily until the pair of footsteps drifted into silence. Carefully, she closed the library door behind her and raced to her room to get dressed.

James held his horse's reins with a firm grip. His heart hadn't settled since she'd thrown her arms around him in the library. His stomach leapt into his throat when he began thinking how easy it could have been to embrace her back. The temptation was so strong, but he had stilled, not daring to move with how indecent the situation had been. What did she think of him, wandering in the home? She could hardly look at him after they spoke on the cliffs. Add her vulnerability of being in a nightgown, he'll be lucky to get a smile from her. His grip tightened. He should have known better than to listen to Miss Keaton's plea to search for her.

He flexed his sore, bitten hand in his glove. She certainly knew how to put up a fight. He glanced over and saw Thomas staring at him with his ridiculous mischievous smile. *Not this again,* he grumbled to himself.

He glanced up, watching Jane confidently stride with her vibrant curls loosely pulled back at the nape of her neck. Her brows rose with surprise as she observed everyone mounted on their horses. Everyone except him. She avoided looking in his direction.

"Jane!" Jenny whispered. "Isn't this exciting?"

Jane's brow arched with question. "Sneaking out?" she asked in a hushed tone. One of the horses snorted, stamping its foot impatiently.

"I didn't get a chance to tell her," Elaine explained, giving a sheepish smile.

Jenny nodded with understanding then exclaimed, "The Aurora Australis are shining tonight!"

James brought Jane's saddled horse to her side. She still looked confused.

"Also known as the southern lights," he whispered to her. In the dim moonlight he watched her cheeks darken. She looked at him briefly through her lashes before darting ahead.

"I've always wanted to see them," she directed at Jenny while eagerly lifting her skirts to take a step on the stool he set by her hem. "I didn't realize we'd see them this far north," she spoke under her breath.

His hands gripped her tiny waist to assist her up. She let out a surprised gasp that only he heard, causing him to still. She appeared flustered staring down at her lap while adjusting her footing and skirts. He tilted his head to the side remembering this reserved side of her a few weeks back—their first night at the plantation playing cards and on the pond in their rowboats. How he tried everything to get her to look at him. He swallowed, alleviating the parchedness. The same desperation from those times burned within him—if not more.

He leaned on her horse's side by her legs and stared up at her. She didn't turn his way, too fixated on the reins in her hands.

"Normally we aren't blessed with such a phenomenon," he spoke softly, only for her to hear. "It's only on rare occasions when the unimaginable happens and we become so fortunate that the colors travel further north," He offered her a smile when she peered at him from the corner of her eye.

He pulled down on the reins in her hand, causing her to lean closer to him. She looked to the ground as he took a step and his lips drew nearer to her ear.

"Truthfully," he husked. "Its beauty is the most captivating of all the sparkling lights in the firmament."

He could hear her breathing quickening, matching his own. Her lustrous eyes trailed down to him. He swallowed, staring earnestly in return. Her mouth parted then quickly closed as if she knew not what to say. Her horse turned its head towards him and blew out its nostrils. Patting the mare on its shoulder, he offered Jane a small smile and strode to his horse.

Mounted, he whispered to the others while they quietly conversed with each other, "Let's go."

They all set off at a steady trot away from the house across the manicured lawn. Their horses' hooves thudded softly across the padded ground. Once the home was out of sight, they cantered across a field up a large hill. James squinted in the dark, trying to make out each shape they passed. The waning crescent moon eliminated very little light before them, making it a prime time to see the lights but difficult to navigate through the ferns and trees.

He slowed his horse to a trot as they ascended a hillside. A large tree stood firm at the top of the mound, marking the spot he wanted them to be. From the top of the hill's clearing, they'd have an exquisite view of the southern horizon.

As Jane was the last to pass him, he hastily whispered to her, "Wait for me."

She raised her brow with questioning. He trotted his horse to the tree by the others. Jumping down he threw his gloves in his saddle bag and hurried over to her. Patiently she waited on her horse as the others left, disappearing into the darkness somewhere on the hillside.

"Would you care for some assistance?" he teased, grinning up at her. She bit her lip, holding back her smile. He loved it when she did that.

"No, thank you, I can manage."

Of course, she could. James lunged forward, grabbing her waist before she could hop down on her own. Easily, he glided her to the ground, bringing her face ever so close to his. He kept his stance, not wanting to be further apart from her. Her horse's tail flicked at him as though to remind him to behave himself. James rolled his eyes. If anything, he wanted to redeem himself.

"I want to apologize for earlier . . . in the library." She peered at his chin. "I was attempting to catch you—after you stumbled into the room. By no means did I intend to startle you like I had."

"What were you doing in the library?" The corner of her mouth lifted in a taunting manner.

The soft curve of her lips drew him closer like he needed to examine them more thoroughly. Remembering she had asked a question, he tore his eyes away and glanced at her curls, trying to remember what he was trying to say.

"Miss Keaton, she was determined about receiving help to find you." His eyes traced down to her beautiful curls. A few strands had escaped from her over her shoulder. Instinctively, he brushed the curls back. His fingers tingled as they grazed across her irresistibly, soft skin. Goosebumps arose in the moonlight from where he touched. "She . . ." he swallowed, trying to focus. "Mentioned it would take all night to find you." He riveted his eyes on hers, using all his strength to refrain from glancing at her full lips. The desire battled him, pleading to give into the temptation as he fought to maintain his focus on speaking with her. He was only to apologize, nothing else, he reminded himself.

"I imagine she did. There's no need to apologize."

Her gentle smile tugged at his gaze, defeating his weak fight, for his eyes eagerly surrendered to her lips. They were so soft and enticing. Desire filled him as he longed to feel them pressed against his. She tilted her chin up in an inviting manner, her eyes flicked to his mouth. His heart pounded in his ears.

"James!" Thomas cut through the darkness, breaking his trance. James exhaled the breath he had been holding. "Would you mind bringing the blankets? They're on Jenny's horse."

"In a moment," James hollered back. Jane bit her lip, holding back a smile, making his stomach tighten like a rope around a bollard.

"And James!" Thomas taunted. "Hurry up, man!"

James rubbed his face and let out a heavy sigh. "Thank you for understanding," he whispered. "About the library, I mean." Far as he was concerned, Thomas was a whole other issue.

She smiled, "Of course."

With the blankets in hand, they strolled a few feet to the top edge of the hill before it descended steeply down the other side. Jane paused, gaping at the scene before her. Her gaze brightened while sweeping over the view as if she were studying a piece of art.

"James," Thomas called from a few feet below them. "Just toss them to me."

He threw one of the two rolled blankets down to Thomas who was sitting next to Jenny. Further away on the dark hillside sat Richard and Miss Keaton. Never in a million years did he think those two would ever connect. He smirked, shaking his head at the thought.

"Come, Jane, James. We'll scoot over to make room for you two," Jenny offered.

"Jenny," Thomas whispered, exasperated.

Spreading out their blanket, she looked at him. "What?" she asked innocently, in the same hushed tone.

In the darkness, James saw Thomas shake his head with disbelief. James smirked at his friend's daftness. If he only knew.

He laid the blanket next to Jenny and followed Jane to sit next to her. They leaned back on their arms and stared across the horizon. It was a spectacular view. Down from where they sat, laid the dimly lit town. The hill was high enough up that they could see where the black water met the skyline. The luminous southern lights swayed a vibrant display of orange, pink, and green glow across the horizon, stretching further south of the ocean. The scattered, speckled stars shimmered bright in the dark sky as the moon scarcely made its presence. The lights were mesmerizing with their depth of color, but James kept finding himself distracted.

He stroked the wool threads of the blanket and took a deep breath in, trying to calm his nerves.

"This is so breathtaking," Jane whispered through the stillness of the night.

"I told you, you were going to love it," Jenny sweetly murmured.

Tall grass danced around them as the gentle wind swept through. He could feel Jane shiver next to him.

"Are you cold?" he asked softly. She grabbed hold of her cloak and pulled it tighter around her body.

"I'm fine, thank you. I just need to adjust my cloak." She offered him a bashful smile then continued to peer at the mesmerizing lights. "I'm told navigating by stars is fairly simple, but I'm overwhelmed by their countless numbers, I can't fathom how one's to do so."

James glanced at her. She was gazing across the sky, appearing to be on the hunt to find something particular. "Ah," her face brightened. "Is that the Southern Cross?" Her finger pointed up to the vast sky. He leaned closer to see if she indeed pointed to the small constellation.

"How many stars do you see in the crux?" he challenged. She bit her lip as she counted the bright stars that formed an x.

"Oh, I only see four," her voice dropped with disappointment.

"Yes, hence the name the False Cross." He scooted closer to her on the blanket with their arms touching each other. He focused on the stars to keep his concentration from solely being on her. "If you continue your gaze a little further south," he briefly reached across her and drew his finger down from where she had pointed, "you'll discover two bright stars—Alpha," he crossed to the other, "and Beta Centauri. Do you see them?"

"I do," she tilted her head to the side.

"Follow along their path and you'll come near Gamma Crucis, one of the brightest red stars in the night sky." James's gaze dropped down on her as she peered to where he directed. "He is the top star in our Crux constellation." His voice quieted as his eyes traced every feature of her face. "The one we keep a watch for while we navigate."

"I see—" her words caught when she turned towards him. His body tensed as he fought to keep focus.

"The sky is also our guide for the seasons," he husked. He swallowed, pushing aside the sudden desperation of wanting to be the only ones on the hill.

"Spring is my favorite season," Jenny spoke on Jane's other side. "That's when Andromeda's constellation makes her appearance." Fabric rustled together as Jenny shifted on her blanket. "Her story is one of my favorite love stories from Greek mythology." She let out a sigh. "Being rescued on the rock from Perseus before the monster Cetus could kill her, such chivalry."

James laid on his back and chuckled to himself.

"Yes, well we shall never forget your love for that story," Thomas's words dripped with sarcasm.

"Please, it's a great story," Jenny defended.

James smiled at Jane who looked to him perplexed.

He answered her questioning stare. "Jenny's love for the story ran so deep, she used to act it out."

"*We used* to act it out," Thomas corrected, sitting further up.

"Yes, well you certainly didn't do a fine job with it," Jenny reprimanded.

Jane tucked her lips together, appearing to be holding in a laugh. "I'm not sure, I can picture any of this."

James chuckled when her shoulders began to shake with her laughter. "Then I better paint it for you." He sat up. The grass bristled against the blanket from the cool breeze. "When we were children, we loved going to the shore to skip rocks. On days when it was hot and muggy, we would go for swims." He glanced over at Thomas who laughed, shaking his head. "After studying a course of Greek mythology, Jenny decided to swim to a large rock from across the shore."

"She was immersed with the story," Thomas joined. "She hollered at us to save her from the sea monster."

Jenny tsked and straightened up. "Jane, don't let them fool you. Thomas and James were just as inspired with the stories. Sword fighting with sticks as though they were in battle."

James smiled from the memory. "Yes, well after a few attempts of—"

"Being coerced." James could sense Thomas rolling his eyes in the darkness.

He laughed, "Yes, being coerced into rescuing her from the rock, we decided we had enough."

"Coerced?" Jane then sat up.

"I did no such—" Jenny began to protest.

"Oh yes you did," Thomas interrupted. "Don't you remember threatening to tell our parents that we let the Millard's cows out of their pasture?"

Jenny remained silent. Jane raised her brow again at James.

He shrugged and gave her a guilty smile. "We did bring them home."

"After missing a day's worth of work in the orchard," Jenny muttered.

"Anyway, we had enough," Thomas continued. "And we decided to leave her—considering she had enough passion to fend for herself."

"That's when she started screaming hysterically that there really was a monster in the water," James laughed.

"It was a shark," Jenny piped in.

"It was a dolphin," James corrected. He knew a shark fin from a dolphin and it was definitely a dolphin.

"No, it was a shark," she stated firmly. "I saw its eye."

"Its eye?" Jane's voice caught in a conflicted laugh. She cleared her throat and looked away from Jenny, hiding her smile.

How could she still be persistent about its eye belonging to a shark? More curiously, how does she even know the difference between a dolphin's and a shark's eye? He chuckled.

"Yes, Jane. I saw its eye. He stared right at me while I sat on the cold rock. Then he had the audacity to stalk me for a time while I had to wait for over an hour until they arrived with the row boat."

"Just like Andromeda." Thomas gave her a cheeky smile. "We were your knights in shining armor."

Jenny let out a groan of irritation and laid back on the blanket.

Chuckling, Jane adjusted her cloak, her body trembled next to his. Swiftly, he removed his frock and draped it over her shoulders.

"But you'll freeze," she objected.

"It doesn't bother me. I've grown accustomed to the cool temperatures from our patrols."

She smiled up at him and wrapped herself further into his frock.

"Thank you," she whispered.

Tugging on the cravat around his neck, he managed to offer her a half smile.

"Miss Sawyer," Thomas casually called out. "Now that everyone on this hillside, besides Captain Richard, has the honors of addressing you by your given name, may I as well?"

James felt her shoulder shake as she laughed. "Very well."

"Thomas."

"Thomas." He could hear the smile in her voice as she replied.

"Excellent. Now, Jane," mischief threaded Thomas's tone. "Did you ever figure out the chess piece James holds so dearly to his heart?"

"I haven't," she mused.

James flashed Thomas an annoyed glare as Jane and Jenny stared at him expectantly. He could see Thomas's white smile against the darkness as he grinned from ear to ear. He didn't understand why he felt the need to insist on bringing it up to her.

"There is one piece that stands out, but I'm not certain if or how it's relevant." Jane bit her lip then continued. "Usually, the charm would represent someone or something dear and close and perhaps, it does. Is it a queen?"

Feeling vulnerable, James sat up and rubbed the back of his neck. His heart beat fiercely in his chest. *It's just a metaphor. Nothing more.* He wiped his palms on his legs.

"Right you are, Jane!" Thomas exclaimed when James didn't respond.

"James? You carry a chess piece around?" Jenny looked at him perplexed. "Since when?"

"Since Thomas mentioned I had one," James exasperated.

"Why would you say that, Thomas?" Jenny inquired.

"I have my reasons," he smirked. "But I do believe he holds a queen dear to his heart."

James shifted uncomfortably on the ground. He looked over at Jane who sat unnervingly still, staring in front of her like she was deep in thought.

"You can be so daft, Thomas." Jenny shook her head. Thomas gave her an innocent shrug.

Everyone grew quiet for a time, particularly Jane who still hadn't looked at him.

"Are you still cold?" he asked. She briefly glanced at him through the corner of her lashes.

"Not at all," she finally spoke, breaking the silence. Sliding his frock off her shoulders she handed it back to him. "I'm rather warm now, thank you."

James hesitantly accepted his coat back. She may be warm but she was acting cold towards him. Not even a minute went by before he noticed her shivering again.

"Would you like this back?" he offered, holding out his coat.

"I'm fine," she spoke steadily, though James could make out her chattering teeth. He began to feel panicked.

"Are you sure?" he pressed.

"Mmm hmm," she nodded, though he could see her chin quivering. James ran his hand through his hair. Why was she being so stubborn? She'd probably freeze to death just to avoid having his coat.

"I think it's best if we headed back. We're going to have an early start this morning." His voice wavered ever so slightly.

"Captain Richard, Miss Keaton, we're heading back!" Thomas hollered.

Miss Keaton groaned in the shadows with disappointment.

Jenny appeared disappointed as she stood with the help of Thomas. James reached down to assist Jane. After she stood, she immediately slid her hand back and took long graceful strides towards the horses with Jenny. James stood baffled. What was wrong?

"First fight?" Thomas asked, nonchalantly strolling to his side. James gave Thomas a stern look of warning. "Don't give me that look," he replied defensively. "I was only trying to help."

James scoffed at him. "Thomas, what makes you think she doesn't already know how I feel?"

"Please. In all the years I've known you, never once have you sought after a woman." He paused. "Though, I guess you've never really had to. They always came running to you, you lucky devil."

"I can't wait for the day until you find someone that unnerves you to the point you forget how to talk, let alone think. And when you do, I'll be more than happy to be there every step of the way." He patted his friend on the back.

Thomas laughed, "I can only imagine what you'd do, but rest assured it's never going to happen, not while I'm stationed here."

James nodded at the truth of the matter. There wasn't any lady on the island who captured their attention. At least not the way Jane had held his. As horrible as it was for her to go through the storm, meeting her was a godsend.

"You never know. Whenever it may be, I'll make certain to be a part of it." James gave Thomas a mischievous smile.

Gathering their blankets, they headed towards the horses. Everyone chatted cheerfully as they rode back towards the plantation. Everyone except for Jane and James.

❧ Chapter Twenty ❧

James vaguely noticed Jenny and Thomas saying their goodbyes as they parted ways to the orchard. He rode in silence next to Jane, following behind the conversing Richard and Miss Elaine.

"Jane," James whispered. "Is everything alright?"

She briefly glanced over at him, her face conflicted and pained. His stomach twisted with unfamiliar knots of agony.

"I hope so," she softly whispered.

She hopes so? He wanted to press further but feared they'd gain an audience.

They rode to the stables in daunting silence. Richard lit a lantern, assisting Miss Elaine off her horse and guided her animal into the dark stables. James steadily followed suit with haste in an attempt to calm the unfamiliar fire burning inside him.

Discreetly, they escorted the ladies across the manicured grass towards the kitchen's entry. From the corner of his eye, he watched Jane as she continued to stare ahead with a look of confusion. Her hand had laid limp and cold on his arm.

He stood in the doorway, Jane by his side. Richard and Miss Elaine had already disappeared into the darkness of the kitchen. Contemplating what to say to her, she glanced up at him.

His stomach dropped like an anchor through stormy waves. Uncertainty and hurt filled her eyes.

"Goodnight, captain," she whispered, staring at his chin.

He stood dumbfounded. There was such sadness in her voice. *Why?*

She drew a deep breath and turned to disappear into the kitchen's darkness, never to be seen by him for weeks. Instinctively his hand flew out to clasp hers. He wasn't going to let her go. Not like this. She peered at him, furrowing her brows.

"Wait," he whispered to her, before turning to his friend who stepped outside. "Richard, go on without me. I need a moment with Miss Jane."

He gave him a nod, and swiftly made his way back to his horse.

Grateful she'd walk with him, James led Jane towards a grove of trees that hid them from the estate's windows. He paused behind a large tree and faced her.

She continued to emotionally stay guarded as she stared past his shoulder.

"Jane, I can't depart knowing something's amiss. Have I offended or hurt you in any way?" Desperately, he held his breath waiting for her reply.

"I suppose the best way for me to answer your question is to have you answer mine." She looked directly into his eyes as though she pleaded for the truth. James's stomach tightened.

"By all means, please, ask away."

She nodded, keeping her manner tight and guarded. "I do not wish to offend you by asking this, but I must hear it from you."

He clasped his hands to keep them from fidgeting with the buttons on his sleeves. His heart beat rapidly in his chest as though he was facing a court martial.

Her eyes saddened while briefly turning his way. "It's in regards to the chess piece."

He let out a staggered breath of relief. Of course, she needed to know. He rubbed the back of his neck. *How to explain it?* Every time it was mentioned, he grew more and more uncomfortable with an unfamiliar yet somewhat exciting feeling.

"Is there someone waiting for you?"

Jane's solemn voice pierced through him, sucking the wind from his sails. His eyes widened, staring at her with disbelief.

He took a step back, "What do you mean?" he stammered.

"The chess piece—is she whom you've kept close to your heart . . . before I came?" Sadness and betrayal pained her face. "There were times in the beginning of our encounters when you were distant towards me, almost as though you were torn. Now I realize it was perhaps because there was someone else."

Dumbfound, he forced the words out, "Someone else?"

Plucking a leaf from a tree, she twisted it in her fingers as though it was his heart. She shook her head and turned her back to him while she wiped her eyes.

"Please, don't hide the truth from me anymore. I've already heard the rumor about your relationship."

"My relationship?" James raked his hands through his hair. Desperate to understand what she was told. "With whom?"

He watched her shake her head, unable to give him a response. Gently he placed his hands on her shoulders and turned her to face him, but she kept her eyes on the ground. Desperate to understand, he whispered, "Jane, please look at me."

Blinking back the tears, she met his gaze. Her watery eyes looked to him as if what he was going to say would hurt. "I know about you and Miss Harrlow," she whispered.

He closed his mouth and shook his head no. "What you know is a deceit. Jenny told me what Miss Harrlow said to you, about she and I being together. I know she assured you it wasn't true but with Miss Harrlow's lies, I can see how you would question my honor. Had I known you had any doubt, I would have corrected it right away."

"Then it's not true?" she asked.

"I would ask you to be more specific, but knowing what I know about her I would have to say no."

"Then you're not courting her?"

He winced at the thought of ever being with the woman. Not only would his life be turned for the worst but so would those around him. "No. I want you to hear this from me so you'll never have to question my honor ever again. We've never courted. Nor do I desire to. There has only been one lady that's captivated me and she's standing in front of me." Jane stared at him with wide eyes. He took her hand and held it close to his heart. "The only reason I appeared torn at times was, because I was." He lowered her hand and ran his thumb over her skin, amazed at how soft it felt to his touch. He gazed into her eyes. "Jane, I promised myself to stay clear from any young lady passing through because I never wanted to mislead them with any false hopes. I've seen firsthand what it could do to one's spirit. And after witnessing how it happened to my friend, I promised myself to avoid any situation that could result in a similar matter."

"Jenny," she whispered with dawning.

James closed his eyes and nodded. "Jane, I tried to stay away from you, but I couldn't." She cautiously studied him. "Truth be known, the impossible task of staying away only tormented me each time I was near you. It wasn't until I saw you before the festival that I knew I was fighting myself over a battle that only added agony to me and was pointless. It appears Miss Harrlow saw that shift in me and attempted to dissolve anything between us."

He carefully studied her, uncertain if he spoke too much. "My feelings for you run deeper than some infatuated encounter, Jane. Forgive me if my actions ever caused you to doubt my honor."

Her lips parted. Short shallow breaths passed through as she continued to stare at him. He shifted in his boots as the silence settled between them. He swallowed, trying to alleviate the dry sensation that consumed his throat.

"I'm sorry. I shouldn't have assumed like I did," she finally spoke with an unsteadiness in her voice. She cleared her throat and glanced away. "And what of the chess piece Thomas keeps mentioning?" She leaned against the tree's trunk. Shadows from the branches above danced across her face. Her shoulders began to tremble as she let out a little shiver and she crossed her arms as though to warm herself.

James removed his frock and took a daring step forward, holding it up as a peace offering. The corner of her mouth twitched. She leaned forward, gazing up at him while he wrapped it around her shoulders. He held the lapels snug around her then stared into her beautiful, vulnerable eyes.

"Do you remember that night at the governor's dinner party? The one after you fell into the harbor?"

She raised her brow, giving him a challenging look.

"Of course, you do," he muttered. "Well, Thomas and I got into a discussion of chess. I told him I needed my knight to help me out of a predicament and he became insistent that I needed a queen instead. I was going to argue but then you walked into the room."

She tilted her head to the side, her eyes squinting with confusion. Of course, she needed more information than that. Flustered, James rubbed the lapels with his thumbs. Staring down at his hands, he continued, "You see, Thomas was the queen and you were the knight. No!" His head snapped up. He looked into her bewildered eyes. What was he saying? "I mean Thomas was the knight and you, well . . ." James felt heat rush to his face.

"I was a chess piece to your game?" Jane questioned, biting her lip. He couldn't really blame her—he was all over the place. He shook his head to clear the perplexity of it all. *It's so much easier talking with my crew.*

"Jane, what Thomas was implying that night was how I needed a queen by my side. Not a game piece. He saw how taken I was with you that day on the pier. When he offhandedly stated a queen, like you, I didn't object. I didn't say anything. His suspicions about my feelings for you grew after his ridiculous challenge that morning of the race."

James caught one of her curls that blew freely across her face. Gently, he tucked it behind her ear. His eyes followed his fingers as they softly grazed along her jaw.

"After my win, he insisted on the chess piece. He felt you were my good luck charm."

"What was the challenge?" she asked suspiciously. Her lip twitched as she fought a smile. James's heart lightened. By the expression alone, he knew all was forgiven.

"I'm afraid that is a secret I cannot tell."

"Is that so?" The corner of her mouth raised.

He gave her a quick nod.

"So, tell me, captain. How would one pry this information out of someone such as yourself?"

She stepped forward, filling the gap that was between them. Her eyes danced in the moonlight as he tightened his hold on the lapels that hung below her neck. He swallowed.

"A gentleman will never surrender his secret." His voice became hoarse as his eyes traced down to her lips. She leaned towards him. His heart hammered in his throat. She had him, and she knew it. He took a quick breath, desperately wanting nothing more than to feel her lips against his. He closed his eyes leaning forward—

"That's a shame," she breathed, turning her head. Swiftly she stepped to the side and out of his grasp. Reaching above her, she began observing some leaves on a low-hanging branch.

His jaw dropped. He stared dumbfounded at the spot she had been standing. His lips twisted to one side.

"Now just a moment, Jane." He grabbed hold of her waist and twirled her around to face him. In the light of the moon, her eyes brightened with surprise.

"I see I have no choice," he said, his voice lowering.

"You don't?" She staggered, taking steps back as James pursued her. "But you're a gentleman. You said you'll never surrender a secret," she taunted, jumping as her back pressed against the tree. James trapped her in his arms, placing one hand above her head and the other by her shoulder. Instinctively, she pressed her hand against his chest. Lightly he covered it, cradling it against his pounding heart. She stared up at him, eyes wide, gleaming in the moonlight.

"Sometimes," he whispered, "I have to make a sacrifice for the greater good."

"So, you're saying you'll talk?" she breathed.

James's blood raced through his veins like rushing water, awakening all his senses. One of his hands lowered and, ever so gently, wrapped it around her waist. His other cradled her velvety face. She gazed up at him with longing. Tenderly, he traced his thumb across her perfectly soft lower lip that had been tempting him for far too long. Fire ignited within him. The desire was too strong to resist. He leaned in, pressing his forehead against hers. Their breath was fast and staggered.

"For this, my sweet Jane," he whispered. "I'll tell you anything."

Determined yet ever so gentle, he pressed his lips against hers. An exhilaration rushed from his lips, down through the tips of his fingers and toes. Her lips were better than he imagined—softer, fuller, with a hint of peppermint.

Then unexpectedly, she kissed him back. Desire consumed him. He grabbed her waist and pulled her closer. He weaved his fingers through her soft curls, gripping them firmly in his hand. He didn't want to part from her embrace as her body pressed closer into his, causing his arms to tighten around her. They kissed as though they never wanted to part.

Gathering all the self-restraint he was capable of, he ever so slowly lifted his chin, separating from her lips. They held each other in their arms, not daring to break the blissful feeling between them. Their hearts beat together in a frantic rhythm, gradually easing their way back to their steady pace.

"Jane." He tenderly held her delicate face in his palm. "Will you promise me something?" He ran his thumb across her darkened cheek.

"What is it?" His chest swelled as she stared adoringly into his eyes.

"Promise to wait for me? Until I get back. This trip will take three weeks."

"Wait for you? Of course I'll wait for you, James."

She gave her answer so freely, he wasn't sure if she understood what he implied.

"What I mean is," never having asked this before, he shifted nervously in his boots, "I'd like to call on you when I get back. I'd like to take you riding through some of the countryside. There's a lot more to explore on Saint Helena than what you've seen."

"I would like that."

He ran his thumb over her irresistibly soft lips. He desperately wanted to kiss her again but fought the temptation for fear he wouldn't stop.

Affectionately, he clasped her hand in his and gave it a quick tender kiss before they began to walk back towards the kitchen door.

"Wait here, before I forget," Jane whispered to him through the open doorway. She handed back his frock, then turned and hurried inside.

Patiently he waited on the manicured grass. Welcoming the cool breeze against the warmth of his cheeks. Staring up at the night sky usually made him feel so insignificant to its vastness. Being with Jane changed that. With her, he felt so invincible. He became so lost in his thoughts that he didn't notice her approach the open door.

"James," Jane whispered through the darkness. Startled, he turned towards her. "Did I scare you?" Humor filled her voice.

"Not at all," he casually smiled.

"Mmm hmm."

James took a few strides, stopping mere inches away from her. Placing his arm on the door frame, he leaned forward.

"What was it you were wanting me to wait for?" he whispered, hoping to change the topic.

"What . . . did I . . ." Flustered, she struggled to find the right words to say. James released a soft chuckle, pleased with his successful distraction.

With a sly smile, she thrust a mango into his chest, causing him to lose his balance. His hands covered her hand with the fruit.

"For good luck." She smiled proudly.

He flashed her a crooked smile. "My crew and I are extremely grateful." He brought her hand, with the mango in tow, up to his lips and planted a kiss on her soft skin.

"I'll see you in three weeks time."

She smiled, then grabbed his other free hand. Turning it over, she placed a wooden carving in his palm. Bringing it to the light, his heart never felt so full.

"Now you'll have a piece of me while you're gone," she whispered.

James wrapped his arms around her waist, pulling her towards him. His mango in one hand, the queen in the other, and Jane in his arms. He was certain he was the luckiest man alive.

"Thank you." His voice was low and rough against the stillness of the night.

"Three weeks," she confirmed softly.

James smiled down at her.

"Three weeks."

Epilogue

James's pounding heart echoed in his ears as he awoke in his dark cabin. He lifted his dampened shirt off his chest and started shaking it out. The cool air whisked over his clammy skin, raising little bumps across his body. He shivered and sat up. Releasing a shaky breath, he threw open the drapes that fell next to his bedside. Light seeped into the dim cabin as a thick gray cloud enveloped his window.

He grunted, flinging his covers off. It would be impossible for them to spot any ship. Particularly an enemy's vessel. Shaking out his uniform from off his chair, he dressed and pulled on his boots. Patting his left pocket, he smiled to himself as Jane's chess piece laid secure in the wool material. He crossed the room and kissed his fingers before pressing them on his other good luck charm—his mango. Ready to carry on with his duties, he left his quarters to head on deck.

It had been two weeks since he'd last seen Jane. His stomach leapt every time she came into his mind. And to no surprise for him, it happened a lot during his quiet time at sea. Thoughts of her helped ease the stress that weighed on him. There had been reports of two more attacks within the week. The pressure to find the ghost ships was taking a toll on him and his men.

He stepped onto the saturated deck. The salty air from the ocean spray misted the ship where his somber crew administered to their tasks. The ship creaked as it swayed over the waves. The sound added to the uncanny stillness of the atmosphere. Holding onto the rail, he ascended the stairs to the quarterdeck.

Thomas manned the wheel of the Ebony through the murkiness. The sails above rippled in the breeze.

"Good morning, lieutenant," James's voice carried deep into the mist. He couldn't help but notice the uncomfortable stance Thomas took. His eyes, though weary, were alert, his jaw clenched and his shoulders rigid. He wasn't his usual chipper self.

"Captain," Thomas replied in a solemn, apprehensive tone. His thick brows furrowed with unease.

"Any reports for me?" James inquired, sensing the severity in his mood. Thomas's knuckles whitened as he shifted his grip on the handles of the helm.

"We've been in this fog for hours. Something doesn't feel right." Thomas peeled his eyes from the sea and looked to James. "The further we go, the more unsettling it's become."

James glanced around the deck and stepped forward to take over the helm. The hair on the back of his neck began to stand. Whenever Thomas had an inkling, he was usually right. The last time he had one of his impressions, they were swimming in the ocean. They were cooling off from the sun's heat when he ordered everyone out of the water. As the last man climbed the ladder, two sharks appeared.

"Alert the men. Ready the crew and loose the cannons," James ordered.

"Aye, aye, captain." Thomas's pinched expression relaxed with relief.

"Lieutenant?" James spoke in a hushed tone. "Order the men to be as quiet as possible. If they are out there, I'd rather have the element of surprise, not a loud announcement."

"Yes, sir."

James observed the orders carried out as his men darted to their assignments. All sixty-four of their eighteen-pounder cannons rumbled below deck, rolling into their portholes. Their ship was one of the largest in Her Majesty's Navy. It carried the second most cannons of any ship in the world. James felt a sense of honor to be assigned to such a magnificent vessel. And, at the moment, he never felt more relieved.

Feet scurried across the deck as the crew hovered into positions with their weapons in hand. Thomas hurried back to James's side and offered a salute.

"The crew is ready and are waiting for further orders, captain." His caramel-colored eyes were bright and eager.

"Thank you, lieutenant." James broadened his stance. He squinted towards the sky with hopes to see any sign of the fog lifting. Nothing. Nothing but a white, heavy mist. Disappointed, James shifted in his boots.

He held the wheel steady, continuing to navigate them north towards the latest attack. Only twenty miles east of Saint Helena's cliffs. *Too close to home.* He scowled, tightening his grip.

Their ship creaked and moaned, filling the silence as it splashed through the choppy water. A bead of sweat rolled from under his hat towards his temple. He wiped it off.

They had been scanning the dense fog for over an hour. Some of his crew grew restless as they fidgeted at their posts. James threw his head side to side, attempting to loosen the stiffness in his neck. Since awaking that morning, his body had been tense.

"Look," Thomas whispered, pointing to a patch of blue sky.

James's thoughts lightened with hope to be free from the white, encompassing snare. Beautiful blue sky trickled through the mist as the fog dispersed. Prying his fingers from his handle, he adjusted his cravat. The disturbing feeling since he had awoken that morning continued to manifest.

"Lieutenant Daniels, take over the wheel," he ordered. Grabbing his spyglass, he stalked to where Thomas stood.

"Do you still feel it?" James asked.

Thomas lowered his hand from his squared chin. "I can't seem to shake it. You?"

"I thought it was from a dream, but I'm beginning to have my doubts."

They were emerging from the last bit of fog. Even with the welcoming sight of the bright day, something was amiss. James dashed to the front of the quarterdeck. Raising the spyglass, he scanned the glistening water. Eager to search for the cause of the unsettling feeling. Sweat began to prickle his back. His heart pounded in his chest as the anticipation grew. He held his breath, sensing he was getting closer. *There!* His pulse raced in alarm.

"Thomas," he called to his friend in a hoarse whisper. Thomas rushed to his side. "Look, a little on the starboard side." James didn't have to give Thomas the spyglass for him to see.

"Two of them," he exclaimed. James tightened his grip on the spyglass. "One of them has sixty-five, sixty-six . . . seventy-four cannons! That ship alone could annihilate us with one blast!"

James swallowed the lump that made its way into his throat. He took a side glimpse at his anxious friend.

It would be a fool's errand to pursue the two frigates by themselves. James rubbed at his stiff neck. They were less than twenty miles from shore.

If they're brazen enough to be this close to the island, what's stopping them from attacking Jamestown next? How many more innocent lives would they lose?

"Get the men ready. We still may have the element of surprise."

Thomas looked to him with wide eyes. He regarded James's uniform for a moment. James took a deep breath as he read what was in his friend's eyes. Had he not been his captain, Thomas would have been blunt and spoken his mind. He knew how foolish they were for not waiting for reinforcements. Unfortunately, so did James. Yet as sailors for Her Majesty's Navy, they had a specific duty to protect their country and crown. Turning around now would make their months of searching for these ruthless barbarians all for naught. It could take weeks to find them again. Within that time, who knew how many innocent lives would be smote by their hands. James wasn't willing to risk that. He wanted nothing more than to inflict every lead ball and cannonball they had before these mercenaries could cause any more harm. He gazed across his crew, feeling humbled to be serving among them. They had given years of their service under his command. He knew where their hearts stood. They were ready. James clenched his jaw and gave a curt nod.

"Aye, aye, captain." Thomas saluted with respect. He gave James a squeeze on the shoulder for support and hurried to the other officers on the deck below.

Twisting the spyglass, James peered through it. Both French frigates sat anchored side by side with their stern facing them. He released a ragged breath as luck appeared to be on their side. There was a large enough gap between the two frigates that their ship could squeeze through. With their cannons in position, they'll fire thirty-two shots from each side. It would cause a great amount of damage to both the French ships. A perfect setup. Perhaps they did stand a chance. Unless they went through with the French expecting them. Then it would be a suicide mission. James wiped his forehead again. He prayed they'd go unnoticed.

"Captain, the crew is ready," Thomas reported. James gave a nod.

"Lieutenant Daniels," he took confident strides to the lieutenant at the wheel, "I want you to steer her right down the center of those ships."

"Captain?" Lieutenant Daniels's eyes widened with confused panic. James peered through the spyglass. He wanted to double check that the enemies' gun ports stayed closed. *Excellent,* he mumbled to himself. *Even their decks were quiet from the morning hours.*

"It's too late to turn back now. This is the only shot we have to survive. Their gun ports are closed. Most of the crew are below deck. If we hesitate and shoot at only one ship, we have little chance of surviving their cannons." He turned to Thomas who listened with determination.

"I'll go give the order," he responded.

James adjusted his constraining cravat. Beads of sweat rolled down his back. Lieutenant Daniels steered them towards their passageway. James gripped the spyglass tight to control his trembling hands.

"Come on, come on, a few more yards," James muttered to himself, peering through the glass. Thomas returned to James's side, panting as he had run back up the deck. He gave James a curt nod, letting him know the men were ready.

A bell clanged rapidly in the distance. The alarm blared from one of the French frigates. James's head snapped forward as shouts from the other ships erupted. Blast! They spotted them. It was too late to maneuver elsewhere. There wasn't enough room as they drew closer to their point of entry.

"Steady!" James bellowed down to his men. Their muskets and pistols were in close range, but not close enough to make a difference. The sailors on deck obeyed with anticipation as they crouched behind the ship's sides. Their muskets loaded and ready to fire. The Ebony's sails fluttered as a gust of wind blew from the south, increasing their speed. The French began to raise their anchors with great haste. This might work. It had to!

Hunched behind one of the masts, James glanced over at his lifelong friend. His stomach took a turn for the worse. Thomas's face was fierce and uneasy with anticipation of the battle at hand. His cheeks tightened. He was serious. Too serious for his own good. No, he can't focus when he's like that. *This isn't good. I need him focused.* Panic rose in his chest.

"Thomas," James whispered, staring at the ships. With their enemies' gun ports now open, he could see the Frenchmen frantically readying their cannons. They were about to enter the death trap. "I have a confession," he took a breath. "I was the one who told Miss Elaine you liked her when we were younger."

Breaking from his frightful state, Thomas looked at him dumbfounded. James knew that year in grade school had taken a toll on Thomas. The other kids had been ruthless in their teasing. Taunting whenever Miss Elaine was around. It had been a constant thorn in his side.

James pulled out his pistol and cocked it back in its ready position. "Steady!" he ordered.

Their ship started to ease its way through the narrow gap of the two frantic ships. Shouts rang from the French quarterdecks. Members of their crew scrambled aloft to release the gaskets.

"Why did you do that? That was the most miserable year of my life!" Thomas hissed.

"You stole my lunch." James shrugged his shoulders. "She asked me if you did and at the time, I obliged and said you did . . ."

"I never stole your lunch!" Thomas argued. Of all things to get Thomas fired up, James knew that this topic would ignite him.

Cries bellowed through the air. The Ebony's stern entered the alley between their enemies' ships. James wiped the sweat on his face. The French scattered across their decks in a disorganized. *Right where he wanted them.* Loud cracking of musket fire erupted on either side of their ship. He ducked as splinters of shattered wood exploded off the rail next to him. With the sails unfurled and rippling in the wind, the French vessels had a stronger chance to keep pace with The Ebony. Their escape from between them would be narrow, if not impossible. James tightened his trembling fingers around his pistol.

"Fire the muskets!" James roared, shooting off his pistol towards the helmsman on the ship to his right. Entering between the two ships, they had just a few more meters before they were positioned at the heart of their hulls. His gun's smoke filled his nostrils as he loaded the pistol with more gunpowder.

Deafening sounds of shots rang from all around them. Lead balls whizzed by, striking the timber of their ship. Pieces of wood shredded, exploding into the air.

"Thomas!" James shouted over the heavy gunfire. "I lied!" He cocked his gun and fired towards the French's quarterdeck. The sharp loud crack from his gun echoed through his ears. He ducked once more from shattering lumber. He'd never spoken to Miss Elaine about Thomas. Quite the contrary, he'd gotten himself in a few tussles with the other lads for standing up for his friend. He had even faced quite a few thrashings from their headmaster that year.

Crouched down, Thomas smirked at him as understanding crossed his face. He chuckled and fired another shot.

James watched in alarm as their enemies rolled their guns through the gunports. He rushed through the sulfur-filled air towards their bell. With both ships taking sail, they were a few meters from where he wanted to be, but with the heavy fire they were receiving, they were going to have to make do. He rang the shiny brass bell two times, signaling their cannons.

"FIRE THE CANNONS!" he thundered.

His chest pounded with the vibrations from explosions they inflicted on their enemy. He gripped a post, holding himself steady as their ship jerked with each eruption from cannons below. BOOM! BOOM! BOOM! Timber cracked sharply and popped from the French vessels. Glass shattered through the air. A powerful blast erupted on his left, rattling their ship. James covered his head with his arm as debris poured down on them.

Black smoke curled through the air, watering his eyes. Opening his eyes, he noticed an orange flickering light in the thick black air from the ship on his left. Fire! His heart raced with triumph. If the fire spread, the French would be down forty-eight cannons!

"Keep her steady, Daniels!" James yelled out to the lieutenant as their bow passed the sterns of the other ships. James squinted through the thick vapor to be certain he heard him. Crouched behind the wheel and covered in debris, Daniels carried out the order. James wiped at his stinging, watery eyes.

Gunfire ceased from both sides while men attempted to gather their bearings in the smog. James rubbed his ears in an attempt to stop the high-pitched ringing caused by the blasts. Coughs, screams, and crying groans echoed all around them. With heavy heart, he knew the battle had only just begun.

Acknowledgments

There have been many people who've helped me in this journey, and because of their encouragement, time and wonderful feedback, I have gotten this far.

To my husband Sam, thank you for giving me your honest opinion and helping me bounce ideas off of you. And my sweet Miles, you are the sunshine in my world. Love you, kiddo.

Xela Culleto, there was no mistake we were suppose to sit at the same table for bunco. After discovering your love for writing, I knew you came into my life when I needed guidance the most. It was because of you and your shared experiences as an author that I was able to get this far. Thank you for your encouragement, your wonderful feedback, and your friendship.

A special thanks to Kyenna Weston. You gave me the direction I needed to be able to add more depth to the story. You taught me how to dig deep in becoming a better writer. Thank you for your inspiring words and council that helped me stretch and grow.

Jenna and Beth, I love having you two in my corner. Thank you all for your kind words. I appreciate how you've supported me since the beginning of my journey.

A much appreciation to my sister in-law, Ariel Fisher. Thank you for sacrificing a second of your busy schedule to help me navigate through the tech world. Girl, you have an amazing talent and may I add, wonderful taste.

Many thanks to my friends and family for your love and encouragement. Mom, Colin, Sarah, Jenn, Kristen, Josh, Erica, and Travis, thank you all for listening to my excitement as I tell you the "cliff notes" of my stories.

And most importantly, I want to thank my God, for helping me navigate through my own uncharted waters.

About the Author

Heather Fisher grew up living in some of the most beautiful parts of the country. While living in the Northwest, her family would go on many road trips to camp. On those long road trips, daydreaming and reading became her favorite pastime as their destinations were always, "just around the corner." She currently lives in Utah with her husband, their fun-loving son, and their cat, Leo. After becoming a mother, she was reminded of her childhood dream to become a writer. When these thoughts and dreams persisted, she began putting them into words. She is grateful for the opportunity to become a writer, and for those long road trips that first inspired her.